ONE OF
OUR BRETHREN

By Ernest Raymond

CASSELL · LONDON

CASSELL & COMPANY LTD
35 Red Lion Square . London WC1

and at

MELBOURNE . SYDNEY . TORONTO
JOHANNESBURG . CAPE TOWN . AUCKLAND

Printed in Great Britain by
Cox & Wyman, Ltd., London, Fakenham and Reading
F.463

ONE OF OUR BRETHREN

Archdeacon Alanside was a brilliant and well-loved figure in
the cathedral city of Casterton, and it seemed evident in all
the parlours of the diocese and indeed in Church circles
everywhere that he was destined for a bishopric. To Richard
Oliver, the young ordinand who tells us the Archdeacon's
story, he was the exemplar and hero on whom he secretly
hoped to model himself.

It was impossible to countenance, therefore, the idea that
someone should have accused the Archdeacon of immoral
conduct in a London hotel, or to credit so bizarre a rumour.
But the news of a forthcoming arraignment in the Bishop's
Consistory Court excited dismays and misgivings as well
as passionate loyalties, not only in Casterton but over the
whole country.

Richard's admiration did not falter, and the ties of sympathy that had developed were strengthened by his love for
the Archdeacon's daughter, Julie. The drama to be enacted
in the Bishop's Court would decide what the future held for
a man whose illustrious career now toppled on the brink of
destruction.

In this new novel, Ernest Raymond evokes the atmosphere of the cathedral city – its dignitaries, churches, lower
clergy and ladies of the Close – with that deep feeling for
place and character which lies so close to his creative
imagination and, in this case he assures us, to his memories.

BOOKS BY ERNEST RAYMOND

NOVELS

A LONDON GALLERY *comprising*
We the Accused
The Marsh
Gentle Greaves
The Witness of Canon Welcome
A Chorus Ending
The Kilburn Tale
Child of Norman's End
For Them That Trespass
Was There Love Once?
The Corporal of the Guard
A Song of the Tide
The Chalice and the Sword
To the Wood No More
The Lord of Wensley
The Old June Weather
The City and the Dream

Don John's Mountain Home
The Five Sons of Le Faber
The Last to Rest
Newtimber Lane
The Miracle of Brean
Rossenal
Damascus Gate
Wanderlight
Daphne Bruno I
Daphne Bruno II

OTHER NOVELS
Mr. Olim
The Chatelaine
The Visit of Brother Ives
The Quiet Shore
The Nameless Places
Tell England
A Family that Was
The Jesting Army
Mary Leith
Morris in the Dance
The Old Tree Blossomed

BIOGRAPHIES, etc.

Paris, City of Enchantment
Two Gentlemen of Rome
    (The Story of Keats and Shelley)
In the Steps of St. Francis
In the Steps of the Brontës

ESSAYS, etc.

Through Literature to Life
The Shout of the King
Back to Humanity
    (*with Patrick Raymond*)

PLAYS

The Berg
The Multabello Road

For

Paul, Madeline and Judy Knowlson

Author's Note

Casterton in this novel is an imaginary city, but inevitably it owes, in its painting, not a little to my memories of a cathedral city I lived in long ago and know best. It seems incumbent on me, therefore, to state that no character in the story had any original or model in real life – except, perhaps, Bishop Gregory Griffyn, and he only in parts. Nor is any incident in the story based on anything that ever happened in that city. There are echoes in it of a celebrated case that excited the country many years ago, but this had nothing to do with the diocese I knew and, in any case, they are echoes and no more. Further, since the whole is fiction, I have allowed myself the licence of telescoping time a little and picturing, for dramatic purposes, the system of examination for ordinands as it existed a year or two before the apparent opening of the story.

E. R.

CONTENTS

PART I

THE CITY OF CASTERTON

Chapter One

ST. CUTHBERT'S CHAPEL
AND THE SOUTH CLOISTER

When in these latter days I recall the city of Casterton I see always
its two straight roads (which the Romans laid) crossing each other
at the centre of what was once the old walled city; and just west of
this crossing, the grey towers and spire of Casterton Cathedral
rising from their green lawn. Usually, too, as I recreate this picture,
I hear in imagination the low-throated bells sounding from the bell-
tower – were they not intermittent eternally in my Casterton days?

One week-day morning, forty and more years ago, the clock in
the bell-tower chimed a quarter to eight, and immediately a single
bell began to summon to early service the few who cared to come.
It would ring for its fifteen minutes and then the great Hour Bell,
seventy hundredweight of it, would silence its junior with its own
deep voice like some ancient and ruthless headmaster. This early
Mass (how we perfervid Anglo-Catholic youths of the Theological
College loved the word 'Mass'!) was said daily in St. Cuthbert's
Chapel in the Cathedral's south aisle, and perhaps no more than
four or five people would be there to hear it. In term-time one of
these was usually myself. Another might be Tom Arrowsmith, my
good and simple-minded friend at the College, but Tom was fat
and lazy and did not always awake to the summoning bell, or,
awaking, did not obey it. This morning, while the single bell still
tolled, I came alone out of our hostel door, dragging on my
scholar's gown, and I hurried along the straight West Street towards the Cathedral's cliffs of mottled grey and moss-greened
stone, readjusting the gown as I went. Early birds like myself were
flying about the spire's peak, high in the sky.

This day must have been the twentieth of October, or there-
abouts, for it was the first full day of our Advent Term, and autumn
was everywhere in West Street. The sun, still low, threw long blue

shadows on a carriageway sprinkled with leaves of yellow, bronze, and green and framed with similar leaves of orange and gold in the gutters. Other wet leaves, varicoloured, lay stuck like postage stamps on the top of a pillar box and the roof of a car. The sycamore on the Cathedral lawn was all in yellow dress, but the broad poplar was still green, its leaves asway and twinkling in some unfelt breeze. This early sun was not yet high enough to floodlight the towered Cathedral cliffs. Their ancient stones, where they were not mottled or moss-greened, kept the hue of dusty milk.

Nobody but me seemed to be approaching the Cathedral, and when the door in its Galilee Porch swung behind me I walked into a silence as deep as that which the great church must have known in the night. No footstep broke it so that I was almost ashamed of mine. As I saw the Norman arches of the nave, I felt as if I had left eight hundred years behind me in the sunlight outside and was moving in the silence and subdued light of some morning of the Middle Ages still held and housed here.

I walked into the long avenue of the south aisle and through the screen and gates of the Cuthbert Chapel. Two women were kneeling here with their heads in their hands. Two candles alight on the altar awaited the celebrant. I stepped softly to my customary chair right at the back, knelt, and all was silence again.

Only these two women. Disappointment pressed on my heart. Where was *he*? My occupation in the chapel on these mornings should have been nothing but prayer, but some of it – nay, all too much of it – was a watching of *him*. I tried to worship God more or less consecutively, but hero-worship of *him* came more easily to a youth of twenty-two. The one was effort, the other ease. *He* was the famous Archdeacon of Casterton, the Venerable Edwyn Alanside.

'Venerable' suggests silver and wrinkled age but Archdeacon Alanside, though approaching sixty, had dark hair, a face little lined, and a figure hardly less neat than that of his athletic days on Isis or Thames (he was an Old Blue). I had never dared speak to him but nowadays he was my model in all things, and I hero-worshipped in secrecy. Indeed my current habit of hearing Mass daily in the Cuthbert Chapel was more a matter of reproducing him, who was always there, than of exceeding other ordinands in piety. This, of course, explains why Tom Arrowsmith was less likely to leave his bed and come to week-day Mass; his big clumsy breast held no such adoration as mine. To be sure, I think he came to early Mass, if come he did, because in his simple way he was fond of me and just now was my pupil in all things Anglo-Catholic.

The single bell was still ringing but it must be near the hour. Could it be that the Archdeacon had left Casterton during our vacation between Summer and Autumn Terms, and that perhaps I should never see him again? It humbles me to remember now how poignant a thing was this anxiety as I knelt there. I suppose only twenty-two can engender for itself such devotion and such distress. But it was a brief anxiety. I heard the door of St. Edward's Porch come open, and this would be he, for this was the way by which the dignitaries came from the Close. They came through the Cloisters into the Cathedral. Quiet steps, and – yes, it was the Archdeacon, well groomed as ever in his caped cassock, pleated from the waist, and girdled with a black leathern belt.

An aristocrat by birth, his father an earl's younger son and his mother a baron's daughter, Archdeacon Alanside's clean-cut face, his walk, carriage, and graceful ease of manner suggested stately homes; and I have to confess that this aura of aristocracy around him had its part in his fascination for me, who was a comparatively poor boy from a middle-class home.

Today he went to a humble place near the back and knelt there, sinking his face into his hands. It was because he always knelt here that I had gone to the back row of all from which I should be able, at times, to study him.

The chimes of the clock stopped the single bell and prepared the outside world for the great Hour Bell. Luckily for Tom Arrowsmith its notes were slow and dilatory, with intervals between them so long as to seem forgetful, and he had time, though with his gown awry, to reach a chair and kneel. No sooner had the Hour Bell dropped its last heavy note than footsteps came from the Chapel of St. Polycrate, which was now used as the canons' vestry, and the Chancellor, Canon Chadwin, in alb and linen chasuble, with his server in apparelled amice and alb, came out of the south aisle dusk into our illuminated chapel. Together they went up to the altar beneath the arcaded reredos from whose centre arch the small figure of St. Cuthbert looked down on them. Holding his crozier, St. Cuthbert blessed with uplifted hand all who worshipped here.

'Almighty God, unto whom all hearts be open, all desires known, and from whom no secrets are hid . . .'

The little service began for this congregation of five, two women, two ordinands, and an archdeacon.

Whether worshipping or hero-worshipping, how I loved those quiet early-morning services of long ago. No sound beneath the lofty, echoing vaults except the voice of a celebrant in a little side-chapel and the whispered responses of a few kneeling people. I loved the drama of the sanctus bell sounding far away for the people of Casterton to hear at the Tersanctus – 'Holy, holy, holy' – and the sacring bell at the yet more solemn moment of the Elevation – the Host uplifted in offering for all ten thousand in our city.

Rarely did any of us communicate. We were of the kind that came to 'hear Mass' only.

The gentle service over, I would often stay on my knees pretending further prayer but really waiting to rise soon after the Archdeacon so that I could leave the chapel behind him, and he perhaps turn and speak to me. This had never happened yet, and it did not happen today. In the south aisle he turned eastwards towards St. Edward's Porch, I towards the west doors and the Galilee Porch. Here I found Tom Arrowsmith waiting for me: a good fellow, an affectionate fellow, but a poor fat substitute for the famous, elegant, priestly – even saintly – figure which I had enthroned for homage in my private world of dreams.

§

The Cloisters were empty and very quiet. Cold too, because of the old damp stone shutting away the sun, and the open Perpendicular windows that looked inward upon the Cloister Garth. The hour was about fifteen minutes to four, and only the wind was astray in the Cloisters. It was rare for a student to be near the Cloisters at this time, but I had just come from the Priest Vicars' Hall at their eastern end. It was in the old cold Priest Vicars' Hall that we had our morning lectures and said our Sext before returning to the Hostel for lunch. Normally this ended lectures for the day, but three of us were doing Hebrew with Canon Victor Scholes two afternoons a week, and today in his enthusiasm he had kept us till nearly four. The others had run home and I came alone along the Cloisters.

I remember that, as I entered the South Cloister, I was looking up at the barrel vaulting which always fascinated me because its splendid old wooden beams looked so like the ribs of an upturned ship. I brought my eyes down to look through one of the cinque-foil windows at the green Garth enclosed by the Cloisters, and was stopped in my walk as by a revelation. The October sun lit the Garth, and the light seemed happily imprisoned there by Cloisters and Cathedral. Immediately before me, on the other side of the Garth, was the great Decorated window of the Cathedral's south transept, and a rose window above it. Hardly a stone in my sight, whether grey or mottled or touched with moss-green, was later than the fourteenth century, and many must have been laid by rough Saxon hands while Norman masters watched. The silence seemed complete, Cathedral and arcaded Cloisters guarding it from any trespass of sound. I can only explain what I felt by saying that I had a sudden sense of Time's basic stillness, and of rest in acceptance of mystery. The Cloister window had a stone bench for a sill, and I sat on it to gaze out at the Garth where the few listing tombstones stood forgotten on the grass.

While I was dreaming, footsteps sounded in the distance. I looked towards them. The Archdeacon was coming out of the bottled sunlight by the Bishop's Palace into the dimmer light of the Cloister. Doubtless he had been in conference with the Bishop and was returning to his home in the Close for tea. He must come by me and see me, seated on my sill. And because we were alone in the Cloister, and because I wore my gown, and it was odd to be

B

sitting there on a stone sill with books on my knees, it was likely he would speak to me. My heart began to tremble.

Of course he did so. He accorded me a shy smile as he drew near – and, oh, I was pleased; this was the first time he had noticed my existence; nevertheless my responding smile was even shyer than his.

He stopped before me. 'So the College is back?'

'Yes, sir,' I answered. And was empty of further words.

'Don't I see you sometimes in the chapel for early service?'

'Yes, sir. I am trying to hear Mass daily.' Remembering that caped cassock and his signs-of-the-cross during service, I guessed that the word 'Mass' was safely placed with him.

'Well, that's fine. I could wish more of your boys did. There's another lad comes sometimes, a – may I say it? – a rather fat boy.'

'Yes, sir. Tom Arrowsmith.'

'Oh, that's Tom Arrowsmith, is it?' He smiled as if he had long wanted to know which was Tom Arrowsmith. 'And your name is . . .?'

'Oliver, sir.'

'Christian name or surname?' The same smile.

'Surname, sir. Richard Oliver, in full.'

'And have you been at the College long, Richard?'

We had exchanged but half a dozen sentences, and yet already I could feel an immense goodwill pouring over me, probably because I was young and an ordinand.

'This is my sixth term, sir.'

'*Really?* Then you're not so far from your ordination.'

'I hope to be ordained next Trinity – that's to say, if I pass my exams.'

'Oh, you'll do that all right. Anyone can see that.' The pleasure this remark gave me! Did he then think I looked intelligent? Bright? The words had sounded genuine; need I think them mere social flattery?

'Oh, I don't know . . .' I demurred.

He was not in the caped cassock today but in the frock coat, apron and gaiters of an archdeacon, and from some inside pocket he now gathered spectacles to look at the books on my knees, which he picked up. While he looked at them I was resolving to wear a caped cassock when I was ordained and to look as much as possible like him, even though my hair unfortunately was brown rather than dark and my height a little above his.

'Goodness gracious me!' he exclaimed. 'Hebrew! You must be much cleverer than I am. Rose's *Introduction to Hebrew Grammar*. Gesenius's *Hebrew Language*. Does Leedes know Hebrew?'

'Who, sir?'

'Canon Leedes, your principal.'

'No, sir.'

'Oh, I'm glad of that. I'm greatly relieved to hear that. I don't know one word of Hebrew.'

'I only know about six. It's just that a few of us do Hebrew with Canon Scholes.'

'Yes, Scholes *would* know Hebrew. There's nothing that man doesn't know. Dear me, I'd have liked to be a scholar like him.' Suddenly he changed the subject. 'Any idea where your title will be?' The 'title' is the guarantee of a curacy from an incumbent which the Bishop requires from every ordinand.

'Oh, no, sir, not yet. But I'd like it to be somewhere in this diocese.' Thinking that I could now in my turn say something flattering, and very much wanting to do so, I said, 'I'd like to be in *your* archdeaconry, sir.'

'Well, my dear boy, I hope you will. We could do with boys like you. I must remember this, and perhaps look around for some title you'd like.'

'That'd be terrific, sir.'

'Six terms! A year and a half. How is it I've never encountered you before?'

'Because, as we say in the College, an ordinand is the lowest form of life.'

'*What?*' His eyebrows came together in an amused frown.

'The lowest form of ecclesiastical life, I mean, sir. Lower even than a curate who's still only a deacon, and you can't get much lower than that.'

'A verger?' he offered.

'Oh, no, sir. A verger can be quite impressive.'

'That's true. That's very true.'

'I mean, people speak to vergers sometimes. No one ever speaks to us.'

'No one ever speaks to you? What do you mean?'

'No one from the Close speaks to us.'

'Oh, but this is all wrong. This is awful.' Now the immense goodwill had clearly changed into a real pity. He frowned and seemed to be troubling about his own record in this matter. 'It's all wrong. I'm glad you told me that. I'm glad you said it. Well, Richard, when can you come to tea with us at the Residentiary?'

'Oh, sir, I didn't mean that.'

'*I* mean it. I most certainly mean it. Look, my wife has some Close people coming to tea on Friday. Could you come then?'

'I could, but I didn't mean —'

'You're coming on Friday. Bishop Griffyn'll be there. Do you know Bishop Griffyn?'

'*Know* him? No, sir. Not *know*. I see him in the town sometimes, and in his stall in the Cathedral.'

'You mean he's never spoken to you, either?'

'No, sir.'

'We ought all to be ashamed of ourselves. We must remedy this at once. It's strange because old Gregory Griffyn is one of the best, even if his tongue is a little – er – caustic. Anyhow he'll probably amuse you on Friday. Get Friday next into your diary.'

'Oh, yes, sir. That'll be absolutely terrific.' So it was in some ways, but already my heart was throbbing with fear of Bishop Griffyn and the others.

'And in the meantime, my dear boy, I apologize to you for the whole of the Close.'

'No, sir . . . please, sir . . .'

'Yes, they ought all to be ashamed of themselves from the Dean down, and that includes the Venerable Edwyn Alanside, Archdeacon of Casterton. Till Friday then. Good-bye and God bless you.'

I hurried back to the hostel, filled with an excitement not wholly unlike that which a youth feels when he's first encouraged by some girl he's admired from afar. In my room in the hostel I looked into the glass to see if it was true that I looked intelligent. On the whole I thought it was.

Chapter Two

A HOME IN THE CLOSE

Friday afternoon, and ten to four. In my best suit, well brushed,
I stepped out of the hostel door, followed by the jeers and cheers
of Tom Arrowsmith who stood on the threshold, and of other
students who leaned out of the first-floor windows like doves from
the openings of their columbarium, to watch this astonishing
episode of a student going to take tea with an archdeacon. I yelled
to all, 'Oh, cheese it, you idiots!' with an adjective improper in an
ordinand, and I was glad when all the heads returned within their
holes, and the long street was quiet again.

My heart was at an uneasy beat because I was unaccustomed to
circles as aristocratic as the Archdeacon's. The son of a country
vicar who had died when I was ten, I had lived since that day with
my mother in a basement flat by Putney's Thames, that basement
expressing well our fall into a straitened and struggling gentility.
St. Edmund's, Canterbury, a school for the sons of clergy, had
been my school. My mother had longed for me to be a clergyman
like my father and since at nineteen, like so many other boys in
those days, I was an ardent capture of the Anglo-Catholic Movement, that gay and coloured rebellion against all unlovely Protestantism, I was now in full agreement with her. I was eager to serve
the great Cause as one of its officers, eager to attempt the Catholic
holiness; but also very ready to wear, on the right occasions, an
embroidered chasuble or cope. Very ready, too, to bear the title,
'Father Oliver'. Or even 'Father Richard'.

After working enthusiastically in my basement bedroom I won
an exhibition to Casterton Theological College and was further
helped, Casterton having been my father's diocese, by the Diocesan
Board of Finance. So my humble Putney heart was shaking as I
turned into the Cloisters and drew nearer the Close, but my head
was instructing me to enact a perfect social ease. Often my hand
straightened my tie or my hair (whose fore parts were always

unruly) and brushed again the lapels of my jacket. Out of the Cloisters I turned on to the Wych Walk, a flagged path between castellated brick and flint walls – and there before me was the Close.

And there the Residentiary. The Residentiary was so called because it used to be the periodic home of the canons when in residence, but of late it had been made into the permanent home of the Archdeacon of Casterton. Like many other houses in Old Casterton, it was Elizabethan within and Georgian without. It presented a gracious white façade to Chantry Lane, the single street of the Close. There was no knocker, so I pressed the shining brass bell. My heart did the only knocking.

A manservant opened to me (oh dear, a butler or footman or some such!) and I said with a sustained ease, 'The Archdeacon is expecting me, I think.'

'The Archdeacon is not in, sir.'

'Oh. . . .' This rocked my ease on its most unstable base. 'Oh . . . but I . . . I think Mrs. Alanside is expecting me.'

'I see, sir. Your name?'

'Mr. Richard Oliver. I . . . perhaps you'd better say I come from the Theological College.'

'Oh, yes, sir. Will you step this way.'

He led me through a low, timbered hall that seemed to glisten with black oak and brass ornaments, and along a passage to a closed door. It was a thick door but not thick enough to hold behind it a noise of high, entangled, feminine voices. He opened it and announced loudly (as was necessary), 'Mr. Richmond Oliver. From the Theological College.' The announcement truncated, as with an axe, the whole high blend of voices.

I went in with a thumping heart and probably a wild, beaten look in my eyes. I found myself in a large white room which with its panelling and tall windows had an eighteenth-century air. The furniture, Sheraton, Hepplewhite, and some of it French with gilded ormolu mounts, confirmed the Georgian mood.

A very small woman, small as a small twelve-year-old child, jumped up from a chair and came towards me. I recognized her as

Mrs. Alanside but hitherto I had seen her only in the distance, and I was surprised to learn how creased was her little face and how crumpled and folded her neck, which looked like a receptacle that was fast contracting as it emptied. Her neat and expensive dress could not hide the roundness of her back. She was, I knew, the same age as the Archdeacon, but to me she looked fifteen years older.

'Oh, yes,' she greeted me. 'Edwyn said you were coming.' (Edwyn? Oh, of course: her husband.) 'How very nice of you. Now whom do you know here?'

'No one, I'm afraid,' I said – and, alas, with a stutter.

'Well, we'll soon alter that. This is Mrs. Prosdick – you certainly know *Mr.* Prosdick, the Vicar of the Good Shepherd. This is Mrs. O'Byrne – or Manon Thérèse to us all. Perhaps you don't know Mr. O'Byrne, the Chapter Clerk so well. And this' – her voice was loud to the point of being noisy, and I knew at once that it was a talkative voice, though so far she had spoken only a few sentences – 'this is Miss Emmeline Harvie' – did she pass over Emmeline Harvie carelessly as over someone of small importance? – 'and you are not telling me that you don't know our Bishop Griffyn – all the world knows Bishop Gregory Griffyn.'

'Of course, I know you by sight, sir . . . my lord,' I said with a bow to a lean old man sitting cross-legged in a winged armchair.

Dr. Gregory Griffyn had been the bishop of a great northern diocese which for centuries was a feudal princedom with bishop for lord, and to this day has a coronet round a mitre for its arms. From this fine strategic eminence he had won a national reputation, but rather as a mordant wit than as a saintly ecclesiastic. His sardonic utterances were reported with delight in every vicarage or clerical circle throughout the land. Often they were ceremoniously polysyllabic, and it was only after the sonorous locution had sunk well in that you realized someone had been incised and deflated. None the less when he resigned his see at seventy-two ('before senectitude and its attendant senility begin their loathsome demolition') the affectionate tributes to 'a great and generous episcopate' surprised all those who had heard only tales of a puncturing tongue. His hint of an early senility had not prevented him from consenting to be a canon residentiary of Casterton and Treasurer of the Cathedral. 'I can still read the services and add up,' he had sighed. Today as he sat hunched in this large chair you would never have known that, on rising, he would shoot up, like a tugboat's funnel, to some six-foot-six from the carpet. In his retirement he no longer wore episcopal attire. No neatly buttoned gaiters enclosed the crossed legs, but long trousers, baggy and a shade dusty. Bishop Gregory Griffyn was a widower, and his married daughters were far away.

'And I, young man,' he now said, staring at me from under grizzled and bristling eyebrows, 'know your face. I know it well. You sit opposite me in Choir.'

'Yes, sir . . . yes, my lord.'

'And you have observed me opposite you, I take it. At least I hope so.'

'Oh, certainly, sir.' (Did one call a retired bishop 'my lord'?) 'Of course. Regularly, sir.'

It was true. In Cathedral services the College sat in the Choir in the long carven pews before the prebendal stalls. Almost in front of my usual seat was the yet more elaborate stall, or throne, of the Treasurer, and there Bishop Griffyn would sit with 'Thesaurar' arching over his head in gold Gothic lettering like the first hint of a halo.

'And this,' continued Mrs. Alanside, 'Mr. . . . . Mr. . . . . I didn't quite catch your name.'

'Oliver. Richard Oliver.'

'And this is my daughter, Julie.'

'Oh, yes?'

A slender girl of nineteen. The Archdeacon in a smaller feminine edition – he, so to speak, the octavo library edition, she the slighter, soft-covered, India-paper edition, suitable for leaving about in drawing-rooms. Same dark hair, same grape-blue eyes set in natural shadow, same nose and chin, reduced for feminine beauty, same shy smile. It was almost ludicrous, the likeness. I had never seen her before because hitherto in term-time she'd been away in Paris at a finishing school. She alone had risen to greet me; a little awkwardly because she was even shyer about it than I was – and I was certainly shaken. But it was a relief to find someone in the room even younger than myself, and I felt a rush of liking towards her for being there. And for being so young. I was pleased to find a chair beside her.

And from that moment till the Archdeacon entered half an hour later no one took any notice of either of us. From that moment neither Julie nor I, thirty years younger than anyone else, intruded one complete sentence into the uproar of entangling voices. What she was thinking I don't know, but I, as curate-to-be, sat there watching, listening, silent, unaddressed, amazed.

It appeared that I had arrived in the midst of a discussion about the Greater Chapter which had met the previous day. As soon as Mrs. Alanside had disposed of me in a chair by her daughter, Manon Thérèse, the Chapter Clerk's French wife, small and plump and pink, shrilled archly, 'But, dear Bishop, you *must* tell us. You just must. How dare you attend the Greater Chapter and not tell us everything they talked about. I always want to know. My beloved Pat will never tell me anything.'

'Of course he won't. Neither shall I, dear lady. In any circumstances whatever.' The long lean face with the bristling grey eyebrows never disclosed by a smile whether he intended any statement to be humorous. Before sentences and after them it stayed a meaningless mask. 'The decisions of a capitular discussion are never submitted to the consideration of the vulgar.'

'*Oh!*' Never an 'oh!' more shocked, or more delighted. 'He's calling us vulgar now.'

'In this ecclesiastical context, dear lady, the word "vulgar" has no derogatory implications. It merely defines the ordinary people as distinct from the ecclesiastical fathers. In this case the Holy Fathers of Casterton. Do you really suppose their decisions can be debated in the licentious freedom of a tea-party conversation such as we are enjoying now?'

'Yes. Why not?'

'Well, I must confess, on second thoughts, that I have noticed, now and again, that some of the fathers don't interpret this rule of secrecy with any disabling literalness.'

'Very well. Nor need you. Need he, Natalie?' (To Mrs. Alanside.) 'And, anyhow, if you can't tell us what you were all talking about, you can at least tell us who did the talking.'

'Prebendary Imbraham was moved to make a somewhat irrelevant speech which seemed to go on for an hour —'

'Oh, Prebendary Imbraham! Trippy Imbraham! I adore Trippy.' This from Mrs. Prosdick.

(Prebendary Imbraham's initials were 'T.R.P.' Hence the nickname 'Trippy Imbraham' in the Close.)

'Yes . . . well . . . at any rate he sat down in the fullness of time, and his speech was fervently applauded, though whether in enthusiasm for its substance or delight at its termination I was unable precisely to distinguish. For my part I had been listening after the first half-hour with a certain sombre aloofness and naturally I sat up with astonishment when I heard the applause.'

'Probably he deserved it, and you weren't listening properly. What happened then?'

'The Dean, madam. The Dean happened then. We were discussing Lord Hugh Grace's Haffendenden Lectures on the Higher Criticism – ah, I see I have divulged one of our subjects now – a lapse which always happens sooner or later in licentious chatter like this – and the good Dean's dislike of all the latest Biblical Criticism is, to say the least of it, warm. But I am never certain how far this hostility arises from intellectual considerations and how far from a disapproval of unwarranted intrusions into credal matters by mere academic lords. His desire for some prompt official condemnation seemed to me to savour a little of Star Chamber disciplines, and since I was now, alas, in an argumentative mood, I was provoked into a speech which slightly ruffled the fathers.'

'Oh, but why? Oh, no, Bishop,' Mrs. Alanside interposed, as she sat in her chair with hands linked on her lap. 'I'm sure you were tactfulness itself.'

'I fear not, dear Natalie. I fear I allowed myself an unworthy sneer at the extreme Fundamentalists, which description hardly excludes the Dean himself. I *did* submit that, however revered some of our highly placed dignitaries might be – and most justly – it was possible for their vision in these matters to be clouded by a lifetime of prejudices – something like that, which was certainly not tactful.'

'No, Bishop, it wasn't.'

'No – I agree, Natalie – and I fear I further suggested that it might be possible, after a long period of being *primus inter pares*, to indulge too high an estimate of decanal authority. Whereupon Canon Leedes, whom I always consider to be the only saint in our Chapter but who has a pretty tongue notwithstanding, submitted quite rightly that this might also apply to episcopal authority, especially after it has been exercised for long years in a prince bishopric – a remark which delighted me. I have a great reverence and affection for Canon Leedes.'

Nothing could better show the exclusion of myself from any part in this merry talk than that no one, at this mention of Canon Leedes, not the speaker nor the laughing ladies, glanced my way, though Canon Leedes was the principal of the College from which I had come.

The Bishop just went on. He went on to say that, after Canon Leedes's speech, the aged Canon Roskill, father of the Chapter, had felt called upon to liberate his soul in a long dissertation, and was rather more impressive in his years and honour than coherent in his words and phrasing.

'Nevertheless,' said the Bishop, 'after the necessary period of probation, I thought I had arrived at a plausible theory of his meaning. But the effort exhausted me, so after a very little while I found an excellent pretext for abandoning my duties and achieving an unobtrusive exit.'

These reminiscences and the ladies' banter were presently interrupted by the entry of the manservant with a large silver tea-service on a large silver tray. The clatter of tea-cups was now accompanied by a clatter of women's voices: Mrs. Prosdick's loud and eager, Manon Thérèse's loud and shrill, Miss Emmeline Harvie's less loud but struggling, and little Mrs. Alanside's loudest and noisiest of all.

I longed to contribute one or two witty remarks but seldom accomplished much more than the parting of my lips. Once I got as far as 'I always think . . .' but immediately Mrs. Alanside took my voice out of my mouth, so to speak, and contributed instead something of her own. A little later, having framed in my mind a really intelligent remark, I began, 'I always feel that the *Benedicite* in Lent . . .' only to have my feeling snatched from me by my hostess and converted into something I hadn't at all intended to say. Again and again I watched my little inchoate offering go far away on her tongue, and at last was quite interested to learn what it would become in the end. She seemed, perhaps because she was so small, to have a nervous need to take everyone's subject, if possible, out of his or her mouth and, lifting her voice, shoulder him or her aside with it. Once I saw Julie grin at me because of this unkindness by her mother, and I was most grateful for that sympathy. So far this grin was her only contribution to the noisy causerie. Probably she knew better than to attempt anything more.

I soon noticed that those of us who could have our subjects taken from us and improved were arranged by our hostess in a kind of descending order. The Bishop she didn't dare interrupt; to him she listened with her hands joined on her lap; but, for the rest of us, Manon Thérèse's words were treated with some respect – was she not the Chapter Clerk's wife? – Mrs. Prosdick's with less; poor Emmeline Harvie's with hardly any at all; and this strange young man from the Theological College with none. I decided to get my only amusement from watching someone's subject snatched away, appropriated, and translated, and wondering what its final transmogrification would be before it died in the clatter. And more than once I got that grin, or grimace, from Julie, which showed that she was exactly perceiving the nature of my amusement.

§

I have to set down a great and sad disappointment in this matter of Mrs. Alanside. That *he* should have a wife so noisy, so assertive, so silly, and (to speak plainly) such a bore. She had all the vivacity that thin, tiny women often do have, and occasionally a gay remark lit up a point in the rush of her talk, but only occasionally; for the most part it was a spate without sparkle. How could he have married her? I sat studying her and saw that she must once have been very petite and pretty. This noisy bossiness had probably flowered late and luxuriantly as he rose higher and higher in the Church. But her talk, her talk! Exalted by it, she was unaware that hardly any of it was properly reasoned out. Since she preferred the joyous business of talking to the difficult business of thinking, most of it was only emotionally created and therefore emotionally distorted.

And this seemed hardly less true of the other women's talk. None of them seemed to worry whether it was rooted in thought. Why worry so long as it was talk? So long as it was fascinating gossip? Leave thought aside, or it might show that this was dangerous gossip. How in pity, I wondered, could the Archdeacon, famous writer, preacher and orator, bear such talk in his home?

Bishop Griffyn's talk, of course, was different. If it often ran a few points for'ard of the truth, or abaft of it, it did so, not because he hardly cared what exactly he was saying so long as he said something (as was the case with the ladies) but because he cared very much for rounded and well-shaped utterances with a sting in them somewhere for someone.

'Do go on, Bishop,' cried Mrs. Alanside, almost at the same time as she addressed a remark to Manon Thérèse. 'Isn't he a joy, Nina?'

Nina proved to be Mrs. Prosdick. And now I, unable to insinuate a single bright remark of the several I had prepared in my chair, gave myself to a study of Mrs. Prosdick; and I soon felt that I was seeing into the depths of her. Her effortful, over-careful enunciation of certain vowel sounds revealed that she was conscious of not being in the same class as Mrs. Alanside, Dr. Gregory Griffyn, and the Chapter Clerk's wife (of Emmeline Harvie she was unsure, like me, what to think) and that she was resolved this inferiority should not sound in her speech. Mr. Prosdick, her husband, recently inducted as Vicar of the Good Shepherd, had been ordained only late in life after some obscure career in a great London store. So, to avoid any trace of her native Cockney, Mrs. Prosdick, a fresh, full-bodied, red-faced woman, rounded her 'o's with care, levelled out her 'ay's till they sounded more like 'ee's – 'I'm so sorry my poor hubby couldn't come; he's awee in London' – but the syllable which seemed to perturb and strain her most was 'oy', and the nearest I can get to representing what she made of it is to write 'ah'. For instance, bravely trying to be as vivacious as Manon Thérèse in this fine room and among these gilded chairs, she explained that her poor hubby was a terribly busy old bah just now, what with the Men's Society and the Mothers' Union and the Bahs' Brigade.

Since I too had been anxious to hold my own and even cut a figure in this company I had every sympathy with her. And now here was her hostess throwing this most troublesome of all syllables at her. 'Isn't he a joy, Nina?'

'Of course he is, Natalie —' I saw that she was proud of addressing an aristocratic hostess by her Christian name and determined to do so with ease, but unwisely she went bravely and bull-headed at the difficult syllable – 'I always enjah the Bishop. Though I think he's a wee bit naughty sometimes, don't you?' Such ease in high circles!

But Mrs. Alanside was no longer listening to her. She was chattering to Manon Thérèse, and Mrs. Prosdick, who had leaned forward to offer this piece of coy gaiety, lapsed back into her chair, defeated.

The cups circulated again; and the rolled bread and butter and the sugared cakes followed them in a three-decker brass cake-stand, carried by me who, unable to use my tongue, had stood up to use my feet, Mrs. Alanside saying, 'Oh, thank you, Mr. . . . .' and then remembering that she'd forgotten my name. 'It is most kind of you.'

The visitors helped themselves to buttered bread or cake, saying thank you, but usually without looking up at my face, because they were talking to someone else. Only Julie, to whom it gave me an oddly sweet pleasure to offer cake, looked up as she said her thank you and gave me her shy smile.

I sat myself beside her again and was wondering how to address a witty aside to her – I was arranging some witty words – when Manon Thérèse introduced an alarming subject into the talk. She cried out (her mouth not wholly unoccupied), 'Do tell me, Natalie, tell me, *please*, that there's no truth in this frightful rumour I've heard – I meant to ask you before.'

'What rumour?'

'That you and the Archdeacon may soon be leaving us.'

A sensation in the room. No one else, it seemed, had heard it.

'I know very little about it. Edwyn never tells me anything about these matters. He simply never discusses them with me.' To my surprise, almost to my shock, a note as of indignation that approached hostility sounded in her abrupt answer. 'Don't ask *me*.'

'But what's this, what's this, what is it?' cried Mrs. Prosdick, eager to be taking her part too. 'Our Archdeacon going awee? Oh no, we can't have that. We won't let him go, will we, Manon Thérèse?' I could see that she was pleased to speak these two French names like the others and took pride in her pronunciation of them, but the pronunciation was so careful and deliberate that it issued in something like Man-Ought-To-Raise-Her. 'Bishop' – she was proud too of calling the great Gregory Griffyn 'Bishop', and here I again had sympathy with her, for I too should have liked to be in a position to do this – 'Bishop, what are they talking about? You will certainly know. What is this rumour?'

The Bishop finished sipping from his cup and laid it down. 'We should certainly not be discussing any such rumour, as our hostess so rightly implies, but let us do so —'

'Oh yes, let us,' encouraged Manon Thérèse. 'I mean, it's important. I should be desolated if the Archdeacon and Natalie went. Please go on, Bishop.'

'Well, I take it you've read that the old Dean of Northumberland died the other day —'

'Yes, yes!'

'Well, the whisper is going around that this deanery, which I may say is extremely well found, is to be offered to . . . well, to one of our brethren in Casterton.'

'The Archdeacon?' asked Emmeline Harvie, getting a word in at last. Emmeline Harvie was easily the biggest woman of them all; she was a very large animal in bones and breasts, though with small soft girlish features; her body, so round and soft and cushiony, was what is usually called 'comfortable', and yet she was un-questionably the least socially comfortable body in the room. 'Not the dear Archdeacon? Oh, *no*!'

The Bishop spread his palms open. 'Who else?'

'Oh, no, well, he mustn't accept it,' said Manon Thérèse. 'Oh why did the tiresome old dean want to go and die?'

'He was very old, madam, and there are those who think it would have been well if he'd withdrawn from office a little earlier. Of course he was greatly loved, but I suspect – indeed I've been told – that there's been a certain sense of enfranchisement in the Chapter since he passed on —'

I did not catch the rest of what he was saying because I was so alarmed by the rumour that I turned and spoke to Julie without the least wit. 'There's nothing in this, is there?' I said. 'He won't go. Oh, please say he won't go.'

'I simply don't know.' A light in her eyes showed that she was pleased to have been spoken to at last. 'Daddy pooh-poohs the whole story, but I rather think he does that because he thinks he ought to. I've a horrible feeling he'd half like to accept, but I hope and trust he won't. All that way up north! Miles from all our friends. And where's Northumberland, anyway? It's practically in Scotland, isn't it? Do get me another cake.'

I jumped up, delighted to be given this task but as at this moment the Bishop was saying, 'I don't think we need shed any tears at the old gentleman's death. He was nearly ninety and it seems obvious to me that if the verdict of Heaven endorses that of *The Times* and the *Telegraph* his passage to felicity will be among the easiest,' Julie whispered, 'Aren't you bored to tears with all this church shop? Don't you think it's awful?'

'No,' I said promptly, in part because she must be considered one of my hostesses, and in part because it hadn't bored me. 'I've been enjoying it rather, especially when the old Bish does the talking.'

'Oh yes, of course, he's bliss, isn't he? But the others – Golly! – don't you find them sinister, rather?'

'Sinister?'

'Yes . . . *you* know . . . deathly, rather.'

'No. I think I've found them amusing. I'll get you that cake.'

'Thanks awfully, but offer it round to the others first or they'll guess I sent you.'

'Rightho.' I did this; and bringing the cake-stand to her, I said, as she took an éclair, 'I do most awfully admire your father.'

'Yes, he's rather terribly sweet, isn't he?'

'He comes every day to early Mass in the Cathedral.'

'I know. Isn't it terrific?'

'He's the only one from the Close who does.'

'But do you mean that *you* go every day?'

'I try to.'

'Gosh! Are you then frightfully holy too? *I'm* not – at least, not frightfully.'

'Heavens, no! It's just that I like to hear Mass, if possible.' As usual I was proud of the phrase 'hear Mass', and pleased to be saying it to her. 'Your father's quite the best preacher of them all.'

'Oh, yes, of course he is. But then he was always rather brilliant. He must have been one of the few people up at Oxford who was both a Blue and a First Class Lit Hum, whatever that means. Some people are naturally brilliant. I'm horribly afraid I'm not.'

'But he told me he was no scholar.'

'Well, that was just a whopper. You can read all about it in *Who's Who*. *I'm* in *Who's Who*. I'm the "one *d*".'

This defeated me. 'One "d", did you say?'

'Yes. One daughter.'

'I must be rather wonderful to be his only daughter. I suppose he spoils you terribly?'

'Oh, sure – thank God. I'm what is known as "the apple of his eye". And if you can tell me what that means, you're cleverer than I am.'

Since this was a Biblical phrase from the Psalms I was able to be clever. 'Actually "apple" means "pupil" there.'

'Does it really? I've always wondered. It also means that he's been much too soft with me always – rather to my satisfaction and Mummy's disgust.'

This last word surprised me. Till today it had not occurred to me that anybody could disapprove of, or criticize, the Archdeacon. But even as I thought this I heard his wife doing the very thing. She was running on to Manon Thérèse, as endlessly loquacious and not-too-scrupulous wives do when they have the ear of a willing listener, about those habits of her husband that were disappointing and even inconsiderate. 'I hardly ever see him at all, my dear. I often say I might as well not be married to him, because he's really married to the Diocese or the whole Province of Canterbury. If he's not preaching or lecturing somewhere, he's shut up in his study, writing. From eight o'clock in the morning when he goes to church till twelve o'clock at night when he goes up to bed, I see almost nothing of him.' ('Goes up to bed' – had she carelessly disclosed that he slept alone?) 'Look at this afternoon. He promised he'd be here to meet you all, and lo and behold, he suddenly rushes off somewhere. Why and where, and what about, Heaven only knows. *I* don't know. He never tells me.'

'Of course he doesn't. He . . .' Julie had found courage to raise her voice in this company – but her right of speech was snatched away by her mother who now addressed Mrs. Prosdick. So Julie, in a dropped voice, completed her sentence to me. Her cheeks had flushed with anger, and her eyes hardened. 'As an archdeacon he has all sorts of jobs that are absolutely confidential. He's responsible to the Bishop for the behaviour of all the clergy in his archdeaconry, and sometimes he has to go chasing after a scandal that's going the rounds in some parish. Is it likely he'd tell Mummy? As you can hear she's absolutely incapable of keeping anything to herself.'

Since I could not admit of my hostess that she was untrustworthy, however much I might be thinking it – and indeed I was quite shocked that she should be volubly complaining of the Archdeacon in the presence of a young ordinand – I stayed silent. And I heard her saying, 'We never go out together anywhere in the evenings – to a theatre or a party or anything, he and I and Julie —'

'Oh, Mummy . . . *no* . . . please! I don't agree.' An impatient arrow from Julie's corner had gone singing through the room. One of her feet had beaten on the carpet. 'That's not *true*.'

'Oh, well, we very seldom do.' Mrs. Alanside didn't seem to mind her daughter's corrections. Perhaps she was used to them. 'As a rule he's either shut up in his study writing to the *Hibbert Journal* or *The Times* or something, or he's at the other end of the country, preaching. I always say it's less than fair to Julie. Granted that he thinks the world of her and has always spoiled her shockingly, but that's not what I mean. I mean a girl of her age ought to be taken out to parties by her father, or we ought to do a lot of entertaining here for her sake. As it is, she hardly meets anybody of her own age. We never entertain at all in the evenings – he's too wrapped up with reading for a sermon or something, and Julie and I sit alone —'

'I don't agree with *any* of it – any of it —' but her mother gave no attention to this from Julie. She just went rattling on, and Julie, turning to me, said, 'Mummy never lets anyone speak. And what she says isn't true. Daddy's always perfectly sweet to me.' Her eyes had tears in them.

I was just wondering whether this fixed loyalty to her father had any physical roots in the fact that she was such a fantastic reproduction of him in smaller and slighter size, whether it could be similar, in some way, to the loyalty of identical twins, when the door handle clicked; all talk stopped; the door came open, and the Archdeacon came in.

§

He came in with a jest on his lips. 'I apologize to you all, my lords, ladies and gentlemen. I was suddenly called away. On a conspicuously futile business. Ah!' Looking round the company, he had seen me, and he addressed me by name before anyone else. 'Ah, Richard! I'm so glad you were able to come. I hope everyone's looking after you properly. Julie, are you looking after Richard? Bishop, since I made the acquaintance of Richard Oliver the other day when he was reading Hebrew in the Cloisters, or perhaps meditating on the Seven Deadly Sins or something – he was certainly looking very thoughtful – I have been asking Canon Leedes about him and he says – well, perhaps I had better not say in front of him what his principal said, but it was flattering. When he's ordained next year we must do all we can to keep him in the diocese.'

All were now looking towards me. I existed, as it were, for the first time. Mrs. Alanside smiled at me; Manon Thérèse smiled, and Mrs. Prosdick, and Emmeline Harvie. He had changed the whole attitude of the company towards me, almost certainly because he'd guessed at once that I had so far been neglected; and if before this party I had enthroned him somewhat blindly, I now felt a delight that this blind fealty was being so completely justified. Julie, her eyes brightening like lamps towards me, whispered, 'I'll find out exactly what Canon Leedes said about you, and I'll tell you.'

'Oh, do,' I begged, for, ordinand though I might be, I craved praise like the weakest of laymen.

'I'll have it out of him in no time. Directly I get him alone this evening. Reading Hebrew! Gosh! When shall I see you to tell you? Or shall I put it in an envelope and send it to the College?'

'Oh, no, you mustn't take all that trouble.'

'But I'd *love* to. I think people should know when people say nice things about them. One gets quite enough beastly things said about one.'

'*You* don't,' I protested. But it was a piece of false flattery, this protest. Really it was designed to provoke her into telling me the 'beastly things' which she'd obviously implied were said about her.

'Oh, don't I? That's all you know. Quite a lot of the old biddies in the Cathedral congregation think I'm a mistake as an archdeacon's daughter. They're distinctly snooty. I can see it in their eyes.'

'But what nonsense! Why?'

'Chiefly, I think, because I ride The Reverend astride.'

'You *what*?'

'Oh, I'm sorry. I forgot. The Reverend is my horse. You must meet him some time. He's a perfectly divine creature. A chestnut. Fifteen hands. And I insist on riding him astride and in jodhpurs. Which they don't think at all nice in an archdeacon's daughter. Mummy isn't sure that it's altogether nice, either.'

'And Daddy?' I felt pleasantly dashing and impudent, saying 'Daddy?'

'Oh, *he* doesn't mind. He's got too much sense. *He* isn't living in 1888. And as long as Daddy doesn't mind I don't mind what I do. I'm afraid I find it rather fun showing myself in that unseemly posture and in those dubious garments to the old dears. I slow up The Reverend so that they shall get a nice view of the shocking spectacle. Then yesterday I got into an awful row with Mummy for smoking in front of them in the street – but I suppose that really was rather wrong. But you don't know what it's like, living in a Close.'

'I only live a hundred yards out of it.'

'Yes, well . . . but probably you don't hear the cackling from there. Wouldn't you say it's been quite noisy in the hen-run this afternoon?'

'A little, perhaps – yes. But the old Bishop's crowed quite a piece too,' I said, hoping this sounded witty. And thinking it did.

'Oh, but he's such a darling,' Julie countered, as if this justified his part in the gossip. 'Do you think hunting's wrong? Because I awfully want to hunt on The Reverend, but Daddy won't let me, and I suppose he's right. I suppose it *is* cruel, really. But it's a pity; The Reverend would take the fences beautifully. He jumps like an angel.'

'I should be delighted to meet The Reverend,' I said, attempting wit again, but at that moment the Archdeacon, speaking, drew my eyes to him.

'Natalie, give me tea,' he said; and he went and sat by Emmeline Harvie, obviously because he thought that she, like me, was probably being neglected and that, anyhow, she was less likely than the others to be at ease in this drawing-room. He had scarcely sat down and begun to talk pleasantly with her before Manon Thérèse, gaily tactless, called across the wide carpet, 'Archdeacon, tell us once and for all that you are not going to leave us for this silly deanery ten thousand miles away; tell us, please, and put us out of our misery.'

'Oh dear, oh dear.' He laid down his cup. 'Has that silly rumour even found its way into this room?' I suspected an unwitting criticism of his wife beneath these words, but perhaps I was wrong. 'Any such rumour, dear Manon, can never be anything but guesswork. Nobody in Casterton can possibly know what names the Prime Minister may choose to submit to the King, and even if something did leak out, it would be wholly wrong for anyone to pass it on. Julie, give me cake. Even if I had received the offer of some deanery and accepted it, I couldn't say a work about it till the P.M. chose to publish it. Any such disclosure would probably result in my nomination being withdrawn.'

'Well, now, isn't that ridiculous?' was all that Manon Thérèse commented on this. 'Aren't men foolish? He's our Archdeacon, not the P.M.'s, and where on earth can be the harm in letting us know what they're up to with him.' She spread despairing fat hands. 'I think they're all like so many schoolboys with their secrets. Depriving me of my peace of mind.'

'Let me restore your peace of mind, dear Manon,' said the Archdeacon, a shade tartly, 'by reminding you that rumour has been pleased to name many persons of far greater distinction than myself as likely recipients of this offer.'

Now my eyes at this tea-party may have been wide open to the frailties of the women, but they were wilfully averted from any weakness in the man I needed for a hero – especially after his considerate treatment of me a moment since. I see now, all these years afterwards, that his show of indignation at a flattering rumour masked his pleasure in it. It was rather what he felt he ought to say than a true picture of his private thought. Had I allowed myself to, I might have perceived at once that he would like the honour of being offered a deanery by the Prime Minister, even though he purposed to decline it. But on that afternoon, long ago, I didn't choose to think him capable of even this small human weakness.

'Are you aware, ladies,' he was now saying, so as to change the subject, 'that the Subdeanery will have one of the most famous preachers in England for the whole of the four Sundays in Advent? He will empty the Cathedral. All our congregation will simply rush across the road to the Subdeanery.'

'Who is it? Who is it?' they all chorused, excitedly.

'It's —'

But Mrs. Alanside took the words off *his* lips now. She took his story from him and told it, leaving him high and dry and silenced. Cast away on a lee shore. She explained that the preacher would be the very famous bishop who had just resigned his see in a University town to become a humble curate; the most revered name in the Anglo-Catholic Movement and far beyond its bounds; far beyond even the frontiers of the Anglican Communion.

The Archdeacon caught my eye, saw that I had observed this shouldering of him aside, and he grinned. As it were at me, privately. As if to say that it was really rather irritating to be treated like this, wasn't it, but one couldn't say so in public. For a second he and I were in alliance against his wife. It was a very fine moment.

Across Chantry Lane, the single street of the Close, the Cathedral clock chimed the three quarters, and immediately there happened quite the most surprising thing of the afternoon. Emmeline Harvie rose from her chair, an enormous soft woman with big soft breasts and small soft features, and, standing there like a monument made of velvet she said firmly, 'Are you coming, Bishop?'

As one who spoke with authority. As a wife might.

And the Bishop answered, 'No, I'm not. I'm enjoying myself'; sharply, abruptly – nay, almost rudely – as one might to a wife.

'Well, I must go, if you won't,' said Emmeline. 'I have a lot to do with Anna and Mary. That was a quarter to six striking.'

'All right. Good-bye, Emmeline,' acknowledged the Bishop cheerfully. And Emmeline, nodding good-bye to all, even to me, went from the room, leaving the others talking.

But despite the Bishop's enjoyment, and the women's enjoyment too, her departure was like the first crack of a thaw: gradually the gathering broke up; crack after crack sent the others drifting away, and, last of all, the Bishop, rising from his cosy chair to his fine and unexpected vertical, all six-foot-six of it, contributed yet another surprise to my afternoon. 'Young man,' he said, 'I am coming with you. I am going your way as far as Canon Leedes's house and if you can accommodate your feet to a senile pace we will walk together.'

'Yes, sir . . .' I said '. . . my lord,' a little alarmed at the prospect of this *pas de deux* through the Cloisters and West Street, but in no position to decline the company of an episcopal canon.

Chapter Three

THE PRINCE BISHOP AND THE ORDINAND

There was nothing senile in the pace of Bishop Gregory Griffyn. His long-legged stride was easy, and confident; and I, though I am tall, had to stretch mine sometimes to keep it in step with his. Together we walked along the flags of the Wych Walk, between its battlemented walls, and so into the dimmed light of the Cloisters. And all the way the Bishop talked happily with a companion half a century younger than he.

'Fortunately, Richard – that was your name, wasn't it? – fortunately, by coming this way, through the Cloisters and along West Street, we achieve your College hostel and Canon Leedes's house without once leaving a pavement and stepping into the ghastly perils of the roadway. Only yesterday I was nearly destroyed in North Street by an inept lorry overtaking a horsed vehicle, and my observations as I extracted myself were hardly episcopal. I fully expect to come to my end in or around the little car in which I am driven by my housekeeper – who is excellent in the home but somewhat less skilled with an internal combustion engine. As for me, I can no more understand these astonishing machines than she could understand, say, Bishop Fotheringay on the Septuagint – which I mention because I was reading it last night with a succession of confusions, frustrations and defeats that can only be attributed, I imagine, to a waning intelligence. Time was when I penetrated all such obscurities with comparative ease. As doubtless *you* do. I gathered from Alanside that Leedes had told him – but never mind that. High praise is a heady drink for youth. How is it that we have never met and walked before?'

I made my joke about the ordinands being the lowest form of ecclesiastical life, since he had not heard it, but only the Archdeacon.

'Oh, dear no!' he protested generously. 'I won't listen to that. Not at all. In some ways you are the most important because you have a huge capital of life to expend on the Church, whereas I have hardly anything left in the bank at all. And a little more of this senile decay and I shall have an overdraft.'

'Oh no, sir,' I protested in my turn. 'It is kind of you to say that about us, but as it works out in practice we are the poor relations of the Close.'

'The *what*? Who are?'

'We, sir.' I had abandoned 'my lord', unsure of its rightness and deciding that 'sir' would meet all needs. 'The Theological students. No one takes any notice of us. All the Cathedral dignitaries pass us by on the other side, like the priest and the Levite. And the ladies of the Close are still worse.'

'Never heard such rubbish. Haven't you just been drinking tea with the Archdeacon's lady?'

'Yes; that's because the Archdeacon took pity on us. He's different from all the others.'

'Nonsense. He's no different from me. You must come to tea with me. I should enjoy that very much. Would you like to, or would you be utterly bored?'

'I should love it.' And, in truth, I was thrilled by the invitation. What a thing to tell the lads! Here was I advancing from point to point in my sudden conquest of the Close.

'Well, so should I. I'm quite as amiable as Alanside. Yes, now I come to think of it, no one did talk much to you over the tea-cups. *I* didn't. It was wrong and I apologize. If you come to tea with me there'll be no women, so you'll get a chance to say something. I take it you've observed that it's impossible to complete a sentence in the presence of Natalie Alanside. Unless you are a bishop. I think I completed a sentence or two.'

'You did, sir.'

'What? Do you mean that I talked too much?'

'Oh, no. It was all awfully —'

'Awfully what?'

'Amusing, sir.'

'I am glad to hear that. But it was all ecclesiastical shop.'

'I love ecclesiastical shop.'

'Well, you must have enjoyed the ladies this afternoon. And even me too, I suppose, for I can only confess that I have a perilous tendency to indulge in reckless speech when I'm in the company of loquacious women. Let me tell you, Richard, that the talk of women is a spring of corruption for all clerics from the humblest curate to His Grace of Canterbury in his palace at Lambeth. Doubtless these ladies mean well, and the Church could hardly exist without them; but doubtless also they are a danger to us all. Let me explain why. It is because they debauch our minds and to a certain degree our souls – which is extraordinary because, speaking generally, they are immeasurably superior to us in piety and character and self-sacrifice. But there it is: they debauch our minds because their talk is wild and emotional and irrational, and they debauch our souls by deferring to us and obeying us and flattering us in a way men very seldom do – unless they are the very silly ones. They crowd our congregations because they are congenitally more prone to worship than men; they fill our meetings because their habit of mind is by nature ancillary; and they inevitably flatter us because it is a matter of one sex talking to another; and so it comes about that we see the Church through a magnifying-glass of women, which is to see it enlarged and distorted and looking much better than it is. Further, my dear boy, it is by reason of this deference and veneration that so many vicars – and, yes, bishops – become the pompous asses they are. When you are ordained make it your business to belong to at least one institution from which women are happily excluded – and if there is such an institution, one in which clergy are few and far between. Such an arrangement may help to impede the corruption to which you will be exposed when you are moving for most of the day in an ambience of women and parsons. Such, by the way, as you've just enjoyed. Well, I shall look forward to a visit from you. You will come when? This day week?'

'Oh, yes. Thank you, sir. Sir, will the Archdeacon really go?'

'Go?'

'Yes. To this deanery? This Northumberland deanery?'

'I do not know. Edwyn Alanside is in some ways an enigmatic divine. I should have thought that, as he is already in archidiaconal gaiters, and it would be no change to get into gaiters decanal, he would prefer to remain where he is, lest he should endanger his chances of changing his sleeves. A deanery has proved too often the end of the journey for an ambitious divine.'

An enigmatic divine? An ambitious divine longing for episcopal sleeves? This of my loved archdeacon in the Cuthbert Chapel! I wouldn't listen to it; and the affection I was beginning to feel for this amusing and kindly old gentleman suddenly depreciated there in the Cloisters. I went silent as we turned out of the Cloisters into the open and sunlit pathway by the Cathedral's Galilee Porch. Bishop Griffyn, unaware of this recent fall in my love for him, went on talking. And all the time as he talked, walking at my side, his eyes were not looking at me but steadily ahead.

'Then, of course, few clergy are eager about going north. They think many times before transferring their allegiance from Canterbury to York, as I should know only too well, having governed, somewhat incompetently, a great industrial diocese in the north. It is always difficult to lure either newly ordained deacons or long-established incumbents from the comforts of the south to the rigours of the north. They naturally prefer the fleshpots and the warm suns of the south – though by fleshpots I wouldn't have you infer any fat temporalities, for these hardly exist any more in our Ecclesia Anglicana, notwithstanding the fact that the Ecclesiastical Commissioners and Queen Anne's Bounty must handle between them some three or four million. Why, with all this lucre available we should have to sweat our clergy I shall go to my grave without understanding. I acquit them all of avarice; it is merely that a priest's life is pleasanter and more socially satisfying in the home-county dioceses like this of ours. Also I suspect, for the whole earth is weak and all the inhabiters thereof – or as St. Augustine put it more vigorously, the human race is sunk in sin – that few are insensitive to the fact that the chances of preferment are greater in Canterbury than in its sister province of York. When you are older you will

have digested the distressing fact that, whether it is in the Armed
Forces or the Civil Service or the political parties or the Church,
the nearer you sit to the Headquarters of the Commander-in-Chief,
the greater your chances of promotion and of a few medals for
your breast. Go to the remote Front Line where there are danger
and discomfort and death and, while you may be rewarded by your
Father in Heaven who seeth in secret, it is likely you will be left
and forgotten by your fathers-in-God who sit below in the seats
of power. How can the great generals in the centre see you far away
on the circumference, surrounded as they are, twenty deep, by
their staff officers and all the other satellites who rotate around
them? One is weak and gives the few rewards to those one meets
and knows and probably loves.'

Again my youthful idealism was bruised by this affirmation of
self-seeking in the one profession whose members should at least
be aiming at selflessness. I stayed silent as we turned into the broad
evening sunlight of West Street.

'That was why, my dear Richard, I did not unreservedly agree
when Alanside said we must keep you in our diocese. I felt I would
like you to take your youth and idealism into the forefront of the
battle where others are chary of venturing, say among the satanic
mills of Halifax or Oldham or Wigan. But I find it difficult to
believe that Alanside will easily turn north at this stage. Still, he's
been Archdeacon now for seven years and he may be bearing in
mind the psalm which we sang only the other day: "Promotion
cometh neither from the east nor from the west, nor yet from the
south." So let the needle swing to the north. On the other hand it
it quite possible, even though these questions of high preferment
are supposed to be absolutely confidential, that some well-informed
party has warned him to wait. To wait for something that will
involve the lawn sleeves.'

He could not know how such words were hurting me. I could
see well enough that his desire was, not to hurt, but to help; to step
down from his great position, and be friendly and amusing, while
he offered truth and good counsel to a young man. I could only
walk at his side, still saying nothing.

Most of the houses in Casterton's West Street rise straight from the pavement, and the College hostel used to be one of these, its threshold the pavement. There, on and about its step this evening, stood five of the students. Their gowns told me they had come from Evensong at St. Thomas-sub-Castro, the small medieval church of which Canon Leedes held the vicariate together with his headship of the College and the prebend of Entwit-in-Pascua. Mattins was compulsory for us all in the Lady Chapel of the Cathedral. Evensong we were expected to attend at least three times a week either in St. Thomas's or in the Cathedral. These lads now ahead of me had plainly chosen the shorter service in St. Thomas's where it was 'said' by Canon Leedes and not sung with full choir.

Of these five students one, most disturbingly, was Tom Arrowsmith, plump and round and loudly laughing. Not a doubt but that he and the others, while suppressing the laughter, would be quietly merry when they saw me approaching the hostel side by side with Dr. Gregory Griffyn, retired Prince Bishop and Canon Residentiary. I could imagine Tom saying to the others, 'Crikey, will you only look at what's coming? Richard, not content with calling on the Archdeacon, has now got a bish in tow.'

So aware of this bishop was I that my cheeks grew redder as we drew near. The lads stood back and were silent as lordship passed by in apparently co-equal conversation with one of their number. I made as if to enter the hostel, but he, with his eyes never deserting the road ahead and so hardly perceiving any students, objected, 'No, no. I'm enjoying this. Come as far as your principal's house and we can enjoy further converse.' Canon Leedes's house was another fifty yards along West Street so I had to pass these wondering students with the Bishop in a full flow of converse at my side. I contrived a wink with my left eye at Tom Arrowsmith as we passed. And I just managed to hear Bill Brickhill, who was one of our newly joined Oxford graduates (and sounded like one) drawling wearily, 'He'll be bringing the Arch along next, Cantuar himself.'

§

After parting with the Bishop before our principal's doorstep (where he'd stayed in converse with me for two more minutes before saying, 'Well, good-bye, Richard') I hurried back to the hostel and up the stairs to its common room. There among a row of books on the mantelshelf was an outdated *Who's Who*. I took it down to read 'one *d*'. What was to be derived from having 'one *d*' before my eyes I don't know. But there it was, and I stared at it. I had just been talking with the one *d*. Since the book was open at 'Alanside' I read the whole biography of the one *d*'s father. 'ALANSIDE, Ven. Edwyn Neville, Canon Residentiary and Archdeacon of Casterton; *s* of Hon. Neville Alexander Alanside and Mary Caroline, *d* of 5th Earl of Nesborough; *m* Natalie Jane, youngest daughter of 12th Baron Kerries. . . .' There followed his school, college, first curacies and incumbencies, his many publications and his present address, 'The Residentiary, Casterton', which gave me a small pleasure because I had just been taking tea in it.

After another look at 'one *d*' I was about to turn the pages and study the career of Bishop Gregory Griffyn, my other new friend of the afternoon, when for an unhappy second I observed that the Archdeacon had omitted from his record both the date of his birth and the date of his marriage. Vanity? – no, instantly I thrust the thought away. I would have no truck with it. Impossible to associate a worldly vanity with that figure kneeling, head on his arms, every morning in the quiet Cuthbert Chapel. So turn happily to 'Griffyn'.

'GRIFFYN, Rt. Rev. Hubert Gregory, Canon Residentiary and Treasurer of Casterton' – and thereafter a whole column giving his distinctions, preferments, and publications. '1st Class in Classics in Moderations and in Greats; Chancellor's University Prize (Latin Essay); Fellow and Tutor of Corpus Christi College, Oxford . . . select Preacher at Oxford; Examining Chaplain to the Bishop of London. . . . *Recreations:* reading, gardening, agitating for sanity and precision in controversy, walking, talking.'

Chapter Four

THE HOUSEHOLD OF ONESIPHORUS

At those daily Mattins in the Lady Chapel and those Evensongs in St. Thomas's one student was detailed to read the Lessons for the week, and there had been a time last year, in these first days of the Advent Term, when Tom Arrowsmith discharged the duty. Tom was the son of a small ironmonger in Croydon and one of those among us whose training at the College was being entirely paid for by the Anglo-Catholic parish where he had been a devoted young server. His earlier education had been limited to that available free at the church school, which he'd been obliged to leave at about thirteen. Thenceforward he had helped his parents in the shop till one of the priests of the parish, delighting in his simple, honest nature, and in his single-minded loyalty to his church, took it upon himself to teach him just so much Latin, Greek, Logic and History as would get him through the Common Entrance to Theological Colleges. Since all the parish loved him, its Vicar, Father John Martin, had little difficulty in finding the funds that would keep him at Casterton. Tom was not less popular among us than among the clergy and workers of this Croydon parish, but his huge areas of ignorance, which, being voluble, he often revealed, provoked some of our loudest (but not unaffectionate) guffaws.

And on this past occasion, at Mattins, when he must read the Lessons, he was unfortunate enough to have within his assignment the last chapter of Colossians. Here occur St. Paul's moving words of farewell. 'All my state shall Tychicus declare unto you, who is a beloved brother and a faithful minister and fellow-servant of the Lord: Whom I have sent unto you that he might know your estate and comfort your hearts: With Onesimus, a faithful and beloved brother who is one of you.'

Tom, after a brief hesitation, did well enough with the name Tychicus, though he did pronounce its first syllable as he would have pronounced the name of the comedian, Little Tych. With the name Onesimus he did not hesitate at all, believing it of no difficulty; he read out to the assembled college, including its principal and chaplain, '. . . that he might know your estate and comfort your hearts with one Simus, a faithful and beloved brother.'

Canon Leedes, who had been following the Lesson in his office book, sat up at 'one Simus' like a man stung on the forehead by a passing bee. His lips, though compressed at the time, moved one small degree up in the centre and down at the sides; and then the palm of his hand curtained the whole lower half of his face. He affected, magnanimously, not to have heard any titters that had burst from other lips. And Mattins proceeded, with the early sunlight slanting through Decorated windows between an assembly of deep-voiced young men at morning prayer and the bays of lierne vaulting above.

Service over, Canon Leedes, in cassock, surplice and scarf, went out of the Lady Chapel before us all and into the Retro-choir. Where he waited. Now in the Retro-choir of Casterton there are two twin glories of the Cathedral. These are two composite columns which rise up on the north side and the south to support the round arches beneath the triforium. They are remarkable because their shafts of Purbeck marble, instead of clustering close to the large central column stand away from it leaving the light of day to shine through. It is said that they have no equal in the country for grace and dignity, nor parallel for this open arrangement; and there are even those who say they have no peers in the world. They rise in the midst of the Retro-choir, north and south before the gates of the Lady Chapel, like Jachin and Boaz, the vaunted twin pillars before the porch of Solomon's temple.

Let us then call them Jachin and Boaz and say that Canon Leedes went out and stood in front of one of them, Jachin, the pillar on the right; my point will then be that Canon Leedes, standing there robed, grave, stationary and lonely, was worthy of this majestic background. For he was a fine figure of a man with a beautiful grave face on which sanctity was written and, above it, a luxuriant supply of prematurely white hair, of which, had he been less saintly, he must have been proud. I say he made a wonderfully fitting spectacle

c

beneath the cold white arches and before the Purbeck marble shafts, waiting for Tom Arrowsmith.

Tom was almost the last of us to come through the gates of the Lady Chapel, because the good fellow really did say a stretch of private prayer after the Grace. Canon Leedes, seeing him, said, 'Mr. Arrowsmith, please.'

'Sir?'

'Spare me a moment, Mr. Arrowsmith.'

'Certainly, sir.'

'Mr. Arrowsmith. "O-nē-simus" in future, please. Not "one Simus".'

'One who, sir?'

'Simus, a faithful and beloved brother to whom you introduced us this morning. Hitherto we have only known Onesimus.'

'Oh . . . I see, sir. I am sorry. Thank you.'

'Not at all, Arrowsmith. You had not met this brother before.'

That was last year. This year, and this Advent Term, I learned from the notice board that it would fall to me to read the Lessons, including 2 Timothy 4, one morning in the near future, and I recalled that in the past I had had some doubt about a succession of names in 2 Timothy 4. You will doubtless remember that verse 19 runs, 'Salute Prisca and Aquila, and the household of Onesiphorus.' Onesiphorus. On the evening before that morning I invited Tom to relieve me of my task, just for once, because of a wretched and disabling cold. The good fellow, ever glad to do a kindness, ever trustful, willingly agreed, and we all went to our Mattins with a certain readiness to hear him. Canon Leedes's eyebrows lifted when he saw Tom, instead of me, go up to the lectern for the First Lesson, but he couldn't open a discussion about this half-way through Mattins. So Tom went back to his seat untroubled and issued again to read 2 Timothy 4. We all waited, myself in an inconspicuous position at the back.

And Tom read, 'The Lord shall deliver me from every evil work' – an untimely statement – 'and will preserve me unto his heavenly kingdom; to whom be glory for ever and ever. Amen. Salute Prisca and Aquila, and the household of . . .' here he stopped as if to prepare for the difficult jump of Onesiphorus – for, as it were, a Beecher's Brook before him. And inevitably, being our Tom who learned slowly and forgot much, he made his brave dash at the name and gave us all what can only be rendered as 'the household of One-Sigh-For-Us'.

No titters were heard for we had all prepared ourselves with an armour of riveted lips. Only Canon Leedes abruptly turned his face to the east and out of our sight.

And now, service over, there he was, standing again before the splendour of Jachin; standing like Pompey's pillar 'conspicuous by himself and single in integrity'. But waiting for me this time.

'Mr. Oliver, please.'

'Sir?' As who should say, 'Now what can you want with me, sir?'

'Oliver, it is your week, I think, to read the Lessons?'

'Yes, sir. But I —'

He did not wait for me to go on. 'And yet Mr. Arrowsmith read them this morning.'

'Yes, sir. He very kindly relieved me.'

'So? But, Oliver, you were present in the' – he restrained a tremble of the thin ascetic lips – 'in what it would hardly be amiss this morning to call the audience?'

'Oh, yes, sir. I'm not *ill*.'

'Your cold – is that it? – has affected your throat, perhaps?'

'No, sir. I —'

'I must say I detect no great loss of voice. But I did notice that you obeyed the Evangelical counsel to avoid the chief places in the synagogue and to . . . to sit down in the lowest room. You were right at the back, were you not?'

'Yes, sir.'

'And no one said to you, "Friend, go up higher"?'

'No, sir.'

'I see. Could it be, Oliver, that you had studied the Lessons beforehand and developed ideas about Onesiphorous?'

How was I to answer this? Impossible to lie. So I stuttered out the truth. 'I suppose it could, really, sir.'

'In other words, you detected in the distance the manifest possibility of One-Sigh-For-Us?'

'Well, no, sir . . . not exactly. . . . I thought he'd say something like "One-Easy-For-Us".'

'Oh, no. "One-Sigh-For-Us" is much better.' For the moment he had forgotten that this was a business of rebuke, not of joining in the fun.

'Yes, sir,' I agreed, and certainly thought it was.

'Ah well . . . I have little doubt that the Blessed St. Paul enjoyed the joke, and possibly the Blessed Timothy too. But I think I must put it to you that the Lady Chapel is not to be used as a theatre for frivolity – though it is possible, of course, that Our Lady – however . . . Now go back to College, and will you kindly in the course of the day make me a translation of the first four pages of St. Augustine's *De Civitate Dei*. It's a most improving work and I shall be glad to see what you make of it. I have always been very fond of it. And may I add that Mr. Arrowsmith will be in Heaven before you?'

'I have no doubt of that, sir.'

'No. It is one of those facts that stare one in the face, is it not? I have made it clear, I hope, that I shall want your version of St. Augustine by five o'clock this afternoon, if you can complete it between luncheon and Evensong at St. Thomas's – where, I take it, you will be well enough again to read the Lessons. You will find a St. Augustine in the Library.'

Chapter Five

NO. 6, THE PALLANT

'1st Class in Classics in Moderations and Greats . . . Fellow and Tutor of Corpus Christi College, Oxford . . . Select Preacher at Oxford . . . Examining Chaplain . . .' I was recalling all these distinctions as I walked towards Bishop Griffyn's home in the Pallant, and my walk was not without apprehensions. 'Agitating for sanity and precision in controversy. . . .' God send that my talk would be sane and precise. The Pallant, its strange name coming from a Roman word akin to Palatine, was not in the Close; it was in the eastern half of our city, but, of course, well within the old Roman framework. Cathedral and Close were on the other side of the Romans' four-way crossing. The Pallant was a long quiet street of gracious eighteenth-century houses, and No. 6, Bishop Griffyn's, was one of the most gracious of all. It was a long house of deep-red brick under a steep, tiled roof, its white, well-proportioned windows set flush with the brickwork and its doorway acting as the only ornament, with its pillars, pediment, and delicate fanlight. I felt that there was something in this long, dignified house that suited well with the Bishop's formal, balanced, unsmiling, almost stately talk; and my hand shook as I rang the bell. But I straightened myself up and resolved to show no fear. No; on the contrary, ease; the perfect social ease.

The door opened, and I started back. Emmeline Harvie had opened it. So all was explained. She was his housekeeper. 'Anna and Mary', with whom she had said she had much to do, must be the servants. She was the lady whose driving of his car alarmed him. She was his frequent companion. 'Are you coming, Bishop?'

She smiled at me pleasantly. 'Oh, yes, the Bishop is expecting you. Mr. Oliver, isn't it? We met at the Archdeacon's last week. Do come along.' And she led me through a panelled hall, past an elegant Queen Anne staircase, to a room at the back.

'Young Mr. Oliver, Bishop.'

I found I was in a room much longer than it was broad. Its old oak panelling was cracked in places and almost certainly contemporary with the house's deep-red brick. A long refectory table below the three garden windows exactly fitted the shape of the room. Covered with large leather-bound books in tall piles, other books lying open, two foolscap MS books also open, and a small typewriter, it seemed, in the same way, to fit the Bishop's mind. He was seated in a chair before the typewriter, where he looked quite an ordinary size, but, as usual, on rising, he seemed to extend most of the way to the ceiling. And the typewriter beneath him, when he had reached that height, suddenly looked extremely small.

'Ah, yes. Young Mr. Oliver. Or Richard. How very kind of you, Richard, to come and call upon me. You know my invaluable Emmeline, don't you? She will bring us tea. Thank Heaven you've come and I have now an adequate justification for withdrawing from this difficult machine. Do you type? I am told one should employ all five fingers of both hands but I seem to be temperamentally limited to the index digit of each hand, with an occasional contribution from a thumb. Come and sit down. You are fortunate in having half a century to run before arriving at an age when one's only relief from the squalid tedium of senectitude is to write one's autobiography. That's what I'm attempting. Foreseeing throughout my life that this dismal time must come, I have always kept a diary, so that in the days of enforced leisure I might be able to review the long years of labour and, by assembling their lessons, provide, not only some aids to my own repentance, but a handsome garland of warnings to other men. That is a thought which removes a little – but only a little – of the task's disgusting egotism. Sit here.'

On either side of the fire-place at the end of the long, narrow room were two long, deep, comfortable chairs. He sank his great length into the lap of one of them, and I, still nervous, sat on the billowing arm of its buxom sister opposite. The fire glowed and flamed between us.

He removed his spectacles from under the grizzled and bristled eyebrows. The spectacles had a frame so thin it looked to be made of steel wire. 'Thank God I can now be quit of these. Smoke? No?

Not now? Well, thank God I can now. Smoking and typing I find
the most incompatible of partners.' There was an occasional table
at his side, and on it a tin of expensive-looking cigarettes. He took
one and lit it. By the tin was a glass ash-tray stacked with the stubs
and ash of twenty others. Behind tin and tray stood a framed photograph of a grey-haired woman. I guessed who she was, and that
the expensive cigarettes, ceaselessly smoked, had to be wife and
helpmeet now.

Striving to be a social success, I said how beautiful his house was.

'Yes, all the houses in the Pallant are beautiful because in the
Augustan age – unlike ours – the big merchants and money-makers
had some taste. But for me the Pallant has an additional advantage
in that it is a sufficient distance from the Close – and the brethren.
Only on the other side of the city, as you will have noticed, do the
clergy really swarm – rather like rooks gleaning in the stubble.
Archdeacons, canons, prebendaries, curates – to say nothing of
your students issuing from their lecture hall like bees out of a hive.
Now tell me all about yourself. Tell me everything you hope to do.
It would be very pleasant if I could be of any help to you.'

This so surprised and touched me that my heart which had been
beating treacherously, stilled, and I found myself after a while
telling him a great deal about myself; about my father's vicarage in
the country, my school at Canterbury, my recent surrender, total
and delightful, to Anglo-Catholicity, and (I regret to add) slipping
in the fact that I had managed to get an alpha-plus in every subject
in my Common Entrance to Theological Colleges. No sooner had
I inserted this little brag than I blushed warmly for it, because the
'C.E.' in those days was a very easy exam and, remembering
'1st Class in Classics in Moderations and Greats', I saw how almost
pitiable to him must seem this potty little success of mine. But he
only nodded approvingly, and I hurried on to other subjects so as
to drown the piece of braggartry beneath a stream of new words.
I told him that one of my ambitions – after, of course, serving for
a time in some difficult urban parish (a sop to him) – was to end up
in a country vicarage like my father's where I should have some
leisure to 'try my hand at writing' – an ambition which seems to

afflict one young man in every three, until he gives it up in despair. But then, suddenly, I *heard* my own voice and was shocked at the speed and volume of its flow – so conducive to fluency is talk about oneself. So shocked was I at what I had just noticed that I quickly deleted all that was to have followed, and submitted instead, 'But, sir, it would be much more interesting if you told me all about —' and I named the diocese which he had ruled in the north.

'Now, now!' he protested. 'Must I really do that?' He swung a hand towards the long table and the typewriter. 'I thought you'd come to rescue me from the perils of autobiography. Let me make clear to you first that I'm not deceived by such preferments as have come my way into thinking they were due to capabilities which transcended those of other men. Not at all, dear boy. If a long life has taught me anything, it is that there are a great many men of high ability in every profession – Law, Stage, Literature, Church – but only a few whom fortituous luck lifts to the narrow places at the top. You must have *some* ability, certainly, to get there but you must have luck too.'

'Did you then have luck, sir?'

'Most surely. I apprehend that, apart from some undoubted ability, I owe everything to two extraneous facts, and the first was that my parents, less by design than by accident, gave me the Christian name of Gregory. Thank you, Emmeline. Just put it there, and I will cater for Richard. Let me explain, Richard. You will recall how that irascible philosopher, Tristram Shandy's father, held the view that the Christian name given to an infant could determine its future for good or ill. Unless my memory fails me he insisted that it would be a crime to call his child Tristram when it might be called Trismegistus. Well, in my old age I'm no longer so sure that this notion was as crotchety as we have been disposed to think. I mean, "Gregory Griffyn" is an extremely memorable noise, once heard, seldom forgotten, and people from the beginning have liked hearing themselves utter it. Thus the patrons who held the advowsons of good benefices, and the bishops, the prime ministers, even Majesty itself, had all chanced to hear of me; and in this unjust world, to have been heard of is always half-way to being elected or purchased or decorated, as the case may be. I think that is clear, Richard?'

'Perfectly, sir. And what was the other extraneous fact?'

'Simply, Richard, that I was provided at birth with a wholly irrelevant talent – highly irrelevant in a divine – of arranging slightly uncharitable words in a sequence that was memorable, and since there was generally a slap for someone in any such arrangement, people have always rejoiced to report it everywhere, with the simple result that the Prime Minister and the King have both heard, and I think enjoyed, more than one of my unchristian remarks and therefore, when a bishopric was vacant, remembered me. Do you take sugar?'

The Bishop had listed 'walking and talking' among his recreations in *Who's Who*, and I began to see that he enjoyed delivering a spoken essay whether his feet walked the pavements or whether his hand poured out the tea. Walking from Close to hostel he had treated me to an essay on Women in the Church and one on Ambition in the Clergy; now, dispensing tea for both of us, he was occupied with an essay on Fame as a By-product of Fortuitous Luck.

'But, sir, in addition to luck, you had scholarship,' I submitted as I took my cup.

'What makes you think that?'

'I looked you up in *Who's Who*, sir.'

'Oh, *that* splendid anthology of human exhibitionism. Yes, I suppose I was something of a scholar. I have not contended that luck is enough alone; only that it is as indispensable as it is irrelevant. But here again there was a pretty element of luck. I did well in my exams chiefly because I had a remarkable visual memory, which has precious little to do with scholarship. I just saw whole pages of Lucretius or Aeschylus or Hooker's *Ecclesiastical Polity* or What-not in front of my mind's eye as I wrote. Very useful. And there you have the whole story, my boy.'

'Yes, sir, but may I suggest —'

'But rather than that I should corrupt your youth, I think I must say that, on the whole, I don't apologize for those remarks which I have called unchristian. It is simply that in the Christian Church emotionalism and sentimentalism and hot irrational prejudices flourish most exceedingly, and it has always seemed to me necessary to puncture all such blown-up nonsense with words that were uncomfortably precise and pointed.'

'Yes, sir. "Sanity and precision in controversy".'

'Aha! Yes, I put that in *Who's Who* when I was young and bumptious, and I am always forgetting to take it out. But I must warn you, my dear boy, that this habit of deliberate precision garnered for me a fine harvest of resentments all over my diocese.'

'Oh, no, sir,' I protested. 'Canon Leedes has told me all about the hundreds of tributes you received when you retired.'

'Yes, it is true that a wonderful chorus of gratitude accompanied my retirement from episcopal activity, but this, Richard, could surely be interpreted in more ways than one.' He cut a slice of cake for me, and another for himself, delivering as he did so an essay on Appointments to the Episcopal Bench. In this detailed thesis – it was delivered as he handed the cake to me, took a piece himself, wiped the cake crumbs from his fingers with a handkerchief, and replaced the thin-rimmed spectacles to see his slice better – his chief point was that prime ministers suffered from an illusion that they must choose bishops for their scholarship, their administrative ability, their force of will, their social gifts or other mere worldly attributes, instead of for the one thing needful – their sanctity. *Porro unum est necessarium.* If only they would seek this first, he said, all the other things would be added unto them. But one had to be a saint to know and fully realize this. And whenever was a prime minister a saint? 'And, look, Richard, there are forty-three dioceses in England, but are there forty-three saints? Or if there are as many, or more, are they known? There are six sees in Wales. Are there six saints in that barbarous part? Surely not?'

Here I came in promptly with, 'I always think we have at least three saints in Casterton.'

'Three?' The grizzled and bristled eyebrows went up in surprise.

'Yes, sir.'

'Well, that ought to be enough to save the city. But who, pray, are they?'

'The Bishop. . . .'

He nodded.

'Canon Leedes. . . .'

He nodded quickly, two or three times, so sure his agreement.

'And Archdeacon Alanside . . .?'

This he met with silence, eating his cake and flicking its crumbs from his finger and thumb. Strange what a sudden, sharp pain that silence was to me. A pain along the heart. I stared at him, waiting for him to speak again. Oh, stop this silence. Why be silent? I began to feel angry with him, and was sorry to be so, for I had been building up a plan for loving him as well as the Archdeacon, and here he was – apparently about to breach the dam which I had built around the Archdeacon's figure to preserve it from all criticism. Waiting, I decided that the only thing to do would be to forgive the Bishop for anything he might say; because in this way alone could I keep both the plan and the dam. And I really did want to love this new and kindly friend.

He spoke at last, having finished a mouthful. 'I'll give you two of those: the Bishop and Leedes. Yes, we are fortunate in that our bishop is the real thing; he is certainly one of the most humble and gentle of Christians and therefore, as I have just contended, one of the most truly successful. His humility is all the more remarkable, because that man is a *real* scholar; he is a walking arsenal of erudition. Yes, I give you George Casterton – every time. And Geoffrey Leedes too. George Casterton showed the wisdom of his sanctity when he decided that none but a saint must rule over a theological college. Would that more diocesans could perceive this, but they, you see . . . however let's leave that. . . . Two saints. Well, say there are a hundred clergy in Casteron – I'm sure it always seems like it; one can't enter a house without meeting a curate on the stairs – well, two per cent is not a high proportion.'

'But Archdeacon Alanside, sir. Surely you would say he has sanctity?'

Silence again; and I looking at him, could see right into his mind. Today, recalling that distant afternoon, I suspect that I can provide almost the actual words that were clothing his thought.

'A romantic young man's idealism. I must not tarnish it. There is something humbling to us all in this hero-worship of the young.' The silence continued while he thought of all the good things he could say about a romantic young man's hero. It was a long minute before he spoke, after picking up a cigarette, but retaining it unlit.

'Sanctity is a huge word, Richard. Edwyn Alanside is a very good man, I know – one of the best – but the sanctity of which I was speaking is a title that one must serve very hard to win; and I still think I can award it only to our bishop and to Leedes. Alanside has the enormous merit of always loving the person he's talking to —'

'Oh, yes, yes,' I interrupted, remembering how I had felt this when he first spoke to me in the Cloisters.

'Yes, and in this he's a much better man than I am. I do not always feel an abounding love for the person I'm addressing. He does. He really delights in meeting every shopkeeper in Casterton and asking him how trade's going; and the farmers too, who come in to market; he asks them about their pigs and their cows. I've never been able to engineer a real interest in either. I mean in the pigs and the cows. The farmers, yes – I hope. He has a joke for every girl behind every counter, and for the children who all run to greet him – excellent – all excellent – he has the expansive heart that goes out to everybody. And by the same token he loves – really *loves* – the great audiences he addresses from pulpit or platform. It's this that helps more than anything to make him the popular preacher he is. I've heard it estimated that he's the third most popular preacher in the country. But – here's the point – I think this reputation means a great deal to him and that he labours to serve it; and it's on this account only that I would withhold from him the title of saint. We have to allow to him, I feel, the "last infirmity of noble minds" – the ambition for fame. The saint gets rid of the last shred of this, and is ambitious only for God. But which of us ever gets quite as far as that? Not myself, Richard. *I've* never really crossed the frontier into that far country, that lonely desert of Libya.'

Here he lit the cigarette.

He said little more about the Archdeacon that day, but all this was so generous that I was delighted to find I could comfortably place Bishop Griffyn in my pantheon alongside the Archdeacon, if a step lower down. When he escorted me to the door in time for Evensong, he said, 'Come again, Richard. I've greatly enjoyed your talk. Come any time.' I shook his hand with an obvious affection that elicited an obvious pressure from him. And I walked home happily, though pondering over the difficulty of modelling myself on both Bishop and Archdeacon; of incorporating, that is to say, a dry biting humour, distinctly ungentle, in a struggling sanctity. Somewhere between East Street and West Street I decided that it could be managed.

Chapter Six
THE CENTURIES

The Cathedral of Casterton with its constellation of satellite buildings in the Close may be medieval, but the grace of the eighteenth century stands all around it. The classical eighteenth century embraces the Gothic, and both, oddly enough, stand within a frame of Romano-medieval walls. I used to walk along the streets of Casterton marvelling that I could so have the Gothic centuries on my right hand and the Georgian on my left. I would notice how almost every house had a Georgian face like Bishop Griffyn's home in the Pallant; every doorway of a standard pattern, with pillars or pilasters, fanlight and pediment. And because, like many immature but idealistic young men, I tried at times to write poetry, often getting no further than what seemed a good title for a poem, I brooded over a poem about Casterton to be entitled 'The City of Beautiful Doorways'.

Every morning I had to swing out of the eighteenth century and walk through the fourteenth, by which I mean the barrel-vaulted Cloisters whose quiet even the birds on the Garth seemed to respect. After the Cloisters I met the fourteenth century again in the shape of our Priest Vicars' Hall where we had our daily lectures and which stood, let us not omit to say, upon a vaulted undercroft of the twelfth century. Century upon century like the strata in the hills. The Priest vicars, or vicars choral, were the clergy whose duty it was to sing on behalf of the canons the daily offices in choir; and this hall had once been their refectory. It was a long, rectangular hall with cold stone walls that seemed to smell of five centuries gone. A fine open-timbered roof crowned the cold empty spaces. There was a dais at the far end where once, I imagine, stood the high table, but where nowadays Canon Leedes, or Chaplain or Tutor, sat in loneliness to lecture to us. In the long south wall, under a four-centred arch, was a tiny elevated chamber, or pulpitum, from whose window one of the priest vicars used to read a holy book so as to stir uplifting thoughts in his brethren seated at their meal.

Lectures over and Sext said, we came out of that old, cold quiet to encounter the façades of the eighteenth century and the noisy traffic of the twentieth. I am speaking of more than forty years ago when there were far more horses among the traffic than can be seen now – especially if the day was a Wednesday and the farm wagons were coming in for the cattle market – because Casterton is not only the principal market in the diocese for clergy but also one of the largest in the county for cattle.

One among the horses might be Julie Alanside's. Now having made her acquaintance, I would recognize her astride the handsome animal which she had named 'The Reverend', inappropriately, since its silken flanks were not black like a parson's, but a glossy brown chestnut. Her father might forbid her to hunt, but on this tall horse, amid the Casterton traffic, she wore a Quorn hunting-cap of black velveteen, a black hunting-jacket, a white hunting-stock with a gold pin, and carried a race whip or a Whangee cane. Sometimes she saw me on my humble pavement and waved the whip, or she just grimaced, remembering our conversation and her present straddling of this beast and her jodhpurs. Once she drew the horse to the pavement and stopped it for a talk with me.

'I've just had the most *marvellous* ride,' she said. 'Miles and miles into the country. Right into the Menwode.' (We must explain the Menwode later.) 'Gosh, it's the most marvellous country to ride in – flat as twenty pancakes and smelling of the sea, and with hardly anyone in sight. Steady, Reverend! I've seen about two people in the whole morning – one a man on a tractor plough-ing a field miles away and the other a ditcher mending a hedge in the middle of nowhere. Just perfect for me because I'm naturally unsociable, on a horse. Whoa, Rev! And gosh, the country's lovely now, with the autumn tints decking up all the woods in twenty different colours. Honestly, Richard, you could almost think some of the trees were on fire. Gosh!' she could only just breathe out this final 'Gosh!' in her fervour.

I said, 'You looked like Joan of Arc when you rose in your stirrups and waved your whip at me.'

'Did I?' she said. 'How ripping. Joan rode astride, didn't she? And that was fourteen hundred and something. Which just goes to show that all the old sillies in the Close are exactly five hundred years behind the times. Which reminds me: I've been getting into a really imperial row. I'm only just emerging from it.'

'Whatever for? With whom?'

'With Mummy. I was smoking a cigarette as I rode home, simply because I felt so happy, and as bad luck would have it, The Rev and I were just coming towards the Close when Mummy came out of it and saw me. She saw the cigarette. That really turned the hot tap on. I suppose it did look rather awful, smoking on board The Rev, so I said I was sorry; but don't imagine that stopped the row. Once Mummy's got going with a real first-class cataract you don't stop it by saying you're sorry or that you meant no harm and that you'll never do it again. It's natural, I suppose: having started an imperial cataract she doesn't want to waste any of it. I stayed till the end, as was only polite, and as I was in bad odour and must try to get everyone sweet again. But The Rev got a bit impatient, I *must* say.'

'And it's all over now?'

'Oh, I think so. I hope so. The great thing is just to stay still and keep quiet and let it disperse. Once Mummy's got rid of it all, things are quite bright again. We were allowed to ride on.'

Another horse that I might see on certain days was the Dean's stately high-stepper which he drove himself from the high seat of his pony carriage, for our Dean, as might be gathered from his square grey beard, his top hat, and his cockaded groom at the back of the carriage, was an old-fashioned gentleman, a relic of the nineteenth century. He would have nothing to do with the racket and stink of a motor. Accordingly you might often see, waiting before the Prebendal Gate which led into the Close, this high-wheeled chariot with the top-hatted groom holding the bridle of a nervous, head-tossing horse.

One car that I might see on the roads was Bishop Griffyn's. This was a model some years old now, its body uplifted far from the ground, its roof high, and its colour black, so that it slightly resembled the London taxis of the time. Emmeline drove it for him, as he had told me, and he was usually to be seen sitting beside her, probably with an anxious expression. Often she drove him far out, across the prairie-flat country south of the city, to the deeps of the Menwode and the sea. No doubt he felt safer in those empty and quiet roads than amid the traffic of the Casterton streets.

One afternoon Tom Arrowsmith and I had gone on a long walk to Selham to visit once again the ruins, seemingly lost in a meadow, of the twelfth-century Cistercian Abbey. We delayed there too long, wandering with our thoughts in the bare, ruined choir where late the sweet monks sang, and through what was left of their refectory, calefactory and cellarium, which were now little more than fragmented stretches of grey flint wall, islanded in tall grass. The sky thickened above us, our watches told us that it was late, and we made haste to walk, at five miles an hour, home to Casterton where we must attend Evensong. The spire of Casterton, rising above a distant wood, seemed a long hour away, across these level fields. Spire, wood, and skirting of red-roofed houses were but miniature things at the far end of all this wide savannah land.

We had been hurrying for twenty minutes when Bishop Griffyn's car passed us at a diminishing speed, drew into the verge in front of us, and stopped.

His head came out of the near window. 'Thought it was you, Richard. Can we give you a lift? Or would you feel safer on your feet since Emmeline's driving?'

'Nonsense, Bishop,' said Emmeline coyly. 'I drive very nicely. I'm getting better and better.' Her coyness always seemed misplaced in anyone so tall and broad and monumental.

'We should love a lift,' I said. 'This is Tom Arrowsmith, sir. We were going to be late for Evensong.'

'Good evening, Mr. Arrowsmith. Come in, both of you by all means but the contract between us says that all travelling in this car is entirely at the passenger's risk.'

'You are so silly, Bishop,' said Emmeline, remaining coy. 'It's not fair. What will these boys think of me?'

'We will willingly trust ourselves to you,' I said, attempting a gallantry in tune with her coyness. 'Won't we, Tom?'

'Not half!' said Tom; and his crudity shamed me.

'Well,' said the Bishop, 'it's right for youth to be venturesome. Get in at the back. You remember Richard, Emmeline, don't you? Go at a reasonable pace because these boys are valuable lives. I must explain, Richard, that Emmeline is at the stage of being impressed by her skill with these machines and is inclined to put it to the test ever and anon by progressive increases of speed.'

'I do nothing of the sort, Bishop. You *do* exaggerate. You really do. I'm a careful driver.'

'With intermissions, my dear. We did nearly destroy that family yesterday. It was in East Street, Mr. Arrowsmith, as we swung out of the Pallant. It was a near thing. Are you both quite comfortable?'

'Yes, sir,' I said.

'Yes, sir,' said Tom, and I was relieved that he hadn't said 'Not half!'

'Very good. Full speed a – no, I mean, Lead on, Emmeline. What time is your Evensong, Richard?'

'Five-thirty, sir.'

'Well, we ought to be able to get you back in time for that. The time now —' He leaned forward to look at the clock on the dashboard. 'Oh, I forgot. This clock only works when the car's going up hill. It does nothing on these flats. Curious; you'd think that it'd only work going down hill – by gravity or something, but no: it only achieves its real purpose when its works are climbing upward – in which, of course, it may be a parable of our human condition. Try to get them back in time, Emmeline, but be careful – be careful.'

There seemed little amiss in her driving while we were in the country roads, so the Bishop, turning round to us in his seat, began an essay on Extempore Prayer. This because they were returning from an interdenominational congress in a seaside town. He stressed the enormous advantage of our set Anglican prayers over 'the extemporaneous vapourings of verbiage which the Nonconformists address to the Lord in the most awful sanctimonious undulations – which I personally, Richard, can only hear with an almost physical anguish.'

'Oh, you are awful, Bishop,' said Emmeline. 'I think the Nonconformists are sweet.'

We had got to this point when a sudden sight of Casterton's spire much bigger than before showed the Bishop that we were on the last mile or so leading into the city, and that from now onward there would be more complicated traffic for Emmeline to negotiate. It was, so he had just remembered, Wednesday, and the farmers in their wagons and carts would be returning from the cattle market.

'Oh, dear!' he gasped; and he abandoned the essay because of this present emergency, and kept his eyes ahead.

'Oh, dear!' he repeated, and his thumb went between his lips, when he saw a crush of sheep crowding unhappily and unintelligently towards his radiator. 'Go slow, Emmeline.'

Emmeline went slow and got the car past the sheep, not without some dubious moments for the Bishop during which his thumb remained at his lips. But we had not long left the sheep behind us when we saw a little dozen of cows approaching, not in a crush but in a scatter, visiting frequently at an alarmed trot the wrong side of the road. They seemed as alarmed at the approach of our car as the Bishop at the approach of them; and soon they were further demoralized by the idiotic yelling of the farm boy behind them; so, what with us in front and this village idiot behind, they were soon scampering all about the road and the grass verges.

'Oh lord, oh Emmeline!' the Bishop gasped, hand still at mouth. 'Oh ... Oh, dear me, dear me! ... *Oremus invicem ... Ora pro nobis....* These ... these execrable machines.'

Emmeline made her way past the cows by taking their convoy on the flank, visiting the grass verge in a quick meandering way, nearly visiting the hedge, and collecting one bump from a distraught cow, wildly adrift, at which the Bishop exclaimed, 'Oh God! Oh Montreal!'

Tom and I, in the back, were hard pressed to hide laughter,

especially as the Bishop's left hand was now gripping the car's doorway, probably for consolation only, but it looked as if he were debating whether to abandon ship.

After these strains with sheep and cows, our further progress through mere carts and cars seemed easy and, as we came into the city, Bishop Griffyn said, 'We'll take these boys to their Evensong. We can just make it – only don't go too fast, Emmeline. So far we've arrived safely, *laus Deo*.'

It was kind of him, and I didn't like to demur, so we were obliged to come to St. Thomas's in an ex-prince-bishop's car, *en prince*, while other students were entering the church and turning round to see who we were. On second thoughts I was pleased.

§

The last Sunday of October and the Feast of Christ the King. In our gowns we students of the Theological College sat in the Choir, filling our two long carven pews in front of the prebendaries' canopied stalls. I had managed to get myself near the eastern end of the pew on the *decani* side because from there I should be able to see the Archdeacon in his stall opposite, which was that belonging to the prebend of Icklingham, and Bishop Griffyn in his even handsomer corner throne, that which proclaimed 'Thesaurar' in Gothic gold above his head. The Archdeacon was the preacher announced for this morning, and I think no girl student could have been much more eager than I for her current idol to justify her adoration.

The eight bells were still clashing from the tower and the people were filing on soft feet into the nave beyond and below our Choir screen. Sunshine, piercing through the clerestory windows, laid lodgments of light beneath the triforium arches and bright oblique shafts along the Norman piers. Droplets of colour, flung from the stained windows, made patterns on the south aisle floors. The clock in the tower clicked; the bells stopped to let the half-hour chime. Half-past ten. Bells silent, and only the organ playing. It raised its volume; we all stood; and the choir, priest vicars, canons, archdeacon and dean, came in procession from their vestries in the transept. The clergy diverged to their separate stalls, Archdeacon Alanside to Icklingham, Bishop Griffyn to Thesaurus.

For how much of that service I was woolgathering rather than worshipping! Always the canticles, psalms, and anthem, rendered by a choir whose boys were trained in their choir school and whose lay vicars were professional singers, would drown me in their surge and swell of harmonious sound, so that I could do nothing – nothing – but dream. My eyes wandered through the openwork of the screen to the people below, and I set them in their sober Sunday clothes against the thick white-stone walls which the Normans had built. The Conquest had been but a recent affair when those stones were laid one upon another by Norman masters and bob-haired Saxon serfs in their coarse tunics and cross-gartered stockings. From my place in the Choir I pictured them on their rough scaffolding, with their crude wooden cranes or treadmills hauling up the heavier blocks. Then I looked again at the people of today, eight hundred years later, kneeling below those heavy, well-placed blocks while a priest vicar chanted in the Choir.

A hymn. One which I liked, and I gave myself to a hearty sing-ing of it, not without an untimely pleasure in the improved quality of my voice this morning. And as I sang I looked round and about the Choir and thought how strange it was that these lofty arches had been lifted high by our conquering Normans so that Richard Oliver might worship among them in eight centuries time. At this point, in loyalty to the builders, I tried to worship more properly. With application, and with no more relapses into vanity.

But all too soon I was sunk in dreams again: in memories of my father preaching in his tiny country church (which had its Norman arches too); in memories of cold mornings in chapel at school; and memories of a high church in Holborn where, for a time, I had worked in one of the great Insurance palaces. It was the priests of that church who had excited my ardour for a Catholic Revival in the erring old C. of E., a revival which should bring back to her all the glories of sacrament and ceremonial that had once been hers. I had never seen Father Stanton, who had been curate of this church for more than fifty years, resolved to live and die in the humblest rank, but it had been the countless stories of that laughing, tender saint which had helped to send me where I stood this morning. He being dead had yet spoken to the insurance clerk.

But since fewer occupations are pleasanter than dreaming, time's footsteps today were giant strides, and here we were at the hymn before the sermon. My eyes went to the Archdeacon in his stall, and I saw him kneel for the usual prayer before preaching. A verger stood waiting with silver-headed wand to lead him to the pulpit. The last couplet of the hymn, and this little procession of two, black-gowned verger and white-surpliced priest, passed out of the Choir and into the nave.

As I watched the Archdeacon in choir habit follow the little gowned verger I thought that no man, unless it was Canon Leedes, could look his part more perfectly. Though not so tall as Bishop Griffyn, he was tall enough and seemed the taller for the smallness of the verger. Dark-haired, fine-featured, of erect carriage and grave walk, he was such a figure as might have appeared on the stage, in robes like these, to represent an historic churchman of Tudor times. As he passed before me I saw his shadowed blue eyes and perceived again his likeness, almost laughable, to his daughter Julie. Remembering her for the first time this morning, I looked through the screen to see if I could find her in the congregation. Yes, there she stood, among the people near the pulpit, with her mother beside her. Till this moment I had never thought of her as tall, but just as her father seemed taller than usual behind the verger, so Julie at her small mother's side.

When all the people (and the nave was fuller than usual) had subsided on to their chairs, and all the canons and prebendaries (a good attendance for a good preacher) had arranged themselves comfortably in their stalls, and silence sat waiting everywhere for the Archdeacon to begin, he said softly but audibly, 'The thirty-third chapter of the book of the prophet Isaiah. The seventeenth verse. "Thine eyes shall see the king in his beauty; they shall behold the land that is very far off."'

A pause for these words to sink into every mind.

Then he began. 'The prophet is promising the deliverance of

Judah from the hosts of the Assyrians encompassing her, and when he speaks of the king in his beauty, he is imagining King Hezekiah no longer kneeling in sackcloth but throned in splendour and triumph. "The land that is very far off" might be rendered, less rhythmically perhaps but more accurately, as "a land of far-stretching distances".'

'Far-stretching distances . . .'

Instantly I was with Tom Arrowsmith in a country road, many miles from Casterton, and seeing across a far-stretching country of level pasture and ploughland the spire of Casterton rising above an autumn wood.

'Isaiah was proclaiming,' said the voice from the pulpit, 'that when the Assyrian should be driven away by the might of the Lord, the people would see the land going on and on to the horizon with never an enemy in sight anywhere.

'Now today is traditionally the Feast of Christ the King. Well, once see Christ in his beauty, and inevitably your eyes behold great distances that at first seem too far, much too far, for poor halting humanity to reach. I am going to show you a few of them today and I suspect that most of you will think that you would have to journey very far, and with great difficulty, even with dislike, if you are ever to attain the farthest you can see. Because, alas, wherever you look over one of these far-stretching distances, you see the Assyrian encamped to hold and drive you back.'

Bishop Griffyn in his study used his steel-rimmed spectacles only to read his book or consider his cake; Archdeacon Alanside in the pulpit used his horn-rimmed reading-glasses, most skilfully, for oratorical purposes. He would whip them from his eyes so that he could lean forward and declaim his point with a particular emphasis. Sometimes he would take them off so as to use them as a kind of extension of his pointing finger, or so as to tap them on the palm of his other hand while he made a series of points. But most of all he used them as a means to a musical pause. He knew the value of pauses, and after making an all-important point he would enforce the pause by replacing them before his eyes and slowly settling them there. He had the platform sense, innate or acquired.

Now, re-settling the glasses, he continued, 'Let us strain our eyes to look down some of these distances. Here is one: the sacred duty of forgiveness, incumbent on all followers of Christ the King. It is not a matter of choice for us, whether we forgive or whether we don't; we have our orders. The royal orders. To forgive till seventy times seven. And that means, I'm afraid – oh, yes, I'm afraid so – that we have to forgive every one of our enemies in the late war, even those we conceive to be the worst.'

Seated next to me in the carven pew was Bill Brickhill, wearing over his gown his Oxford B.A. hood, to the disadvantage of most of us who had earned no such impressive decoration. He had a notebook and pencil in his hands and appeared to the clergy behind to be a serious-minded and studious young man jotting down notes of the sermon as he would of lectures in the Priest Vicars' Hall. Actually I could see with my right eye that he was doodling. And when this word about the Germans came from the pulpit, I felt his elbow nudge mine and saw that he had written for me, 'That, my dear R.O., will vex quite a few.'

But the Archdeacon continued, 'If we are to extend our sight to cover the whole of this distance, which is the whole brotherhood of man – and our royal orders are nothing less – then we simply must achieve firstly, a forgiveness based on pity for a people who, after yielding their souls to leaders who seem to us evil, are now suffering accordingly; and secondly, a forgiveness based on the knowledge that our hands were not wholly white when we took up our sword against them. *They* may have fired the fuse that set the world alight, but how much, just how much, did *we* spread of the tinder and the explosives lying around?'

Yes, Bill Brickhill was right. There was no bodily restlessness in the congregation yet, but, unless my imagination deluded me, I could apprehend an impatience here and there in the nave, and even in the prebendal stalls behind me. At this date the wounds of the First German War were still inflamed.

And now, unsparingly, the preacher was dealing with another 'far-stretching distance' whose consideration could be hardly less unpopular than this business of forgiving Germans. 'Besides forgiving the enemies of our country,' he was saying, 'we have to forgive the enemies *within* our frontiers, the enemies of our community and our peace, the criminals. Difficult, isn't it? Especially if I stretch the distance to its utmost and say we have to forgive the most cruel of murderers. What, even those? Yes, even those. This is not to say that there is to be no punishment for them; but only that it must be punishment without joy, without hate, without vindictiveness. We are ordered by the King to get beyond *that*. If our eyes really look far enough can we see any stopping-place anywhere this side of "Father forgive them . . ."? Do we see anywhere a permission to kill the murderer because he has killed another? Only look far enough, with your eyes that the fingers of Christ have touched, and can you see a gallows anywhere?' He lifted off his glasses, as if to get closer to them all with his question. 'Anywhere between yourself and the horizon?' He shook his head. 'Only Christ's own gallows.' This time without replacing the glasses, just holding them in his hand, he paused long, disturbingly long, so as to isolate and stress the next words. 'But perhaps . . . some of you do not want to look so far. No, no; it would be thinking too far. Too far.'

I shall not give you the whole of this deliberately provocative sermon. He passed on to assess the social sins of those who were so ready to feel a 'righteous indignation' against more obvious offenders. He talked of luxury proudly displayed though it was little more than the gift of privilege; of the ugly greed which some men in business justified by the gross statement that there was 'no sentiment in business' – a statement impossible to a true follower of Christ the King, since he must needs stand forth as the stern champion, at whatever cost, of a Christlike sentiment in business. And let not the women and wives leave this matter to the man in business; it was the duty of all whose comfort was largely the gift of profits and dividends to repudiate all those advantages which they knew to have been extracted by oppression or exploitation of the weak. 'All this you will see in the distance if you strain your eyes enough, but . . . perhaps you do not want to see so far.'

Was there now an actual bodily restlessness in parts of this comfortable and well-dressed congregation?

None the less he went on to disturb their comfort in another matter. Our county was a hunting and sporting county; was not Lord Lailand's pack in its kennels at Stormwood, not five miles from Casterton? Had not some of these well-dressed gentlemen their game preserves? And if this last Sunday in October was the Feast of Christ the King, was not the first Monday in November the opening of the hunting season? But the Archdeacon was telling them they must extend their sight, not only to cover the brotherhood of all men everywhere, but also their brotherhood with the dumb animals. He went so far as to ask of them, Could they imagine Christ the King taking a gun to shoot agony into a flying bird and to bring it down in agony to an agonizing impact with the earth. Or Christ striving to be 'in at the death' of a groaning animal torn apart by dogs. 'Do you really think He would murder for sport? But perhaps you do not want to think so far. Perhaps you would rather save your conscience by calling those of us who take this view "cranks". But surely it looks then as if "crank" merely means someone who wishes to be humaner than you.'

Along the pew came Bill Brickhill's notebook, and I read, 'A nasty one, that.'

This time I wrote on the pad. I pencilled, 'A hit. A very palpable hit' – hoping that my quotation was clever – 'and now behave yourself, B.B.'

The sermon's peroration I thought, with my eager partiality, a prose poem. '"From henceforth let no man trouble me," said St. Paul, "for I bear in my body the marks of the Lord Jesus." The Church is the Body of Christ and I hold it the duty of the preacher to trouble the Church till it shows, for all to see, the marks of its king. I thank God that in some parts of its body those marks are there: in Sisters of Mercy, in Franciscan saints, in men and women who help those in prison, in clergy who live in poverty so as to minister to the poor; in men and women who are not afraid to be reviled as sentimental and soft and weak because they will not countenance the breaking of our brotherhood with our small fellow-creatures by killing them for a little social fun, nor abate their censure of any man who "blends his pleasure and his pride With sorrow of the meanest thing that feels".'

The Archdeacon folded up his notes, turned, and descended.

§

Four of us walked home together to the hostel, Bill Brickhill, Tom Arrowsmith, Alec Raines, and myself, talking of the sermon. Alec Raines was a very small youth, and as self-opinionated as he was small. I still think of Alec as the most argumentative little man I have ever met. In those days he was but twenty-one and looked from behind no more than a schoolboy, so short his body and so small his head. But that head held a store of arguments on all subjects suitable for disputation. Bill always maintained that Alec must have been an impassioned arguer from the moment he discovered ratiocination, say at four years old; and that this unfortunate disease had been made doubly worse when, for the purposes of the Entrance Examination to the College, he had read Jevons's *Logic*. Now in any argument he would accuse his opponent, almost compassionately, of this fallacy or another which he had recently learned, with a ravening appetite, from Professor Jevons. God help us when he got to the Rules of Logic. 'But that's a *petitio principii*,' he would insist. Or it was a *circulus in probando*. Or 'Good heavens, Tom, that's a *circulus in definiendo!*' 'Is it?' said Tom, surprised and no wiser. Or to me: 'But, my dear chap, you don't seem to understand that your major premise was a disjunctive conditional proposition.' And once to Bill Brickhill, 'But that's nonsense, Bill. Your middle is undistributed'; to which Bill: 'My middle is perfectly all right. Don't you worry about that.'

Not but what we encouraged him in his vice for the fun of it. And it so happened that the sermon this morning had dealt with at least four of those subjects about which he was always hot to argue. In such matters as German atrocities, capital punishment, trade unions and blood sports, he took always the High Tory line. So I, charmed that the Archdeacon should have touched on so many subjects that would exasperate Alec, asked him, hoping to fan up a really fine heat, 'Well, Alec old boy, what did you make of that sermon?'

'I am very clear what I made of it.'

Good. The fat was ready to flame. 'Explain further, Alec. Tell us what you made of it.'

'Must he?' Bill sighed.

'Yes. Come on, Alec. What were you so clear about?'

'That the man's an exhibitionist.'

'Oh, rubbish. No, no. No, I won't have that. It's not fair.' The Archdeacon kneeling every morning in the quiet of Cuthbert's chapel, head in hands. . . .

'He's a publicity hunter. I think every one of those subjects was chosen because they make the headlines. It's long been obvious to me that he likes to preach controversial sermons because they get his name into the papers. I noticed the *Casterton Herald* and the *County Times* were there. Don't you suppose he gave them the tip to come? Don't you suppose he's hoping now that they're busy telephoning Fleet Street?'

'My God, I suppose nothing of the sort!' Unfortunately I found that it was I who was catching alight instead of him.

'A first way to fame is to be a storm-centre of controversy – isn't that so, Bill?'

'Alas, that's very true,' Bill agreed. 'But I fail to see as yet what grounds you have for attributing such an unpleasant motive to our excellent Archdeacon.'

'It was a foul suggestion,' I said. 'A filthy —'

But Alec wasn't listening to me. He was intent on spitting out, as we walked along, more and more of his excited opinions. 'And what's more, the man talked a lot of clotted nonsense. He tries to suggest —'

'I agree with everything he said. Every word. Every bally word.'

'And I disagree.'

'So we perceive. And so you're entitled to do. But, as Bill says, you're not entitled to attribute beastly motives to him just because he takes a different point of view from you. You're so blasted proud of your logic, but you're showing yourself now to be about as illogical as —'

'*I* am?' *He* was alight now. '*Me?* How?'

'In being unable to disagree with someone without attributing, not only error to him, but moral turpitude as well.' (I was proud of 'moral turpitude'.) 'For my part I can't see that there's any valid answer to a single thing he said.'

'Oh, *I'd* give you the answers.'

But now it was I who, furnace-hot, was not listening to him. 'Unless of course you don't take the Christian position but the Nietzschean or the Fichtean or the Machiavellian or some such.' I was glad to hurl these learned-sounding names like pepper into his eyes, though I should have been at a loss just then to say what these gentlemen professed, except that it was anti-Christian.

'I am perfectly ready to argue from the Christian standpoint.'

'Yes, well, don't,' Bill petitioned.

'What Richard never realizes —'

'Richard realizes everything perfectly well,' I said. 'Go and get lost.'

'Now, now! Children, children!' Bill remonstrated.

But I persisted, 'I have the utmost admiration for a priest who has the guts to get into the pulpit and say terribly unpopular things. And I'm damned if I'm going to hear him called an exhibitionist just because he has more courage than most. And more true holiness. You should see him every morning at Mass on his knees. The only one . . .'

'What you two quarrelsome boys don't realize,' said Bill, 'is that it's quite possible you're both right. It's possible to have a true love for the Church and its services and to be an exhibitionist as well —'

'But *he's* not!'

'Allow me to finish. It's quite possible to be a passionate and courageous preacher of unpopular truths and at the same time to be not averse to the publicity that accrues from such boldness. It is quite possible to have an abounding love for all one's fellow creatures and a reasonable love of oneself too. Richard won't allow that he's a bit of an exhibitionist —'

'Richard certainly won't,' said I.

'But I don't know. He's always so perfectly dressed. What does that imply?'

'Decency; that's all. A love of decency and order in everything.'

'And not a love of attracting people's eyes?'

'Certainly not.'

'Well, I'm not sure. And preaching can be a form of self-decoration too.'

'And I think that's a wicked suggestion. As bad as Alec's.' All this hovered so near to something Bishop Griffyn had said, and it was so sensible, that I had to repudiate it more and more hotly. 'Of course it's possible to be both brave and egotistic, and a keen churchgoer and egotistic, but it doesn't happen to be the case with the Archdeacon, does it, Tom?' Tom had said nothing so far, being always ready to listen to 'you well-educated chaps' in humility. 'You've seen him at Mass, haven't you, Tom? I hold that the Archdeacon is as near a saint as anyone we've got in Casterton.' I think the angry tears were almost in my eyes as I said this.

'A saint?' Bill began dubiously – but at this moment, when we were only ten yards from the hostel door, I saw Julie running towards us. She must have been given by her mother some message to deliver in West Street and to be now hurrying home to the Close. In any other girl I might have made fun of her way of running, arms held outwards, legs swinging sideways, but just now, after all this argument, I felt fond of her because I knew she would be on my side. And in fact, as she saw me, she stopped abruptly, and said breathlessly, 'I saw you in the Cathedral. Wasn't he wonderful?'

'Absolutely,' I agreed, glad that the other three had heard this. They had stopped with me, in dismay at this sudden confrontation by a girl unknown. 'These are Bill Brickhill, Alec Raines, Tom Arrowsmith, and old Uncle Tom Cobley and all.' She gave them a formal smile. 'Yes, I agreed with every single word of it.'

'Of course you did.' She was still breathless. 'Because you're nice. But some of the old biddies didn't. You should have heard what they said to Mummy, walking home. Oh, I do think people are silly. How is it possible to go regularly to church and still argue about anything he said?'

'I agree. I agree absolutely.'

'I mean, I'd simply love to go hunting, as I told you, and I tend to hate all Germans – criminals I rather love – and I'm afraid I should like to have all the luxuries I could get, but I still know he's right and that I oughtn't to. I can at least *see* that. Why can't they? I'm not sure that I shan't start trying to be better as from tomorrow. Shall you? Or perhaps you don't need to. Being an ordination candidate and all that?'

'You bet I need it a lot more than you do.' And further to annoy Alec Raines, I said, 'You must be proud of your father, aren't you?'

'Just a little. I don't see how I can help it really. I go all twittery when he's preaching like that. Shivery.'

'Well, I should be proud of him too if he were my father,' I said, partly to please her, partly in continuing hot defiance of Alec Raines at my side, and partly because it was true.

Chapter Seven

THE ARCHDEACON'S AGAPÉ

That Advent Term ended in mid-December. Casterton had been full of colour in the term's first days: brown and crimson leaves, brilliant green grass; pale sunlight washing over the spire as it tapered into a clean blue sky. Now in the December frosts, when we must leave the city, the hoar was a white sediment on its roofs and lawns; all colours were dead or dulled; and no sunlight touched the spire because, whichever way you looked down the four Roman roads, you saw a pale grey haze investing the city. Only a few last leaves, brown and brittle, hung from hardly visible twigs so that they seemed to be afloat on the air.

And one day before we left I was bidden to dinner at the Archdeacon's. To dinner. No less. So far as records went no such huge pebble had ever before been tossed into the still waters of our College life. There was bewilderment. There was banter.

In South Street one morning, near the Prebendal Gate, Julie in her black hunting-jacket and cap came reining her horse towards the pavement where I walked. She halted it at my side. 'You're coming to dinner with us,' she said. 'You're coming to dinner with us.' And with the horse tossing its head and plunging a hoof, she pursued, 'It's because Bishop Griffyn told Daddy how frightfully you admired him, and Daddy was naturally braced by that. Who wouldn't be? I love anybody who admires me. Don't you?'

'Nobody does,' I said.

'Oh, what absolute rot. Bishop Griffyn does. Like anything. So Daddy said you must come to dinner one day, but you know how time passes, and it was only yesterday, when he heard that your term was ending, that he said, "But, golly, we haven't asked him to dinner yet." Or words to that effect. And you're going to be asked to come and say good-bye, as it were. You *will* come, won't you?'

'I shall be terrified,' I said, standing on the kerb and looking up at her on her high but unstable and pitching seat. 'Will other people be there? I'm not used to High Life.'

'Only Lucille Eavry, and she's adorable. And —'

'But who the devil – I mean, who's Lucille?'

'She's a widow woman but quite young and gay. And pretty. Daddy and her husband were at the House together.'

'What house? The workhouse?'

'No, don't be silly. Christ Church, Oxford, and he, Mr. Eavry, I mean, became something rather tremendous in the Diplomatic Service; anyhow, he and Lucille have been all over Europe together, attached to this Embassy or that – Madrid, Rome, Constantinople, and so on – and about a year ago he died suddenly in Constantinople of whatever it is you die suddenly of in Constantinople. And now Daddy, in the course of archidiaconing, found her living in a marvellous old Tudor house at East Helwood, with some marvellous old servants to more or less match it, and only about fifteen miles away. I think she's rather lovely without being beautiful, if you see what I mean. Steady, Rev dearest.' She stroked the horse's long tossing neck, but it continued to plunge a hoof and champ its clinking bit. And Julie continued to talk, looking down at me on the kerb, while the pedestrian life of South Street passed behind me and I felt its eyes on my back and on the horse's rider. 'Lucille's nothing to be frightened of. She's one of those who put you at your ease directly she speaks to you and makes you like her at once. I adore her. Then there's darling Bishop Griffyn coming. That was me. I told Daddy how much you liked Gregory, and how much he liked you, and Daddy said "We'll have him along too, so as to make it really nice for Richard." That'll be the lot. Just six of us. But all delightful people. Daddy says it's going to be an agga-pee. Do you know what an agga-pee is? It's a kind of love feast for Christians who really love each other.'

'Of course I know what an agapé is,' I said, a little grieved that she should think I didn't know that much.

'Well, I didn't know till yesterday when he told me.'

'Yes, but you aren't a theological student. It was a love feast

D

among the early Christians, and generally you brought your own food.'

'Oh, for pity's sake don't do that.'

'And it ended,' I said, with a certain relish as I looked up at that pretty face, and with a desire to show my learning, 'it usually ended with the *philema hagion*, the holy kiss.'

'Did it? Oh, that should be fun. Let's all do that.'

I thought I'd better change the subject. 'I'm glad Bishop Griffyn'll be there. I go to tea with him sometimes.'

'I know. He says it's so kind of you to come and sit with him.'

'Does he indeed?'

'Yes. He says he enjoys your talk; it's bright.'

'But it's *he* who does the talking.'

'Yes . . . well . . . I expect you laugh at his jokes. Probably that's what he means.'

'I certainly laugh sometimes. Quite often, in fact.'

'Exactly; so no wonder he says you're witty.'

'But it's the other way about.'

'All the same, you must have said something remarkable once, because he says you've got insight. Steady, Rev darling! Don't be so impatient. I *will* talk to Richard, if I want to. He says you have "perilous eyes".'

'"Perilous eyes"?'

'Yes, because they see far too much. They see what's really going on inside people, no matter what they're saying or pretending.'

'He's thinking of himself. That's certainly true of him.'

'And he calls you the "nice tall brown-headed boy" when he can't remember your name, which is frequent.'

Nice tall brown-headed boy – my affection for the man increased.

'Mind you,' Julie insisted, 'he often says nice things of me too.'

'And with far greater justice, I'm sure.'

'No, no; it's just that I'm the world's best listener when he gets talking. Anyhow, with him at the dinner-table – *and* Lucille – there should be bliss. I'm looking forward to it.'

'And I'm still a bit terrified,' I said.

We sat down that evening, six of us, at a table richly dressed, but what kind of table it was I don't know, because these were the days when people shrouded their table-tops in glistening white linen. I imagine it was a Sheraton extension table because we sat on six elegant Sheraton shield-back chairs, and the long mahogany sideboard with its slim tapered legs was certainly Sheraton too. Three great portraits in heavy gilt frames, by Lely, Gainsborough, and an unknown, looked down upon us. I learned later that they were ancestors, not of the Archdeacon, but of Natalie his wife.

Since Lucille Eavry sat on the Archdeacon's right, and I on Mrs. Alanside's left, opposite Bishop Griffyn, I had her at my side. Contrasted with her tiny hostess, she seemed a woman of large but graceful shape. Her shoulders were wide and her features large as if to match the wide shoulders, but, large or not, they did nothing to lessen the feminine softness of her face, with its round cheeks, clear skin and large, deep, soft brown eyes. The eyes were the more remarkable for the paleness of the skin. I agreed with Julie in thinking that she won your liking the moment she smiled at you with those eyes and spoke to you.

We were none of us in dinner dress, and she wore a cross-over afternoon gown of black silk, with sleeves of fine black lace from shoulder to wrist. Her only jewellery was a long rope of pearls which drooped over the black silk almost as far as her waist, and which she was constantly fingering.

The room was not as large as the white-and-gold drawing-room, so with a fire in the Regency grate which threw rippling lights on walls of warm rose, it was a cosy vessel for incubating good talk; and the Bishop was soon in form. Lucille had bewailed, 'But, Mr. Archdeacon, I am not clear what a Lambeth Conference is.'

'Ask the Bishop, Lucille. He must have attended more than one in his time. Tell her, Gregory.'

'A Lambeth Conference, dear lady, is a swarming of bishops into Lambeth Palace – all the bishops of the Anglican Communion from all over the world. It is indeed very like a swarming of bees at their proper season because they all cluster in a compact mass in

His Grace's palace at Lambeth, which I think therefore we can honestly describe as the skep. The swarm-catcher.'

'But why Lambeth, Bishop? Am I deplorably ignorant, but I always thought Lambeth was a mass of South London slums and that the Archbishop's palace was at Canterbury.'

'Explain Lambeth to her,' said the Archdeacon. 'Unless, of course, our Richard will.' As at the tea-party he had noticed that no one was speaking to Julie and me, and he was determined that I at least should not be left unheeded. Again and again, in the drawing-room before dinner he had directed the talk towards me that I might be happy and feel one of them, and each time I had felt his great good-will, a kind of temporary love, pointing towards me, because I was the person he was addressing, and, even more perhaps, because I was young. In some of my silences I had meditated on a difference in quality between him and his wife. Little Mrs. Alanside had hardly spoken once to me, and not once to Julie. 'Richard is freshest from studies of English Church History and will know all about Lambeth.'

Most happily I did know all about Lambeth. We had been 'doing' the twelfth and thirteenth centuries in our lectures, and greatly was I pleased about this, because so far I had found nothing witty or valuable to contribute to the talk. 'Lambeth Palace,' I told them, 'used to belong to the Bishops of Rochester but they exchanged it with the Archbishop for another property in the last years of the twelfth century. The Archbishop at the time was Hubert Walter, but he was soon succeeded by Stephen Langton so it's not impossible that Magna Carta was debated in a conference at Lambeth. The . . . the actual buildings as we know them at present were probably begun by Archbishop Boniface early in the thirteenth century.'

'Good heavens!' exclaimed Bishop Griffyn at this erudition. And Julie muttered, 'S'truth!'

'There! What did I tell you?' triumphed the Archdeacon. 'No wonder Canon Leedes has a high opinion of Richard. How splendid a thing is real scholarship.'

I, having distinguished myself, blushed all over my face and promptly said, 'But I don't know anything about the Lambeth Conferences of today,' retreating, you see, quickly into modesty.

'It's early yet, Richard,' said the Archdeacon. 'You may come to know all about them. As Bishop of Casterton, perhaps. Or even – why not? – as the Chairman. The host at Lambeth. In the meantime, continue, Gregory.'

'Yes, Dr. Griffyn, please,' begged Lucille. 'I'm so thrilled by it all.'

'I don't know that there's much to be thrilled about in a Lambeth Conference. As an assembly of nothing but bishops it is usually – and perhaps properly – treated with a certain amount of popular suspicion. And if I may be forgiven for speaking the exact truth of my heart, madam, I would say that I can think of few institutions more grandiose in conception and more void of results. I wish it were not so, but there it is: as far as I can see, after some thirty years as a bishop, no person in the country, except a few parsons, attaches the smallest importance to the deliberations at a Lambeth Conference. Even the great majority of the ungaitered clergy take no notice. They just go their own ways, often lawless, as if their Fathers-in-God had never spoken.'

'But what do the Fathers-in-God talk about?' demanded Lucille. 'What do they decide, even if nobody pays any attention?'

'What do they talk about? Let's see.' The Bishop ruminated for a few moments with the hand that held his fork pressed against his mouth. Then the fork descended to his plate again and pursued its proper occupation, as if satisfied that it had provided help. 'Well . . . I remember that at the last conference the Bishop of Plaistow gave us the substance of his *Commentary on the Colossians*, which he said had engaged him for a period of years, and certainly engaged us for a period that seemed as long. Then the good Bishop of London addressed us with his celebrated charm on approximately the whole duty of man. Oh yes, and there was a Negro bishop, a fascinating creature with a smile like the sun breaking through the clouds. He spoke with fluent incoherence about African problems and was loudly applauded, but more, I suspect, for the colour of his skin than for the clarity of his remarks.'

'Bishop, you are rather wicked,' said Lucille, delighted that he should be so.

'Wicked, madam? How can truth be wicked to adult minds? We are all grown up here – even including Richard and Julie. They indeed are probably more ready for truth than any of us, having escaped the Victorian pruderies and insincerities. You too, of course, escaped them, Mrs. Eavry,' he added quickly and gallantly.

'The pruderies, yes. But I'm not so sure about insincerities. Some insincerities seem inevitable to me, especially in the Diplomatic Service. Still, give us some more truth, since we're all adult.'

'I don't know that I remember much more. I recall a white South African bishop who addressed us on Paganism and Taboos among the Bantu, which proved to be a subject of quite portentous dullness (since you want the truth) and was presented with a regrettably boring prolixity. These episcopal jamborees are held in midsummer; and the afternoon was atrociously hot, which was perhaps not noticed by a South African, but we bishops of the more temperate north were susceptible to it, and I noticed more than one of the Fathers – but you can gather what I mean. I nodded once or twice myself. The room was the Palace Library, dreadfully congested —'

Lucille interrupted, 'I was just wondering about that. Surely you can't get all the bishops of the Anglican Communion into a library. There are hundreds of bishops in America alone, aren't there?'

Still remembering with pleasure my recent success, I here injected, 'The Library at Lambeth Palace used to be the Great Hall; it's a hundred feet long,' and then wished I hadn't, since everybody looked at me.

'You see?' gloried the Archdeacon. 'Richard even knows the architecture of the Palace.'

'Perhaps he's thinking of it as his future home,' said Bishop Griffyn, while the Archdeacon turned to the butler at the sideboard. 'Give Mr. Oliver some more wine, Wilson. His glass is empty.'

'Oh, oh, thanks . . .' I stuttered.

'Natalie, I hope you're keeping Richard happy down there, while I look after Lucille. Is she, Richard?'

'Oh yes, yes. Rather!' I assured him – a fine example of diplomatic insincerity.

And Bishop Griffyn, his eyes in the thin-rimmed glasses following his fork, resumed his essay on Lambeth, plainly anxious to do so. 'You mentioned the Americans, madam. There was an exceedingly odd prelate from America who described to us how, on his seventieth birthday, the congregation in one of his parishes surprised him by bringing a vast cake up to the altar for him, just before the Blessing. He was greatly touched, if perturbed, and he submitted to us, with some wit, that our liturgical experts would be hard put to find the correct ceremonial and the right collects for such an unexpected extension to the service. He had wondered whether to make a wave-offering of the cake before the cross as our more romantic clergy like to do with the alms basin: the – er – dibs. But they're charming, the Americans, and they add something strange and new to the rather frightened and strait-laced manners of the old world.'

'Go on, Dr. Griffyn. Tell us more.'

'More? Well . . . at the end of the Conference, the Archbishop closed the proceedings with a summing-up that remarkably resembled a judge's summing-up in a criminal trial in that he was obviously on the watch all the time lest he should say something that might commit him to something. No Primate of All England has ever better understood than our beloved Randall Cantuar that you can only escape offence in the Anglican Church by remaining ambiguous. In concluding he congratulated us on having arrived after long discussion at some agreed decisions and bade us give our thanks to God for this – rather prematurely, I thought. However, the Fathers assented enthusiastically and sang the Doxology, but I couldn't help thinking, even as I sang it too, that we were now in a dangerous mood of idolatry since we were singing a hymn to some very doubtful creations of our own hands. But I decided that it would be unkind to suggest this to the Archbishop.'

'And that's something you'd never be, Dr. Griffyn,' said Lucille, with raillery in her eyes.

'What, unkind? No, no. Certainly not. Never, never.'

'No, I see that,' said Lucille, with a smile that said the opposite.

'Dear lady, I have given you nothing but simple, photographically accurate truths. I allow that they are such as I might not tell to babes. But to you —'

On hearing the word 'babes', the Archdeacon, perhaps by a natural association of ideas, asked me, 'What do *you* say to it all, Richard?'

'Oh, dear . . .' I began, in despair of having anything intelligent to say; and before I could find words Bishop Griffyn came, deliberately, I think, to my rescue.

'Richard and I have had many interesting talks together and I know he's one of those who are not afraid of the truth. He knows, for instance, that we can love our ancient nursery and home, the C. of E., not only because it is far and away the greatest and oldest of this island's historic institutions, but also because, wherever he goes in it, and whichever of its Fathers he hearkens unto, he will get only the same lively impression of regnant and vibrant chaos. And that's exactly the way he must love it if he's going to be a good priest in it. Still more so, if he's going to be an archbishop.'

'Oh, I think that's rather a frightening way of looking at it,' said Mrs. Alanside, who was certainly not one who liked to live in the company of photographically accurate truths. 'I don't think a young man ought to think like that.'

But her husband said softly, almost to the pudding on his plate, 'But it's true. It's true. And we *do* love her. Gregory's "chaos" is only his dinner-table word for her great comprehensiveness.'

Not liking to be corrected, however softly, by her husband, she snapped – though softly too, 'I don't care if it's the truth or not. I still don't believe Mr. Oliver should think like that.'

It was over the dessert that the great argument arose – and an astonishing argument for a table in the Close I thought it, though neither Bishop nor Archdeacon seemed to think so. And certainly not Lucille. The subject was nothing less than the propriety of using contraceptives. It was Lucille who, without conscious design, brought us to it. I, the son of a country parsonage, was startled and a little shocked; and I felt uncomfortable that Julie should be listening, who sat there looking much too young for it. But after this first shock and seeing that it was not shared by either of the famous churchmen, I felt ashamed of my suburban pudency. Lucille had been describing, not without a gathering heat, the 'heart-rending' state of the children pullulating in the slums of cities to which she and her husband had been sent: Madrid, Rome, Constantinople. And she told us how, only a few days ago, she had heard from 'one of the greatest men in British aviation' that he and his doctor-wife were about to found a 'Mothers' Clinic for Birth Control'.

'Yes, I know,' said the Archdeacon. 'In North London. In Holloway.'

'That's it. It's the first in the British Empire, and I only wish we'd set about it years ago. For the children's sake. And for their poor wretched mothers too.'

Mrs. Alanside stiffened in her chair. She was a high officer of the Mothers' Union at its headquarters in Westminster as well as in Casterton. 'Oh no,' she began. 'I don't know about that. It seems to me a fearfully dangerous thing to do.'

'If you'd seen the children in the outskirts of Rome,' interrupted Lucille, now more than a little hot, 'I can't think you'd hesitate. Edwyn, why don't you preach about it?' This was the first time I'd learned that she was on Christian name terms with him. Presumably when earlier she had called him 'Mr. Archdeacon' it was in jest. 'Everyone tells me that you're never afraid to say things in the pulpit, however unwelcome and disturbing. Well, preach about this now.'

Mrs. Alanside's lips tightened. Her head shook as if she were pronouncing her disagreement to herself.

The Archdeacon's shoulders lifted. 'I'm afraid I must wait for the Lambeth Fathers to speak – don't you think so, Bishop?'

But Lucille didn't allow the Bishop time to answer. 'If you wait for them, Edwyn, you'll wait for a few hundred years. Haven't we just heard from Dr. Griffyn that, even when the Archbishop does speak, it is only to say something that can safely mean two things at once, if not more. I'm for the courage that'll really wake the Church up.'

'As Father Stanton used to put it,' said the Archdeacon, who loved quoting: '"I sometimes think we shall never know for certain that we're doing our duty till we're afraid to go out into the streets".'

'Just so! Exactly! I see exactly what he meant.'

'And that was how it ended for our Founder.'

'Except that *He* wasn't afraid,' said Lucille.

'A little, I think,' the Archdeacon suggested. 'Remember Gethsemane.' This sacred name enforced a second or two of silence, after which the Archdeacon said, 'And I thank God that He was a little afraid. It brings Him so much nearer to me.'

'Yes, yes, I see that,' said Lucille.

Mrs. Alanside, annoyed that her husband and her guest should be apparently allying themselves against her, burst in with, 'As far as I can see, there's only one thing the Archbishop ought to say, and to say unequivocally and with the utmost clarity.'

'And what is that?' asked Lucille.

'I should have thought it was obvious. That the only proper birth control is self-control. That's what he should say. Plainly.'

'As does Rome,' interposed the Bishop. 'But I'm afraid – if truth may be heard again – that Rome contrives, with her strange and wonderful elasticity, to reconcile an unyielding theory with an all-accommodating practice.'

But Lucille, really angry now, was not listening to anything from the sidelines. She was complaining to her hostess, 'All that is easy enough to say in a comfortable home like this —' at which I couldn't help wondering, as I sat there, what methods the Archdeacon and his wife might or might not have adopted, since there was only one child sitting over there. I thought also that the Archdeacon's Love Feast wasn't going too well.

Meanwhile Lucille, her tongue loosened like those of the others by the butler's wine, said, 'I would go further. A lot further. I fully suspect that the time is coming, and soon, when all our morality will undergo a change.' Prompted to say what she meant, she explained that she herself could see no reason why unmarried women should be denied the fulfilment of their womanhood that a lover would give them, now that it need not result in children. 'Once the question of children is removed, surely it is a matter simply for the lovers themselves. And if no one is hurt by their love, where lies the immorality?'

'I think that's a quite terrible doctrine,' said the Mothers' Union at the foot of the table; while I was wondering what this Lucille might do, or be doing, since she was still young and, in effect, unmarried.

Incensed by the words 'terrible doctrine', she shot out, 'Well, I could tell you of any number of greatly respected women who are determined to exercise their own private right in this matter.'

'You mean: exercise their right without marriage?' said her host.

'Of course. Isn't that what I'm saying?' The answer was defiant.

'Well, I don't think we can countenance that, Lucille, my dear – can we, Gregory? As regards artificial controls within marriage, I may have two minds and be waiting for Lambeth to speak more clearly. But I agree with you in one thing – that sexual perfection is no fair measure of a man's worth.'

'A man's! Listen to him! It's women we're talking about. I hope what you've just said goes for women too.'

'Certainly it is not the only measure of a woman's worth.'

'Ah! Even you modify it a little for a woman. Even you can't give her the whole of your charity.'

'I think I can.'

'Well, all I know,' exclaimed his wife, 'is that, in my humble view, the matter simply isn't open to question. The Bible is enough for me. The Bible has only one word to describe what you're recommending.'

'And what word is that?' asked Lucille, a little sulkily.

But Mrs. Alanside, suddenly ashamed of her heat, recovered her sense of a hostess's duty. And she remembered perhaps that this was her husband's Love Feast. Heroically she flung aside all anger, and said in the friendliest way, and with deliberate gaiety. 'It's not a nice word, Lucille dear. And I think we'll leave it where it is. In fact, now I come to think of it, doesn't the Bible say somewhere, 'Let it not be once named among you'? You see I know my Bible almost as well as Edwyn or the Bishop. Or young Mr. Oliver here. Come, Lucille, let us go into the drawing-room.'

§

After this second visit to the Residentiary, and after I'd sat listening to the post-dinner conversation over coffee and cognac in its white-panelled and gilded drawing-room, I came away with a very clear view of the relationship between the Archdeacon and his wife. As often happens, the first general conversation split a length into two fragments, man drawn to man, woman to woman: the men, bishop and archdeacon, talking ecclesiastical or secular politics together; and the women, Mrs. Alanside and her guest, enjoying an ardent gossip, unheard by the men but not by Julie and me who sat there seldom addressed, silent for the most part, but listening. It was from all this drawing-room talk that I slowly assembled my picture of the Alanside home.

A mutual impatience showed at times between husband and wife. He could not always control his impatience with her wilder talk, nor she her impatience with this impatience or with his courteous but irrepressible corrections. She was not so self-confident as not to perceive that some of her talk he despised, and this perception forced her to argue and disagree ever more warmly, wildly, and at length. Sometimes, instead of correcting her more irrational assertions, he just sat in silence and sadly, as if suffering a foolishness as gladly as he could. This naturally infuriated her – she told Lucille so in the course of their hearty gossip, when they were dealing with husbands and other domestic matters. 'I know he's ever so much cleverer than I am; there's no cleverer man in the whole diocese, I know that well; but I often wish he'd *throw* something at me rather than just sit there practising a Christian patience. He never does that sort of thing with Julie, but then of course Julie can do no wrong in his eyes.'

Here then, at least in the wife's case, was the common pattern of a love-hate union, if by 'hate' one meant no more than a complex of resentments, jealousies, impatiences and irritabilities, all too few of which were secreted in a private chamber, most being available for drawing-room and street. Love partnered by antagonism, with love most probably the senior partner.

Chapter Eight
IN MY HOSTEL ROOM

My room at the hostel was small, but it had an alcove which hid the narrow bed and the metal washstand behind a curtain. Let this curtain be drawn, and the room was a 'study' which I tried to decorate and be proud of. As I look back on it now, I see it furnished with many affectations. The statuettes! All intended to convey to a visitor my Catholicity. The B.V.M. in several versions; St. Francis with his wolf; St. Richard, my patron saint. And the pictures on the mantel! The Curé d'Ars whose bony, ascetic face, radiant with love and spirituality, has always haunted me; Father Stanton, my hero dead; Soeur Thérèse of Lisieux, whose Cause for Beatification was then going forward. This picture showed a young girl with a face grave and sweet, and I wonder now how far my delight in her – and indeed the worldwide devotion to this sweet-faced girl – had not a sexual element in it, unaware. Books paraded around every wall, and my pleasure in the scholarship they suggested was far from saintly. In the grate was a small gas-fire with broken asbestos, and in a creaking wickerwork armchair before it I would read and read and read.

To this coop and chair I returned for the Lent Term. Each night, after abandoning study when eyes and brain were weary, I wrote in my diary, before pulling the curtain and unveiling the bed. That diary, a long foolscap book, with its leaves now browned and wilting, reveals a period in this Lent Term of doubt and heaviness. Trinity was only months – weeks – away; Trinity when I must accept Ordination. Ordination! I had begun to be ashamed. Doubts about my fitness for such a calling had been abruptly joined by devil-raised doubts about my faith and everything in it. The soiled and breaking pages of this private book show the relief I got from pouring on to them my dejection and dismay.

'*Feb. 14. St. Valentine, Bp. and M.* Gosh' – as Julie used to say – 'my heart is sad tonight. I have just been walking up and down the room in a depression very like despair. I started by thinking that my enthusiasm for service in the Ch – or, more accurately, in the Anglo-Cath part of it – was precious little different from any other boy's enthusiasm for combative activities in this or that political party. One of them longs to fight for Socialism, another for Conservatism, and R.O. for Anglo-Catholicity. And how much of R.O.'s zest was a strong fancy to walk the pavements in cassock, cape, and cincture? Like E.A. Wasn't much of it a desire to copy the outward side of such as Father Stanton rather than to copy Xt who demands so much? I am no saint, and I don't want to "sell all that I have and follow Him". What am I to do? I have just turned to the Form and Manner of Making of Deacons. "Do you think that you are truly called according to the will of our Lord Jesus Christ?" Well, do I? "Do you trust that you are inwardly moved by the Holy Ghost to take upon you this office and ministration . . .?" I *trust*, perhaps, but no more. "Do you unfeignedly believe all the Canonical Scriptures of the Old and New Testament?" Do I? . . . Do I? . . . Do I? "Will you diligently read the same unto the people assembled in the Church where you shall be appointed to serve?" Is this the only question to which I can unfeignedly say "Yes"? Am I really in a state to take Orders, but how can I give it all up now, after so much money has been spent on me? Or is all this perhaps much the same thing as the sudden fear and emptiness of love that a girl often suffers before marriage? No, it is more important than that. . . .'

'*Feb. 22. St. Margaret of Cortona, Penitent.* Oh God whose will alone I must seek to obey, pour thy guidance down on me that I may know what to do; pour thy strength into my heart that I may do it. Help me to see thy purpose. If I must withdraw, give me the desire to do this, for I have no strength to do it now. With all my heart I pray thee, "If thy Presence go not with me, carry me not up hence." But if I should continue in my present path, even though unworthy, oh grant that I bring no harm to thy people anywhere. On this day of St. Margaret of Cortona, let me come for counsel to thee in my perplexity even as the Blessed Conrad of Offida came to her in her mountain home. . . .'

The first part of that prayer was truly sincere, but what are we to make of the Blessed Conrad of Offida and St. Margaret's mountain home? As I see them now in their faded ink, I detect a young man's display of his Catholicity and his knowledge – but to whom, since this book was to be strictly private? To myself alone, I suppose. Hardly to God. You will not find 'St. Margaret of Cortona, Penitent' in the Anglican Calendar; I got it out of Father Stanton's little manual of Catholic Prayers. I detect also in that mountain home symptoms of my youthful view of myself as a poet or a writer.

§

I carried this sick self-distrust to the Cathedral Evensong one weekday afternoon, but I did not take my usual seat in the Choir; I sat instead far away at the back of the nave near the doors of the Galilee Porch. I knelt there so as to be alone, quite alone, with no student or stranger near me. In my present mood I did not feel, and did not want to feel, one of the happy Faithful up there in the Choir: the canons, priest vicars, students and choristers, all untroubled by questionings. Looking at the Norman and medieval walls all around me, I forced myself for a while into the twelfth or thirteenth century when all the world from king to cotter believed in God, and all held that their deeds, in palace or cot, would, if good, take them up into heaven or, if rascally, down into hell. Some depth in me craved the simple securities of such a world, at this time when I was but twenty-two.

Quite alone, then, I knelt there, in a part of the Cathedral that was nearly dark, for its hanging lamps were unlit. There was only a box of light between openwork screen and high altar, and very far away it looked. At first I could discern only gowned students in that haze of light, but there were footsteps in the aisles of a few faithful laity coming to attend service in Choir. Or could they perhaps be – so my fancy wandered – footsteps that were not of today? Footsteps of people long dead, good Saxon women, for women were always faithful, or – let the fancy run – shaven and tonsured priests from monastries still unsuppressed . . . and why not a knight in armour like the crusader on his tomb in the north aisle – perhaps even that knight himself?

The tower bell stopped, the clock struck, and the white figures of choir and clergy filled their places in a part of that light. Now the picture was complete, framed by the chancel arch.

The voice of a priest-vicar said words well known but not to be heard from here, and then the singing began. I listened on my knees and thought that this distant singing was like that distant light made audible. It has always been the part and task of a cathedral that the praises of God in the Divine Offices should be sung in it daily by its collegiate body, whether or not the people of the outside world are there to hear. And so, as I knelt there this evening, I knew that I was listening to a singing that had risen in that same lighted place, morning after morning, evening after evening, for eight hundred years. It was beautiful in its own right because of the trained choir, but it was the more beautiful because of this thought which put its own light within it.

Was it more beautiful when it was at its softest as if on tip-toe for a cathedral or now when, suddenly, the organ blared forth, and the choir gloried in a mass of sound, and my heart, at the drama of it, rose high with them and turned into air? But exactly at this moment the devil attending me intruded his question, 'It is beautiful, yes, wonderfully beautiful, but is it possible that it is all based on a lie?' For lie is the hard word for an illusion, a false comfort, a story written for themselves by men lest otherwise they despair. Sadly, I was half-believing that the answer to this was Yes, when a thought that was some comfort came down upon me; and it was this: 'Does it matter greatly to God if one's beliefs are accurate so long as one has been singing to Him, whoever He is, for eight hundred years?'

Atheist I could never be, however agnostic I might become, so this thought was truly solacing then, and has remained so. But it

was not enough for a young ordinand who could see Trinity
drawing near.

§

Julie on foot, not on horseback, meeting me one day in East
Street, exclaimed, 'I say! The time's getting short. You'll be a little
parson soon. Isn't it rather terrific?'

Attempting melodrama, I said, 'I don't know that I shall be
ordained at all.'

She stared at me. 'Why *ever* not? Of *course* you will be.'

But I stood there on the pavement and told her of all my doubts
and glooms and self-distrust, while half the population of Casterton
passed by and around us. Often we had to shift our position to let
them get by, while she was saying 'Nonsense' and 'Oh, *no*' and
'Everybody says you'll make a lovely priest. *Daddy* says so' (as
though that settled it), or otherwise pouring feminine comfort
over me. She was now twenty, and I found her comfort soft and
warm but quite unconvincing.

Next afternoon, however, as I sat reading in my hostel room,
'Brockers' – old Tim Brockhampton, our 'scout', as we called him
so that we could feel like undergraduates in Oxford rooms –
appeared at my door in his green baize apron and said, 'The Archdeacon is here, Mr. Oliver. He has come to see you.'

'Archdeacon? Which archdeacon?'

'Archdeacon Alanside.'

'To see *me*?'

'Yes, sir.'

'Where on earth is he?'

'Down in the hall, sir. I came up to see if you was in.'

'Good lord!' I ran down the one flight of stairs, and there he
stood, examining the large colour print of Dürer's *Maria mit dem
Kinde*. 'Hallo, sir.'

'Richard, you have shamed us all. It shames me to think that
this is the first time I've entered here. How right you were to tell
me we all ought to blush for our iniquities.'

'Oh, I never said that, sir.'

'Well, anyhow, you've taught two of us at least to drink the cup of shame and mend our ways, Bishop Griffyn and myself. Julie tells me that you're worried, and I'm wondering if I can be of any help to you. She's been betraying all your confidences to me —'

'I don't think they were confidences, sir.'

'Well, I'm glad, because she poured the whole boiling lot over me. She told me everything you said, and I remembered my own days just before ordination. Dear me, a long time ago.'

'It's frightfully decent of you, sir.'

'May I come up and see your room?'

'Yes, of course, sir. It's not much of a place, I'm afraid.'

'In a seminary, my dear boy, one only expects a cell.'

'Well, do come up to the cell. I'll lead the way. It's awfully nice of you.'

'Not at all. You're going to tell me all you're thinking.'

I led him to my room and thrust the old wicker chair towards the gas-fire which was glowing blue and orange within its broken asbestos, for this was a March day and cold. After glancing round at my books and saying 'Quite a library', he put on the horn-rimmed glasses to study the holy statuettes. Also the pictures: Soeur Thérèse, the Curé d'Ars, and Father Stanton. Of the last he said, 'Ah, Stanton. The man we'd all like to be.'

'Oh, yes, sir,' I agreed enthusiastically.

'One of my heroes.'

'And mine too, sir.'

Then he sank into the old listing, creaking chair, inquired if it was safe and, being reassured, stretched out a hand towards the unattractive fire. I took the only other seat, a small bedroom chair.

'Well, Richard, what is it? Feeling a bit adrift and lost? Well, let's see if, between us, we can get the bearings again.'

I told him how I felt overwhelmed by a doubt lest I had no vocation at all. I said I could see nothing much in my vocation except a kind of artist's love for ceremonial and a puerile pleasure in being a combatant member of the Anglo-Catholic party. I said that a faith springing from little but a love for beautiful services and a hostility to Protestantism didn't seem enough to justify taking Orders. I likened it to the 'party line' of a communist.

'Go on,' he encouraged.

I said I liked Catholic services when 'the whole works were piled on' – incense and processional lights and gorgeous vestments, but so far as I was concerned, this was only the outside of the platter. I was nothing like so possessed by the life these things should imply. For example, I knew that as a Catholic I ought to go to Confession, but I didn't: I was too frightened to.

'You don't seem frightened of telling everything to me.'

My eyes sought the floor. 'Not everything, sir.'

'Well, go on. Go on with what you *can* tell.'

I said my trouble was not only doubt of my character but – and this seemed such a terrible thing to say to *him* that I stopped.

'Yes?'

'Not only doubt of myself but doubts of everything in the Creed.'

He nodded gently. 'And does this add up to the whole matter?'

'Most of it. But no. Just to make matters worse, there are all sorts of doubts about the C. of E.'

'Yes. Of course.' His eyes had a smiling friendliness – I would say more, a love. I can never recall this hour in my small room without remembering – and all the more so because of the darkness that fell so soon – remembering without shame St. Mark's words about Jesus and the young man: 'Jesus, beholding him, loved him.' The Archdeacon was looking at me while his lips moved to the smallest fraction of a smile. And his words were, 'Richard, you are describing me as I was in the weeks before ordination.'

'As *you* were?' I asked it, amazed.

'Yes. As I was then. And as I've been a hundred times since.'

'Do you mean you had doubts about your fitness for Orders?'

'Of course I do. Many a time I despaired of myself before I was ordained. *And* since. Often and often since. Even, sometimes, to the point of thinking I ought to give up a service of which I was unworthy.'

'But . . . why unworthy?' I had said this softly because I had hardly had the courage to ask it.

'For many more reasons than one. But I think the chief trouble has always lain in the popularity which came to me as a preacher. One begins to long to be preaching somewhere or speaking somewhere, but, alas, all too often it's for one's own glory rather than for the glory of God. One's reputation becomes one's god.' He looked into the heart of the monotonous, uninspiring fire. 'It'll always be a fight, Richard, your time as a priest. But you'll win it. We win, somehow.'

I dared not ask what the 'many more reasons' might be, and I could not imagine for him any other weakness than the one he'd described – 'the last infirmity of noble minds'. Remembering him kneeling daily in the Cuthbert Chapel I could not suggest to myself even one.

So all I said was, 'But you never feel any doubts about *Christianity*, do you, sir?'

'Is anyone ever really free of them, Richard? Fortunately the other things, our trust and faith and our experience of God are stronger in most of us. That's all, and thank God.'

'But do you mean – are you saying that priests like Canon Leedes and our bishop can still experience doubt? Bishop Griffyn agreed with me that both of them were saints.'

His eyes went up to the picture of Soeur Thérèse of Lisieux on the mantel.

'Was Sister Theresa a saint?'

'Good heavens, yes! If ever there was one!'

'I think so too. And the whole Catholic world agrees with us. She only died twenty or so years ago and yet, against all the rules, she is to be beatified at once. And canonized. Saint Thérèse of Lisieux. None the less, poor child, she suffered torments of doubt in her last months before death. She tells us so. She says it was like a great wall between her and heaven. And that a voice within her was for ever saying that there was nothing after death, and that all her life of sacrifice, all her worship, all her hopes, were vain. Her actual words, I think, were "May God forgive me. He knows I *try*

to live by faith, though it does not afford me the least consolation."
Like all the saints she called it God hiding Himself from her and
making her wait in the dark – on which she commented with the
laugh of the little hero she was, "But He'll get tired of making me
wait sooner than I shall get tired of waiting." And through it all,
whatever else she doubted, she never doubted that love was the
only thing that mattered. *You* don't doubt that, do you?'

'No, sir,' I said. It was a true answer then; and it would be so still.

'She died telling the Sisters so. They asked her for a last message,
and she whispered, "It is love alone that counts." The very last
words to be heard from her were, "My God, I love thee. . . ." And
that, Richard, is the whole inevitable picture.'

Perhaps it was because I chose to admire him so, perhaps because
of some quality in his voice, but perhaps also because he really was
wise, but sentence after sentence, as it came from him, seemed an
illumination.

'Look, Richard,' he said. 'I think these doubts and darknesses
are often God at work. They may be His exacting but loving discipline at the last. There was once a wise and witty principal of a
theological college who used to tell his students, "There are more
men than you think whom God has called to be priests because it's
a good way to save their souls." And it was our great Bishop Gore
who said he didn't mind his ordinands feeling the pressure of doubt.
"It's quite a good thing," he used to tell them. "Most young men
are far too cocksure. You can be ordained in faith."'

'I see, sir. Yes . . .' I said it hesitantly.

My alarming new doubts about the C. of E. he resolved completely, more completely than the doubts about myself. He began
by saying I mustn't identify the Visible Church, wherever it might
be, with the Kingdom of God. The Kingdom, of course, was
within all its members, but in some far more effectively than in
others, so that the Church, whether of the Roman Obedience or
the Anglican, could often be in error and defective. When I worried
about Rome I was to remember sometimes that even that stern
Church in her strange wisdom had a doctrine of the Invisible
Church. I asked what exactly this was, and he said, 'Well, they say

that the Church of Christ must be visible in the world as His body, but it has a soul as well as a body, and all those who sincerely call themselves Christians, and devoutly act as if they were, are in ignorant but invisible communion with its soul. The eyes of the organized Church are necessarily too narrow, you see, but no one knows the limits of God's eyes. God knows His own.'

I felt my heart thrill to this, and he went on, 'In other words, the Invisible Church must be ultimately one with redeemed humanity, and only the King will know who they are.'

I nodded, feeling happier than I'd been for some time.

'So don't worry any more about the validity of our Anglican Orders. We believe them to be valid but, in any case, validity and efficacy are not the same thing. Even Rome allows that God can use irregular instruments as He will, whether they are Anglican priests or Nonconformist pastors. The walls between the Churches, you know, are not quite as high as Heaven.'

How that sentence has remained with me!

'The old Ecclesia Anglicana is really a rather glorious old Church,' he said. 'It has its weaknesses and faults, of course, but this is partly because it has taken the courageous road of holding tight to the past and treasuring it, while at the same time keeping itself adaptable to the present and prepared for the future. Yes, it is *truly* a Church to attract one's love and loyalty. Try to see it, Richard; try to see that your feet are really set in a rather splendid place.'

My heart leapt in happy agreement.

'Don't try to force things too far, dear boy. Just be humble about yourself and wait quietly. For God, you see. Wait for Him.'

'Yes, sir.'

'Just say quite often – and blindly if you like: "Where Thou, my Lord and King, shalt be, even there also, whether for death or life, will Thy servant be."'

I was happy in the thought of saying such heroic words; inspired by them.

When he had finished talking he rose out of that creaking old wicker chair and asked 'Well, have I helped you at all? I should like to think I have.'

'It's been . . . abso-*lutely* . . . *terrific*, sir,' I said.

'Good. Try to come in and help us. We need you so badly. "Come over and help us,"' he laughed, quoting the man of Macedon.

I was now standing too, and I answered, 'I don't think there's really much doubt I'll be coming.'

And indeed I felt, as I followed him out of my room and down our bare stairs, that I'd go with *him*, wherever he led.

§

Last year I revisited Casterton and looked from the street at the old hostel. It was now an office building, housing a firm of Chartered Auctioneers and another of Business Consultants. Evening was falling as I looked at it, and the stillness within suggested that all the clerks had gone home. But there were some lights in the windows, the door was half open, and I walked in. I was met by a middle-aged man, some chief clerk, I imagined, and in the excellent Bible word he was 'astónied' ('stunned, benumbed, paralysed' says the dictionary) when I told him that this house had once been a theological college and I had lived as a student in one of its rooms 'a hundred or so years ago'. He had heard nothing of its religious past.

'Well, it's given over to Mammon now,' he said, almost regretfully.

I asked if I might go up to my old room on the first floor.

'Of course,' he answered. 'But there's no one here now except me. I'll come too. I'm quite interested.'

So I led him up that single flight as I once led the Archdeacon, and I opened my room door. With a strange feeling like a gentle hand about my heart, I looked in and went in. All its walls were as white-painted as the ceiling and nearly as bare. The only furniture was the steel filing cabinets and the steel office desk. On the mantel the only ornament was some firm's complimentary calendar, replacing my statuette of the Blessed Virgin and my pictures of Soeur Thérèse and the Curé d'Ars. A neat steel desk-stool stood where once the Archdeacon had sat in my old listing basket-chair and talked of God.

Chapter Nine

TITLES AT SUMMIT AND BASE

A little later in that term he preached in St. Paul's Cathedral a sermon that was reported at length in all serious papers and 'featured' as news in all sensational ones. It stirred for weeks afterwards, like a spreading fire, letters in the correspondence columns, some merely smouldering letters, but others flaming. Only a few were in support of him.

Parliament had lately passed the Church Enabling Act which set up the Church Assembly with its Houses of Bishops, Clergy, and Laity, and delegated to it wide powers of self-government. The passing of the Act had been acclaimed as a triumph for the so-called 'Life and Liberty Movement' in the Church of England, and the 'sensation' in the Archdeacon's sermon was that, in the pulpit of the metropolitan cathedral, he poured doubts on this acclaim and attacked the Act as it stood. His subject was 'Discipline in the Church' and the explosive warhead of the sermon was its suggestion that Disestablishment might be necessary if discipline was to be established in the Church.

The Act was useless, he said, so long as it preserved the veto of Parliament on all the more serious decisions passed by the Assembly. This subordination to the State, still maintained by the Act, was inconsistent with the proper spiritual autonomy of a Church; it rendered the Church contemptible in the eyes of many; and it disabled, even paralysed, its internal discipline.

'The spiritual independence supposed to be enshrined in the Act, is fictional. This fact will not appear while the Assembly deals with minor measures that are of little interest to our secular House of Commons, but the minute the Assembly passes a serious measure, and such a one as I have in mind for establishing discipline in the Church, there will be no such easy complaisance. It becomes more and more clear to me, as I go about my archidiaconal duties, that the Assembly sooner or later will have to initiate a measure moderating the excessive freedom now practised by so many of our extremer Modernists, on the one hand, and our extremer Romanizers, on the other. Do not mistake me. I glory in the tolerant and comprehensive character of our Church but the boundaries of toleration must be erected *somewhere*. And I find it impossible to believe that Parliament will refrain from vetoing any incursion into any such liberties. Therefore I say that to me it is beginning to seem as if Disestablishment would define and preserve our true comprehensiveness far more fairly than the present Establishment, which will paralyse us from honest action.'

The correspondence stayed fine and fierce in *Times*, *Telegraph*, *Morning Post*; in provincial papers, Church papers, and weekly journals. It raged warmly in our hostel. And whether I read the papers or listened to the students, I was on the Archdeacon's side in everything. He was my friend; he was right in everything. Our argumentative and assertive Alec Raines declared that the whole thing had been 'publicity hunting', which raised in me a fury near to tears; the sardonic Bill Brickhill merely said that the Archdeacon had antagonized two-thirds of the Church by attacking it at both ends which naturally produced a storm of *odium theologicum* among the clergy and would probably issue in the offer of a bishopric from the P.M.

And then, only a day or so after this, reading *The Times*, I saw 'BISHOP OF LOUGHBOROUGH. The Bishop of Loughborough, Dr. Staples, who is seventy five announced last night that he would retire after Easter of this year. At the time of his elevation to the see of Loughborough he was Archdeacon of Hallowfield. . . .'

'Archdeacon of Hallowfield. . . .' Now the word was everywhere that the see, when it became vacant after Easter, would be offered to the Archdeacon of Casteron. All the know-alls and the gossip writers – and the cynics – were pretty sure of this. Had not Archdeacon Alanside, for months past, been, as it were, the next name on the list for high preferment; was not his name on everybody's lips just now; and was it not a recognized trick to promote a man who was rebelling against the Establishment to high and responsible position in it; to make of the poacher, in short, a head-gamekeeper.

Easter came early that year, but March was not dead before, most suddenly, Spring was a pale glow, a clear light, and a warm air in the streets. Only yesterday it seemed the hoar frost had powdered the roofs of Casterton and so bleached the flat pastures and ploughlands around the city that the grass was a dull Lovat brown and the overturned earth the dull yellow of sand. Now the grass was a full green again and a flush of green buds tinted all the trees, otherwise still naked and gaunt. The birds began fluting on the naked branches. Every morning at six o'clock a thrush let loose a fine canticle in our hostel garden. We were all glad that he was happy but held it inconsiderate of him to wake us all up with his good spirits. Anyhow, here was Spring. A cloud-blanket which had overlaid the city for weeks had been rolled up overnight, leaving above the spire and towers only this pale, bright, sea-coloured sky.

And one day Julie, meeting me in the street, invited me to a tennis party 'at the Prebendary MacMasterses', who had a hard court in their garden. 'They asked me to provide another male,' she said, 'and I immediately thought of you. You *will* come, won't you? I asked Mrs. MacMasters, did she want one of the old attractive sort, but she said, No, it was to be a young persons' party.'

I was happy to be taken to tennis at the MacMasterses, even as one of the less attractive sort, but not once in that party, loud with the voices and laughter of young persons, did I ask her about her father and his possible departure. It had seemed the worst of luck that the Alansides should leave Casterton just when I had accepted the offer of a title there.

Before this talk broke about the Loughborough bishopric I had been summoned by our Bishop of Casterton to his palace. George Auberon Falls, 'George Casterton', as Bishop Griffyn liked to call him, was a little man with a broad and upturned nose and, I should think, the gentlest eyes in the diocese. We know how Bishop Griffyn, that agitator for sanity and precision in talk, allowed him the title of saint. The Palace is an extensive battlemented mansion comprising all the centuries somewhere within its front and its wings. These wings partly embrace a garden which leads to a high battlemented wall, lichen-padded and creeper-hung. This is none other than the old bastioned city wall with the Roman stones in its base. So here the illustrious Lord Bishop of Casterton sat among the centuries, and yet when I was shown into his study, I found that it must be one of the smallest rooms in the great house, and surely the untidiest.

'Ah, my boy!' he greeted me, rising in his purple cassock from behind the littered desk, as if I were someone of distinction. 'I tell you what: the sun has made a mistake and thinks it's June. We'll have tea in the garden. I'll make some tea now.'

To my astonishment there was a gas trivet in his grate with an old blackened kettle on it, and he bent down and lit it with some matches from among the photographs on his mantelpiece. 'I like to make my own tea when I'm composing a sermon or a Charge or a Gifford Lecture or something, so that I can drink it when I like. Just sit there and I'll cut some bread and butter.' Out of a cupboard he brought a 'tin' loaf, a butter dish, and an alarming long knife. 'I hope you like your slices thick. I'm going to cut you what we used to call, when I was a curate in East London, some "doorsteps". There's nothing like doorsteps, if the bread is new and the butter fresh.'

'Can I help you, my lord?'

'No, no. This is highly specialized work. There's a table and chairs out there, aren't there?'

I looked through the window at the broad sun-burnished lawns. An old round iron table and some thin iron chairs stood in the midst of the flung sunlight. 'Yes, my lord.'

'Good. Pity to miss this sun. Maybe we shan't get much more this year. Often it's like that if the Spring loses its head and over-does its part a bit. Come on, kettle! Ah, it's beginning to boil.' Taking a coarse brown teapot from the cupboard, he warmed it, poured the water over the window-sill on to a garden bed, and made the tea. 'Do you like it strong? You do? Good. Because I'm afraid I do too. Now if you'll take the doorsteps out I'll bring the tea and the milk. I'm sure you don't want sugar. No person of your taste would take sugar in tea.'

He hustled cheap white cups and plates, and the doorsteps (four of them) on to an iron tray which I then carried out and laid on the little round table in the sun. As I turned round to see if he was comfortably following, I perceived, with a startled admiration, that I was standing in a place that must be as lovely as any to be found among the ancient sites of Europe. There across the lawn and encompassed with a great quiet, was the castellated palace; behind it the towers and spire of our Cathedral rose into the sea-blue sky, with the sun just beginning to floodlight them. Beside me a solitary vast cedar and a giant ilex spread shadows on the great carpet of lawn; beyond it ran the mossed and bastioned city wall.

I exclaimed 'My God!' at this place of quiet beauty, and hoped that my bishop hadn't heard, as his small figure came towards me, purple-cassocked over the grass, with teapot in one hand and jugs of milk and hot water, in the other.

After some easy talk on general subjects, over the tea-cups, he asked, 'And now, what about your title?'

I told him that Bishop Griffyn had suggested I ought to go to some arduous parish in an industrial town. Preferably up north.

He waited to finish a mouthful of his doorstep. 'I know. He told me. And for once in a way I don't agree with him. It's not that I want to keep you in my diocese – at least I hope not. I think my advice is for your sake and the Church's. I want you to go to St. Hugh's with Prebendary Imbraham for your vicar. I would like you to spend your diaconate there and the first year or two of your priesthood. You mustn't think that your education and preparation for a great ministry will finish with your departure from a theological college. Two years at a theological college are not enough. Canon Leedes tells me you are certain to get a First Class in the Universities' Preliminary to Holy Orders.'

'I wish I felt as certain of it, sir.'

'You'll do it. But you must understand that a First in the Universities' Prelim is by no means a First in Greats.'

'I know that, sir.'

'Yes, but Canon Leedes holds out promise of your doing bigger things. And that brings me to my point. I want you to advance much further in scholarship. We need far more scholarly priests in the Ministry. We need what used to be called "learned clerks" – clerks who can speak with the learned in the tongues of the learned. And you see, Oliver' – a gentle smile turned up the corners of his mouth – 'I have an ambition for you to be one of our learned clerks.'

This was so flattering, so unforeseen, and said so kindly, that I put him at once alongside the Archdeacon and Bishop Griffyn on a pedestal in my pantheon. I said nothing.

'I want you to be able to show these learned men – have some more tea – that Christianity, as our Church after the profoundest thought has come to interpret it, is not only acceptable to the intellect, not only impressive to it, but deeply satisfying.'

'I'd love to be able to do that.'

'Yes. Will you want another doorstep? If so, I'll go and cut you one. You don't? No, they *are* rather satisying as I cut them, I think. But it's not only scholarly priests, Oliver – oh, come! What is your name? Richard, isn't it?'

'Yes, my lord.'

'It's not only scholarly priests we want, Richard. Far more important, we need consecrated ones. Well, in the small parish of St. Hugh's, and in the quiet of Prebendary Imbraham's clergy house, you will have ample opportunities for further study *and* for that contemplation and spiritual self-training proper in a young man who really wants to become the best possible priest he has it in him to be. Living, reading, and praying together with Harry Paul, the senior curate, and Trippy Imb – I mean Prebendary Imbraham – will be an extension of your preparation. So you see: I want you to give me four years of your time at St. Hugh's – four years of honouring the double obligation of disciplined intellectual study and disciplined devotional life. Remember St. Benedict insisted that the only true order of things in a religious community was Prayer, Study, Labour. After four years of this with Trip – with Mr. Imbraham – I'll let you go and labour anywhere.'

Of course I accepted his advice, and not only because, touched by his flattery and kindness, I was ready, eager, to be his devoted vassal but, more selfishly, because from where I sat in the sun, I could see the Cathedral towers rising behind the palace battlements and I knew how I had come to love this city and was happy to remain in it.

§

Prebendary Imbraham was a popular mission preacher all over the country, but his preaching was very different from the Archdeacon's. Coming more from the heart than the head, as was natural in a mission preacher, it made no enemies. He was tall and spare, with a face almost Oriental in features and eyes, but radiant with geniality. The features, like a Malayan's, looked as if a roller has passed over them, flattening them, and out of this flatness the eyes twinkled with gaiety and goodwill. A bachelor confirmed, he had turned his large vicarage into a 'clergy house' and here he lived with two curates (needing two because he was in such demand as a conductor of missions) and each curate had his own bed-sitting-room which he called his cell. On the ground floor was a small oratory to remind them of the house's heart and meaning. Here in 'St. Hugh's Clergy House' the life was almost monastic. This was expressed by Sext at noon and Compline at night said by the clergy in the Frater, or, in less monastic terms, the dining-room. I was excited to be going there.

§

It was only as Julie and I walked homeward together after the MacMasters' tennis-party, swinging our racquets, that I told her I should be staying in Casterton and asked my anxious questions, Would her father be leaving it for the Loughborough bishopric, and did she want to go?

'Oh, I don't know,' she said with a little skip and a swing of her racquet as at an inviting ball. 'It would be rather wonderful to have a bishop for a father, and he'd made an adorable bishop, you'll admit. He says he's disgusted with the way his name's being bandied about but I can't believe he's disgusted with the idea of being offered a bishopric. I mean, who would be? I shouldn't. I asked him if he'd accept, and he said I had no business to ask such questions and would I please go and hide my head in shame. He said I wasn't to discuss such ill-informed gossip with anyone – so I'm sinning like anything now. My guess is he'd accept right away.'

'But would you be pleased? Do you *want* to leave Casterton?' I too swung my racquet through the air to conceal that I was feeling hurt at her apparent readiness to leave us – 'us' meaning, more or less, me.

'I don't exactly want to leave Casterton, but Loughborough and Leicestershire could be rather delicious. I've been making my own inquiries – after all, *I* shall have to live there – and I understand there could be heaps of riding and boating and dancing. And, oh dear, the Quorn Hunt is there, and if only he'd let me and The Reverend go hunting with it! The Reverend would adore it so. But I suppose he's right that it's wrong. A pity. . . .'

'You'd take The Reverend with you?'

'Oh, but of course! I couldn't go without him. He'd be miserable. But I haven't told him about the Quorn. I've too much tact for that.'

'When do you think you'd go?'

'Well, certainly not till after Easter, Mummy says. For Mummy's talking about it everywhere in spite of Daddy. What she says is that it's got to happen sooner or later. He's bound to be made a bishop one day; everybody's agreed about that. So it's really a question of when we go and where. Here's your old hostel.'

'I'll walk as far as the Close with you,' I said, feeling sad because all things pass and have an end. I was not in love with her, for my emotions were occupied more with her father, but I didn't like the idea of Julie elevated with him to an episcopal palace, while I remained but the humblest of curates in Casterton.

I walked sadly with her through the Cloisters and along the Wych Walk, leaving her at the door of the Residentiary. I looked sadly at the white façade of the Residentiary and walked sadly out of the Close.

I had not gone far along South Street when a voice hailed me from behind. 'Young Man Oliver,' it called. I turned. Bishop Griffyn had just come out of the Close through the Prebendal Gate. I waited.

'It's many days, my dear Richard, since you've come in, of your charity, and broken my loneliness with your excellent talk. The sun's below the horizon; come and have a glass of sherry with me – if such a dissipation is allowed to you by Canon Leedes. Even if it isn't, I am fully competent to grant you a dispensation. You've been playing tennis, it appears, so you'll need a little refreshment. Who plays tennis in March?'

'I've been playing with Julie Alanside, sir.'

'Ah, "Jephthah's one fair daughter". Well —'

I was certain he'd been about to say something like 'Seems we shan't have the Archdeacon much longer', but had decided that the remark was not yet admissible. Instead, following an obvious train of thought, he said, 'Well . . . the clock's about to strike for you, isn't it? Less than two months to Trinity.'

'I've got to get through my exams first, sir.'

'Oh, you're going to do that on your head. And then you're going, I believe, to Trippy Imbraham's?'

'I hope so, sir.'

'Well, come in and tell me all about it. It's most interesting.'

We said little more till we were in his long narrow study with its view of the garden – a garden awake now to the spring, with crocuses purple and yellow and hyacinths white and blue. As he was drawing decanter and glasses from a low cupboard, he said, 'Take your customary chair. By the fire. Father Medwith would cry anathema on me for giving you this, but I think we won't tell him.' The Rev. Dai Medwith was the vicar of Casterton's most Protestant church, St. Bede's-without-the-Walls, and for that reason Bishop Griffyn, when in mischievous mood, liked to call him *Father* Medwith. 'I can find no support, Richard, for Tee-totalism either in the teaching of Christ or in the practice of the Church. I have sought it diligently, almost, I might say, with tears, but in vain. None the less Father Medwith seems to regard our current neglect of it as standing between the British nation and the full love of God. How's this for you? Sit down and enjoy it and talk to me. If I'm to speak truth, I must say that I recoil from Father Dai Medwith's brand of ferocious Protestantism —'

'So do I, sir, I'm afraid.'

'Again? What did you say? Dear me, my deafness increases with my senility. It had its advantages once, in the Upper House of Convocation, protecting me from hearing a great deal of nonsense; but I'm eager to hear what *you* say; I enjoy your talk, you see. You dislike his extreme Protestantism, you say? So do I. And he's altogether too Draconian for my liking. He was lately a headmaster, you see, and is still a bachelor – a disastrous combination. A headmaster enjoys too damaging an immunity from correction, and so does a bachelor. So do I now as a widower. Emmeline is excellent in the house but no good in that field.' He sipped his sherry and sat down in the deep fireside chair opposite me. 'It was not the situation when I was a diocesan. I reaped then all the correction I needed – and deserved – and perhaps a little more. But a sense of surrounding derogation can be healthy and humbling.'

'How goes the Autobiography, sir?' I asked, having noticed his manuscript book on the table.

He shrugged. 'I go on writing it but wondering all the time whether such disgusting egotism is justified. Perhaps if these post-war years had any interest in the causes for which my generation fought, this sorry business of public confession might be legitimate. Once I indulged the hope that such a narrative of personal experience and activity might interest a son of my own, but when that hope fell from' – as he was saying this I saw in a lightning flash why he was fond of me and liked to call me into his house – 'fell from my wife and myself, I could only regard the work as something to amuse me in the tedium of senescence. But let us talk of you. I gather that your particular hero, the Archdeacon, is threatening the nation with Disestablishment. That won't endear him to his Anglo-Catholic friends. They *talk* about Disestablishment, but there is really nothing they dread more, because they know that the comfortable anarchy of our paralysed Establishment gives them a measure of licence that no disestablished church would tolerate. Alanside certainly has his point there. Now let's come to you. Trippy has offered you a title. I am glad. There's no man with a better heart anywhere. Or a more unquestioning faith. I once suggested that you should go north and work in some harsh industrial parish instead of in our warm and comfortable south, but – yes – I see once again that George Casterton is a better man than I am. And therefore a wiser. Imbraham's natural piety and exuberant geniality will be the right atmosphere for your first few years. I, of course, am a man of somewhat colder temper than the excellent Trippy and apt at times to think that so much geniality verges on the intemperate. And, for a like reason, I suffer a slight malaise when sitting under him as a preacher. I agree that he's one of the finest mission preachers we've got, but that could be due, Richard, to the fact that his outflow from the pulpit is so splendidly untroubled by the exigencies of logic. Even, in his more excited moments, by the exigencies of sense. Moreover there is no chastening weight of scholarship to halt or hamper the glorious fervour and flow. In that he is so fortunate. Finish up that glass and have some more.'

'Thank you, sir.'

'Yes, I am wanting to hear your views about everything. There's the decanter. It always interests me that Imbraham, who is certainly English should have that Asiatic cast of countenance, not unlike a Javanese monk's, and, as if to accord with it, his preaching should have such an Asiatic richness of style. Mind you, the richness works. Beneath the honeyed orgies of sentiment there comes a paralysis of the hearers' reason which will suffer any sugared folly to pass. That's why he was so great a Bishop's Messenger in the recent National Mission. He carries his fiery cross to innumerable companies – largely composed of well-intentioned but puzzled women – and pours over them such splendours of assurance and exhortation that no one is in any mood – so uplifted are they all – to notice all the gay indifferences to logic and sense. But of course – have you taken that sherry? No? Take it. I'm much too comfortable to get up and give it to you. It's so nice to have you sitting there and to hear your views. But of course such magnificent lush oratory is less well suited to an audience of his brethren. He is accustomed to addressing audiences as if he adjudged most of them to be ignoramuses or infidels or both, which (though possibly accurate in many cases) is hardly suited to – or is at any rate discourteous to – a congregation of his brother clergy. But it is this blithe vehemence, coupled with his real and overwhelming love for souls, which made him, I suppose, the remarkable chaplain he was in the war. You knew that about him, I imagine?'

'Oh, yes, sir.'

'Yes, I was associated with him in an Armistice Day service last year, and he made a most excellent figure among us, being medalled across his chaplain's scarf all the way from west to east. It was a most impressive display and seen to great advantage on his tall person. I was proud of him. Less so the other day when I read his new book, *The Impatience of a Prebendary* and so wasted a morning.'

'But why, sir?' I asked, for I too had read the book, since I knew I was to be his curate, and I had thought it good. Was I then – not really intelligent? Intelligent enough to see its faults?

'Because, Richard, His Gay Reverence is quite unaware in it of the risks which attach to the fact that a preacher of his popularity can be certain of immediate publication for any book. It has therefore been written too quick. It is too hurried. Impatience is the word. But the impatience of a prebendary, though admirable in the sphere of action against the devil, is undesirable in the sphere of philosophical thought. Trippy has, you see, far too hospitable a mind. He's ready to give instant bed and breakfast to any gay or consoling idea that comes to him while he's writing his book. But that's not to say I don't love and admire Trippy. Or that I'm not glad you're going to him. He has a fine heart if not a . . . he has a very fine heart.'

Chapter Ten

MR. PROSDICK'S QUESTION

Easter, and at any moment we might hear if Archdeacon Alanside was indeed the Elect of Loughborough. This too was our Easter Term which would contain my final exams. Almost immediately after its close, if I passed the 'Universities Prelim' and the 'Bishop's Exam', I should go with other ordinands to a three-day Retreat in the Palace and on Trinity Sunday be ordained in my familiar Cathedral.

It was the custom of the vicars in Casterton to invite ordinands, for practice' sake, to read the Lessons at their Evensongs and perhaps, as their ordination drew near, to preach at least one sermon from their pulpits. That term Tom Arrowsmith and I were reading the Lessons for the Rev. Benjamin Prosdick (Mrs. Prosdick's 'Benjy') in his Church of the Good Shepherd. This was a little low-roofed barn of a church with a toy-like shingled steeple. Built in the fourteenth century, it stood in its little garden of long dead tombs at the end of a brief narrow twitten between two big shops in East Street. Fortunately for our nerves the Good Shepherd's seating capacity was small, so that our reading of the Lessons from an oaken eagle, and our preaching of a sermon from the pitch-pine pulpit, were not too terrifying. I got through my sermon with only a little unseen tap-dancing of my heart, and only a little dampness about my hair roots, of which, thank God, I alone was aware. Thereafter, next Sunday, I was able to sit in comfort and listen to Tom preaching his sermon, which I thought most awful nonsense.

After these Evensongs Tom and I, as a rule, went home with Mr. and Mrs. Prosdick, to a simple but kindly supper.

Mrs. Prosdick I had met on that occasion of my first visit to the Alansides. I had observed then, you may remember, her hidden consciousness that she and Benjy were not really of the same class as many in the Close, and her consequent striving to sound all her vowels with care lest the Cockney, lately and properly dismissed, should shoulder its way in again and make itself heard. This striving was still noticeable, but less effortful, in the company of two mere ordinands; indeed it was clear to me that she was happy to be at ease with Tom, and to be able to patronize him, since his father was only an ironmonger in Croydon. No question but that she was the superior there. With me she was rather more careful, remembering that my father had been 'at Oxford' and a country vicar.

Mr. Prosdick was a little fussing man whose brief, quick steps towards his immediate aims exactly suggested his native, and therefore unconscious, relish for officiousness, explanatory know-all displays, and a general bustling busybodiness. If there is an opposite to leisurely striding, these quick, truncated steps of Mr. Prosdick were it. Much of his talk was as polysyllabic as he could make it, probably for reasons akin to those that so carefully shaped his wife's vowels. Volubly argumentative, he reminded me of our champion arguer at the College, Alec Raines, but, of course, he was thirty years older. Both these were small men; did this perhaps necessitate an outsize cocksureness? Not only a fussy little arguer but also a fussy little gossip, he was ever in possession, with palpable pleasure, of some new and still-secret information or of some new and engrossing whisper in the Close. But an eager, friendly, smiling little man withal.

And his wife no less a friendly smiling little woman, round-faced, florid and bright-eyed.

On the evening of Tom's sermon I went alone to the Prosdicks' for supper because Tom was spending the evening with his parents, who had come all the way from Croydon to hear his 'first sermon ever'. We three, Mr. and Mrs. Prosdick and myself, had a pleasant little supper, and after it, as was our custom, assembled at Mrs. Prosdick's upright piano to sing hymns, she played the accompaniment with vigour and dominating our chorus with her high treble voice. The guarded, predetermined vowel-control was very evident tonight as she sang. Lost in the sentiment of the hymns, she had forgotten, I suppose, that the company behind her was not important.

'Come to the Sea'viour, m'eke no del'ee —'

(Only thus can I render her 'ay' sounds; no combination of letters from our alphabet will reproduce exactly these socially corrected syllables; possibly 'e-ay' would approach them sometimes.)

> 'Hear nah His accents tenderly se-ay
> '"Come to your Se-aviour, come."'

Both Mr. and Mrs. Prosdick had been Salvationists before his ordination, late in life, to the Anglican Ministry, and it was from their old *Salvation Army Song Book* that she still loved to sing. Most of our hymns tonight were addressed, I noticed, not to God, but to sinners; presumably, therefore, to Mr. and Mrs. Prosdick and their guest, since there was no one else to hear. 'Sinner, whereso'er thou art, At the Cross there's room . . .' and 'Come, sinner, wash your guilty soul In your Redeemer's Blood. . . .' One was addressed to the Soldiers of the Cross, again implying, I imagine, us three: 'God's trumpet is sounding. "To arms" is the call.' I enjoyed it. At last came one addressed to God, and Mrs. Prosdick seemed as careful as ever not to distress him with any of the old Cockney. 'O God, my God, in whom combane,' she sang, 'the heights and depths of Love Divane. . . .'

Mr. Prosdick had sung his part heartily, but all through the singing I got the impression that he would be glad to be done with it because he was anxious to tell me something. Something which was best not spoken before his wife. Not that I had the least doubt he had already told his wife; it was just that he didn't think it seemly to tell me about it in her hearing. At length his patience with the hymns failed him and he said, 'Molly, my darling, I think I should enjoy a little converse with Mr. Oliver alone —' he never called me 'Richard' or 'Oliver' as other clergy did but always 'Mr. Oliver' – 'I suggest he and I now adjourn to my sanctum. It's getting near his ordination. You appreciate that, my dear, I'm sure.'

'Why, of course, Benjy. You two talk awee and I'll wash up.'

'You don't mind, my dear?'

'Of course not. Why should I? You two 'op off and enjah yourselves.'

I was sure it wasn't my ordination he wanted to talk about; it was something else, something secret; and I followed those busy little steps of his with mine hardly less eager. His 'sanctum' was a small ex-bedroom on the first floor. It was even smaller than my room at the hostel, and it had a gas-fire like mine. He bent down and lit it and then turned the one easy chair towards me as I had for the Archdeacon. Like me again, he pulled for himself the only other chair in the room, from beneath the knee-hole of a small desk. And, having sat down with me, he did talk for a little of my ordination and of Prebendary Imbraham, as Bishop Griffyn had done, but – well, I knew from the first that this wasn't his real business. It was only to justify this talk behind a closed door. Our commonplace subjects failed; silence fell, and I thought, 'Now we shall hear it. The words are germinating. He is in travail with them and will be delivered of them soon.' He looked at the china ornaments on his mantel; he dusted something off the shoe of his crossed leg; he looked at the fire and his finger-nails; then said, as if merely breaking for my sake an awkward silence, 'Have you heard an unhappy story about one of our brethren?'

My eyes had been straying in the silence too; I swung them towards him. 'No.'

'A most unhappy story.'

'You mean about a —'

'Yes, about one of our brethren.'

'Here? In Casterton?'

'Yes.'

'But who – which – what is the story?'

'The usual story.' He paused, waiting for me to ask more detail. I did not, because I didn't like to. I felt a little frightened by his tone. Something in his words, his manner, his dropped voice, seemed to shadow our whole town. He was obliged to continue his story, unencouraged, for who can leave a fascinating story 'in the air', once he has begun it? 'Yes, alas, the usual story. The way we all fall, if we do fall. He is said to have stayed more than once

with a woman in a London hotel. A woman who certainly wasn't
his wife.'

'But who is he?' I was now staring, and not less fascinated than
he.

A silence – charged. 'It'll surprise you when I tell you. And
shock you, I'm afraid, because it's someone you've always talked
about in the most laudatory manner. One who seems to mean a
lot to you.'

'Who?'

'The Archdeacon.'

'Archdeacon?'

'Yes. Archdeacon Alanside.'

§

'*What?*' And then '*No!*' I cried, the answer flinging me to my
feet as I realized what he had said. I stood before him immobilized.
'I don't believe it. I'll never believe it. It's some ghastly lie.'

'I sincerely hope so.' But he slightly shook his head. 'I most
sincerely hope he can prove it is. Naturally we all do. He emphatically denies it, of course. As soon as the statements of evidence
were sent to him he —'

'*Evidence?*'

'Yes. Evidence of a private detective and a hotel manager and
his servants —'

'There can be no such evidence. Not *true* evidence.'

'So he says. He went straight to the Bishop and demanded his
right to refute it in open court —'

'Court? What sort of court?'

'The Bishop's own court. There can be nothing else. What it
amounts to is that he has demanded to be arraigned in the Consistory Court.' I thought my little host, sitting there with his hands
joined between his knees and his body leaning forward, was proud
of his knowledge, and that word 'arraigned'.

'I don't know what a Consistory Court is.'

'No, you wouldn't. But every bishop has this statutory jurisdic-
tion in ecclesiastical matters. Usually a Consistory Court deals only

with questions of illegal ceremonies or unorthodox doctrine, but occasionally, alas, it has to try a clergyman accused of offences against morality.' Yes, undoubtedly the little man was proud of his well-informed language and his accurate legal knowledge, probably acquired only yesterday and *ad hoc*. 'It's all done under the Clergy Discipline Act.'

Discipline. That sermon of his in St. Paul's on Discipline. How his enemies would rejoice now, when they remembered that sermon. And here was little Mr. Prosdick repeating his proud words to me, even adding a date. 'Yes, done under the Clergy Discipline Act, 1892.'

'In public? In *public*?' I stood with my hands joined before me and quivering. In all my life nothing had shaken my heart like this.

'Certainly. In open court. If he'd admitted guilt the whole thing could doubtless have been kept quiet but once the Archdeacon had denied it all, declaring the evidence to be lies and perjury —'

'As it is. As it is —'

'— and insisted on being promptly and finally cleared before the whole world —'

'Good for him! And he *will* be —'

'— the moment he took that line the Bishop had no course but to, as they say, "present the facts" before his Chancellor in the Consistory Court. The lay Chancellor of the Diocese I mean, of course: Sir Robert Treevil.' He uttered the titled name with appreciation. 'The Chancellor acts there as the judge appointed by the Bishop, and the Bishop acts as prosecutor. In his own court. It's all very strange and sad.'

'And it's all lies, lies, lies!'

'We sincerely hope so. Naturally.'

'But who's behind it all? Who's been employing private detectives? Who's been collecting witnesses against him?'

Mr. Prosdick did not answer at once. But I knew that he was glad to have been asked this and to be justified in telling me all. His first words were deliberately dramatic. 'One of his brother priests. He is the enemy.'

'Enemy?'

'Yes. Some years ago, in the perfectly proper exercise of his archidiaconal functions, the Archdeacon had occasion to report to the Bishop certain things that were being whispered about this particular priest. The man denied them, just as the Archdeacon is doing now, and the matter went to a Consistory Court. The man was acquitted, but ever since that day he has said — some of us have heard him say it – that he'd "get" the Archdeacon at the first chance that offered; that he'd ruin the Archdeacon just as the Archdeacon had tried to ruin him. That was how he put it.'

'But who is this man? A fine priest, I must say.'

'We have such priests, unfortunately. He is the Rev. Clide of Little Lockhampton. You'll hear more of the Rev. Clide in the next few months.' Though a priest himself, Mr. Prosdick, like Tom Arrowsmith, still kept the habit of his youth and called any parson incorrectly 'The Reverend So-and-so' without benefit of Christian name or initial. 'Mr. Clide must have been waiting his opportunity for years, and if the Archdeacon has but once fallen —'

'Which he certainly hasn't.'

'No – well, let us say the moment there was some suspicion against him, you can be sure the Rev. Clide set his detectives to work. He's a man of great wealth, what's called a "squarson", since he's both squire and parson of his village.' I detected his vicarious pride in that 'great wealth', which he probably exaggerated.

'He must have a great wealth of filthiness in him. It's obviously a plot. He's suborned these witnesses. Probably he's paid them large sums.'

'If that's so, skilful lawyers will certainly ferret it out in court. The Archdeacon will employ the finest lawyers to defend him: K.C.s, you can be sure. The Rev. Withycombe mentioned Sir Gerald Harbon, K.C., to me.' So impressed and happy he was with his 'K.C.s'! One could imagine him dashing about Casterton in search of all such information from clergy in the town.

'When will the case come on?'

'In a couple of months or less, they tell me.'

'Where?'

'Wherever the Bishop or the Chancellor decide. In the Palace perhaps, if there's a room large enough. In the Council Chamber or the Corn Exchange – who knows? It rather depends on the public interest —'

'The public interest'll be there all right.'

'I fear so. I greatly fear so. And the Chancellor must provide room for public and Press.'

'God!'

'Yes, a terrible business. A very sad business.'

'Who's the woman they say he was with?'

'No one knows. Not even the Rev. Clide, I gather. She's a mystery.'

'Because there's no such person. And never was.'

'The witnesses describe her.'

'Oh, maybe. They can lie, I suppose, if well enough paid.'

In a sudden access of despair I rested my hand on the back of my vacated chair and drooped forward over it. Tight-lipped, I forced back mad tears. Mr. Prosdick looked up at me, frightened. He said, 'Look, Mr. Oliver, I knew how fond you were of the Archdeacon, so I thought I'd tell you all this myself – break it to you, before you heard it in some cruder form. I felt a strong desire to save you from that and to give you no more than the truth.'

'It was kind of you,' I said. And at this point I sat down again, with my despair and because I felt overcome with weariness. 'Thank you very much.' So I said; and I had no doubt he had meant kindly; but at one point I was wondering that anyone could be so lacking in introspection as not to see the little busybody in himself.

§

The next day, in the quiet afternoon, I walked, fascinated, to the Close, alone. I walked towards it guiltily, furtively, slowing my steps as I drew near the Residentiary.

And there it was, the white Residentiary – so silent, so still. Or was it perhaps no different from any other day, and only I had painted on it this tragic face? I looked quickly left and right along Chantry Lane: was the whole Close invested with a silent sense of crisis; or had I but thrown the shadow over its roofs and streets? I remembered that I had not seen him for many days at early Mass in the Cuthbert Chapel, nor had I once seen Julie on her tall chestnut horse among the traffic. Were they keeping hidden because of the shame of it? An enemy in my own heart was saying, 'How can he ever overthrow the evidence of hotel witnesses, how can they all be perjurers paid?' But I wouldn't listen to this treacherous voice in my heart. 'He will do it. He will do it. Of course he will.'

If he was in there, what must he be feeling? For this stroke to fall just when the world believed he was to be made a bishop. And when, no doubt, he believed it too. But now, whatever the issue of the trial, *that* door had closed. And probably all doors to preferment. Mud sticks. A trial may heal, but a scar remains. The guillotine had fallen on his career. Oh God, help him. Help him. Was there nothing, nothing, I could do? If ever in my life I have felt like a knight's squire, burning to do battle with someone for his master's honour, it was as I walked quietly past the Residentiary that day. But what could I do? I was even afraid to encounter him. When the door of the Residentiary seemed to click I hurried from the Close and out of sight.

The only battle I could do was with any living soul who suggested the allegations might be true. And there were many of these souls among those who were discussing the scandal – which is to say every adult above twelve years old in Casterton. There were some in the College. Once poor Tom Arrowsmith, in his simple way, said to me, 'But, Ritchy, what will they do if it *is* proved against him in a church court? Proceed against him in the criminal courts?'

Like a snapping dog I said, 'Don't be more of a bloody fool than you can help, Tommy. Can't you see that it's only because the standards of the ministry are rather higher than those of the laity that he's done anything wrong at all? Put that in your stinking pipe and smoke it.'

'Anything *wrong*?' He frowned at me, bewildered.

'Yes, anything for which they could put him on trial in a criminal court. Have some sense.'

'Oh, I see, I see. Yes, of course you're right.'

'Of course I'm right, ass.' But why had my lips allowed in this angry moment that in the eyes of the church he *might* have done something wrong? When he had done nothing . . . nothing . . . and it was all lies.

'But if he's found guilty in the Bishop's court —'

'He'll *not* be found guilty.'

'No, but just say he was, what would the Bish have to do? Unfrock him?'

Even in my blinding impatience, my self-showmanship was enough to make me want to display some of that legal knowledge which Mr. Prosdick had proudly exhibited before me. 'I imagine the most our bishop would do would be to deprive him —'

'But isn't that unfrocking?'

'It is not. You've got a mind like a newspaper. Unfrocking is to depose from Holy Orders. Depriving is to dispossess of all preferments and of the right, for many years at least, to practise as a priest.'

'You mean he wouldn't be an archdeacon any more?'

'Of course I do. Don't you understand English?'

'He'd just be plain "Rev. Alanside"?'

'Just be plain "Rev. Edwyn Alanside". One happens to put Christian names or initials between "Reverend" and a surname.'

'And he wouldn't be unfrocked.' Tommy never minded being snubbed by me. 'I always thought they were publicly unfrocked in a service in the Cathedral.'

'Not by our bishop. Not by George Casterton.' Now I was copying Bishop Griffyn. 'He's not quite so barbaric as that. He happens to understand mercy and pity and love. He happens to understand "Go and sin no more".'

The mockery of the Cathedral bells. They rang for daily Mass in the Cuthbert Chapel, and for me they rang out of tune, for that figure in the caped cassock would not be kneeling there. They rang loud for Mattins on Sunday mornings, and their clanging, clashing loudness bruised me: one prebendal stall would be empty. It was told us that the Bishop, understanding well that his Archdeacon could now hardly bear to be seen by people who had revered him, had said, 'Go and rest in a place by the sea where no one'll know the story.'

The story was everywhere in Casterton but it had not exploded over England yet. That would come with the public announcement of a trial.

I did once see Julie coming towards me along the pavement. Instantly I wanted to turn some corner so as to escape her, but there was none, and our meeting was inevitable. She saw me and put forth a sad smile. Her eyebrows lifted to show me frankly her dismay. Courage to speak came upon me when we were opposite each other. 'Julie,' I said – and my head shook, tears of which I was ashamed sprang to my eyes and caught shamefully at my voice – 'Julie, I want you to know that I'm with your father in everything. Absolutely. Absolutely.'

She saw the hint of tears in my eyes and, allowing herself the sad smile again, said, 'You are a very dear person.'

It was then, I think, that my heart discovered and chose her.

§

My sadness and disruption of mind did not damage my work for our final exams. Rather did I find an escape, a forgetfulness, in work. I escaped the streets of Casterton and read for hours and hours in my hostel room, often till after midnight. To help me further in these labours there was a new glowing joy in my heart as well as the bewildering sorrow – strange, ill-matched bed-fellows these. It was a glow at the knowledge that I was in love with Julie; it shone in my heart as the sun's disc might shine, round and roseate, through a deep curtain of fog. And as a cock-bird will begin to show his plumage in advance of the mating season, so did I want to spread before Julie a notable plumage in the form of a First in the Prelim and distinction in the Bishop's Exam.

I remember that, because I wanted this success so badly, I did not dare pray for it. I did not dare, for fear that God would think adversity good for me. I kept the matter, so to say, well out of His mind. Far from His thoughts so that I might secure my triumph while He was busy with larger affairs. I prayed for Tom Arrowsmith instead.

And the result was all that I had longed for. I got my First in the Prelim; and in the Bishop's Exam I passed first of the fourteen candidates for deacon's orders. This meant that I should be Gospeller in the Ordination Service: directly the Bishop had laid his hands on my head last of all and said 'Take thou authority to execute the office of a deacon. . . . Take thou authority to read the Gospel in the Church of God. . . .' I should rise from my knees, pass through the communion rails, and read the Gospel to the great congregation, acting, though but a minister just ordained, as Second to the Celebrating Priest himself.

I was of course pleased with my First, but my pleasure was as nothing compared with Tom Arrowsmith's delight in getting a Third. He had been so convinced he'd never get through at all. Sitting next to me in the Greek Testament exam, he had taken one grim look at the questions, and then slid a shred of blotting-paper towards me on which he had written 'πίπτω, πεσοῦμαι' which, being interpreted, is, 'I am going to fall down' or, if you like, 'I'm about to be pipped.'

And behold he had not fallen down; he had got his Third. Now he could be ordained as deacon to his church in Croydon which had sent him at its own charges to Casterton. He had not failed them. Where was there an excitement, a happiness, like unto Tom's in these last few days before Trinity?

For the days of Retreat in the Bishop's Palace we had many devotional addresses from selected priests of the diocese. The Bishop sat with us at meals and was often present at the saying of the Daily Offices, but he did not address us till he gave us his solemn Charge after Compline on the Saturday night, the Vigil of Trinity Sunday.

We assembled in his chapel, a little thirteenth-century building annexed to the Palace. None but the ordinands were allowed in, for the Charge is given behind closed doors. We sat in the old choir-wise seats against ancient walls. Waiting for the Bishop, I thought how this little shrine had been built in the reigns of Richard and John when the twelfth century was dying and the thirteenth was coming in with its procession of great sinners and saints; and how Casteron's own great saint, St. Roland of Wych, must have loved it and used it in those troubled but inspiring times.

St. Roland's successor, our little Bishop with the upturned nose and doubling chin, took his place on a chair just within the sanctuary, facing us, and while our last night as laymen stood around the chapel, and a rising moon faintly lit the coloured glass of the window behind him, he charged us with a great gentleness in some such words as these (I have never forgotten the substance of them):

'I tell you tonight, my dear sons in Christ, with the utmost solemnity that, as far as I can see, there lie but two courses before you as you stand on the threshold of Holy Orders. They are opposites; direct opposites and mutually exclusive; and in all my life I have never been able to see a possibility of compromise between them. The first is to become – or at least to be ever struggling to become – *utterly* dedicated men who seek only the advancement of God's Kingdom. Within a few hours you are to be ordained as deacons. Now the Greek word, *diaconos*, means a servant, a waiting man, a messenger. In other words, you are to be consecrated tomorrow, not to greatness but to humility – and a lifetime of humility. You do not shake off your humble diaconate when you are made a priest any more than a newly consecrated bishop has ceased to be both priest and deacon. I may be a bishop now, but I am not the less a humble deacon still, a servant, a waiting man, a messenger.'

As he said this, I remember that I looked up at the old sexpartite vaulting above me and wished with all my heart to be exactly like him. Doubts and denials had no place of entry into this little building tonight because of an overwhelming assurance, swelling about my heart, that even if doubters and deniers were justified, I'd rather be in the wrong with him than in the right with all the intellectuals of the world. Such was the power of a sanctity to my youth in those days that night. It was appropriate that as he was speaking thus, and I listening, the Cathedral bells across the garden should chime the hour.

'That is one course. The other, the opposite, is to become a careerist seeking your own advancement. And I should tell you less than the truth tonight if I were to suggest that there is any hope of compromise between these two. Once you attempt a compromise anything may follow. Things that you didn't at all want to happen. Falls that surprise you. Falls that may be known only to yourself but are not less malignant and destructive than those which, in some unhappy cases, become known to the world. For the destructive power that lies in compromise is more likely to spread its infection in the heart of a priest than in the heart of a layman. And why? Because the sense of guilt and the consequent self-despair is greater there. The abandonment in despair of all struggling after goodness comes a little sooner to him. So my last word to you in this most solemn hour of your life, my dear sons in Christ, is this, "Choose ye now what ye will serve." You remember in the Book of Deuteronomy, that most precious and lovely work, these true and terrible words – terrible because the truth is terrible – you remember how the inspired author relentlessly repeats them: "Behold I set before you this day a blessing and a curse" – mark that last word. "See, I have set before you this day, life and good, and death and evil. . . . I call heaven and earth to record this day that I have set before you life and death, blessing and cursing; therefore choose life that both thou and thy seed may live." Your seed will be your people. Let them live. See that they live. After we have said a last prayer together I shall leave this chair and this chapel, but I want you to stay on your knees for some while, meditating on the words I have left with you, "Choose ye what ye will serve."'

§

Next morning before a great congregation, because the Cathedral was always crowded for an ordination service, I knelt before the Bishop at the entry to the sanctuary and with the others felt his hands on my head and heard his words, 'Take thou authority . . .' Then, alone of the new deacons, I passed through the communion rails as through a gateway, and, turning, faced the people, one of their clergy now. I read them the Gospel.

All the dignitaries of the Cathedral, and many incumbents and clergy from the city were in the prebendal stalls to listen to one of their number, the newest and lowliest, play for the first time his part as their brother – all except one.

§

'Who's in, who's out. And take upon us the mystery of things.'

PART II
ECCLESIASTICAL COURT

Chapter One

THE FIRST DAY

St. Hugh's Clergy House, Westgate, where I now had, with pride, my bed-sitting-room or 'cell', was only a few hundred yards from the College hostel, so I often met students on the pavements who had been junior to me and still had their exams before them. Sometimes I met them in my new caped cassock which was an exact model of the Archdeacon's, having been bought for that reason both sadly and defiantly. And my pride in this uniform, which I cannot deny, was both ashamed and unashamed; ashamed because it savoured of my still too-active self-showmanship; unashamed because it amounted in my heart to a declaration that I believed in him and intended to continue modelling myself on him.

In this elegant uniform (and in truth there are few more elegant robes than a caped and cinctured cassock) I encountered Bill Brickhill one morning, loitering on the doorstep of the hostel.

'Hallo, Reverend,' he said. 'How's it feel? Do I genuflect, or something? What are you doing? Out visiting?'

'Yes. And I've no time to stay gassing with you. And why aren't you at lectures, anyway?'

'Aha! Why not? Strange things have happened. Would you wish to hear something really interesting?'

My heart slumped. I seemed to know beforehand that the 'something really interesting' would be something that hurt.

'What is it?' I asked, sharply monosyllabic.

'We children have been cleared out of the Priest Vicars' Hall. It's wanted for more serious purposes. We're having our lectures here in the common room.'

'What do they want the hall for?'

'Can't you guess? They are preparing it with all sorts of thrones and chairs and benches, rather as they prepare the Abbey for a coronation. For *there* is the seat of judgment; even the seat of the house of David, my boy.'

'You mean the trial is to be there?'

'I mean that exactly.'

'And when?'

'Wednesday next. Ten-thirty. Am.' A joke, you see, turning 'a.m.' into 'Am'.

'Oh well. . . .' I was in no humour for jokes. 'Well, there it is. . . .' Raising a hand in farewell, I left him.

In our Priest Vicars' Hall. The Priest Vicars' Hall had once, in the fourteenth century been known as the Gildenhalle because it belonged then to the Merchants' Gild of Casterton, before being given to the priest vicars, or vicars choral of the Cathedral. I have told you how it was long and rectangular with an open-timbered roof crowning high stone walls, dank and cold. Behind the dais where our lecturers would stand was a half-timbered wall with a small door leading into the old Vicars' Parlour. I could only imagine that they would place handsome chairs on the dais as thrones for the Chancellor and his Assessors and many rows of lesser chairs on the long floor of the hall. But what with the barristers, the solicitors, the Pressmen, the defendant and his friends, no great number of people would get into those chairs to represent the whole of Britain listening.

As I walked on, turning into South Street, I saw the Archdeacon coming out of the Close by the Prebendal Gate. Oh, he was pale, pale; and I instantly crossed the road and gazed into a shop window to avoid a meeting. Then he had returned from his refuge by the sea to be ready for Wednesday next and his fate.

And Julie was back. I met her later that day. She was walking sadly along North Walls, under the darkening summer trees. She smiled bravely as she saw me, and lifted her eyebrows, not in dismay this time, but in delight at my cassock and collar. 'Oh, you do look appealing,' she said. 'Gosh, you'll win all hearts!'

I said nothing about the trial because I did not know what to say.

Leaving her, I wondered, Did I want to get into the Priest Vicars' Hall on Wednesday next, or would the pain of it be greater than the interest? But, anyhow, whether I wanted to or not, I could not do it in the morning, because Prebendary Imbraham would expect Harry Paul, my senior curate, and me to be busied with other matters. Perhaps one afternoon I would try to get in; and perhaps not.

I did, however, on the Wednesday morning, contrive at about fifteen minutes after ten to pass the entrance to the hall and see what was happening there. This entrance faced the Cathedral lawns, and a chattering crowd of people stood on the sacred grass among the bay trees and the yews: Press photographers, old men who would normally be sitting with their pipes in the park, gaitered farmers (for it was Wednesday and the cattle market), pairs of gossiping women, loafing young men with thumbs hooked on to their trouser pockets, noisy children who for one reason or another were not at school, and a single city policeman. All this because the defendant was a priest and not a layman; no clergy were there; this was the World's invasion of the Close, usually so quiet and empty except for some priestly figure, or ecclesiastical lady, walking alone.

Even as I went by, affecting little interest, I heard a schoolboy ask innocently, 'Will he go to prison?' and at the same moment saw all the Press cameras jump into position – or rush there – to snap a tall and manifestly legal figure in his wing collar and black coat. 'Who's that? Who's he?' I heard; and the answer was repeated and repeated like a ball tossed from each to the next, 'Sir Gerald Harbon, K.C., *his* counsel.' 'Who?' 'Sir Gerald Harborn, K.C.' Always the 'K.C.' was uttered impressively, and some of the romantics explained how great an advocate he was. 'Absolute tops. *He* must cost a pretty penny. But *he'll* get him off if anyone can.' 'Yes but what about the other cove, the prosecutor? He went in just now. Don't go underestimating him. *He* knows his stuff too, he does.'

'But he isn't a K.C.'

'Never mind that. He's a Chancellor in another diocese, and a Sir. Sir William Cummins. You don't become a Chancellor all that easily. *Or* a Sir.'

'I don't know what a Chancellor is, do you?'

'Well . . . he's quite a big cock, believe me.'

Meanwhile a comment by a farmer: 'Well, mebbe I can give the old Archdeacon a job in my cowshed if they unfrock him.'

I caught a woman's eyes following me and I hurried guiltily into South Street where the farmers' carts were clattering along, and a farmer's boy with a stick was shouting at a drove of cattle.

§

But in the afternoon the lodestone drag of that hall was too strong for me. At first I thought of going stealthily towards it as in the morning and trying to work myself in. Did I not know Jack Rivers, the Registrar's clerk, who'd been 'on the door'; had I not played tennis with him at the MacMasters' Young Persons' Party? Perhaps he could work me in. My brain threw up excuses I could offer him. 'But, my dear chap, I'm a friend of the family. Don't be silly.' Or the sophistry, 'Nonsense. It's my business to learn the methods of these ecclesiastical courts.' But then I sickened of all this slyness, I felt ashamed of it, I remembered our Bishop on the moral destruction worked by compromises; and I went straight to my vicar and told him the truth: that I had a longing to attend the trial and was feeling ashamed about this, and would he tell me, please, if it was sin.

Prebendary Imbraham sat behind his large desk in the largest sitting-room of our Clergy House. Bishop Griffyn had spoken of his Asiatic face, and certainly, if he had been half his height, and if his skin had been browner, one might have guessed that one of his recent ancestors had been Malayan or Japanese. Today, as usual, those inset, narrow eyes were alight with geniality – that geniality which, in Bishop Griffyn's view, bordered at times on the intemperate – and he dispersed my mountain of doubt with a fine, merry breath of it.

'My dear boy, go by all means. You are over-conscientious – a good fault in a young deacon. I admit there's a terrible interest in it – why shouldn't we admit this? But you'll be fortunate if you can get in. I'm told the whole of Casterton's trying to get in, and most of the villages round about. Well, you know your Vicars' Hall.

What does it hold? Two hundred? Three hundred at a stretch? The Registrar is talking of only admitting people by ticket if the trial goes on for long. Look: I'll give you my card to show to whoever's at the door. Don't suppose it'll work as a ticket, but it might. Evensong at five-thirty, but the court will have adjourned by then. If you get in, come and tell me all about it. And please: if you can tell me it's going well for Alanside, you'll make me happy.'

I ran towards the hall; at least I went as fast as the dignity of my cassock would allow. The court had resumed at two; it was now nearly half-past. In the Cloisters not a soul was in sight so I did break into a run here; several runs till I was in the Cathedral garden. A queue of people stretched from the door of the hall, right through the little archway into South Street, and sank my heart. What hope? But my cassock enabled me to walk to the door without their murmuring; probably this black uniform suggested that I was some officer of the court.

Jack Rivers was alone at the door. From the Court Room above I heard a man's voice going on and on, much as in these days one hears in the distance a broadcast voice going on and on and on. It hastened my words: 'Look, Jack —'

'No good, old boy. "House Full." Capacity audience. Every inch of standing room occupied twice over. Look at all those silly people there.' He nodded towards the queue. 'Did you ever see such patience? And what hope have they? This is the great social event of the season. Nobody's going to faint in the crush and make room for them. The whole case is much too spicy, according to all that the gen'l'man told us this morning.'

'Gen'l'man?'

'The prosecutor. Sir Bill Cummins.'

'But hang it, Jack. This is more or less *my* lecture hall. It was we who lent it to you for your present ungodly purposes, damn it all.'

'That's no language for a little parson.'

'Never mind language. I'm a friend of the family.'

'So's all Casterton, as far as I can make out. But only about fifty of the family's chums have got in.'

'But damn it, Jack, you and I and Julie have all played tennis together.'

'Can't help that. The reporters have had to have precedence, and it would seem that the Press of the world is here. And some from the moon, I fancy. The interest in this distinguished affair is, as one might say, almost inter-planetary.'

'Is the Archdeacon there?'

'Naturally. Is he not, so to say, the gen'l'man in the dock?'

'It must be rather hell for him.'

'Yes, my boss says he'd much better have admitted to an indiscretion or two so that all could have been settled quietly in the Bishop's study, instead of insisting on *this* how-d'ye-do and so giving Fleet Street the sweetest dish it's had for ages.'

'But he's innocent. How could he admit guilt if he's innocent? He was perfectly right in insisting that these ghastly accusations must be disproved before the world.'

'If he's innocent, there are some majestic liars in the world.'

'Yes. There are.'

'On oath?'

'I suppose so.' Evading the question, I showed him my vicar's card. 'My vicar gave me this. He wants me to report to him on the trial this evening.'

'Oh, good old Trippy. I wish I could oblige him. But there's absolutely no room, old boy. I've been told not to let anyone else in. But listen, sonny: have you no *nous*? Do you never use your loaf? As a regular tenant of this hall don't you recall that there's another way up to it from the Priest Vicars' Close – a way that none of these silly people know anything about?'

It was true. I remembered. On the other side of the great chamber above, through an ancient doorway in its south wall, an ancient windowed stairway led down to the Vicars' Close, which was a row of fifteenth-century houses, low and crumbling and creeper-hung, where once the priest vicars used to live. Thus this old and little-used stair, in those far-off days, was their way up to their refectory and parlour.

'Golly! Yes!' I said.

'Yes, to be sure. And my idea is that you might be able to squeeze in that way. I mean: you're young' – he was perhaps two years older than I was – 'and one doesn't mind discomfort at your age.'

I ran right round – via South Street and the Prebendal Gate – to the Vicars' Close and to a small four-centred doorway behind which was this old stair. I ran up it. The stair-head had no less than two crumbled stone arches leading into the hall. The farther arch allowed me to see the whole long rectangular place from its middle. I was a little taller than the standing people near me, and I saw our familiar hall marvellously transformed. On the platform at the far end the Chancellor, Sir Robert Treevil, sat behind a long refectory table in his black silk gown and full-bottomed wig. On either side of him sat his Assessors, three clergy on his right, two laymen on his left. The laymen I could not recognize; the clergy I knew: Archdeacon Lenham of Silchester and Canons Pearson and Maidwell. The Chancellor, centre of the picture, was a small friendly smiling man whose smile seemed to say, 'Now don't let any of us make too heavy weather of this,' though it was weather in which a man might sink.

Below the Chancellor, at a lonely table, sat the Registrar; and behind this table, at their own tables, counsel and solicitors. Behind them, in the front row of chairs – I had edged myself farther in to look at those chairs – sat the Archdeacon, pale as the great room's cold stone walls, but perfectly dressed in archidiaconal garb while this was still allowed to him. And at his side, also bravely dressed, little Mrs. Alanside.

Nowhere Julie.

The rest of the floor-space was thronged with spectators either seated in chair-rows too close together or standing, two and three deep, along the walls. Sweeping this dense congregation with my eyes, I remarked one women knitting speedily as she watched and listened, another holding opera glasses on her lap or making great use of them, two gawking young men with jaws fallen, and one old man asleep.

Apparently the prosecutor, Sir William Cummins, Chancellor

of a neighbouring diocese, had occupied the morning with a long opening address and was now examining his witnesses. At a small table on the right of the platform a man was being sworn by the apparitor, who was a grey old man in a gown. Sworn, this witness sat at the table, after pulling up the knees of his trousers. He was the manager of the Morland Hotel, Gloucester Gate. A man of forty but white-haired, he looked like a distinguished and expensive consultant physician. A perjurer?

'Your hotel, Mr. Grace: is it on the Bayswater Road?' Sir William Cummins, though a Chancellor, was less distinguished in appearance than his witness. He was a short rounded man with a large, too large, head, ovoid as a melon.

'No, sir. It faces the backs of the houses in the Bayswater Road.'

'In a quieter part, would you say?'

'I suppose so, sir. Yes . . . certainly.'

'Is it a large hotel?'

'Not very. There are many larger in that neighbourhood.'

'I see. And can you remember who visited it on this day?'

'I can.'

'Was there a clergyman with a lady among the visitors?'

'There was. That is right.'

'Could you identify the clergyman if you saw him?'

'I think so.'

Sir William turned towards the Archdeacon. 'Mr. Archdeacon, would you very kindly stand up?'

I dropped my eyes and withdrew a step backwards. I could not endure this. But just before I dropped my eyes I had sent them weakly, inevitably, towards little Mrs. Alanside. Her head too was bowed; her eyes on the floor.

'Is this the clergyman?'

'Yes, sir.'

'Thank you, Mr. Archdeacon. . . . Was the clergyman in any exceptional uniform?'

'I don't understand, sir.'

'I mean, was he in gaiters and an apron, rather like a bishop?'

'Oh no, sir. He was in a dark grey suit with a clerical collar.'

'How would you describe the lady with him?'

'I find that very difficult, sir. To me she seemed like any other well-dressed lady. The clergyman, if I may say so, was the more striking figure.'

'Well, perhaps your wife will have noticed a little more about her.' Laughter. Laughter that rent me; did they not realize that a man was being tortured in their midst?

Sir William spoke to the apparitor. 'Give Mr. Grace, please, his hotel visitors' book.'

The apparitor laid a heavy volume on the witness's table and walked back to his seat.

'This is your visitors' book, Mr. Grace?'

'It is.'

'Will you read the entry that relates to the clergyman's visit?'

'The name is difficult to read. The writing is little more than a shaky line – almost as if meant to be illegible.'

'Please do not comment. Read as best you can.'

'Apparently the words are "E-something" and "A-something", followed by the words "and wife".'

'If you can't read the names how do you read "and wife" so easily?'

'Because I wrote it myself.'

'I see. And why did you write it? And when?'

'I wrote it after the clergyman had asked for a double-bedded room. Because of his clerical collar I supposed the lady was his wife.' Laughter again, quietly rebuked by the Chancellor. Mrs. Alanside's head cast down.

'He was given the double-bedded room. Was there any luggage?'

'Very little. A kind of large black handbag. The lady had nothing.'

'The apparitor will now give you your hotel account book. Will you read to us any entries that cover this visit?'

'Night of the 10th, two dinners debited to Room 14; two breakfasts —'

'One minute! Room 14. What room was that?'

'The room my wife assigned to the clergyman and the lady.'

'In that book is there any name attached to "Room 14"?'

'Well, not quite, sir. Only "Rev. A —". I hadn't been able to read his name and didn't like to tell him so.'

'I understand. And was there any subsequent visit by this couple?'

'Yes. Two weeks later. Fifteen days later.'

'You knew his name then?'

'Oh, yes, sir.'

'How?'

'I had been told it by the man from the detective agency.'

'We shall come to him.'

Remarkable the power of my cassock. A man standing in front of me in the stone archway turned round, saw it, studied it, and assumed that it implied an official capacity. Thinking I ought to be allowed to get into the court, he made way for me. 'Go on, mate, if you have to.'

'Thank you so much,' I answered. 'But I'm only an observer.' This, though I had intended no deceit, sounded well. It sounded official. It suggested some kind of watching brief.

'Well, observe,' he enjoined. 'You can't observe much through my back.'

He let me slither past him, and now I stood in the front row of the standing people. Sir William was still questioning his witness about that second visit. 'Here the entry "and wife" is in pencil, Mr. Grace. Will you explain that?'

'Well, sir, they arrived in the afternoon, and as I had his name now from the detective, Mr. Lake, I said, "Will you sign the register, please, Mr. Alanside?" And he signed it much more clearly this time. I then asked the lady to sign, but he said this was quite unnecessary.'

'And then?'

'I said it was necessary and *he* added "and wife" in pencil.'

'They stayed how long?'

'One night only. They went after breakfast next day.'

'Mr. Grace, on the occasion of this second visit was there anyone with you who saw the clergyman and lady?'

'Yes, my friend, Mr. Gibson. He was sitting in the reception office with me.'

'Thank you.' Sir William sat down.

The Archdeacon's counsel rose, Sir Gerald Harbon, whom I had last seen running the gauntlet of the Press cameras. I saw him better now: a tall, dark man with heavy Hebraic features, though, in fact, he was Irish. His black hair was parted down the centre, a feminine style that looked odd above that strong heavy face. At first one guessed him as sixty; only in a full light did wrinkles like monocles around his dark eyes suggest the nearness of seventy. Because his hair was such a jet black his chin, however closely shaved in the morning, was dark by three in the afternoon. It was a jest in the junior Bar that Sir Gerald Harbon, K.C., strolling the corridors of the Old Bailey, might well be the Prince of Darkness himself, disguised for a visit to his customers hereabout.

His rising stirred all heads because of the many echoing cases whose names were among his battle honours. Would any of them resound further than this?

'Mr. Grace, you have told us that this visitor wore a dark grey suit with a clerical collar. You are sure about this?'

'Perfectly sure.'

'Why I ask you this, and seek your perfect assurance about it, Mr. Grace, is because it seems so strange that, if what the prosecution allege is true, and this visitor was anything but an innocent guest, he should have come in a clerical collar. Surely it would have been simpler to wear a layman's collar, and then none of this business would have started.'

Mr. Grace seemed bewildered by this query, a wholly unforeseen one, and he stayed silent for a time. Sir Gerald did nothing to interrupt the long silence, which so obviously enforced his point; he just stood and stared and waited pleasantly. At last the witness managed to say, and not without pleasure in a suddenly discovered retort, 'I suppose one could say it was worn to disarm criticism.'

'I suppose one could,' Sir Gerald agreed, and if ever those four words meant, 'I suppose someone could be idiot enough to say

F

that,' it was now. He bent down towards his papers and came erect with one of them.

'Mr. Grace, you have told us that it was you who added the first "and wife".'

'Yes, sir.'

'So there was at one time nothing in the book to suggest that the clergyman had a woman with him? You say you wrote it after he requested a double room. *How long after?*'

'That same evening.'

'*How long after?*'

'I can't exactly remember.'

'Bring me the book, usher. Ah, here is the entry. The ink for the words "and wife" looks very different.'

'No doubt. It was from my fountain-pen.'

'It was not written many days afterwards?'

'It was not, sir.'

'To that you swear?'

'I do. Certainly.'

'Not after a man from a private detective agency approached you with inquiries?'

'No, sir. That same evening.'

'Were you busy at the time? Was your hotel full?'

'I was busy enough.'

'People coming and going?'

'Yes. Because there was a conference of some sort in the Great Western Hotel nearby.'

'Exactly. The detective – who sent him?'

'That I don't know, sir. He always referred to his employer as "our client".'

'Did he hint as to whether "our client" was in Holy Orders?'

'No, sir.'

'Did he state what authority he had to ask questions of you?'

'He told me he was a retired superintendent of the police.'

'And you had no hesitation in telling him all that you could about two of your guests?'

'I told him little that he didn't know already, sir.' Laughter.

'How could he know anything already?'

The witness shrugged. 'Watching, I suppose. Keeping observation.'

'Did any money pass between him and you?'

The witness looked at the Chancellor presiding. 'Do I have to answer that question, sir?'

In the friendliest way, and with the kindliest smile, the Chancellor said, 'I think so, Mr. Grace.'

'There was a small sum given me which he called an "honorarium". An honorarium for taking up my valuable time.'

'And how much was the honorarium, Mr. Grace?'

'I forget. Perhaps five pounds . . . ten pounds.'

Abruptly Sir Gerald sat down.

Next to be called was Mrs. Fanny Grace, and she looked the part of a hotel manageress much better than her husband looked his part. Under a large hat she had a mass of hair henna'd to a smouldering bronze; round her fat neck was a collar of pearls, and down the declivity of a her prominent bosom lay a mat of white lace like an expensive apron. As with her dress, so with her speaking; it seemed to come from lower environs than her husband's.

After eliciting corroboration of much that the husband had said, Sir William Cummins asked, 'Mrs. Grace, your husband didn't feel able to describe the woman. Can you enlighten us at all?'

'Well, I didn't see her so clearly at first, like, for she wore a smallish black hat with a black lace veil that fell a little way over her eyes and a longer way down her back. In build I would say she was on the broadish side, but graceful, if you see what I mean, and in dress she was very much the lady, if you see what I mean. At dinner I noticed that her hair was all coiled and piled on the top of her head and I thought, "Very becoming". Her dress was a black georgette frock with a —'

'I see. We see. That will do. I doubt if we shall be able to remember all that.'

'I got the impression that the lady was frightened. Embarrassed, like.'

'Mrs. Grace, I haven't asked you about that. You assigned them a room?'

'Yes. No. 14. A double room.'

'Who took them up to the room?'

'Mrs. Collins. A chambermaid. A thoroughly reliable woman. She's been at the hotel more than ten years.'

'Just limit your answers, please, to the questions. This Mrs. Collins, you say, showed them up to —'

'Yes. And it was she who heard —'

'Please, *please*, Mrs. Grace. We shall hear from Mrs. Collins herself. You remember the visit of the detective?'

'Oh, yes. He come and pressed me for information. It was he who told us the clergyman's name.'

Sir Gerald shot to his feet, much taller than the small and round Sir William. Sir William, after turning towards this dark disturbance at his side, and looking up at it, amended his witness's answer. 'You mean he told you what he thought was the clergyman's name.'

'It *was* his name. We learnt that when the clergyman come a second time.'

'Thank you, Mrs. Grace.' Dissatisfied with his witness, Sir William nodded to her, and turned again towards Sir Gerald, now comfortably seated. But he only grinned and murmured, 'No questions.'

So Sir William called for Mrs. Collins, and a full-bodied woman in late middle age went to the table. In her old-fashioned black hat with protruding hat-pins and her long black coat and skirt, she looked the type anyone would call 'a faithful old body'. The expression on her round, mottled face, with its closed lips moving up and down, seemed as willing as it was nervous. A perjurer? Paid?

'Mrs. Collins, you took the clergyman and lady up to Room 14. Do you think you could recognize the clergyman again?'

'I might, sir. Yes, I think so, sir.'

Again the request to the Archdeacon to stand up before a staring crowd – a man who had been the admiration of vast audiences, an idol of women, a trusted confessor and counsellor to his penitents – to stand up and be identified by the chambermaid. Again I could not bear it and cast down my eyes. I only heard her voice: 'Yes, that is the gentleman.' When I looked up again, it was over; he had sunk back into comparative anonymity by his wife's side.

'Did you do anything for them in their room?'

'Oh, yes, sir. I lit the fire for them at the gentleman's request.'

'Did you hear any of their talk while you were doing this?'

'Oh, yes. The fire wouldn't draw at first, and I was there on my knees for quite a time.'

'Well, what did you hear?'

'I heard him say, in a low voice, like, "You must be careful, my dear. You mustn't tell a soul anything about this. Not a soul."'

'Can you remember anything else?'

'No, but I remember that.'

'You helped in the dining-room, I think, that evening?'

'Yes, sir. We was short and very busy, what with being full and all.'

'Did you wait on this clergyman and lady?'

'Not exactly, sir. But the gentleman did recognize me in the door and ask me, very pleasant like, for a corner table. At the back, he said. Mrs. Irons was doing their table, but I did carry some dishes for her.'

'And did you by any chance hear any of their conversation?'

'Yes, I did. I heard him say to her, "Keep your hands down, darling, or they'll throw you out."'

'And what did you make of that extraordinary remark?'

'Both Mrs. Irons and me thought it was because she hadn't no wedding ring.'

'I see. Thank you.' He looked towards Sir Gerald, but defending counsel only rose very slowly, after choosing from among his notes. When he did rise he had notes in his hand. His dark face was bent over them and he did not look at the witness.

'Mrs. Collins, you have told us that you heard the occupants of Room 14 say' – here he read slowly from the notes: '"You must be careful, my dear. You mustn't tell a soul anything about this." Is that right?'

'That's right.'

Sharply his face lifted to the witness. And stared. 'How is it that you remember so many words in such exact detail? Words spoken, as you told us, in a low voice.'

'I dunno. I just do.'

He snatched off his spectacles to ask the next question. 'You have said the hotel was full. You attended many other persons, I suppose?'

'Yes, sir.'

'When did you first recall in such perfect detail what two of so many visitors said?'

'The very next day, sir, when the detective gentlemen came.'

'Ah, yes: the detective. Did he suggest to you that you might have heard compromising words?'

'He ars't me if I had.'

'"You mustn't tell a soul anything about this." That might refer to any subject on earth?'

'I suppose it could.' But Mrs. Collins seemed disappointed by any such interpretation.

'You will appreciate that it seems extraordinary to be discussing one's immorality, one's fornication, while a maid is in the room?'

'He said it in a very low voice.'

'And yet you heard it clearly and remember it perfectly? Do you not see that the very detail and accuracy with which you report the words lays them open to doubt – I don't want to suggest any intentional misrepresentation.'

'Oh, they said what I said all right.'

'And you are confident that it was the clergyman who said it, and not some other guest in the hotel?'

'Oh, yes, it was him all right.'

'Very good, Mrs. Collins. Well, let us turn to the words you overheard at their dining-table. These were not said in a whisper, I suppose, or you could never have heard them?'

'Oh, no. Ordinary voice, like.'

'I see. Quite ordinary voice. When did you remember having heard them?'

'I suppose it was after the detective gentleman ars't if I'd heard anything suspicious.'

'Just so.' Sir Gerald replaced his spectacles to read from his notes. 'Will you assure me that I'm repeating them exactly.' With slow deliberation he read: '"Keep your hands down, darling, or they'll throw you out." Is that right?'

'Absolutely.'

'*Really?*'

'Yes, he kind of meant that her hands would give the show away.'

'Well, never mind what he meant. Your guesses are not evidence. You are confident about the words. Are you equally confident that it was he who said them?'

'*Yes*, sir.' She snapped this at him irritably, not liking aspersions cast on her accuracy. This reply was like the angry shut of an offended lady's reticule.

'Very good. Well now, what would you say, Mrs. Collins, if later in this trial I produced a husband and wife who were staying in your hotel that same night and who will both say that the husband said these exact words to his wife at a dining-table, because she'd left her wedding ring in the bedroom upstairs?'

My heart jumped with delight. It not only jumped, it beat with delight. I was like a young man watching a match and ready to shout aloud when his side scored in the enemy's goal. The man who'd let me pass him said in my ear, 'That's a fourpenny one. *Cor!*'

The witness for her part looked flabbergasted; but then looked as if she was suspecting a trick on her – a 'try-on' – which she didn't at all appreciate. So she said haughtily, 'I should still say it was him that said it.'

'Very good. We shall hear from them, and we shall have the remarkable situation that two apparently married couples were saying exactly the same things at exactly the same time in exactly the same place. Now I want to ask you something else. You are obviously a very perceptive woman; would you describe the clergyman's lady to us. Was she – shall we say – "broadish"?'

'Oh, no, I wouldn't say that.'

'And "graceful"?'

'Not particularly. No, I don't think so.'

'Was she very well dressed?'

'No . . . no . . . just ordinary, like.'

'Would you describe her as "very much the lady"?'

'Oh, dear me, no. That's the last thing I'd'a said about her.'

A fine stirring now in the crowded audience – rather like the mounting excitement when the popular side is pressing their enemy's goal. A stirring – and silence.

'She was not notably broad or graceful or well-dressed, and certainly not "very much the lady". Good. And she had no wedding ring?'

'None at all.'

'Strange. Very odd, Mrs. Collins. Hasn't it occurred to you that if they were there for an immoral purpose, they would almost certainly have invested, between them, in a sixpenny wedding ring? Doesn't the absence of the ring, and the remark you so clearly overheard, almost *prove* that they were a married couple? And that the wife had merely forgotten her ring?'

Mrs. Collins was as obviously taken aback by this sudden turning of her evidence to face the wrong way, as Mr. Grace had been by counsel's similar employment of the clerical collar. She could only shrug, stare, and say, 'I know nothing about that.'

'Very well. Was this the first time you noticed that she had no wedding ring, Mrs. Collins?'

Not seeing the point of this question, and afraid of it, she hesitated before answering, 'Well . . . yes.'

'You did not notice its absence when you were up in their room, lighting their fire?'

'No.'

'I see. I see. All right, Mrs. Collins; all right. Now another point. I don't want to distress you unnecessarily but my client's character is in issue and I cannot be too gentle with anyone who is helping, inevitably, to deprive him of his good name for ever. I understand that you have given ten years of faithful service to the Morland Hotel and are thought highly of there. I am glad to repeat this. *But were you ever at any other hotel?*'

She paled. She looked at him and did not answer.

'Come, Mrs. Collins.'

'Well, yes, I was. Long ago. At a hotel called the Queen Anne.'

'Where?'

'In Notting Hill Gate, like.'

'How long were you there?'

'About three months.'

'Why so short a time? Why did you leave?'

No answer.

'Mrs. Collins, you are on oath. Were you dismissed?'

'Well, yes, I was, like.'

'Because you had not accounted for money received.'

'Well, it was something like that . . . yes.'

'I won't trouble you about it further. It's, as you say, a long time ago. All I want to ask you now is, Did this detective gentleman give you any money? A tip, as it were?'

'Yes. He give me a tip.'

'How much?'

'I don't remember, not after all this time.'

'Was it a matter of pounds, perhaps?'

'Yes . . . one or two.'

'What does "one or two" mean? Three? Five?'

'I tell you I don't exactly remember. Two, I think.'

'All right. That will do. You are vague about the money after all this time but perfectly clear about words spoken several days earlier. In bedroom and at table. Let us leave it at that. Thank you, Mrs. Collins.'

As she walked away the man behind me said, 'That's finished *her* off. They can now transfer her to the w.p.b. Always supposing this grim bloke lets them. They say he comes from Ireland, but he don't look Irish to me. I should have said his father's name was Moses and his uncle's Aaron. Anyhow he certainly knows how to do his stuff. Hope he chews up the others like that. I'm definitely on the side of the old parson bugger, me'self.'

§

Another hotel maid gave her evidence but added little and was not cross-examined. She was followed by 'the friend, Mr. Gibson', a large and portly man who could well be a brother licensee of Mr. Grace. His testimony was brief: merely that he'd been sitting in the reception bureau of the hotel when the clergyman and lady arrived on the second occasion and had heard the parties ask for a double room. He identified the Archdeacon and stated that he had seen him add the words 'and wife' in pencil. All of it was stuff faded in colour because a twice-told tale. Or seemed so.

But Sir Gerald rose slowly with notes drooping from his fingers and his spectacles dropping down his nose; and something in that slow movement suggested that he had in his hand that which would make matters interesting again. He stared over the spectacles and under the heavy black eyebrows at Mr. Gibson.

'Mr. Gibson, you are a great friend of Mr. Grace?'

'Yes, I like to think so, sir, yes.' Hearty. Pleasant. Smiling.

'You come often to see him and have a chat?' Counsel hardly less pleasant and smiling.

'Oh, yes. Twice a week sometimes.'

'And I take it you have discussed with him many a time this visit of the clergyman and lady?'

Obviously suspecting a trap, and pleased by his quick perception, Mr. Gibson answered promptly, 'Oh, no! Oh, no, I haven't!'

'When you say "No", Mr. Gibson, do you mean "Never"?'

'Yes. Yes, I think so. No, I didn't discuss it.'

'*What?*' The black eyebrows came together. They fell a fraction nearer the eyes. 'Not after you'd heard that a detective had been watching the clergyman's movements; not after you'd heard that the clergyman was to be arraigned in a bishop's court for something which you and Mr. Grace had seen together; not after you knew that the whole country would ring with the story; not after you knew that your great friend would be called as a witness, and, a few days later, that you would be summoned too? *What?* Not a word spoken between you?'

'Well, I suppose I must have discussed it a very little with Mr. Grace – off and on. Yes.'

'*And* with Mrs. Grace?'

'Maybe. I —'

'Well, why deny on oath that you'd ever discussed it?'

'Depends what you mean by "discuss". I may have mentioned —'

'By "discuss" I mean, among other things, deciding what you would both say in court. Did you do this?'

'I suppose we must'a done something like it.'

'You discussed together what you could remember of a momentary event many months old?'

'If you put it like that – yes.'

'Very good. Thank you, Mr. Gibson.' Sir Gerald's resumption of his seat was as markedly quick as his rising from it had been deliberate and slow.

Broken that witness, I thought with something like glee. Oh, good, good.

There was no reason why the next name called should excite the audience – or the laity in it – but every reason why my heart should start at the sound of it. 'The Rev. J. Hanson Clide.' I remembered Mr. Prosdick: 'He is the enemy. The Rev. Clide.' I swung my eyes towards him as he approached the platform. The enemy who had emerged out of the unknown; from somewhere out of the level and quiet pastures that lay south of the city; out of the green Menwode where he was squire and parson of a village too small to be heard of and remembered. A small thin man with a thin peaking nose, bristling grey hair, a determined lip, and a quick precise walk (not unlike Mr. Prosdick's own); a firm and purposeful walk which seemed to say, 'Here I come to do my task, and let no one think I'm afraid of anybody or anything.' All the same, after he'd taken the oath and sat at the table – both briskly – I noticed that he looked anywhere but at people; he looked at the open timber roof above him, at the trefoil windows in front of him, and at the little pulpitum chamber from which, in the old days, some uplifting work was read to priest vicars at their meals. Never once did he look towards the Archdeacon with his wife at his side; hardly once at Chancellor or Assessors; only seldom at counsel, and then straight and, as it were, defiantly.

He testified, in his evidence-in-chief, that he'd heard a distressing rumour about Archdeacon Alanside; that, feeling this to be a serious matter for a man in the Archdeacon's position, for the diocese, and for the Church as a whole, he had wished to be very careful before he 'took any steps'; that accordingly he had employed a detective agency to weigh the truth of it; that after receiving the agency's report he had gone to the Morland Hotel, seen the pencilled words 'and wife' in the visitors' book, and recognized the Archdeacon's hand which he knew well; that he had then gone to Mrs. Alanside, whom he accounted his friend, and asked if she had ever visited this hotel; and that, on receiving her answer No, he had gone to consult the Bishop, leaving with him some statements of evidence offered by detective and hotel staff.

(Thanks, I thought. Now, Sir Gerald.)

Sir Gerald rose. My heart beat and beat in anticipation.

Sir Gerald put on his spectacles. 'Mr. Clide, you employed this detective agency at your own expense?'

'Yes. Entirely.' The 'entirely' was to stress that, if anything, he was proud of this and not ashamed. But he weakened its effect by a quick, nervous and unsolicited explanation. 'It wasn't really expensive.'

'How was that?' For a moment Sir Gerald seemed more interested in this surprising fact than in his brief.

Mr. Clide spread an empty hand on either side of his little table. 'The man's daily payment and his daily expenses were not high.'

For a moment I thought Sir Gerald, in his interest, was going to ask 'How much?' but he avoided doing so.

Mr. Clide pursued, 'And, in fact, there was very little for him to do.'

'He was watching for many days?'

'Twenty perhaps. Little more.'

'Mr. Clide, you knew, of course, that if this rumour was proved to your satisfaction, it would mean total ruin for a brother clergy-man?'

'When one is seeking only the truth of a matter, sir, the question whether the consequences will be agreeable or disagreeable is, at the time, irrelevant.' A good answer, but he spoiled it by adding, 'It might not have been total ruin at all. There have been cases —'

'Never mind them, Mr. Clide. You are an avowed enemy of the Archdeacon?'

'Not at all. I don't particularly like him, but, apart from that, I have no great interest in him one way or another.'

'No great interest. Then you have never threatened to "bring him to the ground"?'

'Of course not.'

'Mr. Clide, did the Archdeacon, many years ago, send papers about you to the Bishop with the result that there were proceedings against you in a Consistory Court like this? That is true, is it not?'

'It is very true.'

'And the Archdeacon acted as prosecutor in his capacity as Archdeacon of Casterton?'

'He did.'

'And you were found "not guilty"?'

'Of course. Naturally.'

'You were acquitted . . . *but* . . . did you swear, on leaving the court, that, if ever the chance offered – that at any cost and however long it took – you would wreck the man who brought you there?'

'Certainly not.'

'What if I produce a witness who will testify to having heard this threat?'

'Produce him and I will answer him. I will say that he has either been dreaming it or is telling lies.'

'I did not say the witness would be a man. You believed, did you, that the Archdeacon had committed adultery?'

'I could do no other. The evidence was there. And not of one occasion only.'

'So you went to see his wife?'

'Let me explain this. I knew Mrs. Alanside well. I was fond of her. I have often been the recipient of her confidences. I might even say she has poured out confidences to me —'

'Such as?'

'Confidences, I'm afraid, largely about her husband and his neglect of her for other interests. She has complained to me many times about his treatment of her; of his leaving her for long periods alone, and of his caring nothing for her but only for his daughter. I have been deeply sorry for her.'

Surprisingly, Sir Gerald said, 'Go on, Mr. Clide. Go on.'

'She has said that she seems to matter nothing to him. It is his career and his work that matter and she is no more than a piece of furniture in the house.'

'Go on, Mr. Clide.'

'So I took her into my confidence and told her about this evidence against him, and that this case was bound to come about. I advised her, as a friend, that to me her course seemed to be to go away from him temporarily and see if he could clear himself.'

'Let me see if I understand you aright. You had an affection towards her – and a Christian spirit towards her husband – and wished to be of help to them both. Is that it?'

No answer.

'As a clergyman and a brother priest, why did you not go straight to the Archdeacon?'

'The Bishop told me to be careful.'

'So in charity towards all and malice towards none, you advised her to leave him till such time as he could clear his name. Did she absolutely refuse to go?'

'She refused, yes.'

'Did she absolutely refuse to believe in these allegations?'

'Yes, I think so.'

'Come, Mr. Clide, your memory is not so poor that you can't recall if she refused flatly to listen to you. Did she, or did she not, declare her absolute belief in her husband's innocence?'

'Yes, she did.'

'And did she say, for example, that if ever there was a time when she intended to be at her husband's side, it was now?'

'She did say something like that.'

'Did she insist that these charges were "absurd and monstrous"?'

'That I cannot remember.'

'Well, we shall hear from her very shortly.' A flutter in the whole rapt audience like a shiver through tall grasses at a lift of the wind.

All heads turned or bent towards Mrs. Alanside, whose own head was down. 'Thank you, Mr. Clide.'

The witness stepped off the platform and walked down the room with the same quick and purposeful steps which seemed to say that his attitude to this case, and his confidence in himself, were untroubled, unchanged.

And the Chancellor, glancing at his wrist-watch, said in a voice that contrasted with all others, so normal, pleasant and unexcited did it seem: 'It is nearly five o'clock. We will now adjourn, I think.' And he smiled round on us all as if we had enjoyed an interesting afternoon; then rose and led his Assessors through the small four-centred doorway behind him into the old Parlour of the priest vicars.

Chapter Two

THE SECOND DAY

Next morning I did not ask Prebendary Imbraham a second time for his approval of my attendance at the trial. I let well alone, choosing to assume that his genial permission yesterday constituted a licence for the whole proceedings. To keep my conscience easy, however, I discharged some parish duties first – vigorously if a shade rapidly – and I did not reach the Priest Vicars' Hall till about half-past eleven. Once again I could secure no more than standing room under the arch of our ancient stairway, but with this I was satisfied. My interest would be too passionate for any physical weariness to trouble me – or even to make itself felt. When I arrived there seemed to be a halt in the proceedings. The Case for the Prosecution, I learned, had just closed, and the Defence was about to open.

When at last Sir Gerald opened his case he said that the defendant would answer the charge with a 'total and emphatic denial'. It would not be in dispute that he stayed on these two nights at the Morland Hotel, but on neither occasion, he would swear, was a woman with him. Sir Gerald then, and promptly, astonished us all by calling first, not the Archdeacon, but a young, comely, modishly attired woman who was half smiling as she sat herself at the table and agreed that her name was Mrs. Ethel Bardwick.

Who was this? Six questions and their answers explained. Had she ever stayed at the Morland Hotel? She had. When? On January 10th. Alone? No, her husband was with her. Did she have any meals at the hotel? Dinner and breakfast. At the dinner was she wearing her wedding ring? No, because – and the half-smile widened to three-quarters – she had been slimming and the finger had got so thin that the ring would slip from it, so she'd left it upstairs in the bedroom. Did her husband make any remark about its absence? Yes, he said, 'Eth, keep your hands down or they'll throw you out.'

'Thank you, Mrs. Bardwick.'

And since prosecuting counsel, who had been listening with interest, pulling his chin, said, 'No questions', also with a half-smile, she carried her smile off the platform and to the back of the room, where she found a seat to enjoy the rest of a captivating trial.

'I do not feel it will be necessary to call Mr. Bardwick,' said Sir Gerald very significantly. 'I will now call the defendant.'

Pale as a sick man not yet convalescent, but groomed from dark head to gaiter-topped shoes for this appearance in a judges' ring, the Archdeacon stood at the table and took the oath with a voice deliberately firm and clear. Every eye in the room, except his wife's, was steadied on him. With my heart thumping I found myself praying, 'Oh God, help him, help him, help him.' Stunned to a kind of stupefaction by all the evidence we had heard so calmly, so decorously, sworn, I felt like one who had taken blow after blow in the face while his hands were tied. How could *all* these people be lying on oath? And yet I was resolved, absolutely, finally, to believe in his innocence. I gave the whole of myself to his 'total and emphatic denial' because I loved him, because my heart was aching for him; and I knew that I would go on doing this against all logic and sense, if necessary; against all evidence, however sworn. 'Oh God, help him, help him, help him.'

Never such a silence as this. The silence that waited for Sir Gerald to speak.

'Mr. Archdeacon, where were you on January 10th this year?'

'In London.'

'Where did you stay?'

'In the Morland Hotel, Gloucester Gate.'

'For what purpose were you in London?'

'For continuous research in the libraries of Westminster, the Guildhall and the British Museum. For a book I was writing on the varying faces of Anglican Christianity in the Civil War, the Protectorate, and the Restoration.'

'How did you come to stay at this hotel?'

'The one I had been staying at, in the same district, was full that night and they recommended me to the Morland.'

'We have heard from the detective that you went into the hotel with a woman. What do you say to that?'

'That there is no more truth in it than that, as I crossed the park to come to Gloucester Gate, a young woman asked me the way to Gloucester Terrace, and I said, "Come with me. I am going in that direction."'

'Where did you leave her?'

'At the corner of Gloucester Gate, by the hotel, after showing her the way.'

'We have heard it suggested, quite improperly, that the writing of your name in the visitors' book was deliberately made illegible. Would you explain its rather shaky character?'

'It is not illegible; it is my name; but the light was bad, the book is heavy, as we have seen, and I had to hold it to the light with one hand and write with the other.'

'What room were you given?'

'No. 14. A double room because the hotel was full.'

'You had meals in the hotel?'

'Yes, dinner and breakfast.'

'Alone?'

'Alone.'

'And you returned home on the 11th?'

'I returned home that evening.'

Sir Gerald bent down to speak to Sir William, who nodded.

So Sir Gerald proceeded, 'My learned friend allows me to take the next questions more quickly. Did you stay in this same hotel two weeks later?'

'I did. I was well satisfied with it, and I was continuing my researches, for two mid-week days, in the Westminster Library.'

'What room did you stay in?'

'That I have forgotten, but I have heard today that it was No. 7 and I have no doubt it was.'

'But you deny that there was anyone in it with you?'

'Emphatically.'

'Then in consequence you deny that you pencilled in the visitors' book the words "and wife"?'

'Of course. My wife was here in Casterton.'

'Mr. Archdeacon, we have heard that my lord Bishop was supplied with copies of statements made by the prosecution's witnesses. Were similar copies sent to you?'

'Yes.'

'What did you do when you read them?'

'I wrote immediately to the Bishop, asking that I might be given the earliest opportunity of rebutting such preposterous charges.'

'Is this' – Sir Gerald gave a paper to the apparitor, who carried it to the witness – 'a correct transcript of your letter?'

After scanning quickly the surface of the document the Archdeacon said, 'It is.'

'Will you read it to the court, please.'

The Archdeacon stood up. With the paper in his hand he half turned towards the crowding audience as he had often turned towards a congregation in the Cathedral, and with his beautiful voice and clear diction so often given to sacred subjects he read for us all, 'My lord Bishop, I have now had time to consider what course to adopt in reference to the grave and baseless accusations brought against me by the Rev. Hanson Clide. Since these have been made by a brother clergyman I venture to hope that they may form the subject of an inquiry by the appropriate ecclesiastical court, where I shall have the opportunity of indignantly and publicly denying and refuting them. And, knowing that you will appreciate the great distress of mind from which I have been suffering since I first heard of these allegations, I do most earnestly beg that the court may be convened at the earliest possible moment.'

'Thank you, Mr. Archdeacon. You are here then to deny and refute the accusations. How do you account for the sworn evidence we have heard?'

'I do not know how to account for it. I can only assume that it is the result of a whole chapter of blunders, or that it is in part perjury and in part mistakes. We have had evidence this morning of one remarkable blunder about words spoken at a dinner-table, and I think it possible that, on a crowded and busy evening in a hotel other mistakes could occur when people have been asked to remember some time afterwards what happened.'

A murmur of agreement flowed up from floor to platform like a thin shallow wave. It meant, to my relief and pleasure, that the audience, in great part, was on his side, hoping all things for him.

'Would you like to tell us something of your relations with Mr. Clide?'

'They have never been happy. I don't think he has ever forgiven me for reporting him to the Bishop and bringing him to a court such as this on a charge of which, I am only too glad to say, the court acquitted him. He has, in fact, said to me, "All right, Alanside, I'll get you yet. And I don't mind how long it takes." I have known recently that his agents were watching me.'

'Are you then suggesting that he has not merely made a mistake but that there is much more to it than this?'

The Archdeacon paused. Then said, 'Since I am on oath and must speak the whole truth, I say quite simply, but with regret and pain, that I believe the whole shocking business to be a plot engineered by him to ruin me as he has long promised to do.'

So many in the audience were those who had admired and loved him, and so taut was their attention, that these words burst their control and drew loud clapping. My heel, without the authority of my head, hammered its excited agreement on the floor. The Chancellor was about to rebuke us all, but the applause stopped, and he looked pleased that he wouldn't be required to say anything unpleasant. I saw the reporters write speedily.

Sir Gerald said, 'I will now leave you for the present, Mr. Archdeacon, to answer the questions of my learned friend.'

Sir William rose. 'You have heard Mr. Grace, the hotel manager's sworn evidence. You say it's untrue?'

'Untrue, except in so far as that I was in his hotel and in that room.'

'And his wife's evidence?'

'Equally untrue.'

'The maid, Mrs. Collins?'

'Wholly untrue. She never lit a fire for me. I never have a fire in my bedroom. She is thinking of someone else.'

'Alanside' – (How dare he call him 'Alanside' without so much as a 'Mr.'?) – 'we have six witnesses to the fact that a lady was with you. Are they all perjurers?'

'Or blunderers. Honestly mistaken.'

'In which case we could be done with the question of perjury. Perhaps we need not wonder any more whether respectable citizens will come into a church court to commit perjury against someone who can mean nothing to them?'

'I can only repeat that, if it is not perjury, then, in my view, they are the deluded instruments of the instigator of the whole scandal.'

'The entry in the hotel book, "dinner for two", is that a delusion?'

'It is not for me to explain the errors or methods used in hotel account books.'

'There is a similar entry for your second visit. Have you perhaps any counterfoil to a cheque showing what amount you paid?'

'No, on neither occasion was the bill large since there was only one person in bedroom and at meals, and I paid in cash. Has Mr. Grace any cheque of mine showing a large amount?'

'*I* will ask the questions, if you please.' (Don't talk to him like that!) 'Is it an accident that No. 7, on the second occasion, was also a double room?'

'Not at all. A quite ordinary happening. If every time a man is given a double room because all the single rooms are occupied, he is to be subsequently accused of adultery, which of us is safe?'

Again the outbreak of happy applause, and this time the Chancellor said regretfully, ingratiatingly, 'Please . . . no . . . I cannot have this. Don't force me to have the court cleared.' And he smiled at the people as a parent at children whom he wishes to be good.

'Alanside, is it your explicit suggestion that Mr. Clide has engineered a plot against you and that some at least of these witnesses have been suborned to commit perjury?'

'I have not said that — I have only suggested —'

'*Will* you answer the question! Yes or no?'

I saw the Archdeacon wince at this tone. It was the measure of how far he had fallen. He was no longer the dignitary spoken to with respect by all who addressed him; he was just one more Accused. My temper fired – how *dare* he speak to him like that – him whom we honoured and loved? None of us spoke to him like that. But the Archdeacon only responded with a cold dignity, 'I will answer your question as far as I can, and no farther. Yes, I believe Mr. Clide to be plotting against me. Of the others I say nothing. Because I do not know.'

From my place in the archway, my voice said almost loudly, 'Hear, *hear*!' and people turned to look at me.

Sir William having finished, Sir Gerald rose for one question in re-examination. It was the kind of question that usually concludes an examination-in-chief in a criminal trial. 'Mr. Alanside, for the last time did you have a companion with you in this hotel at any time?'

'I did not.'

'Your answer to the charge then is a total denial?'

'Total and absolute.'

'Thank you. I call Mrs. Alanside.'

It seemed to me that I'd never seen the Archdeacon's wife look so tiny as when she brushed past her tall husband returning to his seat, and when, after nearly tripping over the step, she stood at the table by the apparitor, also a tall man. Nor had I ever seen her look so old, her skin so sallow and lined, her eyes so recessed in their hollows. She looked many years older than the Archdeacon; a little withered woman. Her arm was trembling as she held the testament and was sworn. I had not in the past loved her but now I felt that I'd have liked to take her into my arms and hold her close like a child and comfort her, as if I were older and wiser than she.

Sir Gerald said tenderly, 'Sit down, Mrs. Alanside. Now when did you first hear of this allegation against your husband?'

'Two months ago.'

'And what did you say when you heard of it?'

'That it was monstrous beyond words. Ludicrous and impossible.'

Evidently Sir Gerald had not elicited all, for he pursued, 'Anything else?'

'Yes. I said, "This is J. H. Clide, of course".'

'And why did you say that?'

'Because it was in my hearing that, shortly after his acquittal, he said to my husband, "I'll get you yet, if ever I can." And "Look out that you're not in a court like this one day." And because it has long been a commonplace in the Close that, as they say, he was "out for my husband's blood".'

'Mrs. Alanside, he has said that you "poured out" confidences to him that were not flattering to your husband. Have you anything to say to that?'

She did not answer directly but bowed her head. She looked at the black testament lying on the table and demanding the 'whole truth'. In the hall the silence was like a great black empty trough, waiting for her answer.

At last with a slight lift of her small shoulders and a slight shake of her head, she said, 'I may have been a little indiscreet at times and complained about this and that – what wife does not, in anger sometimes? But never as much as Mr. Clide has suggested – at least I don't think so – and never meaning that I didn't love my husband. He has all my love.'

I knew then that their marriage might have been one that had worn badly, even to being threadbare in places, but not so that it was no longer a cloak around him; not so that her woman's loyalty was undone; not so that she wouldn't be there when the world attacked. Her voice stumbled as she went on, 'There has always been absolute confidence between us. In all things.'

'Mr. Clide has suggested that your husband is often unkind to you.'

'Nothing could be more untrue. My husband is the kindest man I know.'

'He has told us that you said something like, "He cares nothing for me; only for his daughter".'

'Sir . . .' Her voice shook. 'I may have said things like that – half in anger perhaps – or half in fun – I don't know. But they were not meant. I can only say that if I did say them, I am very sorry for it. I love my husband and I think he loves me.'

The reporters writing, one and all. Go on; write; write.

'Mr. Clide suggested that you should leave your husband till he'd proved his innocence. What was your answer to that?'

'I said that he didn't need to prove his innocence to me.'

Write. Write.

'You accept wholly his assertion of his innocence?'

'But of course!' Her eyebrows lifted as Julie's did sometimes. How could he ask such a question? 'I have lived with him for more than thirty years and know him to be an utterly truthful and God-fearing man. He's not capable of lies.'

'Give Mrs. Alanside the hotel visitors' book.' The apparitor placed it on the table before her. 'Open it at the marked page, please. Now, Mrs. Alanside, do you see pencilled against your husband's name the words "and wife"? What do you say to that?'

'Simply that it is most certainly not in his writing.'

'Thank you. And, finally, have you ever complained to Mr. Clide or anyone else of any light behaviour or anything like immorality?'

'Good gracious, no! Never, never.'

Sir Gerald sat down, and Mrs. Alanside, looking first at him and then at the Chancellor and Assessors, seemed to be wondering, 'Is that all?' The Chancellor smiled sweetly at her and nodded that she might go, so she stepped uneasily off the platform and awkwardly sought her place by her husband's side.

§

Soon after this the court adjourned, and this time I chose to go out with the mass of people flowing down the stairs to the Cathedral garden. Here, standing gowned among a crowd of lunchtime loiterers, I saw Bill Brickhill. He cried, 'Hallo, Your Eminence. How goes it? How goes this little piece of ecclesiastical shop?'

Many of the loiterers rushed towards us to hear my answer. 'Is he going to get off?' asked one or two.

'I hope so,' I said, my words braver than my thoughts, and brief, because I didn't want to talk to them. 'His counsel's making a rare old mess of the prosecution witnesses.'

'Good!' said Bill.

'He'll never get off,' said one dull-faced lout.

This infuriated me. 'How the hell do you know when you haven't been in court and heard a single word of the evidence?'

'They'd never have brought the case if there hadn't been something in it.'

'Oh, I see! How interesting! Then everybody on earth who's been accused of something is necessarily guilty. How simple! I wonder we trouble to have trials at all. As a matter of fact, in this case I believe the accused to be absolutely innocent. A hundred per cent innocent.'

'Innocent or not,' said Bill, 'the whole shindy, as I've been busy pointing out to these gentlemen here' – he looked round at the ring of loafers – 'is no more than a noisy little bit of clerical shop, among clergy, whose standards happen to be a shade higher than theirs. A point which they don't seem to grasp.'

For very shame I felt I must do some parish work before returning in the afternoon. But return I must, because it was accepted by all that the trial would finish that evening. The Chancellor would keep the court sitting till late rather than have it reassemble for a short period the next day.

§

When at last I returned to the hall, too late for my liking, Sir Gerald was making his final speech. Tall, heavy-featured, Hebraic, he stood looking from under the black eyebrows towards Chancellor and Assessors with his spectacles low on his nose and his hands on the back of his hips, so that his coat was thrust back. He was speaking less than loudly, and a kind of white hush occupied the long hall; it seemed a thing akin to the white chalky walls built centuries before. Knowledge that the trial was nearing its end deepened the hush. Chancellor and Assessors would withdraw like a jury to consider their finding and later return to their places for the Chancellor to deliver judgment.

As I worked my way to my usual stance Sir Gerald was saying that he would 'put his client's character in issue'. Here was a man who had given devoted service to the Church for more than thirty years. In the whole country no man was better known as a preacher or more valued as writer, lecturer, counsellor. And it would be no exaggeration to say that, until this moment in his sixtieth year he had been admired and loved as a man who lived a life of exemplary holiness.

Almost I was ready to cry again my 'Hear, *hear*!'

'You have seen and heard him today. Did he not impress you as a man of calm and controlled sanity? And yet, if these accusations are true, they cannot be explained otherwise than by insanity. Madness. To know that one's being watched by an enemy and yet to go to a hotel in clerical collar and sign one's own name – why not a layman's collar and an assumed name? – and two weeks later to return with the same woman to the same hotel and the same eyes, and to sign the same name!'

This incident of the absent wedding ring, did it not throw its mist of suspicion over the whole hotel evidence? Consider the maid's evidence. Why did not she, an elderly and experienced woman, observe the absence of the ring while she was lighting the fire and hearing those words, 'You mustn't tell a soul about this'? Wouldn't any woman turn at once and glance towards the lady's left hand? But not Mrs. Collins. Didn't this suggest that she was recalling another couple in another room, discussing Heaven-knows-what? There had been sworn evidence that the words 'Keep your hands down' had been uttered by Mr. Bardwick to his wife. 'Now if they'd been spoken also in guilt by my client they could hardly have been heard well enough to be honestly sworn to in a court of law. Clearly they were spoken once only and in joke. None the less this maid, this Mrs. Collins, was prepared to swear against my client, "Oh yes, it was him all right that said it".'

He was not going to suggest conscious and wilful perjury against the hotel witnesses. 'Often it is quite possible to have an honest belief that you are speaking truth and yet to learn that what you have averred is not in fact true. Have we not all sometimes said, after being proved hopelessly wrong in our memories, "Well, I would have gone into a court of law and sworn to that."'

The words 'and wife'. They had been told that on their second appearance they were in the Archdeacon's handwriting. But was it not extraordinary that they were exactly the same words as the manager admitted having written, unknown to my client, two weeks before? 'And anyhow, what husband writes "and wife" in a hotel register? Doesn't he write "Mr. and Mrs. Jones"? You may think that the evidence of the Prosecution's handwriting expert was less than helpful. He solemnly told us that these words were either written by the Archdeacon or were an attempt to copy his hand — which left us exactly where we stood before this expert came to give us the benefit of his skill. His expert evidence serves Prosecution and Defence equally well.

'The man Clide. I suffered him to go on and on with his aspersions against my client because I am putting *his* character in issue also. You will have observed the contrast between his loaded statements as to some unhappiness between Mrs. Alanside and her husband, and her frank and honest admissions. Perhaps I may be allowed to say that in forty years of practising in the courts I do not remember a witness more convincing, more obviously anxious to speak only truth, than the Archdeacon's wife —'

A murmur of agreement swept up from the floor.

'You heard the Chancellor ask me to state clearly whether I was imputing to Mr. Clide nothing less than a conspiracy to ruin the Archdeacon. This, he said, would seem to make it inevitable that other witnesses were parties to it. I do certainly suggest that something like a conspiracy came into existence soon after the 10th of January when my client first visited the hotel, but how far these other witnesses were intentional or deluded instruments of the prime mover, I do not know. It is enough that I impeach the evidence of them all.'

Sir Gerald was speaking long through the sleepy summer afternoon, and since much of it touched on things we'd all heard before, my thoughts began to wander and woolgather dreamily as they so often did in the familiar Cathedral services. I looked across the seated people at the fifteenth-century lavabo in our hall's north wall, with its elegant ogee canopy above it and its little impish hooded figure below, supporting the stone basin, and I wondered if so elaborate and ornate a thing could have been used only to bathe the priest vicars' hands as they came into this Refectory for meals. Or could it once have been used in the old Western rite of the 'Lavabo', when the celebrating priest washed his hands at the Offertory, saying *Lavabo inter innocentes manus meas:*

'I will wash my hands in innocency, O Lord; and so will I go to thine altar. . . .

Lord I have loved the habitation of thy house; and the place where thine honour dwelleth.'

Would the court declare *his* hands to be washed in innocency, and would he then go back to the altar and the place where *his* honour dwelt?

With this familiar psalm, so apt, running in my head, I prayed, and prayed again, 'O God help him, help him.' I was storming heaven with this repeated prayer when I heard Sir Gerald saying, 'Who is this woman? What was she like? Where is she?' and my attention raced back to him.

'You will have noticed that the maid denied every single particular in her mistress's description of the woman. She was neither broadly built nor particularly graceful nor notably well-dressed nor "very much the lady". Strange this variation. Can it be that the woman is a myth? The fact that this case was about to be tried has been prominent news in all papers and featured sensationally in the more popular ones, with large pictures of my client. If it is suggested that she was a woman of the streets, should it not have been possible to find her and bring her here to confront my client with perjury? And must he not have considered this when he demanded a public trial? If on the other hand she is supposed to be some obliging friend what are his thoughts and feelings now, as he knows that she is reading each day the whole story of his passionate denial?'

My thoughts strayed again, and so far, that I did not even notice when he was speaking his peroration. It could only have been a quiet and undramatic one while I was thinking of many other things. I saw suddenly that he was gathering up his papers and would say no more.

Everyone stood as Chancellor and Assessors rose from their long table. We remained standing as they passed into the old Vicars' Parlour behind them – the room where, so often, I had sat with other students for an exam. The door closed on them in there, and many of the audience filed out of the hall 'for a breath of fresh air'. No one could say how long the deliberations of the court would last. Fifteen minutes perhaps. An hour. Two. Most people stayed in their chairs chattering. Some laughed at times, and I wanted to kill them. I stared at the backs of their heads instead and hoped they would turn and be shaken and shamed by the indignation in my eyes. The Archdeacon and his wife stayed, speaking occasionally to Sir Gerald or the solicitors. Once I saw the Archdeacon managing a smile though he was sitting at a point between life and death. The best part of an hour went by. The chimes of the Cathedral sounded across Cloisters and lawns, and the heavy Hour Bell struck. Five o'clock. And still that door stayed shut.

Chapter Three

JUDGMENT OF THE COURT

'They are coming back.'

Instantly a rush of people into the hall from stairway and threshold. Most of them were women – women struggling for places as at a bargain sale.

Hastily all sank in their places and, since the Chancellor and Assessors were already seated at the long table, the stage was set again for this last scene. I glanced towards the Archdeacon. He was staring at the Chancellor's face as if to descry the verdict there. His wife's eyes were on the ground. Scanning her more carefully, I saw that she was trembling.

The Chancellor, without rising, began his Judgment. And wonderful was the change in manner, voice and diction of this little friendly smiling man, now that it was *his* time to speak, and with supreme authority, *ex cathedra*. His face became unsmiling, his voice low and laden with gravity, but audible everywhere, so beautifully enunciated the syllables. In the customary fashion of judgments he announced no verdict at once but kept that for the climax and coping of a large, shapely, architectural argument. In words of dignity, built into lapidary periods, he rehearsed before us everything that we'd heard two or three times before, and submitted things wholly obvious that were new only in being arrayed in such sonorous terms. Impatient for the verdict, my toe beating, I could not help believing that he hoped this massive and handsome Judgment would be remembered as a masterpiece of its kind. He must have been speaking for a long half-hour before we could suspect on which side the scale would fall.

He spoke of the Bishop on whom had devolved 'the invidious and painful duty of appearing, under the Clergy Discipline Act, in this, his own court, as prosecutor on a grave charge against one of the most distinguished of his clergy'. His lordship, having been acquainted with certain facts by a beneficed priest in his diocese, had had no option but to appear and present the facts.

(Yes, yes; so we know; so we all know. My foot beat.)

He expounded the part of the Assessors beside him. Under the Clergy Discipline Act they were full members of the court with the right to decide on questions of fact. The decision of the court could result either from the unanimous voice of all or by a decision of the Chancellor supported by a majority of the Assessors.

And so to the defendant. 'He is entitled that an offence shall be proved against him, not on suspicion, and certainly not on some convenient assumption that the Church might be put in peril by a doubtful acquittal, but only on such proof as, if this charge were an offence against the criminal law, would require a verdict of guilty.'

(Quite. That we naturally supposed.)

Having said this once, he said it all again in different but still handsome terms. 'Since a judgment in a Consistory Court can put a defendant in jeopardy of all but his life, it is imperative that the judges must ask themselves no less a question than this: Had the charge been a capital charge, would a jury have found a verdict of guilty? There were certain parts of the evidence which were common ground, and other parts that were in dispute —

(Why, certainly. We had noticed that. Not a doubt about that.)

It was the contention of the Defence that the witnesses for the Prosecution were either victims of a serious mistake or, alternatively, that they, or some of them, were parties, whether consciously or unconsciously, to a conspiracy. If unconsciously, then it could only be suggested that their memories had undergone with the passing of time some process of accretion; if consciously, then the suggestion must be that they had been suborned to invent evidence in pursuance of the conspiracy.

(Why, yes. That one sees.)

And so the elegant prose went undulating on, and we could not discern which way it was tending, till suddenly its goal glimmered in the distance. 'This theory of a conspiracy,' he was saying, 'the court after long discussion has dismissed as impossible. Except in one case, it can detect no motive behind the prosecution's evidence which could, even unconsciously, deflect the desire of the witnesses to deal honestly with the court.'

Here my heart began to fall. I began to see that the course of this stately Judgment was plotted for destruction; and indeed, from now on, it streamed with slow steady force along its chosen channel towards its goal. In that dank and hushed stone chamber all could now foresee the end. And, with the Archdeacon staring at the Chancellor, the end came, the full-dressed crowning words which brought down his house about him.

'We have found it impossible to accept the suggestion that the landlord of the hotel was not only open to corruption himself but able to carry with him his wife, his servants and his friend into a maze of perjury or error. We further cannot accept that the account books showing meals for two have been doctored in pursuance of a plot, and if this is not so, they are powerful corroboration of the hotel witnesses' evidence. I have indicated, I think, all the processes of reasoning which have brought us to the conclusion that these charges of immorality alleged against the defendant are established. We therefore pronounce him guilty; this is the decision of us all, and I shall report so to the Bishop in pursuance of statute.'

With that he rose; the Assessors rose with him; and all walked silently out of view into the Vicars' Parlour behind the timbered wall.

One glance at the Archdeacon on whom a horror of great darkness had fallen. The old aristocracy of temper ensured that he, having risen, was standing erect, as he talked unexcitedly with Sir Gerald and gratefully shook his hand. I could stay no more. I had not even added my note to the loud murmur of dissent which had followed the judges till they were lost to sight and hearing. I could only rush from a place of sickening shock, and I went down my old and little-known stairway, so as to escape into the emptiness of the Vicars' Close. I did not want to be a part of these people now pouring from the Hall as a rabble of chatterers.

At the foot of that stairway, and just outside its ancient door, is

a narrow passage known as the Dark Cloister; it leads from the
old homes of the priest vicars to the main Cloisters. Presumably
when its vaulted roof was in place it was very dark; now it is open
to the sky, but its stone flags remain and some of its corbels in
the walls. Only at one point is it bridged by a house adjacent
to the Priest Vicars' Hall, and here you can imagine, if you care
to, something of what it was like when it was really the Dark
Cloister.

Just within that shaded place, out of anyone's sight and un-
perceived by me, a lonely figure was standing. Julie. Julie needing
to know the end. Waiting for her parents who would return to the
Close this way. And waiting how long? The chattering voices must
have told her that it was over, and her heart must be trembling.
'Richard! Richard!' She had seen me, and was running towards me
with eyebrows raised in frightened inquiry. 'Is it all over? Is it . . .
is it over?'

'It's all lies, lies, lies,' I said; and the tears wanted to gush. My
own words could have raised them like a tide.

'You mean . . .?'

'It's wicked, wicked.'

'Oh, darling' – she had never used such a word to me before,
and I don't think she was conscious of using it now – 'is it . . . is it
guilty?'

'Yes, yes, yes —'

'Oh, no, no!' And she flung herself against my breast to sob
there, and my arm went round her to draw her tight into my comfort. I was able to do to Julie what I had imagined myself doing to
her mother. Her tears started mine but as her head was bent against
my shoulder I was able to stop her from seeing them. So there we
were, the two of us in the quiet and empty Vicars' Close, crying
together. And I said, 'It's all lies. Filthy lies. Don't think it's all
over. He can appeal. We'll go on fighting. No one believes it.
We've hardly begun to fight yet. Oh, don't cry like that, my dear.'
I held her yet tighter, and with my spare hand stroked her head.
'We haven't begun yet. Don't worry. They'll make it all right . . .
all right.'

G

'No, no. There's nothing we can do,' she sobbed, luxuriating in despair since this is the only compensation it allows one. 'It'll be absolute ruin for him. He said so to Mummy this morning. He said that unless he could prove it was a plot, they'd have finished him. Oh, Daddy . . . Daddy. . . .'

'Darling' – now I had said it almost unconsciously – 'this is not the end. Bishop Griffyn told me he could appeal. He can appeal to the Archbishop's court. He can appeal to the Privy Council. There's heaps he can do.'

'Oh, Richard, do you think so?'

'Of course I do.' I was holding her tight indeed, and in the midst of my sick distress there was a core of physical pleasure in having her so close against me. Her face was still bent against my shoulder that she might sob there, so I put a kiss on the parting in her dark hair.

Without so much as noticing this, she burst on, 'I must go to him, poor sweet. Oh, how can people be so wicked? Where is he? Is he up there?'

She had lifted her face, wet with the tears, to ask me this, and I put my lips for a second on her forehead. None of this did she seem to notice, but only asked, 'Is it all right for me to go up there? He said I wasn't to come. That's why I have been waiting down here. I didn't want any of the awful people to see me.'

'Of course it'll be all right now, if he's still there. The trial's all over. Come along, we'll go and see.'

I took her hand, which she trusted to me as a child might, and I drew her like a child through the ancient doorway to the stairs, up which the priest vicars used to go, never wondering who might tread in their steps hundreds of years after them. We found their long white chalky hall empty except for a man clearing away books and papers from the Chancellor's table and a little group at the foot of the platform: the Archdeacon, his wife, Sir Gerald, and the solicitors, talking together.

'There he is, my dear —' but Julie had left me as if I were no one and was running towards him. I saw him pick up her hand even as he went on talking to the lawyers, and I just saw her other hand come over to enclose his in both of hers. Then I slipped from the hall, having no real part among them.

§

Leaving the hall this time by the ordinary stairs, I found that the rain was pouring down as if from a cloud-burst over the city. The air in the Cathedral garden smelt of newly washed grass and wet leaves. On the pavements of West Street the umbrellas of the people were bent forward to breast a way through the vertical, beating rain. From the road's camber came a sibilance and swish of wheels speeding through surface water. I had no umbrella to protect my caped cassock, but the Pallant was not far, and in my desperation I could not wait to get to Bishop Griffyn whose words I craved more than anyone else's. So, head down, I butted and twisted through rain and traffic and pedestrians to the Pallant, pressing at last for shelter against his door. There was delay in answering my ring and I crouched beneath the beautiful doorway, out of the un-relenting rain and the whipping wind. He opened to me.

'Ah, Richard – oh, my dear boy, you are wet. Come in. Come in.'

'You know the result, sir?'

'Result?'

'Yes. The trial.'

'No.'

Dramatically I gave him one word. 'Guilty.'

'Alas, so I feared. I saw it coming. But come in and get dry. I'll put a match to the fire for you.'

'Can I talk to you about it, sir?'

'Yes, tell me all about it. I very much want to hear. Take your usual chair there. It seems ages since I've seen you. How's old Imbraham?' He was bending to light the fire as he said this, and I had no doubt he had mentioned something commonplace so as to dilute my obvious despair. 'I hear he's going to conduct a six days' mission in Chelsea, which I should gather, from all I read, is in need of it. Seven o'clock. Or very nearly. A glass of sherry will be more than legitimate.'

Soon we were in our customary chairs on either side of the

fireplace with decanter and glasses between us. Leaping wood-flames made a place of trembling light for us at our end of the long room, darkened by the stormy weather without.

'Now tell me all,' he said as he poured the sherry. 'You were at the trial?'

'Yes, sir. At most of it.'

'I guessed you would be. You were there at the end?'

'Yes, sir. I've just come from there. Sir, what can he do now? You said something about an appeal.'

'That's right. An appeal lies from the diocesan to the provincial court. And even from there he can appeal to the Judicial Committee of the Privy Council.'

'He'll appeal of course?'

'Will he? I don't know. These verdicts are very difficult to upset. And there's the question of expense. The costs can run into thousands.'

'We'll all subscribe. Everyone in Casterton'll subscribe. Everyone believes him innocent.'

'Many would subscribe, I'm sure.'

'Sir, please, if he cannot appeal, or if the appeal goes against him, what happens?'

'That depends on the Bishop. Of one thing I'm sure: George Casterton'll never sink to the crude and disgusting business of unfrocking. I consider unfrocking a peculiarly revolting example of a "holier-than-thou" attitude in all who have any part in it. Was the Bishop there at the end?'

'No.'

'No, I didn't expect he would be. A lesser man with a love of the limelight might have appeared in his robes, picturesquely flanked by his chaplains, and pronounced his eloquent and dramatic sentence.'

'What sort of sentence?'

'Deprivation, to start with. Deprivation of all preferments and of all right to act as a priest. Then, if it's to be a matter of unfrocking, we go on to a public ceremony in the Cathedral, wherein we solemnly depose and degrade a wretched man from Holy Orders. Heaping misery upon misery. That's unfrocking. George Casterton will never do that. He'll stop at deprivation. And this, maybe, for only a period of years.'

'Then the Archdeacon could come back again?'

'Not as an archdeacon. Only as a humble priest. A curate, perhaps, like you.'

'Sir . . .' I began, but could not go on.

'Yes, Richard?'

'You . . . you don't believe him guilty, do you? You can't.'

Without answering, he twisted the stem of his sherry glass round and round. He drew off his steel spectacles and with one of their arms touched his teeth; then laid them on the table at his side and took a cigarette from the box.

This silence wounded and angered me. 'No, you can't. No matter what this court says, *or* the Archbishop's court, *or* the Privy Council, you can't believe it. You don't, do you?' My words were almost a cry for rescue; for rescue by one whose strength I believed in. And since he wasn't instantly responding, I put my appeal in the simplest words. 'Say that you don't believe it, sir.'

'I don't know what to say, Richard. The Chancellor – it's no good offering you a cigarette, is it? – the Chancellor is a very clever man, and there's no shrewder judge of evidence. What's more, he's an old friend of Alanside's. What can I think? If I'm not to believe the Archdeacon guilty, I must believe other men guilty of a far greater crime than adultery – of destroying by perjury a man who was nothing to them.'

'But they can have been mistaken.'

'Yes . . . well, God knows I don't put the value of human evidence very high. Even sworn evidence if men's passions or interests are there to distort it. But what interests or passions had any of these people – apart from one?'

'Lots of people have an unconscious pleasure in seeing a great man brought low. And I'm not sure that this pleasure isn't greater if he happens to be a priest.'

'Yes, there's something in that, Richard. But . . . is it enough?'

My anger heated against him, and I said accusingly, 'You think him guilty.'

'I did not say so. I said nothing of the kind.' He was now a little angry with me, and he sipped at the sherry as at a lenitive; sipped twice; then sought to defeat his impatience with an unhappy boy by its opposite, generous understanding. *He* mustn't be unreasonable and angry even if I was; so, leaning forward to refill my glass, he said, 'You declared it was impossible, Richard. I only implied that I couldn't go as far as that.'

'But it *is* impossible. Would he have insisted on being arraigned in open court if he knew he'd have to lie and lie on his Bible oath? It doesn't make sense. The Archdeacon do this! On a Bible oath! How *could* he? Think of his preaching, think of the spiritual vision in his sermons and his books, think of the way he goes daily to Mass, think of his terrific love for people which, as *you* once said to me, shines out when he's talking to anyone, especially if they're asking his help. He came once and helped me when I was full of doubts and miseries, and he was perfectly wonderful. I'm not going to believe in this. I'm *never* going to believe in it. I'll never believe a love and a vision like his can lie and lie.'

An empty quiet in the room till he broke it by saying very softly, 'We have the treasure in earthen vessels, Richard.'

But I wouldn't listen to this; I turned my head and looked out at the garden where the rain had suddenly stopped and the sun was bright again on the dahlias and madonna lilies, the tall hollyhocks and canterbury bells. And he, musing aloud, continued in the same low voice, '"Frail children of dust. . . ."' then, seeing my unhappiness, he leaned forward and hung his long arms between the length of his outstretched legs. 'Listen, Richard: with all my heart and soul I hope that what you say, in your great loyalty, is right. Before God, I hope that one day you'll be proved right. But if you're not, and if it's not as you think, then understand that, for my part, whatever the courts may have decided or may yet decide, I shall still believe my friend Alanside to be a good man and one of the best I have known.'

I was a little soothed by this, but not enough. 'Obviously you believe him guilty,' I insisted. 'And he's *not*.'

'God grant we may learn so in the fullness of time. Perhaps we shall. *Veritas temporis filia*, as the Romans had it.'

Even in my real unhappiness I had to show him that I could translate this. 'Truth is the daughter of Time. Yes . . . well . . . perhaps. . . . And oh, God, I hope so. I hope so. . . .'

'Of course you do. Now sit here by the fire for a little and rest.'

When I left him the long wet pavements lay blue beneath the sudden blue sky. So did the streaming gutters, radiating the blue. There was still a thundery darkness in the west, and against this the Cathedral spire, lit by the evening sun, rose like a clean new monument, pale cream in colour as if built but yesterday with freshly cut stones. And it seemed to me wrong, somehow, that it should look like that tonight; timeless and indifferent to change.

PART III
AFTERWARDS

Chapter One

THE STRANGE BLEND THAT SUMMER

That summer of my early diaconate. In memory it is remarkable for the shadow that lay over it and, strangely, for a brilliant light in the heart of the shadow.

The shadow, of course, was the pain and indignation flung over me by the disaster to the Archdeacon's home. Whatever Bishop Griffyn had suggested, my mind stayed shut, its doors bolted against any doubt about the Archdeacon's innocence or the wrong done to him. It was not the mysterious woman in the hotel room I was unable to believe in; to believe in her was difficult but not impossible; one had heard that saints could lapse like this. What stayed beyond belief was that my fellow-worshipper in those early morning Masses, my kind counsellor in my little hostel room, had lied and lied under oath and was now ready to lie and lie again before the highest courts in the land.

For within an hour of the rising of the Bishop's court he had issued a statement to the Press: it announced that he had instructed his solicitors to by-pass the Provincial Court of Arches and to present to the Judicial Committee of the Privy Council a petition for leave to appeal to them; it pleaded for any persons to come forward who might have evidence of his movements on the days in question; it invited financial help, saying that the costs of the trial just concluded and of the coming appeal would be 'crushing'; and it ended with the words, 'I have been overwhelmed by the assurances of unshaken fidelity and the offers of help, and indeed the love, of all those who know me.'

This statement appeared in the papers the next day. And on the same day many of the papers carried an interview with him. In it he said he would know no rest till he had vindicated his honour; that he now held this to be his duty, not only to his family and himself, but to the whole Church; that letters and telegrams, pouring in, showed he had staunch defenders all over the world; and, lastly, that his best and wisest companion in all this trouble had been his wife.

I shut the ears of my mind to a new, strange, slightly hysterical note in these declarations. There seemed a quality of clap-trap in them of which he would have been incapable only a few weeks ago. If I could not wholly shut out the note, I told myself that I understood it.

On the following day *The Times* carried an appeal for funds, signed by several of the higher clergy. And who other than my vicar, with his affectionate, outrushing heart, should be the leading spirit in this appeal? The very phrasing of the letter was his enthusiastic work. 'We, the undersigned, having complete confidence in the rightness of Archdeacon Alanside's appeal to a higher court, are certain that innumerable friends of his, who have profited so greatly from his ministry in the past, will be as eager as we are to give him every financial help. Subscriptions, large or small, should be sent to the Rev. Prebendary T. R. P. Imbraham, St. Hugh's Clergy House, Casterton.

And since the Rev. T. R. P. Imbraham was about to be busied with a mission to Chelsea, and since I was his junior curate, which is to say his general dogsbody and maid-of-all-work, it was I who was the effective Secretary and Treasurer of the appeal. For this I thanked my fortune since it meant that I was fighting in the forefront of the Archdeacon's battle – almost, you might say, leading it.

One of the first subscriptions I opened was from Bishop Griffyn: a hundred pounds. No letter accompanied it; only his usual slip, 'With the Right Reverend Gregory Griffyn's compliments and thanks.' 'And *thanks*' – I did not fail to notice that word. I learned also from the Vicar, who was not good at keeping things to himself, that the Bishop (though the case before the Privy Council would be listed as 'Alanside *v.* the Bishop of Casterton') was finding money from some special fund to help his opponent.

This was the shadow over that summer. And in the very core of it was the brilliant light. When so inapt a blend: a daily, heavy dejection with an excited joy in its heart? And this joy had sprung into existence almost in the very moment when the Archdeacon was overthrown; the moment when rushing away – anywhere – from the calamity, I found Julie waiting for the result and held her close to comfort her. I felt confident, certain, after the way she'd thrown herself in despair on my breast, I *knew* that she would come to me, if I asked her. That *she* . . . *his* daughter. . . . One could not believe for joy. The whole of Casterton, when it was not dark with the shadow, was alight with the bliss.

I had not said a word of love to her yet, out of reverence for her family's sorrow; nor she a word to me; but she had soon heard from my hearty vicar, 'It's that young Richard who's doing all the work in our appeal; *I'm* not doing anything'; and this made a new link between us. Once I saw her in Little St. Andrew's Lane and crossed over to tell her 'how well things were going – the money simply bounding in'; and she said, 'Gosh, you're wonderful. You're doing it all, I know. Oh, I think we shall win, don't you? I'm sure we shall. The world can't be so unjust as for anything else to happen. He's trying not to look too miserable, but oh, he is, he is. His face is so unutterably sad. And I can't bear it. I can't bear it. I want to see him back where he was, and happy and laughing and full of fun again. Help us to get him there, Richard; help us.'

'You bet I will,' I said. 'With everything I've got. And oh, why isn't it more?'

I tried not to find any pleasure in the thought that the disaster to her father had narrowed a social gap between us. Even closed it. No, no; I would fight and fight for him even though victory might open the gap again.

For a long time I saw nothing of the Archdeacon because, though loving him the same as ever – no, more, much more, in his sufferings – I was shy of meeting and talking with a man disgraced. Then one afternoon, on my day off, as I strolled homeward along Sunder Green Lane towards the spire of the Cathedral tapering above a distant spinney, I saw him coming slowly towards me. He too had wandered out to be alone in the quiet country.

Hemmed in by tall hedges, I could not evade him, and my heart drummed its dismay; drummed the more because he had changed so harrowingly in the last few weeks. The fine-featured face was now almost cadaverous, its skin as sallow as vellum; the elegant knee-breeches and gaiters had yielded place to bagging trousers, and the well-cut archidiaconal frock coat to some old frock coat that he must have worn long ago in the days before his preferment. Only the clerical collar was defiantly the same; a proud symbol of the fact that he was still in Orders; that he might have been deprived but he was not deposed.

He approached with both hands joined behind his back over a dangling stick, and as he recognized me, he smiled a greeting.

Like Julie he assumed a mask of liveliness and humour. 'My dear Richard! Where have you been? It's far too long since we've seen anything of you. And I've never once been able to congratulate you on your many successes. A First in the Prelim – *and* Gospeller – splendid! You could hardly have started better. I think it means you'll do big things.'

That he should talk thus happily of my career while his lay wrecked about him! For his sake I decried my success. 'I was just lucky, sir, in my exam questions; that was all.'

'*Oh*, no: *oh*, no. That won't do, Richard. Leedes told me you'd get your First long before the examiners put pen to paper. And you don't get the same luck in *two* examinations. Now turn round and walk along with me for a bit. It's not time to go home yet, and these early autumn days are some of the loveliest of the year. Spring can't touch them for wonderful effects of light.' Ever an apt quoter, speaking poetry with a beautiful voice, he now quoted Donne's Autumnal Elegy: 'No spring nor summer beauty hath such grace As I have seen in one autumnal face'; and went on to Ovid's '"*Saepe sub autumno, cum formosissimus annus . . .*" You must come and have supper with us one evening. You know I have left the Residentiary?'

'No, I didn't know it, sir.'

'Oh, yes, I've found a rather nice little home in Friary Lane. I did it quickly so as not to embarrass the Bishop. It's a bit of a dog-kennel after the Residentiary, but it'll serve. I shall not return to the Residentiary unless this wicked verdict is reversed on appeal. As it will be – it certainly will be. We have the enemy on the run, I think.'

'Oh, *good*, sir!'

'Yes, you really must come to supper and see the little place. Julie would so like it. Do you see anything of her now?'

'We've met once or twice.'

'Well, I wish you could take her out to tennis sometimes. She loves it so, and she's quite good, I believe.'

'She is. She's heaps better than I am.'

'Yes . . . well . . . we seem to be seeing so little of people just now . . . with our move and all.' Was there a different truth behind this: that people were avoiding them? 'The tennis courts are still up in Friary Park, aren't they?'

'There were people playing there yesterday.'

'Fine. Then do play with her there. As my guest. When you see my new kennel you'll see that the Park is almost my front garden. So you can properly be my guest. I'm glad to know that Trippy insists on your having a whole day off. I always did with my curates. "Clear out and don't let me see you again all day." That was my rule.'

Now just ahead of us a field gate broke the hedge. He saw it and said, 'Let's sit down and really look at the autumn. Come along.' And he clambered on to the top bar, hooking his heels on to a lower bar. This lifted his knees high and dragged one of the trouser legs above a falling grey sock, unveiling an inch of pink flesh. I felt a pain at the loss of dignity which this involved – was he more broken than I had known? To sit beside him in the same position, hindquarters humped over the top bar, seemed ridiculous, so I just leaned against the gatepost and laid my arm along the bar.

'There's nothing like it,' he said, gazing far over the green savannah fields. 'The grass saturated and therefore never so luscious and green. The sun warm and the air just flushed with cold – a mixture for gods. And you've noticed, I hope, that on a day like this, the soil turns purple under the trees, and the sun throws mauve-blue shadows on the road. . . .'

My eyes followed his over the green level lands, and I recalled his sermon about the 'far-stretching distances'. There far away, above a long low cape of trees, was his Cathedral spire.

So far he had said nothing about the financial appeal; perhaps because any mention of it would hurt too much. But now, after a silence in which perhaps he decided he ought to express some gratitude, he said, 'I hear from Imbraham that you're doing all the work in that appeal.'

'I am doing some of it, sir, and nothing has ever given me greater happiness.'

'It's kind of you, and I don't think any of the money will be wasted. We've got the enemy on the run.' Had he forgotten that he'd said this before – not five minutes before?

'When will the Appeal come off, sir?'

'Who can say? "The law's delay" you know'; and he continued the quotation, perhaps for the love of it, perhaps as a quiet memorial to his innocence '. . . the insolence of office, and the spurns that patient merit of the unworthy takes . . .' The next kindness that you must do will be to take Julie out and amuse her, poor child. Yes, to tennis. As my guest. It'll be the end of summer all too soon.'

'I could play next Thursday, sir.'

'Well, I'll see about it. And I'll get Natalie to telephone you at the Clergy House about supper. Better be on a Sunday. That's the traditional time for curates to come to supper. The day's work done.'

'I should love it, sir.'

'Well, now I expect you want to get home. I think I'll walk on a little farther. I love walking.'

He clambered off the gate and after lifting a palm in farewell continued his way southward towards the Menwode and the sea. Only once did I dare turn my head to look at him. He was still walking with his head bowed and his stick dangling from hands linked behind him.

§

That invitation to supper did not come. Had it been only words? Pleasing words? Or had there been some difficulty with Mrs. Alanside in her new home, so unready and so small? And 'my guest at tennis'. No more was heard of that. The tennis nets came down

in the Friary Park; the cricket pitch was railed off from use; the
last of Luke's Summer was over; and all lay green and emptied for
winter.

Then a headline in *The Times* which Prebendary Imbraham
provided for his Clergy House.

ALANSIDE *v.* THE BISHOP OF CASTERTON

Appeal Date Fixed

Tuesday the 8th November has been fixed for the hearing
by the Judicial Committee of the Privy Council of the Appeal
by Archdeacon Alanside against the decision of the Consistory
Court of Casterton. As in the lower court Sir Gerald Harbon,
K.C., will lead for the Archdeacon. . . .

So soon? No law's delay here. It was only some three months
since the trial in the Priest Vicars' Hall. No hope of my attending
this new trial which would be in the Council Chamber in London's
Downing Street, not in my own Priest Vicars' Hall. I would only
be able to read it greedily in our *Times*. Soon a further announcement appeared telling us that the appeal would be heard before the
Lord Chancellor and two other Lords Justices, with the Bishops
of London, Gloucester and Rochester as ecclesiastical assessors.
So had our Archdeacon's case soared to the summits.

And it was summit news in all the papers when the case began.
The almost verbatim report in *The Times* crammed whole pages.
Three Lords Justices including the Lord Chancellor, three bishops
including his lordship of London; a K.C. with two juniors for the
'prosecution'; queues stretching from Downing Street past
Colonial Office and Home Office; the world reading – and all this,
as Bill Brickhill had said, about an incident which, in a layman's
life, would have been but a small unpublished domestic affair. In
my sick anger I called it 'a huge medieval pomposity'. Meeting
Bill Brickhill, I said it was as if an array of magnificent fire-engines
were now assembled on a vicarage lawn and dealing with a small
patch smouldering in the grass. Hosing it heavily to protect the
world from fire. I thought this was clever.

Four days of it; four days of fine reading for the newspaper public; twice as long as the Consistory trial, because the Archdeacon had new witnesses to say they had seen him dining and breakfasting alone, and witnesses as to character, who included two bishops and a dean and some canons, all ready to say that they had known the appellant fifteen, twenty, twenty-five years and held the allegations against him to be 'impossible' – 'monstrous' – 'absurd'; and because the prosecution had new witnesses also to testify that they had seen him here or there with a woman answering the description given by the hotel manageress – 'tall, stylish, well-dressed but nervous'; and because Sir Gerald Harbon was putting up a prolonged, exigent, ruthless fight on behalf of his client (God bless and preserve him always).

Every day I read every word of the report, and on the fourth day my eye saw first the headlines, 'Archdeacon's Appeal Dismissed. The Judgment. Heavy Bill of Costs.'

With a deep heart-pain, physical in its effects, I read the Lord Chancellor's Judgment. It occupied two and a half of *The Times'* great pages and had taken, so the paper said, an hour and a half to deliver. Most of it, like the Judgment in the Consistory Court was a carefully balanced review of the evidence, and it was only towards the end that I saw how it would run on to the same lines as our Chancellor's. Their lordships, it declared, could see no evidence anywhere to sustain the allegations of a conspiracy, and none to suggest that the entries in the hotel account books, showing meals paid for two persons, had been either mistaken or deliberately mis-recorded in the interests of such a plot. Sir Gerald in his closing speech had asked 'Where was this woman? Who was she? Why had no one been able to trace her or produce her or suggest who she might be?' But their lordships held there were many reasons why, in colloquial terms, she should have 'kept herself to herself', perhaps in collusion with the appellant – in which case conspiracy could more properly be adumbrated against him.

The formal phrasing, the fine balancing of the long sentences, the steady march of each stately period towards its climax – all this was splendid of its kind; and I could not but believe that the Lord

Chancellor, like any other famous actor, was happy in this fine ceremonial drama which had provided him with so 'fat' and picturesque a part. Enjoying his display of skill in its performance, and the prospect of praise thereafter from Bench and Bar. 'A masterly and memorable judgment.'

National drama, in the highest court in the land, and all about an alleged chambering the other day. No more.

And so to the last words.

'Their lordships, accordingly, have reached the conclusion that the Judgment of the Consistory Court must be upheld, and it has been a source of satisfaction to them that the views which they entertain are shared by the Right Reverend Prelates who have been good enough to give them their assistance on this occasion. The result, therefore, is that their lordships will humbly advise His Majesty to dismiss the Appeal. Costs must follow the event. The appellant's actions have involved the Bishop of Casterton in heavy expenses, and their lordships see no reason why he should not be re-couped for expenditure entirely provoked by the appellant's grave misdemeanours and subsequent stubborn denials, and incurred therefrom as a legal duty.'

To me, so hotly partisan, so hopelessly dedicated to one view only, this remark about the costs seemed a peculiarly nasty exit-line, cruel in its phrasing, with which to leave the stage, after secretly enjoying one's role in the great dramatic event of the hour.

Beneath the Judgment was a paragraph headed 'Statement by the Archdeacon', and I read it – read on with my heart still a throbbing blob of anguish and anger.

Archdeacon Alanside gave the following statement to the Press this afternoon: 'The closing of the case as we have heard it today marks naturally a complete and final change in my career but none in my religious convictions nor in my devotion to what I deem to be the purpose of my life. In other ways still open to me I shall pursue my calling so long as I am permitted to do so, and in this determination I am greatly helped by the confidence of countless friends.'

It was only as I turned other pages, in an idle misery, that my eye was seized by yet another paragraph. Headed 'Edwyn Alanside' – just like that, and in 'quotes' – it said, 'The Rev. E. Alanside has agreed, we understand, to address the Cobden-Bright Debating Society in Leeds on Sunday, his subject to be "The Building of the City of God". He has expressed the wish that he should be announced simply as "Edwyn Alanside".'

Yes, 'Archdeacon' no more. And probably wondering if he would remain 'Reverend' any more.

Chapter Two

TORR BROW

What could I do? I did not like to break in on the Alansides in their distress – nor, more selfishly, did I want to endure the sight of their embarrassment and shame. And yet I longed, I ached, to go to them and say, 'Is there anything – anything in the whole world – that I can do?' but I was paralysed from moving towards their new little house, from being within sight of it or near to it, from speaking any word. And the days went by.

But inevitably the moment came when I met Julie in North Street near her new home. Seeing me, she hauled up as usual her brave little flag of cheerfulness, but – it failed to open out properly today. It hung a little sadly. Trying to joke, she said, 'Stranger, stranger, where have you been all this time? Have you forgotten all about us? I'm Julie Alanside, in case you've forgotten.'

'I haven't liked to worry you,' I explained. 'I —' but all words went from me. I couldn't bear to speak about the things that must preoccupy them now.

'Most people seem to be feeling that, because nobody's coming near us. We're seeing hardly anybody.'

'Julie,' I said, 'some time ago your father suggested we might play tennis together on my day off. Tennis is all finished now, but couldn't we perhaps go together for a nice walk?'

'Oh, I'd love to! Where would we go?'

'How many miles can you walk without getting tired?'

'About forty.'

'Could you do eight miles, all told?'

'Of course I could. I could walk every bit as far as you could. And probably farther. Where?'

'Let's go and climb Torr Brow. Four miles there and four back.'

'Oh that'd be marvellous! And naturally if it's four miles there, it's four back. Oh, I'm excited about it. Will you come and fetch me?'

'No . . . no . . .' I stuttered, still shy of that house and of meeting either her father or her mother. 'No, I'll meet you at North Gate where the North Walls end. That's fair enough, because the exit from my North Walls meets the entrance to your Friary Lane. Thursday, please. But early. The sun goes down soon after four. One o'clock?'

'Good enough. North Gate, Thursday. Oh, how marvellous!'

The old bastioned walls of the city swing round from west to north, and along that sweep of them the city fathers have built them up into a high rampart and furnished them with limes to make a pleasant promenade. At their northern break, where once the North Gate stood, I waited for Julie that afternoon by a yellowing lime, with my heart inflating and deflating because I intended before evening was down to have told her I loved her. And if . . . if . . . I paced the rampart, awaiting a verdict as her father had awaited one, but unlike him, because I was believing, I seemed to *know*, that it would be the incredible verdict I craved. I believed the incredible with an almost sickening state of joy in my heart. Beneath the walls the submural houses hid the country from me, but I could imagine Torr Brow as a grey shape against the sky. All the country south of Casterton is seaward plain, but north of the city the land begins to climb, and the horizon in the distance is a long sweep of mauve-blue hills. The nearest of these blue hills is that fine out-throw of the Downs, six hundred feet high, Torr Brow.

Before I saw her, Julie came running on to the rampart. She was wearing a coat-frock of navy blue with a high collar of fur, and a hat of red felt that fitted like skin to the shape of her small head but allowed a dark curl to fall towards either cheek. I perceived with the same disabling joy that she had dressed for me.

'Isn't it a terrific day?' she exclaimed. 'Who'd know it was November? I adore autumn. It's light can be so wonderful; far more magical than spring or summer.' Julie echoing her father in thought and words as she echoed him in looks.

'Well, come along,' I commanded. 'It *is* November and nothing can stop the sun going down at its appointed hour. We've eight miles to do.'

'I could do twenty on a day like this. Gosh, it's thrilling.'

It was indeed a gift of a day. When we were beyond the city and on an unfenced road the light all around us seemed the very essence of light because the colours scattered over the green country were everything from dull gold to brick-red and crimson and flame. Extraordinarily white the field gates looked in a landscape so clear. Only the ash trees were still a bright green; the elms were emptied of leaves and stood in purple clumps, and much of the newly turned arable was a purple brown, its colour heightened in the clear light.

As we walked on through all this autumn blessing, Julie told me about the last hours of the Appeal, to which her father had allowed her to come because she had insisted she wanted to be seen sitting with him.

'I shall never forget when the horrible old Lord Chancellor —'

'The filthy beast!'

'Yes, but rather handsome, I'm afraid – I shall never forget him sitting there for an hour and a half and saying his stuff, so obviously pleased with the well-turned sentences, and then finishing up with that poisonous remark about costs, which showed that he'd really been against Daddy from the beginning.'

I did not hurt her by saying that I had read the Judgment and thought he had striven to be fair at least till he came to the verdict. That little Parthian arrow about costs had come after the verdict.

'Daddy was wonderful. He just rose when they rose and walked out of the ghastly place into Downing Street, with his hand in mine. Poor Mummy was in despair. Out in Whitehall she said, "Well, that's the end. There's nothing we can do now"; but he said, "There's nothing more in law we can do, but there are other ways of fighting, and I'll fight that conviction till the end of my life." But I knew that, whatever he said, he was suffering horribly, because his hand kept pressing mine unconsciously and rather painfully hard. It hurt, but I pressed his back – pressed it for all I was worth. Mummy persisted in despairing – saying it was all over and there was nothing we could do, but he said, "Oh yes, there could be a petition to the King, and he quoted *Lear* – you know how he loves quoting – he said "Wipe thine eyes. The good years

shall devour them, flesh and fell, ere they shall make us weep."
I did *Lear* at school.'

'But can he petition the King?'

'Apparently so. He says there are hundreds of clergy on his side,
and they are talking of getting up a committee to organize a
petition.'

I had no hope in this petition – who had ever known a petition
to the Crown upset a decision of the courts? But I did not say this;
I said only, 'What's he going to do now? He can't act as a priest
any more, can he?'

'No, not as a priest of the Church of England. Apparently the
Bishop had no course but to deprive him of everything; that's
automatic, it seems, after a conviction of' – here she stopped; she
could not say 'adultery' – 'after a conviction. He's still in Orders,
but they're no use to him any more. As he keeps on saying,
"Othello's occupation's gone." I also did *Othello* at school for my
Senior Oxford, but I never thought I . . .' Here she stopped completely.

'What will you all do?'

'We have some small private means, but not enough. Mummy
has a little money. Daddy, poor darling, thinks he can make some
money by lecturing and writing and perhaps hiring a hall in
London and preaching there – but, Richard, I never like to say to
him what I think.'

'And what is that?'

'That his name would be a draw for a few months, and then . . .
then it'd be all over and people'd be excited about other things.'

'And I'm afraid you're right, wise child. It's hot news now, but
it'll be cold all too quickly. But fancy you seeing that. I should
have thought you'd have blinded your eyes to it.'

'I don't want to see it like that, but if you love someone terribly
and are simply mad to help them, it opens your eyes.'

'Or shuts them. But if he gets this hall,' I asked in a sudden
alarm, 'will you have to move to London?'

'No. He'd only preach in it on Sundays. He says he'll never leave
Casterton till he can go with his name cleared. He says he's not

running from anybody. Mummy wishes he'd go, but she's trying to do whatever he wants. She's being rather splendid. *I* wish he'd go too. It's not too pleasant here now: people either avoiding you or looking at you with a horrid new interest, or coming to stare at your house as if there were a strange animal inside. Or, almost worse still, being so terribly kind. Still, I'm staying here just as long as he wants to stay.'

We were now off the unfenced road and on a path that ran up the shoulder of Torr Brow. There was a sea of russet bracken around us, flecked with dark patches of furze. The nearer grass had rusted to orange but the grass above us was a lush green cap on the summit of the down. Gradually our path petered into a chalky track, and I took her hand to help her up the steep. We climbed till, at last, she panted, 'Oh, dear!' and again, 'Oh, lord! Dare we sit down?'

'We dare,' I said, and produced from my slung haversack a light waterproof. I laid it on the green slope at the side of the track, and we collapsed on to it, sitting there, or reclining on elbows, while we looked down on a vast green lap of England, spread with all the coloured gifts and tawny spoils of autumn. In the middle distance Casterton seemed no more than a brown hamlet crowded with trees, and its spire but a small thing under the sky. Its poor human tragedies, too, but small, diminished things. Small and local and largely lost in that great green expanse between us and the sea.

We stayed silent, I much troubled, because it seemed the moment to speak.

'Julie . . .' I said; and that was as far as I got.

'Yes?' she encouraged.

'Julie . . . please . . . may I say that I'm terribly in love with you? I haven't liked to say anything about it during all these months, but, darling . . . is there any hope that you . . . that we . . .' So awkward was I in this declaration that, unconsciously, I had forced myself into a stiff position by pressing with both hands on the grass.

She put out her ungloved hand and laid it on the one near her. 'Darling Richard,' she said, 'you're the dearest thing.'

'Yes. Maybe,' I agreed, 'but does that mean . . . could it mean —'

'That I'm terribly in love with you? Yes, I think it does, my sweet.'

'Oh God! Oh Christ in Heaven above!' I said, blaspheming a little, trapped into this unclerical practice by so wonderful an answer. 'No, but, Julie . . . do you mean it? Are you sure?'

She gave me no answer at once, which produced a slight but painful undoing of my prodigious bliss; however she quickly undid the pain, reknit the ravelled seams, by saying, 'I think I've been rather sure of it for some time, but I know I knew for certain just now when you were speaking, because my heart simply jumped out of my body, and that's a good sign, isn't it? Gosh, it was something I've never felt in my life before.'

'Oh, my God! Julie! Quite sure you're not joking?'

'Never more sure of anything in my life.'

'Oh, my God!' I took her into my arms, and the rest was kisses and breathless ecstasies for a very long while – till, in truth, we wearied even of them.

'Can we think of ourselves as engaged?' I asked as I let her go; as I almost put her away from me. 'We needn't tell anyone but just keep it as a secret between ourselves.'

'But I *want* to tell everybody,' she cried in protest. 'Oh, mayn't I? It'll be something so wonderful in the midst of all this. I shall be so proud of it. And Daddy'll be awfully pleased too. He thinks the world of you.'

I noticed she didn't mention Mummy, and, nobly though Mrs. Alanside had been behaving, I could still imagine her saying, 'It's hardly what I expected for Julie.'

'Heavens, everything gets better and better,' I exclaimed. 'I never thought you'd kind of care to announce it.'

'But why ever not?'

'Well, I mean . . .'

'You mean what?'

'I mean, I suppose, I thought you'd be ashamed of it. Just a little.'

'Well, of all the silly remarks!'

'But, Julie, you extremely adorable thing, my exquisite heart's delight – though in actual fact, it's almost a pain at the heart at the moment, and I hope it is in yours – Julie, I'm only a junior curate – than which there is no lower form of life except a theological student – I'm not even priested yet, I have an income of precisely two hundred whole pounds a year, with, let us admit, a part of the Whitsun offering. And that's all. No,' I put her with a flat hand farther away. 'It's all ridiculous.'

'Daddy says he thinks you'll be given a good job one day. He says you'll go far.'

'That's only because he thinks I'm much brighter than I am. Golly, isn't it quite amazing, incredible, to think of having him as a father.' I remember I said 'father' instead of 'father-in-law'.

Julie stayed silent at this and picked at the grass by her side. I knew she was thinking, 'Is Daddy anyone to be proud of now?' so I hastened on, 'I've always admired him so tremendously and I can't think of anyone else in the world I'd rather have as a father-in-law. But, Julie, even if he were right, I shan't get a new job for years. I promised the Bish I'd stay four years with Trippy Imbraham. He said I was to do a lot of quiet reading in Trippy's Clergy House so as to become a learned clerk. How can I do a lot of quiet reading when I'm thinking of you all day? The whole thing's absurd. How can I become a learned clerk with you about?'

'Perhaps I could help.'

'Don't be silly, dear. This is difficult reading. No, I should have waited four years before falling in love with you. This whole engagement is a mistake. Let's postpone it for a few years.'

'But, please, I don't want it postponed. I want to let all the world know about it. Oh, yes, *please*. It's the only lovely thing that's happened for months.'

'Ah, well,' I sighed, feigning a sad but brave acceptance of the inevitable, 'you'd better go and discuss the matter with your father.'

'Oh, but that's all in order. Daddy just does everything I want. He always has – rather to Mummy's disapproval sometimes – not that she'll disapprove *this* time,' she added promptly.

'I should think she'll be shocked beyond measure.'

'She will *not*. She likes you awfully. Oh, isn't it all terrific? I've never been so happy. I'm on top of the world.'

'No, you're not,' I said. 'You're only half-way up.' And I jumped up and pulled her to her feet. 'We must get to the top now, or the whole thing'll be unlucky. It's important, this. I've a strong inclination to kiss you on the top of the mountain. Something's telling me that you should never offend a mountain at a moment like this. And certainly not Torr Brow. Come, woman.'

And we began climbing again, each pulling the other in turn, up the steepening slope. When the slope flattened out towards the summit, she clasped my forearm between both her hands, as if it, or the gentleman attached to it, were something of her own now. On the top we walked along, parted, but with fingers interlinked so that our two arms could swing between us, back and forth, violently, happily.

Chapter Three

THE SMALL PARTY IN FRIARY LANE

Whatever may have been Mrs. Alanside's reservations I was accepted by Julie's parents; by her father with joy certainly; by her mother maybe a little despairingly. Mr. Alanside (I can call him Archdeacon no more), somewhat to his wife's dismay, insisted on having a 'small party' in their new home to celebrate the betrothal. I could detect from Julie's and her mother's talk some of the motives behind this insistence: there was, of course, his love for his daughter and his generous affection for me, but there was also a defiance of such ostracism as he had met in Close and Town; a need to see how many friends of yesterday would respond to this invitation and come to his party; and, lastly, so deep had been his fall, a pride – actually a *pride* – that his daughter was going to marry a clergyman. I think I realized for the first time the completeness of his collapse when I perceived, with a pain of compassion and love, that *he* was now proud of *me*.

'It's poor dear old Alanside bravely keeping his end up,' said my vicar when he received his card of invitation.

I studied the card on his chimneypiece.

The Reverend Edwyn and Mrs. Alanside
AT HOME
To meet Julie's fiancé, the Reverend Richard Oliver

The words had been filled in by his hand, and I knew that he had written 'The Reverend Richard Oliver' with satisfaction. I might be the most junior of junior curates, but some of those who would decline the invitation need not know this.

I did not once disquiet Julie by inquiring who had accepted and who had refused, and it was not till long afterwards that she told me of the many who had written in the third person regretting a previous engagement, and of some (God damn them) who had pointedly refrained from answering. When the evening of the party came (it was December now) I went through the dark streets to Friary Lane, very curious to see who would be there.

The new home in Friary Lane was a little red house with a weather-tiled front and a hipped roof, at the corner of St. Olave's Lane and facing the Friary Park. Small and late and unlovely, it was a poignant contrast to the Residentiary in the Close, and the symbol of the fall.

Since the rooms were so small the host had made the ground-floor rooms and the narrow hall festive with red and blue candles so that the guests, if they should be many, would be encouraged to distribute themselves around. Much of the fine old furniture from the Residentiary was forced into these rooms, and the bright flickering candles stood on Sheraton sideboard and escritoire, on Louis Seize bureaux and cabinets, and on a Heppelwhite satinwood commode. On an Adam serving-table he had placed the champagne and the hired glasses. Glasses for many.

The parade of the champagne bottles was a surprise to me, but I learned from Julie that it was all a part of his defiant effort; that the champagne was a cheap brand; and that the wine merchant had promised to take back all the bottles that were not used. Even so, she said, her mother had been worried by the expense.

It looked as if many bottles would go back, because the guests were not many. As the evening proceeded and they remained scarce, I suffered for him and for Julie who, as I could see, was also suffering for him. The evening being mild, the door of his house was now left open in case any arrived and were not heard; and often, even while we were all talking among the coloured candles, I saw him wander out into the hall, so as to look along Friary Lane, and see if someone else was coming.

Those who were there were those on whose kindly presence I would have gambled: my vicar, full of hearty jesting and radiant goodwill to us both; Canon Leedes, my late principal, quieter but not less benevolent; and of course Bishop Griffyn with Emmeline Harvie more or less in tow. Emmeline told me afterwards that he had said, 'Come, Emmeline, we don't visit the sins of the fathers upon the children'; and Emmeline, an ardent defender of her

Archdeacon, had retorted, 'But, Bishop, perhaps there were no sins to visit.'

'Perhaps not, my dear. Perhaps not,' had been his answer.

No one else had come from the Close or its precincts: no Chancellor, Precentor, Dean or canons. Mr. and Mrs. Prosdick were there, Mrs. Prosdick noisily so; I could see that she, however unconsciously, was remarkably at ease now that the Alansides were no longer high above her but even a little below. She bore down upon Julie and me, calling us, with a histrionic registering of ecstasy, 'My dears! My *very* dears! Isn't it all wonderful? And such a nice party!' and assuring me, with her usual studied enunciation of the socially revealing syllable 'oy', that I was an exceedingly lucky bah.

'Don't I know it!' I answered, not very wittily.

'And when will the wedding be, Julie darling? I'm sure he'll make you as good a hubby as my Benjy — and that's saying a lot, you know. Not but what there are times when I could cheerfully murder the little man. When will it be?'

'Oh, not for ages yet.'

'And where will it be? Now *where?*' Her head went saucily to one side. 'Tell me where. I'm so ex-ated.'

'Prebendary Imbraham declares that it's simply got to be at St. Hugh's, Richard's own church.'

'Oh, that'd be lovely. D'you know, Mr. Oliver, I've nipped along to St. Hugh's once or twice to hear you preach, and I must say that each time I quite enjah'd your sermon.' She said this as if it were a rather surprising fact. 'I came back and told Hubby how enjah'able it was, but the funny little man only said I ought to be above sermon-tasting by now, and it was desertion, and, anyhow, the preaching was quite good at *his* church. I think he was quite jealous, the silly old bah.'

Mr. Prosdick at this time was out of hearing. He was being a helpful old bah, carrying with his busy little steps a bottle of champagne round among the glasses.

Mrs. Alanside said kindly words to me, making, I suspected, the best of this business bravely. 'It's going to be so nice for Julie to have someone young. Everyone in Casterton's about a hundred.

She hardly meets anyone of her own age now. We seem to have lost touch with an enormous number of people now that we no longer live in the Close. I'm *so* glad she's going to have you.' Ever carelessly talkative, she scattered words around that revealed more than she knew.

I could almost hear the words she would have used about me to her more intimate friends. 'At least he's a gentleman.' I was a gentleman simply because I was a parson and, for good measure, a parson's son. All her talk showed that her standards of gentility were the oddly illogical ones of her class. You were a gentleman if you were a brewer but not if you were a grocer, even though you had a chain of a hundred shops. You could be a motor salesman and a gentleman, but not a furniture salesman. In other words it was respectable to make and sell beer but not to market more solid refreshment such as bacon or cheese or tinned pears. It was gentlemanlike to sell cars that would stand in a garage but not sideboards that would stand in a dining-room. And I'm afraid I must add that you were a gentleman if you preached the gospel of Christ under the authority of the Church of England but not if your Orders derived from one of the other, unestablished, communions – nay, not even if that communion was Rome itself.

When the congratulations were over, and no more guests seemed to be coming, and the older people were all talking together, having little to say to two of our generation, I was able to speak easily and unheard to Julie in this medley of noisy, playground voices. A group of family friends from afar, standing together by the Sheraton sideboard, had reminded me of that dinner at the Residentiary a year ago; and so vivid was the memory that I asked Julie, 'Where is Lucille What's-her-name? The Lucille who was at that dinner last December.'

'Lucille Eavry?'

'Yes. Why isn't she here? You were so fond of her. And she was so fond of you. And I hoped she liked me. Is she coming?'

'Not on your life, Richard my dear. Lucille's one of those who've dropped us. Dropped us from the first moment the case came on. Nothing has ever surprised me more. I should have thought she was the one person who would have stood by us through thick and thin. But no; it's very clear that our little spot of trouble worked the other way. Never a word to any of us. Not a word of understanding or sympathy or offer of help.'

'Perhaps she's away.'

'She is *not*. I made it my business to find out. She's been in her lovely Tudor house at East Helwood all the time.'

'That's only about fifteen or sixteen miles away, isn't it?'

'Yes. And that makes it all the more pointed. If ever we've received the cut direct, this was it.'

'But I can't believe it of her,' I said, recalling that merry affectionate, friendly, tolerant woman, with the large, deep soft brown eyes in the fine pale face. 'There must be some other explanation.'

'Oh, no. It's diplomacy. You remember her husband was a diplomat, and in diplomacy I'm sure you quickly break your links with anyone in disgrace, whether they deserve it or not. Mind you, it's no great loss to Mummy that she's kept away. After that famous dinner-party when Lucille talked about unmarried women having a right to lovers – you remember, don't you – Mummy was definitely warm and swore again and again that if she'd known beforehand what the woman was like, she'd never have allowed her to cross her doormat. And this in spite of the fact that she enjoyed, as you probably remember, an enormous long gossip with her in the drawing-room after dinner and after Lucille had said her stuff. Well, she doesn't cross it now, so Mummy's had her way.'

'I still can't understand it,' I persisted. 'The Lucille I saw may have had her unorthodox views but there was no utter selfish meanness in her face. I saw only kindliness and affection and jollity there.'

'That's what I should have thought about Lucille, but there it is: she cast us out. And she's not the only one by any means who's thought it best to have no further dealings with the Alansides. And what's so extraordinary, my pet, is that some of the men have been worse than the women. They've sent him anonymous letters of insult, lots of them. And did you know he was hooted by a crowd of loathsome young men in Eastgate the other day, probably lewd,

H

lascivious little brutes themselves? Oh, I wish he'd go from here, but he won't. He just says, "I've done nothing wrong and I'm not running from anybody."'

'Didn't you try to get in touch with her?'

'With who? Who're we talking about?'

'Lucille.'

'*Lucille?* Certainly not. I'm not begging for anyone's sympathy. After all this it'll be Lucille who'll have to speak first.'

At this point two people came up to talk with us and the subject was blown away, just as I was wondering whether I wouldn't, one day, try to encounter Lucille fifteen miles away and learn the truth.

The evening was getting late; some of the guests had gone; Julie and I were sitting on a sofa now that there was a chance to do so, when Mr. Prosdick who'd been in the neighbouring room on a busy excursion with a beer bottle and glasses at his host's suggestion, came bursting in to say excitedly, 'Alanside! The Bishop!'

'*What?*'

'His lordship. Just arrived in his car. His car's outside.' Mr. Prosdick was always impressed by the episcopal limousine as by the episcopal 'lordship'. This handsome Rolls had lately been presented to the Bishop, since he was getting old, by a group of clergy.

Mr. Alanside returned, bringing the little Bishop straight to us two. 'There they are, my lord,' he said.

The Bishop put out his hand to Julie while all the people stood round, including my vicar, Bishop Griffyn, Canon Leedes, the Alansides, and Mrs. Prosdick beaming; and he said, 'My dears, you must forgive me for only coming in as late as this. But I've been far away finishing a rather special Visitation with a Parish Council in session, and, dear me, how some of the good souls did talk. I told them at last that I had another *very* special Visitation to make, a very important one, to two young people who were celebrating their engagement, and one of them one of the newest and brightest of my clergy. They let me go at once, sending good wishes to you both.'

'It's wonderful of you to have come,' said Julie.

And I said, 'Yes, my lord.'

'Yes . . . well . . . God bless you both. I'm greatly pleased for Richard's sake.' He turned to chaff me. 'But don't forget all about that reading and study you promised me to do. Don't be tempted too much away from it. I admit' – he glanced at Julie – 'there's temptation here. You must see that he keeps at it, Julie my dear. You and I have got to make a great scholar of him.'

By this time the busy Mr. Prosdick had arrived at the Bishop's side with a glass of champagne. The Bishop lifted it to us, repeating 'Bless you both. I'm so glad I was able to be here, even if I was disgracefully late. I was so afraid I'd be too late, but Chambers, my good chauffeur, did wonders, encouraged by his bishop. I wasn't sure whether his wonders were quite in accordance with the laws of the State, but I didn't feel they were in any way contravening the laws of the Church, and there are times when the two don't run quite concurrently. I told him this, doubtless to his comfort.'

'Bring him in! Bring him in!' commanded the host. 'At once.'

So the chauffeur was brought in – by Mr. Prosdick enthusiastically – and was the last to toast us. 'Mr. Oliver . . . Miss Julie, if I may so call you.'

('Isn't he absolutely sweet?' whispered Mrs. Prosdick to her Benjy, who was standing by and smiling benevolently upon such an episode.)

Chapter Four

THE REARGUARD SKIRMISHES

Now almost every Sunday after Evensong I came to supper with
the Alansides in Friary Lane and so was able, from my place in the
family, to watch my future father-in-law's fight against the disaster,
which, after the manner of victors, had not only dislodged him
from a fine position but was now pursuing him through the open
country towards a last stand.

To me, as the months went by, it all seemed a pretty hopeless
fight, a mere matter of rearguard skirmishing, but from his talk at
the supper table (and one effect of the disaster had been to age him
into garrulity) I saw that he was indulging hopes above anything
likely or even possible. Neither Julie nor I nor Mrs. Alanside ever
said a word to disturb these hopes. We saw that he had need of
them.

Nothing came of the Petition to the King; there were not enough
signatories to make it a worthwhile project. It was astonishing the
fall-away of his friends after the Lord Chancellor's Judgment.
After the Consistory Court trial he still had loyal friends and sworn
believers all over the country; after the Privy Council Judgment
they faded away.

For two days and one Sunday after the Judgment he received
big money from popular newspapers for articles no matter about
what, so long as they carried his name. These offers of big money
he had accepted, saying, 'I shall need every penny of it. God knows
how I'm going to live now.' For a few months he was in demand
as a lecturer, in northern towns especially, and he would bring
back to Friary Lane ten or fifteen guineas from each of these
engagements but, as Julie had foretold, this demand slowly expired.
His name remained in the List of Standen's Lecture Agency, together with a photograph, the most attractive ever taken of him
which he had particularly chosen for this purpose, though it was
fifteen years old. But no more did the letters from the Agency drop

through the door in Friary Lane with their offers of engagements and fair fees. He went daily to the doormat but found nothing.

It is hardly worth telling of his venture with the Lucas Hall in Plumstead Street, Pimlico; it lasted so short a time. It had been his belief that, even though he was Archdeacon of Casterton no more, and held no more a licence to serve in the Church of England, his past fame as a preacher would fill this hall on Sundays, and the two collections, after hire and other expenses had been paid, would provide him with an income. Even more than this he dreamed of this hired hall becoming a fashionable, if unorthodox, place of worship like that of Edward Irving a hundred years before, who, after being deposed for unorthodoxy from the Scottish Church, had amassed a large, wealthy, devoted congregation of 'Irvingites'.

But the Lucas Hall venture died before it had lasted a half-year. The first weeks had seen the hall filled to capacity and had lodged a big hope in the heart of the preacher, but really the crowds had come, for the most part, to gaze at him as they might at a notorious criminal and they soon dwindled into a sparse company of simple but faithful – even adoring – women and young men. The 'profit' each Sunday sank to less than two pounds, to less than one pound, and finally to submersion beneath a debt. Obliged to abandon the project, he preached on his last Sunday evening a farewell sermon to nineteen tearful women, one aged man, and five devoted lads.

For more months than this he earned money by writing topical articles for popular journals like *John Bull*, *Tit-Bits*, *The Referee*, and *Woman's Friend*. For these articles he received an average fee of three guineas per thousand words. But it always saddened me that one whose long, grave, dignified letters had invariably been given an honourable prominence in *The Times* was now finding his only place of rest in such hostels as these. And of course the months had not numbered twelve before the thousand-word scripts were returning to Friary Lane in company with a rejection slip, and he knew, in the deep of his heart, that it had never been his subject matter which had sold the articles, but his shadowed name; a name now left behind and lost in some cold desert of half-forgotten things.

What then lay ahead? For a while, and this was even more saddening to me, he found a market for fifteen-minute speeches about his celebrated case in small cinemas up and down the country. If his wife expressed a dislike of his doing this (Julie and I stayed quiet and unhappy about it) he would answer hotly that he was resolved to lose no opportunity of keeping his case before the public because he believed this to be his obligation to the Church even more than to himself. But in fact he was allowing himself, because of his need for money, to be exploited as a variety 'turn' so as to get the people into struggling picture houses. Even as he had declined from *The Times* to *John Bull*, so he had declined from the great cathedrals to little cinemas in shabby streets.

I chanced one day to be in the largest seaside town of our diocese at the same time as he was billed to appear all the week at a small cinema called The Queen Street Cameo. This little place was one of the last to engage him, being ready to do so because his name was still a potent memory here. My duty had been with our Diocesan Church House in this important town, and when it was done, I could not resist walking past the Cameo to see how he had been advertised. I walked towards it with apprehension and a feeling of furtive guilt, but I could not stop myself and turn about. I went on, slowing my pace as I got nearer the garish front of the cinema, but soon, and with a shock like a bullet in me, I saw a banner hanging across the width of the entrance and flaunting the legend, 'REV. E. ALANSIDE. "I HAVE PAID – BUT . . ."'

I was sure that he had not sunk to the point of providing this vulgar title for his speech; I knew that no one can control what a theatre manager or newspaper editor, eager for 'impact', will invent as a catch-penny title, but I supposed he must have tolerated it up there and I wondered what were his feelings each day as he came to the theatre from the street: did he draw his eyes from that banner, casting them down on pavement and threshold, as he passed beneath it?

§

'What now?' I asked Julie when all his sources of income seemed to have dried up, and we two were walking a country road together. 'What is there for him now?'

'Nothing as far as I can see. He's over sixty now, and who gives work to a man over sixty?'

'But with all his degrees, surely he can get something. Some men over sixty get jobs, retired bank managers and such like. They become assistant secretaries to clubs and societies and institutions.'

'Yes, but you forget that nearly everybody thinks of him as an ex-criminal, which he isn't, and wouldn't have been, even if he'd been guilty. His name may be getting slowly forgotten, but there's no one in the country who wouldn't recognize it the minute he applied for the job and shake their heads and probably make dirty jokes about him. His very fame has finished him off. Poor lamb, he's basing his hopes now on his slander case, but that won't come on for ages; these law cases never do. He's talking of heavy damages from that – thousands. But, oh dear, I can't help feeling he's deceiving himself, and if he's wrong and saddled with all the costs' – she shrugged – 'I don't know what'll happen. Mummy and he between them have barely enough to live on.'

'Wouldn't some of his friends help him again with the costs?'

'My darling Richard, there are no friends. Only half a dozen here and there. The rest have grown tired of him. Nothing said, mind you; all very quiet; just keep away and leave him to his fate. Oh, the utter wickedness of the world!' She clenched a fist so tight that it trembled at her side as she walked. Her mouth set in a hard, unlovely line. 'Wickedness. Wickedness. Because he was innocent – I *know* he was – and how dare they – how *can* they – do nothing to help him? Daddy was innocent, just as Dreyfus was, and one day, I fully believe, all the world will know it. It will be Dreyfus over again.'

I offered no answer, not because I was allowing myself in these later days to doubt his innocence, for then I must believe that he was leading a lifetime of lies – and I could not believe this of the man in the Cuthbert Chapel – but because I could no longer see anywhere a General Picquart or an Emile Zola who would rise to the defence of this Dreyfus. I could no longer imagine any famous voice lifting the cry '*J'accuse*.' Zola had published '*J'Accuse*' as an open letter to the President of the French Republic, denouncing those who were suppressing truth and justice. Where was there anyone to write such a letter to King or Prime Minister? And, indeed, where was there anyone who was suppressing truth and justice?

Chapter Five

DEATH OF THE LEARNED CLERK

Once Bishop Griffyn had said to me, when delivering his soul of some unsmiling satire at the expense of my vicar, 'Trippy Imbraham is given to boasting that in all his long life he has never experienced disobedience from one of his curates, but this, of course, is because, in his enormous geniality and charm, he has never distressed them with any rules to obey.' Like so many of his comments this was more merry than true, though, like all good satire, it had a kernel of truth. If we didn't have rules in the Clergy House, we at least had a Rule, and one almost monastic in its obligation. The Clergy House Rule said, '7.0 Rise; 7.30 Mattins; 8.0 Holy Communion or Meditation; 8.45 Breakfast; 9.0 Terce, Reading and Study; 1.0 Sext; 1.15 Lunch; 2.30–5.0 Visiting; 5.30 Evensong; 6.0 High Tea; 6.30 to 10.0 Visiting or Devotional Reading; 10.0 Cocoa; 10.30 Compline and Silence.'

I loved the Rule. As I had always loved the quiet Mass in the early morning, so I now loved the joy of disciplined reading, the break for Sext, the social pleasure of visiting (for Trippy's curates were welcomed everywhere, even by the lapsed or the anti-clerical), and the listening rapt, when I was not on duty, to Sung Evensong in the Cathedral. I was not wholly enraptured by the cocoa at ten, but I certainly was by the beauty of Compline that followed it. 'The Lord Almighty grant us a quiet night and a perfect end. *Amen.* Brethren, be sober, be vigilant, because your adversary the devil, as a roaring lion, walketh about, seeking whom he may devour: whom resist, steadfast in the faith. . . .' *Te lucis ante terminum . . .* 'To thee before the close of day . . .' Then the Silence. And bed.

Soon I was priested and able to take the quiet Mass in St. Hugh's, with perhaps only my vicar and senior curate in the church. Soon I was in the second of the four years I had promised to give to St. Hugh's, my 'Four Stretch', as I called it, my 'Bird'. I had now to make the best possible compromise between the learned and clerkly studies in my 'cell' and the most unmonastic fact of my engagement to Julie. Of this compromise Trippy had said with loud laughs, 'Certainly, my dear boy, we must lighten the Rule a little for an affianced man. We can conceive of Visiting, I think, as including an occasional visit to Miss Julie, ha, ha, ha. Visiting, yes; but not Meditation. I think you mustn't let the lady in there or she'll occupy the whole period, ha, ha, ha; ha, ha, ha. And don't forget there's your day off. There's to be no skimping of that. That's under Obedience. And what more recreative than to spend it with the charming Miss Julie? Upon my soul, I envy you. Such beatitude. Dear me, I could wish I were twenty-five again.' Which was an odd remark from Trippy because it was everywhere supposed that he was a congenital bachelor who'd never once been disturbed, or undone, by the soft eyes of a girl.

In these first two years, my reading, almost inevitably, was given to the Greek and Roman Fathers of the Early Church; first to the so-called Apostolic Fathers, Clemens Romanus, Polycarp and Ignatius; then to those of the subsequent but still primitive age, Irenaeus, Justin Martyr, Tertulian, Origen, Lactantius. I was soon utterly fascinated and held by this reading, impatient to get back to it from every less enthralling task. To read in Irenaeus how he had walked and talked with Polycarp, who had walked and talked with St. John – St. John who had walked and talked with 'the Lord' – it was too tremendous – and I use that word in its exact sense: it set one trembling with a strange awe, to be translated from a bed-sitting room in Casterton, over eighteen centuries, to the first years of the Church which I now served; years which had already numbered a thousand before Saxon hands laid one single stone of Casterton Cathedral – that Cathedral which I could now rise and look at from my window.

I saw you, when I was yet a boy in Lower Asia, with Polycarp, and I could even now point to the place where the blessed Polycarp sat and spoke of his intercourse with John, and with the others who had seen the Lord. Everything that he had heard from them about the Lord, about His miracles and His teaching, Polycarp told us, as one who had received it from those who had looked on the Word of Life with their own eyes.

Let me rise again and look from my window at the Cathedral standing there, silent under the stars.

So thrilled was I by it all that I began to play with an ambition, or, rather, an unlikely dream, of writing a learned book on Christian patrology, regardless of the fact that a few thousand others had done this already, from the time of St. Jerome onwards. I even thought of a pompous title for it, *Consensus Patrorum*.

But it was no *Consensus Patrorum* that I came to write. Alas, far from it. Unfortunately, in the course of this delighted reading, I came face to face with a writer of the Silver Age of Greece and Rome who was the very opposite of a Christian Father, being scoffer and atheist, anti-Christian and pagan and immoral. But extremely entertaining. Lucian. Here was wit and mischief and uproarious fun to rival Aristophanes of five centuries before and Voltaire of sixteen centuries later; and all of it in an Attic style most graceful and easy and polished and unpretentious. I fear, yes I confess, that when it would have been more becoming in a curate to be reading Eusebius on the *Canonical Epistles* or Tertullian on the *Testimony of the Soul*, I was reading deep and long, and with loud, lonely laughs, in Lucian's *True History* and his *Lucius the Ass*. I read on and on, hoping that this could be construed as scholarship and telling myself, without conviction, that it was only right and scholarly to get a picture of the age *in toto* and to learn, as a Christian, what the Opposition had been saying.

This view, however, did not suffer me to take my Lucian off the shelf in the hour set apart for devotional reading.

My ambition now, possessing me like a devil, was to write satirico-comic essays in the Lucianic manner, grave, suave, dignified commentaries on the social and ecclesiastical scene, with the fun or the silken invective beautifully dispersed among gracious and balanced sentences. I was not sure that the style I had in mind would not derive from both Lucian of Samosata and Bishop Gregory Griffyn of Casterton.

Secretly I wrote an essay of a thousand words, having learned from Mr. Alanside that this was the length the newspapers liked, and with the blind self-confidence of an inexperienced amateur I sent it to no less a journal than *The New Witness*, because this was the dignified paper which, as a would-be scholar, I read every week.

How my indignation swelled – so inexperienced I was – when the days went by, the weeks went by, four of them, five of them, and not so much as an acknowledgment came from the Editor of *The Witness*! With the sixth week indignation gave place to resignation and a second essay which I had begun was pushed aside in despair. It almost went into the waste-paper basket, but not quite. One day, perhaps, when I should be something more than an insignificant curate, I might make some use of it; but if there was one journal in England which should not receive the offer of it, it was *The New Witness*.

I returned to Eusebius and Clement of Alexandria and Gregory Thaumaturgus – till that morning when I saw on the hall table of the Clergy House an envelope addressed to me with '*The New Witness*' printed along its top. My heart stopped, then sped and steam-hammered up and down as I tore the envelope open. A cheque for seven guineas came out of it, with a courteous letter accepting my article and – if you will only believe it – asking to see more such articles in a similar vein. Seven guineas! And even Mr. Alanside of late had been getting only three guineas a thousand! And 'more such articles'! *More!*

§

This letter was the lethal shaft that slew the learned clerk. I rushed to tell Julie about it; I told her only; no one else; not her father because I thought it might hurt him now that his articles were being rejected; not my vicar, because I felt a little guilty since there was nothing in the Rule allocating an hour for writing satirical articles; nor Mrs. Alanside because she would tell the whole of Casterton. There was no reason why Casterton should know who had written the article. It was signed 'Lucilius the Younger'.

This was a young man's pedantry like *Consensus Patrorum*. In reading commentaries on the satire of Lucian I had found myself referred to the very Father of Roman Satire, Lucilius, to whom we can almost attribute the present meaning of the word 'satire', as the polished ridicule of folly in life and literature. Needless to tell you that I accepted the Editor's invitation to send him more of my essays. All were signed 'Lucilius the Younger', and since the original Gaius Lucilius had lived and laughed in the second century B.C., the present Lucilius was certainly younger. All were accepted and in due course published, and then one morning I opened a letter from the Editor offering to commission a fortnightly article from me at ten guineas a time for a year, and hinting at the possibility of making this a more permanent arrangement.

Death in the Clergy House; I say death because my pleasure was so excited, so agitated, as to resemble the spasms of the dying; and indeed something seemed to be dying, an old life of small means and limited, local repute, while something new and larger leapt to birth. Never a moment in my life finer than this, except that one on the slope of Torr Brow. Twenty-six such articles at ten guineas each! Possibly, if I had known anything about literary agents I could have negotiated an even better commission, but I had never heard of such people, and since I was now effervescing like a shaken beer bottle, I wrote at once to accept the Editor's offer before he changed his mind.

Two hundred and sixty guineas was £273 a year: my stipend was now £210 – there was the Whitsun offering! – why, my income would top five hundred. Five hundred. It seemed wealth beyond easy belief.

Julie? Marriage? I was virgin still at twenty-five – what else could ordinand and curate be? And I could long to bed with Julie.

Five hundred a year. Julie. But then Conscience rose from its couch, stood up, and stared at me. This was not at all what the Bishop had ordered. These essays were not easy to write, so did I polish and polish them, often walking up and down my room with a single sentence or paragraph for an hour and more; like an invading force they occupied great stretches of the day allocated to Study or Meditation or Devotional Reading; they even bestrode my back like the Old Man of the Sea when I was out parish-visiting.

I got so worried and guilty about it that I decided at last to discuss it with Mr. Alanside who had once been so kind a counsellor in my little hostel room. And it was not only for my own comfort that I resolved to do this, but for his too; I saw how pleased he would be to be consulted as if still an honoured priest, and one held by the young to be wise.

So I went and sat with him in his little drawing-room at Friary Lane – there was no private study for him in that narrow home – and we talked together while Mrs. Alanside clattered about in her kitchen on the other side of the wall. More than once, listening to him, I thought how sad was the difference between this consultation and that other when, perfectly attired in archidiaconal frock-coat and gaiters, he had stepped down from his high place to stretch a hand to a floundering ordinand.

Today, sitting there in crumpled black trousers and jacket, with the clerical collar which he wore so defiantly yellowing a little and cracked a little, he was obviously, and as I had foreseen, flattered to be consulted as a priest. Moreover, he was proud to be able to speak with the knowledge of one who had written many articles. Equally and obviously he was pained to learn that I, a junior, a mere boy, a tyro, was being offered three times more than anything he had received of late. Pained yes, but struggling to be generous in his pleasure.

'Richard! This is quite wonderful! I *am* pleased. I thought some of the articles you sent me were splendid, and I do know something about this, though of course the essays I wrote were for the more specialized journals. You certainly mustn't turn away from such an offer. Why should you? Good gracious, are there not deans who contribute regularly to papers of far less dignity than your *New Witness*? And what about other famous Fathers-in-God who, if they don't write for the popular Press, do spend long hours on

their learned articles for the *Hibbert Journal* or the *Quarterly Review*
– I have done so myself. Long articles for both the *Hibbert* and the
Quarterly. And, come to that, I've written for the more popular
papers too. I have received as much as twenty-five guineas for a
brief article – not so very long ago. And look: what about the end-
less books which all the Canons of Westminster write for Mr.
Murray and Mr. Eyre and Mr. Spottiswoode? The good bishops
too, with their Bampton Lectures; those must occupy many, many
days that might be devoted to pastoral care. Isn't that so?'

'Yes, sir. But these are serious works on Theology. Mine —'

'I'm blowed if the Dean's articles are. I should have said they
approached the flippant.'

'Yes, the Dean's are secular.' I was determined to use this good
word, which I had intended to apply to my articles, had he not
interrupted me.

'Extremely secular,' he agreed. Did I detect the ashes of an old
envy here?

'But deans are allowed to take things easy, are they not, sir?
The Bishop's plan for me was that I should give four years to
reading and study at St. Hugh's; not exactly to writing satirico-
comic essays.' I was also determined to get 'satirico-comic' in.

'That may be, but I find it inconceivable that the Bishop will
want you to turn down this offer?'

'I can't turn it down. I've accepted it. By return of post. Do you
think he'll be frightfully angry?'

'No. He may be disappointed, but he'll understand.'

'I don't want to disappoint him. Perhaps I could work as hard
as ever and write the beastly articles too.' So I suggested, but
knowing this would be impossible.

'Will you let me go and talk to the Bishop about it? As your
future father-in-law perhaps I could do so with propriety —' and,
oh, as he said this, my heart knew with a sharp pain that he was
pleased by the idea of being able to call upon the Bishop and discuss
a serious matter with him as in the old days. He still had some sort
of position and authority as Julie's parent and my father-in-law-
elect. It was about all he had.

I felt it was really *my* duty to go to the Bishop – almost as a penitent – but I could not bear to deprive an unhappy man of a little cup he had suddenly glimpsed. So I said, 'It would be frightfully kind of you, sir. You'd tell him, wouldn't you, that I'm worried about it all,' and I added for his further satisfaction, 'You could tell him I came and asked your advice.'

'I'll certainly tell George Casterton all about it.' Deliberately he used the Bishop's Christian name as if nothing had disturbed their old familiar friendship.

'Thank you, sir.' And remembering the Bishop's kindness and encouragement when he sent me to St. Hugh's to study and become a 'learned clerk', I made a great effort. It required time, and there was a halt before I spoke. Then I said, 'Tell him that, if he wants me to, I'll try to withdraw my acceptance and go on studying.'

'He won't ask that, Richard. He'll never ask that. You're perhaps being over-conscientious about this.'

'Well then, sir . . .'

'Yes, Richard?'

'Sir, would it be possible – do you think it would be possible – now that I look like being able to earn about five hundred a year' – I said it proudly – 'possible for Julie and me to get married?'

'Oh, dear! Oh dear! I hadn't thought of that. So soon? Heavens, Richard, this is a shock. I'm going to be miserable without Julie.'

'I know you are, sir,' I deplored, almost as if what I really ought to do was to give up the girl as well as the articles.

'Julie's still very young. She's only just come of age.'

'Yes, that's true,' I said sadly. And, hoping to dissolve a little of this rocky obstacle, I submitted unconfidently, 'I'm nearly twenty-six.'

'Well, we must see how things go. I mustn't stand in your way. I never expected to see Julie going out to work as she is now, but she insisted on doing something to help, and Jack Hardwick simply jumped at her for his social reporter. Do you know Jack, the Editor of the *Casterton Herald*? He's always been a great friend of mine. And of course he was very lucky to get Julie. He saw that she'd be the equal of anyone at any social function, and able to talk with anyone.' Here the buried defiance peeped above ground. 'I should think she's ideal for him. Dressed for a party, Julie's an ornament and an honour to his rather fatuous paper.'

'She certainly is,' I endorsed.

'She's a very beautiful girl. I must say I've often thought at a party that she was the most beautiful girl there, but perhaps that's just parental partiality.'

'I suffer a little from it myself, sir.'

'Ah, well, I never thought she'd have to earn her living and become a reporter.'

'She needn't be a reporter, if you'll let her marry me,' I pointed out with a grin.

'Dear me, this has come upon us suddenly. Still, I'll speak to her mother about it.'

Simple, commonplace words but my heart hammered with an exquisite agitation as I thought of Julie in the bridal bed, soon now.

'It'd be awfully kind of you if you would,' I stuttered.

§

The Bishop summoned me to the Palace one morning, and I went towards his little tatterdemalion study with some qualms – not to say, some shame. The last Lucilius article to be published had surely, in the words of Mr. Alanside, 'approached the flippant', and the nearer I got to the Bishop's door, the more flippant it seemed. Seeing the door, I suddenly lost the last of my pride in Lucilius. 'Lucilius the Younger.' What could be sillier? 'Oh dear. . . .' The Bishop's secretary on the garden lawn had told me to 'go straight to him in his study', an instruction that had sounded alarming; so that now, within sight of his closed door, I went from reason into panic. My last few steps saw me 'deprived' like my father-in-law; 'struck off the rolls for infamous conduct in a professional sense'. Before my knuckle touched the door I was wondering whether the Bishop wouldn't recommend, perhaps, a kind of voluntary deprivation for a year, while I purged my offences. It was a timid, half-willed, shame-filled knock that tapped and trembled on his door. 'Lucilius'. Sickening, beastly name. 'The Younger.' Oh, God . . .

'Come in,' his voice called – not unpleasantly, thank heaven.

He was standing behind his loaded desk as I entered, a little man in a very old and presumably pre-episcopal black cassock. Too small, too snub-nosed, to seem a mighty prince of the Church, and Lord Bishop of Casterton, but a prince among men none the less, I thought, because of the sanctity in him that raised him above us all. So small and undistinguished in feature, and yet – as we had always heard – there fell a hush in the House of Lords whenever the Bishop of Casterton rose to speak, quietly, humbly, and yet with ardour and passion. As he gave me his gentle, welcoming smile I could almost have wept in front of him at the thought that I might have been betraying his trust in me. Now in his presence my desire for money and fame seemed utterly unworthy, and even more, perhaps my eagerness for Julie in my bed and my arms. 'After five minutes in his presence,' a man had once said to me, 'one finds oneself believing in Love and Eternity whether one wants to or not.' And another, an agnostic: 'I came away from him, thinking, "My God, is there really such a thing as Grace?"' The term 'Father-in-God' is lightly used of bishops, and only with my Bishop in Casterton have I known it to come alive and express something that was real and true and very happy. I really felt 'his son' and knew a restful happiness in being his son. Hence my shame and doubt now, and my half-readiness to give up everything.

'Lucilius the Younger.' Such pomposity. Such arrogance. 'Oh dear, oh dear. . . .'

But he was gentle and laughing with me.

'Sit down, Lucilius,' he said. And he sat too, opposite me, pushing aside a cairn of books and papers as if they were an obstacle between us. 'Alanside told me you are worrying yourself to death about your articles and your promise to me. You're not to worry any more, my dear boy. I've read some of the articles, and they are good – they are even very good – you have a gift for this sort of thing, and I'm sure one must be loyal to one's gifts. An opportunity seems to be opening before you, and you must certainly come to terms with it. Without shame, I think, because you will only be one in a great tradition of good priests who've been good writers too. It's quite simple really: you've just got to do your best in the sight of God both as priest and penman. But I have one warning. May I give it to you?'

'Of course,' I said in a low voice.

'It's this. Write . . . write all you want . . . but you mustn't lower your devotional life in the least. You must keep it still on the top rung. Once you start coming down the devotional ladder, your old sins come rushing up to meet you and to leap joyously on to your back. You're enough of a priest already to know *that*, I'm sure?'

'Yes, my lord.'

'Yes, one sees it happen all too often. Well, only be alive to that, and all the rest will look after itself. You'll see to it that nothing interferes with your pastoral duties. They are pre-eminent. It was for them that you were ordained and that I licensed you to St. Hugh's; nothing short of a resignation of that title and the acceptance of a part-time curacy could justify any neglect of them. You see that, don't you?'

'I see it perfectly, my lord.'

'So the only thing that will suffer is the study and research I wanted you to undertake. But it needn't all go. I can trust you to do your best about that. You have a love of scholarship, I know. Well, keep the scholar's mind. . . . And now we come to something that seems to me wholly pleasing in this matter. Can you guess what it is?'

'No, sir.'

'It's just that I'm very pleased to think you may be able to marry Julie. You *do* want to, don't you?'

'I'm afraid I do, rather.'

'And you think she wants you?'

'Well. . . .' I didn't like to say Yes too cocksurely. 'I . . . I think so, my lord.'

'So do I. I'm very sure of it. And I'm sure it's a pity to keep young lovers apart too long. Go and marry her when you feel you can do your duty by her. I particularly want to see Julie made happy. As you know, things haven't been too good for her in the last two years. Help her to be happy again.'

'It's something I've been longing to do, sir . . . my lord.' And I couldn't help adding, 'And if it were possible, I'd like to help her father too.'

'Yes, yes,' he agreed, nodding. And again, later and strenuously he said, 'Yes, oh yes.' But no more.

§

So died the learned clerk, not, alas, full of years and honours, but at least with the comfort and forgiveness of his bishop.

Julie and I were married in the last days of June that year. We had found a tiny house in West Street almost opposite my old hostel. It was a marvellous mixture of a house. Like so many in Casterton it had a white Georgian front with pedimented doorway and fanlight, but the broad window of its one sitting-room was a shallow round bay and surely Regency. In the bay you could stand and look towards the honey-coloured and towered cliffs of the Cathedral, plushed with lichen and moss, but if you turned about and looked behind you, you saw the old dark beams of a Tudor cottage. Being both Georgian in front and Elizabethan behind, it was a small echo of the Residentiary; and how Julie and I loved it. The Alansides gave us many pieces of furniture that they could not house in Friary Lane, and the whole of my parish, and perhaps a quarter of Casterton, gave us almost everything else we needed. The parish of St. Hugh's was agog – at least its women were – for the wedding of their own curate in their own church to the daughter of a once greatly famous (and now scandal-shadowed) name.

June had been chosen for the wedding so that the garden of the Clergy House, joyously and radiantly offered by Trippy Imbraham, could be used for the reception. The Bishop, at his own request, married us, my vicar assisting him. It was certainly an occasion in Casterton, not because I was of any importance but because the bride came to the feet of the Bishop on the arm of a priest he had deprived. This hit the imagination, not only of our city but of places much farther afield, and Fleet Street in the centre of them supplied them with the news. The name of Archdeacon Alanside had long sunk below the horizon of Fleet Street, but it was still good for an afterglow. Nevertheless Fleet Street left it to readers to recognize the name; with that 'sportsmanship' which is often as remarkable as its ruthlessness, it said only, 'The young couple were married by the Bishop of Casterton, the bride being given away by her father, the Rev. E. Alanside.' No word about an old scandal was inserted to spoil a bride's great day.

At first Mr. Alanside had said, 'Listen, Julie darling: I'd better keep in the background. I don't want to be a shadow at the festivities. You can get someone else to give you away. Old Gregory Griffyn, I suggest. That'd be splendid: a bishop to marry you, and a bishop to give you away.'

To which Julie replied, 'Listen, Daddy darling: I'm not going to be given away by anyone but my father. If you don't want to do it, I won't get married at all. And then Richard'll be disappointed. At least, I hope so.'

'Well, I think it's a mistake, but if you really want the old man . . .'

'I not only want him, I fully intend to have him and no one else. Let that be perfectly clear to all. Mummy, make it clear to him. It'd be a pity if there was no wedding after all because, as far as I can see, the whole of Casterton's looking forward to it.'

'All right, my dear,' her father agreed. 'I'll try to do my duty.'

So all of Casterton that could get into St. Hugh's saw their disgraced Archdeacon take his daughter up to his bishop, she resting her white-gloved hand on his arm, unashamedly, proudly.

Our church was filled beyond its capacity; we had a full choir, even the men choristers attending; and I remember thinking, during the anthem they gave us, that all this fine ceremonial served both as a wedding for me and a funeral for the learned clerk. The approaches to the church were crowded by ten thousand; but the company later in the Clergy House garden was small. The Alansides had so few friends now; their income was limited; and I had not liked to list the names of more guests than they. (I had, however, invited the Rev. Tom Arrowsmith from Croydon. And his wife; I ask you to believe it; his wife. A wife with heaps of bronze hair and a ceaseless smile.) But the late June sun was an enthusiastic guest; as enthusiastic and universally benign as Prebendary

Imbraham, and I can hardly say more than that; so the caterers had been able to spread the buffet counter under the trees and distribute garden tables about the lawns and along the rose beds; and the company was soon as vivacious and chattery as a population of brightly plumed parakeets caged in a zoological garden. Little Mrs. Alanside in new silks and a brilliant hat almost as tall as herself bustled among her guests and was happy, but Mr. Alanside seemed – to me at least – a lonely figure on the fringe of the picture, smiling when spoken to, but often left alone, not because the guests ostracized him but because they were uncomfortable in his presence, as if his story made him abnormal.

When a photographer appeared from the *Casterton Herald*, Julie's own paper, and begged for a wedding group, Mr. Alanside hurried from sight. Hearing what was proposed, he went quickly to the other side of our Clergy House, the narrow tradesmen's approach between kitchen door and garden wall where no guests were. My vicar, enthusiastically searching for him, and probably having forgotten, in the joys of the afternoon, that he'd ever been in disgrace, found him standing by the dustbins.

'Come along, Eddie,' he shouted. 'Where the dickens have you got to? They want you for a photograph. We're all waiting for you.'

'No, Trippy, look: I'm best out of this. Tell me somewhere where I can safely hide.'

'Don't talk such nonsense, my dear boy. Can't do without you. Everyone's got to be in it. The Bishop's going to be in it.'

'All the more reason why I should keep away. I'm not going to embarrass the Bishop over this. He was good enough to let me keep my clerical collar, but I'm known to all the world as one of his black sheep. I know he wouldn't offer any objection to my presence, but it just wouldn't do. It simply wouldn't, Trippy. These Press photographers don't only put their picture in the local paper, they try to sell it all over the country. It'd probably sell all the better with me in it, but it'd start up a whole lot of memories that are best left where they lie. More than that, I'm thinking of Julie. A photograph is a terribly permanent thing, and she'll look at it again and again all through her life. She'll show it to other people. I don't want anything in it that'll spoil it for her. Her mother'll be there and the Bishop and you and dear old Gregory. Leave it at that.'

'Well, if you feel like this, old boy —'

'I do. And I think I know what I'm doing. Some instinct tells me I'm right. Just tell them that I've been called away but that I'll hurry back when I can. Meantime tell me where I can keep out of sight. And rest for a bit. I'm tired.'

'You can come to my study, old son. You'll be comfortable there. There's a particularly sybaritic chair in it. And it's on the first floor, so you'll have a grand-stand view of the garden. But it's a pity; a pity; we wanted you.'

So while Julie bewailed, 'Where's Daddy? Oh, where's Daddy?' and while the busy and fluent young photographer arranged us all in front of a giant lime tree, and while Mrs. Alanside said, 'It's no good, darling. You've heard he's gone and won't come back till later'; he was actually in the study, sometimes pacing its carpet, and sometimes standing back from the window so as to see, without being seen, how the picture was faring.

Chapter Six

THE WANDERER

My father-in-law's 'last stand' was his slander action brought against a prosperous ecclesiastical lawyer in our city. This was the action from which, so Julie had told me, he dreamed of reaping 'thousands' in damages. Julie and I had been four months among the Tudor timbers of our little West Street home; it was October and the lime trees on the Cathedral lawns were both green and gold with their leaves lying everywhere on grass and pavement; while, far away, in the High Court of Justice, King's Bench, before Mr. Justice Dorman and a special jury 'Alanside v. Arkenwell' was heard. In it the plaintiff alleged that the defendant had uttered words reflecting on his moral character. The alleged slander was contained in the words, 'You won't hear anything more of Arch-deacon Alanside because it seems he's going to be unfrocked. All very sad, because there's no nicer or kinder man anywhere if only he could keep the seventh commandment.'

At first sight it looked like a good case with the promise of substantial damages. Plaintiff's counsel asked him, 'What is your present position in the Church of England, Mr. Alanside?'

'A priest in Holy Orders,' he answered, looking straight into counsel's eyes. Was not his clerical collar in place for all the court to see? In a nervous moment he fingered the collar.

'What does that answer imply, Mr. Alanside, as regards this assertion that you were going to be unfrocked?'

'That it was wholly untrue. That it was a mischievous lie.'

'To be unfrocked is to be deposed. What do you say to that?'

'That I have never been deposed. Deprived, yes, owing to a verdict which I still emphatically repudiate; but not deposed.'

'You were free then to write articles and to speak on platforms in the character of a priest in Holy Orders. What harm, what damage, do you consider that this statement about unfrocking was calculated to do to you?'

'The damage, sir? Why, ruin.'

'Ruin, did you say?'

'Yes, sir. I don't think that is too stern a word. Such statements put into wide circulation – because they were inevitably reported everywhere – had the effect of destroying in the end my chances of earning an income by writing and speaking and preaching.'

After this, counsel sitting down, it really did seem as if some damages might be recovered.

But defendant's counsel, rising to cross-examine, began, 'Mr. Alanside, let us get this clear. You have suggested that these spoken words were ruinous to you?'

'I have. And I do.'

'Why exactly? Because they alleged adultery against you?'

'Certainly. Yes.'

'So your contention is that if this allegation of adultery were widely circulated it would be ruinous to you? That is what you say?'

'That is what I say.'

'And yet, Mr. Alanside, for many months after your conviction in the Consistory Court and what amounted to a subsequent conviction in the highest court of the land, you were going out of your way – at the very time these so-called defamatory words were uttered – to keep these convictions before the public by writing in journals of the widest circulation' – counsel rested on these two words – 'and by speaking in halls and cinemas all over the country? In a word, you courted the utmost publicity for the convictions? Is that so?'

'Yes. That is true.'

'Then it would seem that the defendant was only doing in a very small way what you were doing in a very great way.'

'*No.* No, sir. I was dealing in truth; he in lies.'

'Lies? Wherefore lies? He stated, to two witnesses only, so far as we have heard, that you were incapable of keeping the seventh commandment; which is exactly tantamount to stating you had committed adultery. And this statement has been accepted in two courts as the proven truth, and published everywhere as such. Is that not so?'

All that plaintiff could reply to this damning question was, 'I do not accept the convictions as truth.' And he quickly left it to assert, like someone leaping on to a safer place, 'There was also the statement that I was to be unfrocked.'

'Agreed. But do you deny that there were rumours everywhere that you were to be unfrocked?'

'I do not know what rumours were abroad, but if people were saying this, the event has shown that they were telling lies.'

'Not, sir, if they were simply stating what the rumours were. Thank you, Mr. Alanside.'

To lessen the impact of this skilful piece of cross-examination, which seemed to have deflated the whole of the plaintiff's case, his counsel rose to ask two questions in re-examination.

'Mr. Alanside, have you committed adultery at any time?'

'Never.'

'Then what was your purpose in keeping the fact of your conviction steadily before the public by every means open to you?'

'It was my intention to affirm my innocence whenever, wherever, and however possible. I regarded this as my obligation to God, the Church, my family, and myself.'

The best answer, perhaps, to leave in the minds of the jury. Counsel sat down.

When the jury retired they were out only twenty minutes. Returning, they found, in answer to questions posed by the Judge, that the words complained of had indeed been spoken to two witnesses, but that their utterance was not actuated by malice, nor were they likely to have damaged the plaintiff more than his own words and actions had done.

'Thank you, gentlemen,' said the Judge, and bowed to the foreman, hinting that he could sit down.

But the foreman, a staring cadaverous little man, evidently wished, before he sat down, to add something for the benefit of the public and the Press (and possibly of himself, since his high-minded and public-spirited statement would be printed in the nation's newspapers, a pleasant experience). So he apologized quickly, 'Pardon', and said, 'We wish, my lord, to add as a rider that in the unanimous opinion of us all, this was a case which should never have been brought.'

The Judge bowed an acknowledgment of this offering, but made no comment.

And on these findings the court pronounced judgment for the defendant with costs.

It was reported to us that the plaintiff on hearing this judgment walked instantly and in silence out of the court room, saying no word to anyone; not even to his wife who had to follow after him, alone. She found him walking up and down the pavement outside the court entrance, up and down, unaware of the people passing him by, unaware of the traffic roaring or trundling past, unaware, apparently, of anything but the pavement flags beneath his feet.

§

The same evening I brought out of the Casterton streets an evening paper to Julie where she sat with her sewing under our Tudor beams. It announced verdict, rider, and judgment in its stop-press column. She glanced at the report but only pushed the paper contemptuously away and went on with her sewing. 'I never believed in any other result,' she said, watching her needle. 'He should never have brought the case at all. But he had worked up such dreams about it. Oh, why the hell was it necessary for the jury to add that nasty, beastly, self-righteous little rider? Why couldn't they keep quiet? Why wouldn't it have been enough just to bring in a verdict and stop talking? I should have thought that silence would have shown some pity, or at least some regret, at what they were called upon to do. Instead . . .' She reached in her work-basket for her scissors. '. . . Oh, why do people rejoice to stand up and display their beastly self-righteous contempts? Filthy Pharisees.'

'Because it makes them feel superior,' I suggested.

'Just so, and how *dare* they be superior and contemptuous because of something they've probably all done themselves? Once, Richard, it was their fashion to exalt Daddy to the skies; now their only idea seems to be to add their kick where he lies beaten and down.'

'Yes,' I agreed, walking to our bay window and looking sideways at the Cathedral where he had been so famous a figure. 'Wonderful how quickly and completely adulation can be dispersed if the wind swings round.' And I quoted, just as he might have done, who was so ready with his quotations, '"Now lies he there, And none so poor to do him reverence."'

'Except Mummy and me,' she corrected instantly.

'And me.'

'Yes. *Dear* Richard,' she said. 'Always there.'

§

After this defeat he surrendered. On his return to Casterton he announced to me in the over-dramatic vein he affected in these days, 'I've hauled down my flag, Richard. There's nothing to do now but kiss the rod,' and, having said this to wife and daughter, once and twice and again, he spoke no more to any of us about his case or his long fight, or his innocence. He went into a lasting silence. One break in the silence there was, when he suggested 'leaving Casterton, now that he had thrown in the towel', but, drifting from day to day, he did nothing about such a move. And he said no more about it. He and his wife had barely enough to live on, even in their present small house, and could hardly face the cost of a move. Presumably he would stay there till he died.

So deep was his silence that he never told wife, daughter or me how he paid the costs of his slander action. I never asked him lest the answer to my question should give him pain. I have always suspected that Bishop Griffyn had a part in raising the money, but I know nothing.

I do not know what his thoughts were in these days. I remarked how he would go alone to the daily Mass in the Cathedral just as he used to when I first saw him. Or if it was a Saint's day and there was an early service at St. Thomas-sub-Castro he went to that little church because it was so much nearer his home. And in either place he would kneel at the back, making the sign of the cross at all the proper moments and bowing his head low at the Consecration and the Elevation; but never did he communicate. Not even on

Sunday mornings did he leave his pew at the far back to take communion; and this was a mystery that Julie and I would sometimes discuss.

He became a wanderer about the seaward plain that lies around three sides of our city. It was as if, all ambition dead and all desires spent, there was little left for him but to enjoy such pleasures as nature offered to eye and ear. An untiring walker, he would usually go on and on till he reached an arm of the sea that came winding into the Menwode peninsula. The Menwode, to which we have referred more than once, is that prairie-flat part of our county which has the waters of the sea, in creek and channel, on three sides of it. Sparsely wooded with feathery trees, and drained by many a winding rife, its level fields may be tobacco-brown ploughland, or green meads lying against fawny acres of wheat, all ready for harvest. It is not possible to wander far along its lanes without suspecting a freshening of the air and detecting the dank, weedy smell of yet invisible tides. Menwode: no one knows the origin of the name. His favourite goal, because of its shows of sea-water, the Menwode lay across those far-stretching distances of which he had once preached in the Cathedral; and the spire of the Cathedral, as he strolled on, became ever a slighter and remoter thing behind him. Coming home, he would boast, 'I must have walked the best part of eight miles, and I'm hardly tired at all. I was always an athlete.'

In the early November days, which were still bright, he put on a long black overcoat and an old black hat with wide, curving brim, and set off for his long walk through the quiet country places. This shovel hat must have belonged to the days before he became entitled, as canon or archdeacon, to a neat felt Homburg with a rosette on its ribbon. It gave him an old-fashioned appearance in the country lanes to eyes that turned to watch him. The long coat, too, seemed rather old-fashioned and loose and worn, as if his old care for a fine appearance was now lost with all the rest. Unconscious of such eyes, he was glad to be clear of city streets and between green hedges, with the sun offering him good cheer while a chill in the wind told a different tale. The crowding trees along the horizons delighted him, setting domes of colour against one another, russet and orange, copper and yellow green. When the November days became dark and dank he wandered on through an early dusk, tinted brown by red-rust leaves, and spoke to no one much, unless they were children. These he often greeted, and when he returned early because the sun went down after four he would see them paddling home from school through leaves still huddled in the city gutters, and would stand still to encourage or chaff them.

Once, returning on my bicycle, from Solmer Hithe, to which I had been sent with a message from my vicar, I saw him leaning over a meadow gate and considering some behaviour in the grass. I dismounted to share his interest. He was watching with amusement a cock blackbird lifting dead leaves and tossing them aside in his hunt for edible treasure beneath. 'Just watch,' he said as the intelligent bird, having moved the leaf, put his head on one side to 'hear' an appetizing worm in the wet soil below. A dab of his yellow beak and the worm was hauled up like a rope and ingurgitated faster than anyone could say 'Cock Robin'; then his head went to one side again. Now, better than a worm, he dived the beak at a snail and shattered the luckless creature's shell on a convenient stone. 'Well, *their* troubles are over,' said my father-in-law of both worm and snail. 'That was the last of Earth for them.'

When at last the trees were stripped bare, and extra sweepers were provided by the city in this 'leafing time', he said to me once, 'Do you sometimes feel an odd sense of comfort when the last of the leaves are down? I always do'; and I wondered what he meant. Was he thinking, perhaps, of a kinship between the stripped, empty trees and himself who was now, by his final surrender, stripped and emptied of all the old ambitions and desires?

When the days lengthened again, one of his favourite walks was to the ruins of Graving Priory. The choir of Graving Priory is still intact and beautiful and makes a noble parish church for the village, but the rest of the old Benedictine monastery – nave, cloisters, frater and guest house – like the remains of the Cistercian abbey at Selham – are but stones and single arches rising from high grass.

He liked to wander between these stones and recreate in imagination the lost aisles about him again; or to dream of all the history that lay beneath this hummocky turf and the feet of these browsing cows.

Sometimes he would be seen walking along the ribbon of tow-path by the weedy Casterton canal. This narrow track went winding for four or five miles, usually with no one in sight, and nothing to accompany a walker except reflections of blue sky and clouds in the slack water, and trees on the opposite bank. Head drooping or erect, he would go on and on by the water, quite alone, between tall weeds and high straw rushes, ever in search of a wilderness.

If on another afternoon he turned towards the westward country, he must pass our bay window, and we might see him go by in his old-time hat and long open overcoat, with his hands joined behind him and stick or umbrella dangling.

'Where's he off to now, poor darling?' Julie might ask; and I would answer, 'Basingham. It's always Basingham if he turns west.'

Basingham is the oldest village among the Menwode creeks, and at high water, when the estuary beside it brims high above the green mud, it is beautiful, with an expanse of sea before it like a vast wind-ruffled lake. Here he loved to sit under the old Tide Mill of Menwode, 'disused like myself', and watch the dinghies and the wherries, or the small yachts with their red sails, making their way down the long channel to open sea. At high-water he watched the tide washing into the streets and lapping against the barriers of the waterside houses. If it was a Sunday he would stroll into the thousand-year-old church and listen to Evensong. His thoughts wandering too, he looked at the coarse round pillars, ten centuries old, and found a strange healing in the thought (so he once told me) that this day of his presence here would also, quite soon, be a thousand years in the past. Such a thought, he said, made him feel ready for his death, ready to go into the past; and he would find himself remembering, with a sense of release, one old friend or another who had finished his time, borne his sorrows and was dead.

Chapter Seven

FENNINGS

It was now three years since the Lord Chancellor gave Judgment in the Privy Council and Archdeacon Alanside's war was lost, no matter what guerrilla skirmishing he might attempt afterwards. And it was more than a year since he finally gave up the fight and went into a silence whose full meaning no one knew.

A total of three years, and now the astonishing thing.

He received an invitation from the Bishop to the Palace. He sat for an hour with the Bishop, his lordship cooking tea for him, cutting him slabs of bread, and plastering them with butter. The Bishop's doorsteps. This interview over, he came out of the Palace into the Close, his head alight; into the Cloisters where he walked up and down, heart thumping, breath shortening; into the Cathedral where he knelt for a minute; then out of the Close and into Grieve's, Heraldic Stationers, where there was a telephone for public use. Here he rang Julie. There was no telephone in his small home, but we had just installed one at my vicar's request in ours, and were proud of it. I was pleased to say that it was necessary for my journalistic work.

'Julie darling – your father speaking – can you come round this evening after supper? I've a piece of news for you. And bring Richard. Yes, you must bring Richard too; it'll interest him.'

'Oh, what *is* it, Daddy? What is it?'

'No, I won't tell you now, my precious. I want to be able to tell Richard myself. In my own words. I've just come from the Bishop's and haven't yet told your mother. I'm in Grieve's, talking to you.'

'Daddy, is it something rather nice?'

'Yes, I think you could call it that.'

'Oh, I can't wait. Can't you ring us again? Richard'll be back from Evensong in a few minutes.'

'No, let's do it properly. It's an occasion for a little drinking together; a little celebration, as it were. Just for the family.'

'Oh, Daddy, what *is* it? Is it something about Richard?'

'Richard? Dear me, no! It's about his father-in-law.'

'Please, then . . . tell me . . . tell me. At once.'

'Not at all. Possess your souls in patience, both of you; and come round at about half-past eight.'

'Half-past eight. Oh, well, that's only three hours. I suppose I can wait till then.'

'That's a good girl. You wait. And in the meantime God bless you.'

I hastened home that evening because I wanted to complete a Lucilius article. These were still a regular feature of *The New Witness*, and its amiable editor (who, I had once sworn, should never again see offering of mine) hadn't hesitated to tell me that Lucilius had 'added his mite' to the paper's circulation and accordingly the proprietors were going to pay the man a little more. Not much, but some.

I took the extremest pains with these essays, and it was impossible to labour on one after Julie had told me about this stimulating exchange with her father. The labour often drained me sick, so was I glad of an excuse to postpone it? Instead we discussed what the news might be, both of us as excited as he could wish. We certainly didn't glimpse what it was.

Punctually we arrived at Friary Lane and there saw that he had spread the dining-room table for the small celebration. He had gone out into North Street and bought two bottles of a sparkling white burgundy in lieu of the champagne which he couldn't afford. The wine shop had lent him four tall tulip glasses appropriate to this wine. With Natalie's help he had laid out a dish of sandwiches, one of cheese biscuits, and a silver porringer of sweets. He smiled at us mischievously as we came in, nodded pleasantly, and kept his new tidings locked somewhere behind the mischievous eyes.

'Please, Daddy,' Julie protested, sitting down. 'Don't be quite unnecessarily piggish. What is it? Tell us what it is.'

'No, let us fill the glasses first. Natalie, you?'

'Thank you, dear; but tell the poor children. Poor mites.'

I

'Julie, yours? A nice burgundy, this. Richard, that all right for you?'

'Marvellous, sir.'

'Oh, come on, Daddy! This is getting childish. Have you even got around to telling Mummy?'

'Oh, yes, he's told me,' said Mrs. Alanside. 'Of course *I* know.'

'Well, *you* tell us. If he persists in behaving like this.'

'No, he wants to tell you himself. And he can explain it all much better than I can.'

'Well, why doesn't he get on with it? For pity's sake?'

But Mr. Alanside only sipped his wine with a smile playing around his lips. As of one who was enjoying this preamble. 'Have a sandwich, Julie?'

'No, I won't. Not till you come clean and tell us.'

'Well, then, a biscuit with cheese? I spread these specially for you.'

'No.' Snappily.

'A sweet?'

'No.'

'Oh, well, perhaps you've had your dinner and are not hungry?'

'Oh, what does dinner matter? Besides, we don't have dinners. Can't afford them. We have suppers.'

'Like your dear mother and me. How do you like this wine, Richard? Is it any good?'

'I've never known anything about wine, sir, but I know I'm enjoying this.'

'Good. Well, children, have either of you got a guess?'

'What sort of guess could I have?' Julie demanded. 'Has someone left you a fortune?'

'No. There's no one in sight likely to leave me a penny. Richard, any idea?'

'None whatever.'

'Well, I must speak, I suppose. It's —' He halted and I thought tears had sprung to his eyes. 'It's restoration and reinstatement. The Bishop has offered me the incumbency of Fennings. St. Olave-at-Hill, Fennings.'

We did indeed stare, Julie giving a gasp at this wholly un-imagined answer. We were silent for a second, and he repeated, 'It's restoration and reinstatement.'

Julie jumped up and flung her arms around his neck and burst into tears, gulping, 'Daddy! Daddy!'

I could only say feebly, 'This is terrific, sir.'

'Yes, the Bishop had me round this afternoon and offered me the living. I confess I was thunderstruck, but he just said, "Go and think about it and pray about it. Give me your answer when you can. Yours is the first offer." Fennings! It's quite the loveliest little church and the loveliest village in the diocese. I —' But he couldn't go on; Julie's tears were infecting him.

To say 'Fennings' was to throw before my eyes a small flint church in a coronal of old trees under Finching Down. It was about twenty-five miles away, under our long race of heaving downs; about half the width of our county away from Casterton. I knew it well and, sitting here in the Alansides' room, I could see its squat battlemented tower, its short shingled spire, and its roof healed with our local stone on which the salt sea-breezes had delighted to fashion cushions of orange-tinted lichen and moss. The enthusiastic Rector-elect was perhaps exaggerating when he called it 'the loveliest little church in the diocese', but it was beautiful certainly, and lovable.

What had happened? Fennings was a cure of only a few hundred souls but fairly endowed; it was the kind of gentle commission often offered to a priest who had laboured well in the diocese and earned his place of ease. I could only imagine that the Bishop had been watching the life of his late archdeacon, that he had heard of his regular attendances at Mass during the last two years, and that he had been impressed by the silence that followed the slander action. He would know that that unhappy action must have been inaugurated years before it was heard, when the Archdeacon was still angrily rebutting the charge against him, and that when at last it came on, the plaintiff could do nothing but take up again the attitude of a man greatly wronged. Since then only silence. Silence, and apparently prayerful attendances at Mass. I did not doubt that the Bishop believed him guilty, and I could only suppose that with his Christlike understanding he was ready to think of his archdeacon's sin as somewhat less awful than the stoners of this world assessed. ('Neither do I condemn thee. Go and sin no more.') He was ready to hope that an erring brother, getting old now, had purged his guilt. My father-in-law was justified in calling it 'restoration and reinstatement'; but it was not acquittal, it was not annulment of an old verdict; it was forgiveness.

'And you will accept of course, of course?' cried Julie, concluding her embrace with a last congratulatory kiss.

'Oh, *yes*,' Mrs. Alanside pleaded. 'It'll be a bit of an uprooting at our age, but it's a lovely part and the living is not at all a bad one. We shan't be so horribly poor. And it's a nice rectory; we've dined there sometimes when Canon Colwyn was the rector and Daddy was preaching for him. I think I could make it very nice with our furniture and we shall at least have more room to move about in than here.'

'We must all go and look at church and house, all of us together,' declared Mr. Alanside. 'The family. When's your day off, Richard?'

'Thursday, sir.'

'Well then, shall we go next Thursday?'

'Yes, yes,' cried Julie. 'Oh, isn't it splendid? Thank God someone is good and kind in this world.' And I said Yes, I could go.

'Fine! Fine!' he exclaimed. 'Come then, Richard, more wine. Julie, drink up. We're going to be happy at Fennings. I feel I'm going to enjoy some peace there at the last. I shall probably be content to stay where I am, taking my walks along the downs, but your mother must have a small cheap car to run about in. I've always been a walker. Another nice thing is that it won't be too far for you two children to come and see the old people sometimes. I hardly knew where I was when I came away from the Bishop this evening. First I walked in a dream along Chantry Lane but then turned back and went into the Cloisters to think over it all, and at last I just had to go into the Cathedral and say my thank-you. It's only a small charge, of course, but it's restoration in the eyes of the world. It is the end of something.'

§

We went all together. I now had an 11.9 Morris Cowley tourer which I had bought cheaply, second-hand. I called her 'Harriet' because, high and black and severe in outline, she made me think – unjustly, I am sure – of Harriet Martineau. Harriet was a family joke but she served well enough to take us all north-eastward through a pass in the Downs and then along the underhill road that wound about the foothills till we were in sight of Fennings. Very quiet seemed the leafy little village with half the steep down above it and this winding beech-bordered road below.

The old rectory was inevitably disappointing because, many weeks having passed since the late rector died and before the Bishop, doubtless after much thought, offered the living to Mr. Alanside, it was now empty of all but dust and splinters and scatterings of old dead news-sheets and parish magazines. But, even so, Mr. Alanside was happy, wandering from room to room and saying, 'This'll be my study' or 'This'll be the prophet's chamber for Richard when he comes to preach here; Elisha's "little chamber on the wall with a bed and a table and a candlestick" – only Elisha's bed must have room for our Julie too.' Mrs. Alanside was less happy about this old-fashioned house whose every weakness was stressed by the uncurtained brightness, but she agreed, for his comfort, that she could 'make it nice in time'.

No disappointment, nothing but joy, in the little church standing among the trees, its steep roof patterned with apricot rusts by the salt sea-winds. 'A little church under a green hill-side,' said the delighted rector-designate, quoting Archdeacon Manning. Its late incumbent might be gone, but not the faithful women who kept it swept and polished and garnished. Small because the cure was small, its walls probably followed the lines of the old Saxon church that preceded it. The aisled nave with its brief but beautiful arcading was certainly of the early thirteenth century, said Mr. Alanside enthusiastically, as he wandered from old leaden font and old oak chest to the sanctuary with its Sarum altar and its three-light lancet window above. Standing in the chancel and looking at the altar, he said, 'I want nothing more than this. Time was, Richard, when I was ambitious for fame and greatness, but not now. No longer. I just want peace and happiness in a tired old age. And I believe I could make a success of my pastorate here, if only because it'll be fine to have a task to do at last after being so long an idle wanderer.'

We came happily home in the car, all of us loud with plans and hopes and dreams. Julie and I left the parents at their door in Friary Lane, her father still full of good spirits; and we two drove quietly to our own home, more than pleased with the work of the afternoon.

But on the Monday afternoon four days later, I came home from some parish visiting, all prepared with a light jest for the entertainment of Julie, and never was joke more completely lost on the heedless air. As I opened the door she came out of the living-room to meet me and I began, 'It seems years since I've given you a present, beloved, so I've brought you a little box of sweetmeats. Is this good of me? Is this character?' but she only warned in a whisper, 'Hush! Mummy's here.'

'Mummy?'

'Yes. What do you think has happened?' Her hands spread outwards from the sides of her hips in a gesture of despair.

'What do you mean?' I asked, halted there in our narrow passage, and laying the unnoticed sweets on a table. 'What are we talking about?'

'Hush! Mummy's there.' She pointed a finger at the living-room wall. 'She's crying. Daddy has declined the offer of Fennings.'

'*He hasn't!*'

'Yes, oh yes, he has. Come in and hear. But poor Mummy doesn't know what on earth to make of it.'

'What do *we* make of it?'

'How should I know? None of it makes any sense to me. But come in and hear the whole story.'

I went into our small living-room under the oak beams and saw the tiny Mrs. Alanside seated on a chair's edge, her shoulders sunken, her back rounded, and one hand on her lap pressing her handkerchief into a ball.

'Oh, Richard. Has Julie told you? Why has he done this? What are we to do with him?'

'Tell me exactly all that happened.' Julie and I sat down to listen.

'I simply can't understand men. Men and their ridiculous consciences. For years he's been saying how much he wanted something like this to happen, and when something comes along that's better than his largest dreams he has an attack of conscience and turns it down. Tells me he's refusing it.'

'But why . . . *why?*' I besought.

'*I* don't know. He was full of lovely plans all Thursday night and Friday but yesterday he turned a little quiet and strange, and this morning after he'd been to early Mass at the Cathedral he came back to breakfast very late, as if he'd stayed in his place long after the service was over and everyone else had gone. He was praying, I suppose. He's been very silent all day till this afternoon when he comes to me in the kitchen and says, "Natalie, darling, I'm going to refuse the Bishop's offer." Just like that. I stared at him, dumbfounded, and he said, "Yes; it's a final decision. I feel sure I'm doing right." I begged, "No, oh *no!*" but he just lifted a hand' – she copied his action, the lifting of a hand to discourage talk – 'and he turned away from me to the window while he said, "Don't ask me too much about it. Don't worry me about it. It's been a tremendous struggle but my conscience tells me I'm doing right." He said, "I just don't feel I ought to take it on because I'm not really equal to it." Not equal to it. But that's nonsense. He's not yet sixty-four and he's always saying he can walk miles and miles without tiring. I tried to argue with him, but he only said, "No one but me can know if I feel equal to a task; and I just don't. I have been feeling very tired of late. May I please leave it at that? There are some things one can never properly explain." When I sank on to a chair and burst into tears he was very gentle, putting his hand on my shoulder and saying, "I'm so sorry, for your sake, my dear. We could have been happy there, but you'd rather I did what I felt was right, wouldn't you?" Right? How can it be right? Richard, what does it all mean?'

I had no answer and could only stay silent. Julie too. So her mother, more than eager to pour forth her cascade of bewilderment and dismay, was able to continue, not without pleasure, 'I said we'd have to go on being poor, and he said, "No, I've thought of that. I've been thinking of that for hours. I'll do something else; some sort of clerical job that will get us a few more pounds." He said he ought to have done this years ago after he'd stopped earning money from writing and lecturing, but that he'd been too proud. He said he was sorry for this and asked me to forgive him. But where's the sense of it all? If he can do a clerical job, he can do all that's wanted at Fennings. I begged him to reconsider it, but that only made him suddenly angry so that he said, "Please, *please*, don't worry me."'

'Couldn't *we* talk to him?' I asked, in almost my first words.

'I suggested this to him. I said, "You often listen to Richard nowadays," but he only got rather angry again and said, "*Please* don't let anyone come worrying me about this any more." Naturally I went on a bit, and he walked straight to the door saying, "Please, please, *please* don't go on and on about it," almost as if suffering. He said, "I've told you this is final; absolutely final," and he went out of the room. I didn't dare go after him, but I did peep into the cold drawing-room later and there he was, just standing and looking out of the window with his hands behind his back.'

'*Poor* Daddy,' Julie bewailed. As for me, I was useless as a counsellor, because I could not see where he or we had got to in this strange business. I was staring into a deep mist. But Mrs. Alanside answered her daughter, 'I suppose the truth is that, between them all, they broke him. They broke his heart so that he can no longer really face the idea of running a parish, however small, or of any sort of spiritual responsibility. They did something very terrible to him, between them all.'

Thus, even when impatient with him or defeated by him, her

words proclaimed her sure, her everlasting and unarguable belief in his innocence.

§

With the passing of the years I had become a little less blindly assured of his innocence, less ready to swear to it hotly before all men, but I had never allowed myself to look steadily at the alternative. The alternative was too painful; I preferred that my mind should idle, without map or compass, in this low-visibility haze. Perjury, followed by years of open lying; how could one think of it? – no, no; leave it; turn away. And he, for all this last year, had said no word about the Case; nor had any of us mentioned it to him. None of us ever did now.

I am walking along North Street towards the Matthew Wyke Hospital and I ought to be thinking of my visiting duties, but instead I am thinking of this recoil from Fennings. I remember his words, 'My conscience tells me I'm doing right,' and suddenly, as I walk, an idea that supports his innocence rather than his guilt bursts into my mind like a joyous thing. I have to do this sort of thinking alone, as I walk the streets or as I sit silent in our living-room, because I would never dare even to hint to Julie at the possibility of his guilt. She would not listen if I did this; nor would she listen to any whisperings that might stir in her heart. What power has mere reasoning to deflect the loyalty of women to their own?

So walk on alone with it.

Can it be pride, a stubborn pride, that lies behind this startling refusal? Has he resolved to say to the Bishop, 'My lord, I thank you with all my heart, but I can accept no office until that verdict is undone. It is not charity I want, but justice.' My heart leaps in the street as I think this, leaps with delight in an idea that will justify me in gripping tight hold of his innocence again. Already I am believing in it again. I argue, 'Look: if he were guilty what is to stop him from accepting the Bishop's forgiveness and trying happily to do good work again? Nothing to stop him.' And here I wonder, 'Did the Bishop mention the Case to him and speak of guilt and penitence, or did he, in his tenderness, leave that question to lie between a priest, long punished, and his God?'

My mind was so exalted by this sudden idea that I longed to discuss it with someone whose intelligence was colder and tougher than mine, and yet generous and understanding withal. And for me to think like this was to see instantly but one figure: the long figure of Bishop Griffyn with the bristling eyebrows and the deliberately unrevealing eyes behind their thin spectacles; eyes which apparently had no connexion with the talk that came in a torrent from his lips. Bishop Griffyn seated cross-legged with the comfort of cigarettes beside him in his long rectangular room. I was restless to get to him. I could not wait one night. That evening, on my return from the hospital I proudly used my new telephone, and got his voice. 'Dr. Gregory Griffyn speaking.'

'Richard Oliver answering. Can I come and see you, sir? Possibly after supper tonight? It's something I want to ask you about. Something rather important and urgent.'

'Why, yes, my dear boy. It's ages since I've seen you. I thought you were dead, and I was sorry. Emmeline will no doubt provide some coffee; and I – who knows? – I may have a small bottle of Cointreau somewhere. Bringing your dear lady with you?'

'No, sir. No, sir.'

'No; I quite understand. Something hardly suited to the extremely odd arrangement which is a female intelligence – not but what their hearts are better than ours. And their perceptions often acuter. But their talk – all over the place, as a rule. It's very strange; very strange indeed. Come for an exceedingly long jaw. It'll cheer me up. Other people's perplexities are meat and drink to me in my empty senectitude, as you must know by now.'

§

When we were seated in the familiar long room, with the blinds drawn and the coffee and Cointreau on a low table between us, and, as so often before, no light around us except that which came from the leaping fire and his green-shaded reading lamp; and when he had sipped the liqueur and lit himself yet another cigarette, he asked, 'Well, Richard, what is it we have to discuss?'

'It's about my father-in-law.'

He just nodded. Without comment.

'We're all so bewildered by his refusal of the Bishop's offer. He was overjoyed when he first received it; up in the air about it like a boy who's just been told he's won the first prize. He insisted on a celebration that same evening. We all went together to Fennings and he was so happy strolling about the village and the church. Now —'

'Now he has told the Bishop he can't accept it. I know.'

I explained how he had come home from Mass at the Cathedral and announced his decision to his wife, and how, when she asked him 'Why, why?' he could only suggest that he was not equal to it – 'Which is nonsense,' I said, 'because Fennings is almost a sinecure. There must be other reasons, and he practically admitted this because, when she went on protesting, he said, "There are some things one can't ever explain." And when she still went on, he got impatient and begged to be left alone.'

'Yes. And did you know, Richard, that he said to the Bishop, after thanking him, that he no longer wanted to be considered for any living, this or any other?'

I had not heard this. It startled me, but, after thought, I hoped it might support my theory about the pride of an innocent man. I laid this theory before him . . . in hope. Could it perhaps be read as the fine pride of one who had been wronged? 'No new office, please, until that verdict is undone.'

Bishop Griffyn did not nod at this, but neither did he shake his head in unbelief. He gazed in front of him rather than at his questioner, and after a time picked up his liqueur glass and sipped from it. He pressed out his cigarette before it was finished, and felt for another. Having lit this, he leaned back in his deep chair with his elbows on its long arms and his fingers now interlacing, now tapping together. 'I'm afraid that's not my reading of the mystery, Richard. I wish it were. But surely, if you're right, he must have said to the Bishop that he would consider no offer of any kind till his name had been cleared. He said no such thing. He said nothing. Nothing but – very sadly – "Neither this living, my lord, nor any other."'

'It could still be pride,' I submitted, though my heart was emptying of its fine hope.

'Perhaps,' he assented; but without conviction.

So after a silence I asked, 'Well, how do you read it, sir?'

He refilled my glass. 'God forgive me, Richard, if I'm wrong. I have a guess, but it's only a guess.'

'And what is it, sir?'

Leaning back and lacing and unlacing the fingers, he said, 'I don't want to hurt you with it. I know your long devotion to him and, what is more, Richard, I believe it to have been a devotion that was wholly justified. So I don't want —'

'Go on, sir.'

He knocked ash from his cigarette too early. "You must understand that the Bishop finds it very difficult to doubt his guilt, but can any of us be absolutely certain? As near certain as may be, perhaps, but no more. That was one more reason, added to the Bishop's natural love of mercy, which, I suspect, made him go no further than deprivation. I know that when he laid this offer before Alanside he said not one word about the Case. He preferred to assume a penitence, if penitence was necessary – and he gave him his chance. Some of my sterner brethren on the Bench would call this a dangerous lenience and think him soft. But George Casterton is not soft. He is merely wiser than most of us because he has advanced into the brighter lights that are found in sanctity, while most of the rest of us are still in a twilit country outside. Personally, knowing that I'm still definitely in the dusk, I'm always chary of questioning the methods of any obviously sanctified person. I just tell myself, "He's probably right, G.G., so hold your peace." What our George Casterton did was to lay a new chance before an unhappy man, whether he was innocent or whether he was guilty, and to tell him to pray about it.'

Having said this much, Bishop Griffyn did not go on for some time. Resting his arms on the long chair-elbows, he looked at me with a faint, kindly smile as if he wished I would now take up the tale, but I was sad because of the failure of my hope, and I had no comment ready. I said only, 'Well, what then, sir?'

'This is the part I don't like to say to you, Richard. Do you really want the exact truth of my thoughts?'

'Please, sir.'

'Well, then. You have just told me how Alanside came home very late from Communion in the Cathedral yesterday and how your mother-in-law perceived at once what he'd been doing. He'd been praying alone. In a place that probably meant more to him than any other place on earth, because it was where he'd known the love of great congregations, and often, I am sure, managed to get very close to God. "Pray about it," the Bishop had said. "Pray about it" – what?'

Lifting his hands from the elbows of the chair so as to beat his fingers together, my host paused and then enjoined me, 'Fill that glass again. These liqueur glasses are so depressingly small. That's right. Have you ever thought, Richard, that there can be no real Tragedy, as the Greeks understood it, without a sense of God's presence? Nowadays we don't write tragedies of the order of the *Oresteia* and *Hamlet* and *Phèdre* because this sense no longer overshadows us. Most people today are troubled hardly at all by thoughts of a great Presence near or within them. It is no longer near enough to touch them. But nothing will persuade me that Alanside has ever lacked this sense. No, no; I'm sure . . . I *know* . . . that he's carried the burden of it all through this long story. And I suggest that, after his first excited joy at the Bishop's offer, he did what he was told and began to pray about it. And, as you know, Richard, to pray is to light all sorts of lamps in our poor, dim-sighted souls.'

Again he paused; I did not speak; and he resumed, 'Look, Richard: you're a priest now and often the celebrant at the altar. You know now, from *inside*, that all priests find it a dreadful thought – literally dreadful – if they think they are going to consume the Sacred Elements with unclean lips. We cannot do it. Or not at all easily; not without a sickness of the spirit. A sickness that if it's left to worsen and worsen will end in spiritual death. We can preach; we can teach; we can give absolution, knowing that the sacrament is valid, no matter how tarnished or broken the instrument. But we cannot easily consecrate the Elements and partake of both kinds, eating and drinking all that is left after the service is over. Better anything than that, we feel. Especially if we are Catholic-minded like Alanside and believe that under the appearances of bread and wine – in some undefinable manner – Jesus Christ, God and Man, is truly present. Well, say – just say . . .'

But he did not say the thing at once. His heavy eyebrows contracted and pressed down upon his steel glasses as he wondered whether to say things that might wound me. He resolved at last to offer them.

'Just suppose, Richard, that Alanside knew he was guilty – don't you think that when he was alone in the Cathedral, with God seeming near, and all the lamps brightening, he must have seen that before going to Fennings to discharge week after week this awful task he must somehow or other be done with the falsity of posing as an innocent man cruelly wronged? Have you not told me that, even though he goes almost daily to hear his Mass, he seems never to communicate? Doesn't that tell us something? I think he must have felt that if he was to take up this living, it was his duty to uncover the truth to the Bishop and possibly to his wife and Julie too – and perhaps – I don't know – even to do a little something in public because of all the people he'd accused of conspiracy or malice or lies. And I fancy he found that this was something he could never do – *never* – partly for Natalie's sake and still more, I suspect, for Julie's. To admit to the adultery might have been possible, but how admit to years of perjury and hypocrisy and public lying? Don't you think that whenever he contemplated doing this he saw always your Julie? And Natalie. And all the thousands who'd sworn by him, all his brother clergy who'd helped him with their witness and their money, and all those simple people who believed in him still. Richard, was it not largely for Julie's sake – don't you think? – that he'd felt forced from the beginning to deny all the charges? But if he could not do this tremendous thing, and yet felt sure that he ought to – or even only partly sure – well, at least he could refuse to offend God further by something that was looking to him like sacrilege. If I'm right in seeing it like this, then surely it was a good deed, so far as it went. It left him a better man because he'd offered a sacrifice to God. Quite a big one. And it showed that the Bishop's unexpected move, and his "pray about it", had worked their good ... Alanside pronouncing on himself his own sentence of Deprivation. Quite a big step ... and God is patient.'

He had been looking away as he spoke these latter words but now he turned and smiled at me. 'Are you very angry with me for reading the riddle like this?'

'Of course not,' I said, though speaking sadly. 'I suppose it is the truth, really.'

'Perhaps. Only perhaps. One cannot know. Probably no one will ever know.'

Maybe not, but it had seemed the truth. And so gently had it been offered to me that I found, to my joy, that it was doing nothing to impair my love for my father-in-law. My obstinate love for the distinguished archdeacon whom I had first chosen to worship when I saw him kneeling in the Cuthbert Chapel remained; even stronger than before, perhaps, because I found myself thinking passionately, 'I don't care *what* he did. He was always goodness and kindness itself to me.'

'May I ask you something more, sir?'

'That's what I am for, Richard.'

'Have you really thought him guilty from the first?'

'No. But after his Appeal failed, yes. The Lord Chancellor is not a man easily fooled.'

'But, sir, I was there at the first trial, and Sir Gerald Harbon seemed to tear a lot of the evidence to shreds.'

'Some of it. Some of it, yes. But, alas, not all. He made mincemeat of that old chambermaid, whose evidence was probably as inaccurate as it was certainly unscrupulous. She almost certainly heard someone else say, "Don't tell a soul about this", and "Put your hands down or they'll throw you out", but she was determined, oath or not, to fasten them on poor Alanside. Harbon put that dear lady where she'd be no further use. And he partially discredited other witnesses, I thought – reading it here in my *Times*. He did his best, a splendid best, but was it enough?' The bishop's head shook sadly.

'But, sir,' I persisted – my words like some last hopeless strokes by a drowning man, 'the Vicar tells me that after the Appeal you and he and a few others came in again with gifts to help pay the costs, and that in the covering letter which *you* composed you wrote something like, "From a few of us who feel that justice has not been perfectly done." Was that, so to speak, just a kindly lie?'

'Did Trippy tell you that? I wonder if he should have done. No, not quite a lie, though I suppose I hoped to deceive him into thinking we meant more than we did. I was incensed with the Lord Chancellor for marring a scrupulously argued Judgment by that nasty little bit at the end about the appellant's costs. Good God, all that his court had found my poor Alanside guilty of was something that every layman admits when he leaves a case undefended in the Divorce Court. All right: state that he must pay his costs but don't leave the court with a parting sneer at him. God in His heaven, was the Lord Chancellor empty of sins himself? Do any of these pompous judicial gentlemen really suppose we don't know them for what they are: men of like passions with ourselves, who stumble quite often. Their white wigs don't imply the white flower of a blameless life. Look, Richard, a layman taken in adultery suffers nil; a priest – unless he has the strength to admit all – is converted by public obloquy into being a hypocrite for the rest of his life. I don't find that perfect justice. There was a deep goodness in Alanside, whatever his fall and his subsequent weakness, and I suggest that we not only chose to damage that goodness greatly, but that the Church's Law, working in concert with the vast hypocrisies of the world, flung it into the gutter.' He was speaking hotly now; all the old cold balance was set aside; and his eyes, under the bristling brows, no longer veiled the risen fire within. 'Confound it, he looked like being down and out; and he was one of our brothers; in the words the good monks use, he was our brother in Holy Religion.

And, I think, one of the best in his day. No; something seemed to me wrong somewhere; it still does; and I take my comfort from putting my good friend Alanside into a Presence where there is a more perfect justice and a wider charity than anything *this* world affords.'

Chapter Eight

THE SOLUTION?

Well, I suppose that now, at last, Bishop Griffyn had enabled me to accept his reading of all the heavy events in this cloistered story. He had enabled me to do so because of his charitable attitude towards them, which everything in me rose to endorse. In those days of my youth I had to be someone's adoring disciple and since I could now give only a filial but utterly forgiving love to my father-in-law, I gave my spiritual adherence to the witty, apparently cynical, but in fact wholly compassionate Bishop Griffyn. I set about combining in myself, as he did, a cold clear intelligence with the warmest charity. At least, that was the intended pattern.

I have always thought that my father-in-law, after his refusal of Fennings, and his request that no other 'call' be offered him, abandoned, unconsciously perhaps, the will to live. As I look back to those days I seem to see him drifting quietly and not unhappily towards the one Call which he could not refuse and which, indeed, he was very ready to accept. He did, for his wife's sake, seek some clerical employment and, after one or two temporary jobs he found a more permanent one. An old and stately firm of lawyers in Lincoln's Inn Fields, Messrs. Hulme, Brunswick and Barrès, gave him the job of receptionist, to which his manner and appearance were well suited. They suited the firm's distinction, its antiquity, and its fine house which had stood in the Fields before Queen Anne. No one need ask the name of the handsome and courteous old receptionist, but one or two clients had had it whispered to them. He quite liked working the switchboard and occasionally typing letters that were sent down to him. To us he would say, 'I am now a doorkeeper, not exactly in the House of the Lord, but in an honest house of which I need not be ashamed.'

But after two years of this he could not go on with it. He was too tired. To be at Lincoln's Inn by half-past nine he had to leave Casterton at seven every day, and this was proving too much for him, for he was sixty-six now, and an old sixty-six. The firm gave him a liberal present when he said his good-bye. Thereafter some friends came to his help with a small pension. Not even to his wife who, as he well knew, could keep no secret, did he tell how this was managed, so Julie and I have never known; but how could I do other than suspect that Bishop Griffyn and the Bishop of Casterton himself were somewhere in the plot?

§

Our county town is a small medieval city on a tilt of the Downs with a castle and priory ruins that even antedate by a year or two the Norman walls of Casterton's Cathedral; and besides these it has houses, churches, and taverns of much historic interest. In the summer of the year in which Mr. Alanside withdrew into final retirement there was a gathering of the County Archaeological Society in the castle grounds, the purpose of which was to escort new, or old but unlearned, members to all these places of interest. I had been for three years one of the unlearned and had always wanted to go on one of these conducted tours but had never yet done so, the county town being fully thirty-five miles along the Downs from Casterton. This year, however, the gathering fell on my day off, and the day was blue and golden, so I set off in Harriet Martineau, my antique car, to go and learn.

Did I learn on that sunny afternoon something very different from anything I'd come seeking?

Arrived in the bailey of the castle, what was my amazement to see Mr. and Mrs. Prosdick among the assembly of thirty or forty women? And more, to perceive that Mr. Prosdick, fussing busily this way and that, with his usual quick, brief steps, was most obviously the conductor of this sight-seeing tour. I had forgotten, if I had ever known, that he was a member of the Archaeological Society; but I might have guessed that he would be. Mr. Prosdick, in his eager sedulous way, and perhaps in a secretly humble way, remembering his schooling had stopped so soon, collected member-ships of our local culture groups, whether literary societies or debating societies or scientific societies. He was, I need hardly say, a Rotarian. How happy, how proud, he must be today to have been held learned enough to act as our instructor and guide. No wonder he was fussing around, hither, thither, this way and that, and back again.

I went straight to Mrs. Prosdick's side and waited for her to turn and recognize me. She did so at last and shrieked.

'Benjy! Benjy! Oh why doesn't the silly little man hear me? Benjy! Look who's here. It's Mr. Oliver.' Not in six years had either Benjy or Mrs. Prosdick felt equal to calling me by my Christian name. Always it was 'Mr. Oliver'. She could not manage 'Richard' nor he 'Oliver' without a handle.

Mr. Prosdick, hearing from the distance, and perceiving, raised a hand in a somewhat pompous salutation and came with the quick little steps towards me, hand still upraised as if he'd forgotten to bring it down. 'Well! What a surprise! *Mr. Oliver!* What are *you* doing here? You've never been here before.'

'No, but I've been an absentee member for years.'

'Well, better late than never. Excuse me for a moment if I rush off. I'm arranging for parties to split at one point. And it's a job arranging anything; they're all talking so much. Some want to do one thing and some another, so —'

'Yes, you run off. Establish a little discipline.'

He ran off, with another lift of the hand, this time in a temporary farewell; and Mrs. Prosdick explained, 'Of course I've done this tour before but never with Benjy leading it. Had to come and see Hubby do his stuff.'

'I'm sure he'll do it splendidly,' I said, hardly lying, because I knew he'd do it so enthusiastically.

And she put my exact thought into words. 'Oh yes, he always manages this sort of thing marvellously because, you see, he does enjah it so.'

We wandered after him, she reproaching me, 'You men ought to come more often to these meetings. Usually it's just a crowd of women with perhaps one old gentleman toddling along among them. The lectures in Casterton I find most improving. A real intellectual treat. But quite often Benjy's the only man in the audience. As he was today till you came. I always call the Archaeological Society, "Forty women and Benjy".'

It seemed the perfect caption for the picture in front of me. I said, 'Why didn't I know you were both coming? I'd have brought you in Harriet.'

'You'd have done what?'

'Harriet is my car. She's a preposterous old girl and bumpy, but she gets there. She arrives. Can I drive you back?'

'Oh, but we've got return tickets,' she lamented. 'What a pity.'

'That doesn't matter,' I said, knowing my Mr. Prosdick. 'You can get a rebate on them. Mr. Prosdick'll see to that.' And I could well imagine him setting about this satisfying little bit of business.

Mrs. Prosdick said it would be *lovely* to go back in a car on such a lovely evening. And through such lovely country. Most enjah'able.

Benjy now started proceedings. He called out, 'Please,' and again 'Please,' and 'Listen, everybody, PLEASE,' till at last he'd persuaded the hen-yard cackling to stop. 'Ladies and' – turning to me – 'the one gentleman.' For he was a humorist. In theory, at any rate. The women tittered dutifully. 'Ladies and gentle-*man*, come along, please. The museum rooms first. And then we'll climb to the very top of the Keep.'

'Oh, dear!' sighed the stouter ladies. For they were humorists too.

'No, you must all come, ladies. You're all young and vigorous. Like me. This way.'

And with his speedy little steps he led his straggling flock towards the Museum. Never a more satisfied bell-wether. It occurred to me that he ought to have had a bell round his neck.

In the Museum he led us from show-case to show-case, speaking with fervour – and profusely – about Neolithic axeheads, Bronze Age urns, Iron Age potsherds, Roman coins and medieval suits of armour. Here and there hung rubbings from brasses, and on these he was especially strong, and boring.

'Now for the Keep,' he called to his flock. 'Now for the Donjon, ladies.'

'Oh, dear!' sighed the larger ladies again.

'Now, now! We don't want any oh-dears. I'm not allowing any

desertions. You're all much too lazy. This'll take the superfluous flesh off some of you.'

'Gracious me, isn't he *ore*-ful?' Mrs. Prosdick pretended to object. 'Such a rude little man. Joo ever hear the like? And him a minister too! Talking about superfluous flesh. But he's quite right. They all ought to go up. The view up there is, honestly, just too divine.'

So I write it, but actually she had said something more like 'just too divane'. And 'Joo ever hear the lake?'

It was while our bell-wether was leading us towards the towering and surly Keep and calling back, 'This was the way the garrison used to retreat to the Keep from the curtain wall and the barbican, ladies, when they were hard-pressed by the enemy. Now it's me hard-pressing you —' it was while he was doing his comedy turn that I saw the back of a woman whom I thought I recognized. Surely I knew those broad shoulders and the set of that silky black hair. Could one recognize a woman by the back of her shoulders, the back of her hair, and her posture and poise? Was I right in placing around her the rose-tinted dining-room of the Residentiary in the Archdeacon's prosperous days? Lucille Eavry? I would not be sure till I should get to her side and see her face.

'Now then, ladies and gentle-man, here we are. No slacking. You're all coming up after me. You'll find it well worth it. Come heavenwards, please. But mind the stairs. They're not quite what they were after about eight hundred years.' With which his little feet went twinkling up the spiral stairway in the western tower.

All climbed and panted after him, and at the top crowded to the battlements where he was standing.

'Look!' he said.

Since the castle was set on a hill, and the keep on a motte or mound, the view from these battlements was indeed remarkable. Below us were the town's red roofs, reminding me of the 'View of Anvers' by Cézanne. Beyond the feet of the tilted town lay water meadows with the black oxen pasturing there; and through them the sluggish River Ease idled and sparkled in the sunlight, gathering lesser streams to take them to the sea. On either side of this broad river-gap the rounded downs looked like separated hills rather than sisters in a range, and one saw what a fine defensive site this castle had occupied, guarding the approach from the tea. Beyond these hills spread the Weald towards a dim blue shadow-line which was the heaving swell of the North Downs. 'Across far-stretching distances.'

'Isn't it too – too – marvellous?' asked Mrs. Prosdick.

'Absolutely terrific,' I agreed.

And my delight obviously pleased the guide and showman in her because she said, 'Yes, I felt sure you'd enjah it.'

Difficult to get near the possible Lucille since all were crowding towards the various points where Mr. Prosdick was indicating one interest after another, with a joyful flood of geological and strategical erudition. We had to hear a shocking deal about the Upper and Lower Greensand, the Gault, the Chalk, and the Wealden Clay, and about William the Conqueror. I did manage, however, to get near after one stampede and make sure. Yes. Lucille Eavry.

I didn't want to speak with her while the women were still stampeding about; so I waited. Till we should all be walking the streets in some sort of crocodile again. At such times as I saw her face in full it seemed little changed from that evening in the Residentiary, though six years had passed. Her rather large features, matching the wide shoulders, still failed to lessen her soft feminine charm. The feminine softness lay in the round cheeks, the clear skin, and the large, deep, brown eyes.

'Now, ladies, *will* you please listen. If you've all seen enough – and said enough, ha, ha – we'll go to the Priory ruins. Come along. You can still gossip to your heart's content as we go down the hill.'

'Heavens, what a rude old man,' said Mrs. Prosdick. 'Just fancy!'

Streaming out of the bailey we went down a perilous steep street, all cobbles in the middle and bricks at the sides, and called very properly, 'Care Street'. It was our way to the ruins in a riverside field below. Lucille was walking with another woman in front of me. I excused myself from accompanying Mrs. Prosdick and gradually got abreast of Lucille and her friend. She turned to see who was now at her side but did not recognize me.

I spoke. 'Isn't it Mrs. Eavry? We met once. About six years ago.'

Her smile was gracious but still unrecognizing. She looked at my clerical collar which had had no existence six years before.

'Where was it we met?' she asked.

'It was at Archdeacon Alanside's, when they lived in the Residentiary at Casterton. We were both dinner guests.' Even now I said this with pride.

I did not doubt she had started a little at the name of Archdeacon Alanside, but this might have been caused by a recoil from that old scandal or by her consciousness that she had avoided her friends, the Alansides, from the moment the scandal broke. Yet hardly a recoil – she who had spoken so warmly that far-away night on the need for more sexual freedom. Since she did not seem ready with a comment, I provided, 'I was only a humble ordinand then.'

'Oh, yes?' – as if she had yet to remember me at all clearly.

'Bishop Griffyn was there too,' I added, to give her time to gather herself together.

She recovered ease, or assumed it, and said, 'Ah, yes, now I remember it well. It's all coming back. Weren't you Richard . . . Richard . . .?'

'Richard Oliver.'

'This is Mr. Oliver,' she explained to her friend. And to me: 'Alice Deakin, Mr. Oliver; a near neighbour of mine at East Helwood. And where do you work now, Mr. Oliver?'

'I'm still at Casterton. Never left. I'm on the staff of St. Hugh's.' Sounded better than 'curate at St. Hugh's'.

There fell a silence. Why? Not knowing why, I did not like to intrude on it. And she spoke at last. 'It was a terrible business about the Archdeacon, wasn't it?'

'Yes . . .'

'Terrible.' She repeated the word in a dropped voice.

'There are still people who believe he was innocent.'

'I know. I meet them sometimes. Or used to. But it's largely forgotten now.'

'Do *you* think he was?'

Obviously not wishing to answer Yes or No to this, she parried it with a half-smile. 'What do *you* feel?'

'I used to swear he was innocent and wickedly wronged, but I don't know. . . . I'm not so sure now. And *you?*'

Since there was no avoiding an answer, she sighed, 'I suppose he was guilty . . . really.'

'If so, the woman has never appeared from that day to this.'

'No,' she agreed; and waited before adding, 'But why should she?'

'It was an old Cluniac priory, ladies.' Mr. Prosdick in front had turned round to call this out to his ladies, and was now walking backwards down the hill as he instructed them some more. 'Cluniac – though I don't suppose that conveys anything to any of you. Cluny in France was about the most famous of all Benedictine abbeys. It has two thousand daughter abbeys, and this – or rather, these few stones in the fields were one of them. So there you are. Now you know.'

'No one has ever known who the woman was,' I said.

'But naturally. Surely. Wasn't there every reason why she should lie low? I should think so.'

'Oh, well . . . perhaps. . . . Yes, I suppose so. Unless, of course, she was a myth.'

'Do many people think she was a myth?'

'Quite a few. Sentimentalists, if you like.'

'You must see the Alansides sometimes since they still live in Casterton.'

'How did you know that?'

'My dear, I don't live all that far away.' She said this with a laugh. 'Less than fifteen miles.'

As *she* had mentioned this I felt justified in applying a little stab. 'Why is it we've never seen you at the Alansides?'

'How do you know I never see them? Do you often go there?'

'Quite often. The ex-Archdeacon happens to be my father-in-law.'

'*What?* You mean . . . you mean you married Julie? Darling little Julie?'

'I do.'

'Oh yes, I think I heard she married a curate. And it was *you*! Oh, my gracious!' She turned to her companion. 'Alice, this is the husband of one of my very dearest friends.'

I would not accept this definition after her total neglect of Julie, and I felt displeased enough to say, even in the presence of a stranger, 'Julie's often wondered why you've never been near her, or near her father since his disgrace. She imagines you didn't want any more to do with them after that.'

'Oh, *no*!' It was a cry forced from her. 'Oh, *no*! She mustn't think that.'

'What else can she think? It's what she *does* think.'

'Oh, but . . . Mr. Oliver . . . she —'

'Come along, ladies. This way. I have your tickets for the ruins. No more gossiping now. Come closer if you want to hear all I can tell you.'

We went massing near to him as he led us under a railway arch towards fields of rich and heavy green turf.

'Believe it or not ladies, this railway runs right over the site of the magnificent priory church which was even bigger than your great mother church at Casterton. Now it's only a few stones. Railway obliterates sanctuary, choir, nave, chapter house and cloisters. And if that isn't a good picture of our modern civilization, I don't know what is. Keep with me now.'

'She must never think that, Mr. Oliver.' Lucille had run to keep up with me and was panting. Her friend, Alice, was left behind like someone of small importance in a sudden emergency. 'Tell her you met me – *do* – and say I said it wasn't that. It was never that. I loved Julie.'

'Why not come and tell her yourself?' I said with a formal laugh. 'She used to love you.'

'Does Natalie . . . does Mrs. Alanside think that too?'

'Certainly.'

'Oh, dear. Oh, no. They mustn't think that. Neither of them must think that. Ever.'

'This, ladies, was the frater or refectory and that yonder the

calefactory or warming house.' We were among fragments of flint-
and-chalk walls, thickly built and ivy-curtained, some of them with
little trees sprouting from their tops. 'There's not much left of 'em,
is there? So just use your imaginations, please. Thank you.'

'Tell her. Tell her, won't you? And Natalie too. I wouldn't have
either of them think I — Oh, *no*!'

'And now come along to the Rere Dorter. Follow me please.
Don't get tired. There's an awful lot to see and learn yet.'

'Whose daughter?' One of the ladies being humorous.

'The dormitory, dear lady. Nobody's daughter. No daughters
or mums or wives were allowed here. The good monks wanted
peace. And occasionally a little silence.'

'*Benjy!*' Mrs. Prosdick had caught up with me. 'Oh, he *is* a rudy!
He really shouldn't! He didn't ought to say such things, really,
I don't think. Joo think they'll mind, Mr. Oliver?'

'No. That's all right.' I had hardly heard her. 'They're loving
it.'

They were all looking at ruined walls with their drooping ivy
or sprouting trees; I was seeing none of these things. I was not
even seeing the marsh-green meadow from which these islanded
ruins rose like dolmens and menhirs, for I was staring with my
mind's eye at a sudden monumental Perhaps. Suddenly at that
poignant 'Oh, *no*!' the suspicion had stood before me. An astonishing and quite unforeseen suspicion. And even as it had arisen
there had come from her those careless, distraught words, 'Neither
of them must think that.' Why 'neither'? Were there not *three*
Alansides? Why not 'none of them must think it?' Why had she
not said, 'Oh, does the Archdeacon think this too? Tell him he
mustn't. Ever. Did the guilty always make one mistake?'

This fine and well-dressed woman at my side – was it she who
had lain with him? If so, what had she felt when I said so innocently,
walking down the hill, 'No one has ever known who the woman
was. Many think she was a myth.'

Not a myth but here at my side?

Was it possible that she, like so many other women, had given
her worship to the handsome Archdeacon and that, after a time, it

had become clear that she was available to him – at a time when Natalie, his wife, as old as he and somewhat estranged, was no longer there for his need?

'Could be; could be,' I was thinking as we followed after our guide to a long stretch of leaning walls, all rubble and flint and ashlar.

Who may not fall? And after a fall how could she ever say a word to betray him?

'Look, Mr. Oliver, I – you must explain to Julie that I have been on her dear father's side all the time – tell her that – all the time, all the time – and that it was only embarrassment that kept me away from them all. I was cowardly perhaps, but I couldn't face the awful discomfort of meeting them and talking to them when the whole world was talking of nothing but his disgrace. Can you possibly understand this?'

'Indeed I can. I felt exactly like that myself at first.'

'It's like the nervousness you feel when you're introduced to someone hideously maimed. Oh, you do understand, don't you?'

Her words sounded so true that now I was wondering whether my suspicion was wrong. 'I felt like that myself at first and kept away for some time like you. But *now*! Why not come and see Julie now? You're so close. Only fifteen miles away. Or I have a shocking old car and I could bring Julie to you?'

'No! Oh, no! I couldn't face any of them after I've been so cowardly. I should feel so ashamed. Women are like that, Mr. Oliver. We are cowards. I go anywhere to avoid feeling shame. Do you really understand?'

'Yes. I'm a bit like that too.' But this second excuse, ringing less true than the first, sent me back to my suspicion.

Could be. Could be.

'Now come along, ladies, to what was the Infirmary Chapel. That really is something to see. They've only lately excavated it. Follow me like good children. That high mound over there to the east is almost certainly where the Calvary stood.'

She was at my side, and so was Mrs. Prosdick as our enthusiastic showman discoursed on the stones of the Infirmary Chapel, raising from these tilted fragments in the grass the great pile as it had once been, with its chancel, nave, and apsidal chapels on either side.

'And with that, ladies and gentle-man, we have just about finished here. Thomas Cromwell didn't leave too much for us to see, and the excellent citizens purloined most of the rest for their own cottages. Come and we'll visit some of the old churches.'

But I walked out of that meadow thinking of other things. With Lucille Eavry on one side of me and Mrs. Prosdick on the other I was thinking that Bishop Griffyn's assessment of the affair was probably near enough, and that this Lucille was perhaps the woman – just perhaps. This is something I have never said, and never shall say to Julie. Most of the world has forgotten the Archdeacon Alanside story in these days, forty years on, and I think Julie and I pretend to have forgotten it too. But there are still some, growing old now, and not all of them the unwise, who, when I offer these thoughts in their hearing, shake their heads and will have none of them.

'No one will ever know the real truth,' I thought that day in the priory meadow; and in fact, as you shall hear, one man only has ever learned it, and he was forbidden to speak.

Chapter Nine

THE BEDCHAMBER

One day in the early spring of the following year when, after weeks of extended and inexcusable cold, there came at last, at last, a sudden warmth in the sun's rays and a smell of daffodils in the city's air, I came home from an afternoon of merry visiting (all of us exulting in this break of spring) and Julie met me at the door to say, 'Daddy's very ill. I'm afraid it's serious.'

'Why . . . what . . .?' I stammered.

'He got up this morning to go to his early Mass but felt so ill that he went staggering back to bed. Mummy says he could hardly crawl up the stairs. I raced round to see him. He made light of it and smiled and joked but' – she shook her head – 'he's very ill.'

'Did they get the doctor?'

'Oh, yes, but like all doctors he was non-committal to both of them. I wish *you'd* talk to the man. He might tell the truth to you.'

'Or to you.'

'No, not to me. He's very young, and what young man takes women seriously? He'd be much more impressed by you, a little parson and all.'

We went at once to Friary Lane. The little red house facing the park frightened us as we approached. And rang.

Mrs. Alanside, a woman without insight into herself, did not perceive that her only relief, her only pleasure, in this time of distress was to make the most of the alarm. 'Better? No. Worse if anything. Come in. I don't like the look of him at all.'

'He's still in bed?' I asked foolishly.

'Good gracious, yes,' she snapped irritably, annoyed because I had sounded insufficiently impressed by the seriousness of it all. 'He's very ill. Every movement seems to leave him breathless. I shall never forget trying to get him upstairs. He had to pause at every step. I don't like it at all.'

'What exactly does the doctor say?'

'Nothing. Do they ever say anything? He said it was heart trouble, of course; and he said something about not knowing whether it was functional or organic, and if you can tell me what that means you're cleverer than I am.'

I didn't feel any cleverer about this, and she continued, 'I suppose it means something, but I don't know what. He did say there was no *immediate* danger but that Edwyn must stay quiet in bed and be waited on hand and foot.'

'Does it mean getting a nurse?'

'Not yet. I explained we weren't rich, and he said he thought I could manage.'

'I'll come and help,' Julie promised. 'Every day.'

'So will I, whenever I can,' I added.

Mrs. Alanside being overwrought, the tears rose easily into her eyes. 'You're good children,' she said. 'I think I'm lucky in you both. Come up and see him.'

She led the way up and opened his door. 'Julie and Richard, darling.'

'Ah, good!' came his welcome in a weak but would-be merry voice. 'Now isn't that pleasant? Come in. Sit you down. I don't think there's anything much to worry about. I feel rather a fraud, lying here. It's just that they won't let me move. Got to keep still. An extremely tedious pastime.'

But there *was* something to worry about – in his appearance at least. Possibly the sparse white hairs, disordered by the pillow, and the open pyjama jacket, showing a pleated throat and a white-haired chest, made him look older and frailer to me than ever before. His eyes were red-rimmed and watering as if the cold airs of this temporal world were already chilling them. His cheek-bones, protruding, shadowed the hollows beneath. The lips were now so thin as to seem hardly lips at all. And yet . . . I thought that his face, shrunken like this, was magnificent. With the fine brow, the firm nose, the sunken cheeks and the sad, kind, thoughtful eyes it was like a sculpture of St. Jean Baptiste Vianney, the Curé d'Ars, whose hollowed ascetic face used to gaze down at me from the mantelpiece in my hostel room. So inescapable is the impress of a man's calling that this one lying here, whatever his failure or his recent unworthiness, was a perfect study for a priest.

He joked with us, playing with Julie's hand which he had kept in his. 'This is spring. Spring at last and I intend to get well and enjoy it. It's dull, lying here. Nothing to do but listen for the next cart to go by.'

'Julie's coming heaps of times to see you,' I said.

'Indeed she is,' said Julie.

'Now you mustn't go putting yourselves out. And I mustn't exaggerate. It's not so bad. I listen to the children playing in the park. And the bells – oh, my dears, I have lived thirty years and more in Casterton and never realized till now how many they are. First the old deep Hour Bell bashes out ten o'clock from the Cathedral, and then all eight bells in the belfry get going, and immediately all the little daughter churches start competing with Mother, opening up with their perky little bells. You need to be lying in bed, rather bored, to hear it properly. I can distinguish the bells of the different little churches after a time. St. Thomas-sub-Castro's is a blithe little fellow – impudent, you might say; the Good Shepherd's is cracked; and Father Medwith's – as dear old Gregory Griffyn calls him – is suitably stern and grim and Protestant – slow, solemn, not given to gaiety at all. Father Medwith over again. I try to catch your St. Hugh's, Richard, but it's a bit too far away. Julie darling, if you do come sometimes, you must do what you can to help your mother. She's being wonderful, as always.'

'You bet I will, Daddy.'

'And me too, sometimes,' I suggested.

'Thank you so much, both of you. I don't think it'll be for long. I feel all right when I lie still.'

And there he lay in this small room crowded with old furnishings from the Residentiary. His bed, a Sheraton bed, was large and wide, with graceful slim posts that supported above him a baldaquin flounced with rose-coloured brocaded silk. A gathered curtain formed the bed-head behind the pillows, and looped curtains hung on either side of them. The valance below matched the flounce above, and a rose-silken coverlet chimed with all these hangings. The chair for visitors at the bed's side was an upholstered Chippendale, its seat, back and arms covered with a flowered silk. And Natalie's dressing-table in the window was an elegant thing, a satinwood table-desk with slim reeded legs and an Italian Empire toilet-mirror standing above its sweeping curve of small drawers.

So much old splendour crowded into a little room.

It was all part of the same irony that Natalie had propped him up with two faded gold cushions from the little-used drawing-room downstairs.

When we had left him in his handsome bed and were out in the last of the evening sunlight Julie said she was frightened because he was so changed, and begged me to 'get on to the doctor at once'. I telephoned to him as soon as we were home and he answered most heartily as if no one was ill and I had suggested a game of draughts. 'By all means, old chap; come round this evening after dinner. It'll be good to see you. How's your good lady? And how's business going with you? Customers coming in well?'

'Not bad,' I muttered gruffly, for his tone annoyed me; I was jealous for the sufferings of my father-in-law, and jealous for the honour of our alarm.

'One of these days *I* hope to do good business with you, padre, but just now I'm far too busy making a living.'

'I see. Well, that'll be fine when the time comes. In the meantime, about my father-in-law . . .?'

Dr. Bob Nethersole was a young man who had entered into his present inheritance when his senior partner, old Dr. Bathwick, retired at seventy. Very tall, with much fair hair and a boyish face, he looked to be in his twenties rather than his thirties; and it was perhaps a consciousness of this unsuitably youthful appearance which caused him to use, whenever he could, the longest, heaviest, and most esoteric words in his trade. It was youth too, perhaps, which suggested to him that the major constituent of a bedside manner should be a dominant jollity. When I sought him out that night, in his house in Little Rome, he greeted me, 'Come in, sir!

K

Take a pew. Here by the fire. Or perhaps in your case I should say, Take a clergy stall. Smoke? No. Sensible man. I will now damage my ageing heart and lungs by smoking the cheapest of gaspers.' Having lit the cigarette, he sank into the chair opposite me, leaned back in it, and asked, 'Well now, what can I do for you, Reverend Sir?'

Still unamused, I said that Julie was shocked by her father's appearance, and would he care to tell us rather more than he had told his patient. We could be trusted.

He took the cigarette from his lips, pursed them forward, replaced the cigarette, and shrugged. 'The whole question, my dear sir,' he answered, and the desire to appear learned glistened in his words, 'is whether the trouble is functional or organic.'

'So I understand,' I said, though in truth I did not.

'If it's merely functional there is no need to worry unduly. It's serious at the moment but it's unlikely to proceed to a fatal termination.'

'You mean he won't die?' I said, unconsciously translating the pompous sentence into time-saving English.

I don't think he thought my version an improvement. But he nodded in agreement that it did convey his meaning.

'And what,' I asked 'if it's organic?'

'If the trouble's organic we must accept that there's some disease or lesion in the organ itself.'

This time I understood well. It was clear to me that organic trouble meant trouble in the organ. 'And what then, doctor? Is the danger great?'

'Yes. I'm afraid so.'

'*Very* great?'

'Not absolutely necessarily, but more often than not, it leads to heart-failure and —'

'Death?'

A shrug. 'Heart-failure is almost synonymous with death.'

'And which condition do you really fear?'

'Well to be frank with you, there are certain cardiac arrhythmias —'

'And they are?'

'Cardiac arrhythmias?' He seemed surprised that I shouldn't know. 'They are irregularities in the heart's rhythm.'

Well, why the hell, I thought irritably, couldn't you say so at the beginning instead of just exhibiting to a layman your professional learning? But he was not to be turned from these displays. He went on to say that cardiac arrythmias might be a transient condition in which case they would pass – (Thank you, doctor. That much I grasped) – or they might be due to some disease in which case he feared an onset of auricular fibrillation. We dealt with auricular fibrillation. It was, he explained, a kind of mutiny and anarchy among the fibres of the heart, all of them going their own way and living their own lives instead of co-operating as a disciplined regiment. Sometimes the mutiny could be arrested, but not often . . . and then . . .

'The end?'

'Probably. Heart-failure supervenes and we must await the worst.'

A great heaviness sank my heart as I perceived that this was what he really feared. I lost sight of him sitting there, and of his comfortable study around him, for I was seeing the great Archdeacon Alanside coming towards me in the Cloisters as I read my Hebrew and inviting me – first of all the dignitaries to do so – into his handsome home; I saw him coming to my meagre hostel room and lifting me out of a despair; I saw him splendid in our Cathedral pulpit; and I remembered him rising courageously in our Priest Vicars' Hall after a verdict that laid his life in ruin. Then I thought of him lying in that wide and elegant bed, with its curtains of faded damask framing him like a memory of lost greatness.

'But, doctor, my father-in-law is not really old?'

'He's coming up to his three-score-years-and-ten, and "the days of our age . . ." but I needn't teach the Bible to you.'

I was now so irritated by his exhibitionism and by his easy readiness, in the brutality of his youth, to write off, almost humorously, the life of someone I loved that I felt driven to batter him down with some heavy esoteric knowledge of my own. 'That psalm, number ninety,' I said, 'is ascribed to Moses but if he really wrote it he went badly astray because according to Deuteronomy he lived to be a hundred and twenty, and even at a hundred and twenty, so the last chapter of Deuteronomy tells us, his eye was not dim nor his natural force abated. Personally, of course, I think the psalm is more properly attributed to the Babylonian exile, much later. Even so, the Exile was in the sixth century B.C. and surely a man's prospect of life has increased a little in two thousand four hundred years.' This, I thought, would be enough for him to be going on with.

He stared. Then offered, 'For some, yes. But we all differ. Every man is a law unto himself.'

'All right,' I said, coming irritably to the main business. 'If it's as bad as I can see you think it is, what do we do?'

'All we can do is to keep him at rest and as free as possible from distress or worry. Sure I can't persuade you to a cigarette? No? Well, another for me, I think.'

'In other words, it's simply a matter of making his passage to death as slow and easy as possible.'

'Yes. That's about it.' He lit the cigarette and threw the match into the fire.

And I said, 'Doctor, I know my father-in-law well and, so far as I have any right to speak, I want to ask you, when you feel sure of the truth, to tell it to him. After all, he is a priest and' – here I turned my eyes away – 'a devoted one. He believes in the Church's Last Rites.'

At these words he showed a sudden sharp interest. Now *I* sat there as the expert, he as the ignorant inquirer.

'But Mr. Alanside is not a Catholic?'

'He certainly is. An *Anglo*-Catholic.'

'I'm afraid I'm not up in these distinctions. What are these Last Rites, for an – "Anglo-Catholic", did you call him?'

'Penance. Or "Confession", if you prefer it. Absolution. And the Last Sacrament . . . which we call the Viaticum.'

'Viaticum?'

'Yes. Provision for the journey.'

'Oh . . . oh, I see. . . .' A statement expressing more of surprise than of illuminated sight.

And I regret that, to surprise him further, I added, 'There is also Extreme Unction, but I don't think he would go so far as to want that.'

'*Unction?* Good Lord! I thought all that sort of thing was out-dated ages ago.'

'Not for one or two. One or two still hold it to be a sacrament of the Church, though less certainly of Dominical institution than the others.'

He no more understood what I was talking about than I had understood some of his ponderous words.

But I was ashamed that, even in the midst of a deep anxiety for a dear friend, I should have felt pleasure in exhibiting a professional learning, just as he had done; but there the small pleasure undoubtedly had been. My better motive, however, on which I now seized as a life-belt from this egotism, was something larger and very different. 'So I beg you, doctor,' I said, 'to let him know when you think the end is coming near. He is a priest. And the Church was the love of his life.

Chapter Ten

THE TRUTH IS LEARNED
BY ONE ALONE

My father-in-law's decline was slow at first, and there were times when we dared to hope; but with the warm summer there came, instead of new strength, a rapid weakening. He no longer sat up, propped against many pillows or against the gold cushions from downstairs, but lay supine with only his face moving to look at Natalie, at Julie, or at the ceiling, while his wasted fingers trifled with one another or picked at the top of the sheet. Always in the daylight Natalie or Julie sat in the flowered-silk Chippendale chair; or they were both there, one on either side of the great bed. They read newspapers to him, and he lay listening; or they read to themselves, giving him only the quiet comfort of their presence.

When possible, I was there, and the family was complete. Then when all of us were silent, I would notice how he turned his eyes to look at Natalie's bent head or at Julie's, and I wondered, Was he asking himself if he ought to tell them the truth before he died? Or was he assuring himself that, even though it meant damnation to maintain the long lie and to carry it out of life with him, well, then, he must be damned rather than hurt them. And rather than lose, at the end of all, their lifelong trust.

The days passed, and the eyes and the bones of his face told of death; and he said no word to any of us. And I was now worrying lest the doctor should fail to do what I had asked.

So much for the daylight. There was a strange thing about the night. Natalie, in the small hours, hearing his cough or imagining his voice, would come towards his closed door and see through the chinks that his room was full of light. She would go in and say, 'Do you want anything, darling?' And he would reply, 'No, no; it's just that I'm not sleeping. You go and sleep, dear. You need all the sleep you can get.' This happened so often that at last she perceived the truth: he had become afraid of the dark and its loneliness. Having learned this, she often, if the chinks showed the light, only stayed outside his door and listened awhile, then returned to her bed rather than let him think she had discerned his fear.

All this she told us, and I wondered if in those long, wakeful hours, when darkness seemed too like death, and he put on the bright light, he was pondering on what he ought to do. I remembered Bishop Griffyn's words, 'Have you ever thought, Richard, that there can be no real tragedy without a sense of God's presence? And I can't believe that Alanside has ever lacked that sense.'

That Bishop Griffyn was right in this I was certain; and if he was also right in thinking that Alanside's first conciliation of that Presence had been his refusal of Fennings, then surely the second and last conciliation was what happened now.

One evening when it was clear to us all, and not least to him, that the end was approaching, Julie sat in the Chippendale chair and often looking at his face because he was so silent, his eyes on the ceiling, his fingers pulling his chin or pinching his lower lip like a man given over to thought. When at about seven o'clock she rose to go, she laid a hand on the coverlet beside him to pat it in a show of merry farewell.

He picked up the hand. 'Going?'

'I must, Daddy darling. I'll come again in the morning. And even this evening perhaps. Just now I must go and feed Richard.'

But he kept her hand and in a voice disturbed by uneasy breathing said, 'Julie . . . send your Richard to me . . . will you do this?'

'Of course I will, dearest. Tonight?'

'Not if it's any trouble. Tomorrow perhaps. Not if he's busy tonight. But it would only be for a minute. I'm just going to ask him to take a message for me. Soon. Fairly soon. That's all.' And he squeezed her hand as if to comfort her and tell her not to worry; it was nothing very important.

'I'm sure he'll come and see you tonight. I think he was coming in any case.'

I went at once that night because the summons was strange. Julie came with me but I went up to his room alone, none of us knowing what this summons might mean. The women remained in the dining-room below, both a little frightened and silent.

He smiled and tried to lift a hand in greeting when I entered the brightly lit room. 'Hallo, Richard. Good of you to come. But this is sick-visiting outside your parish. Hope old Trippy won't mind. I shan't keep you long, I promise, but sit down for a minute. I find talking rather difficult.'

I sat on the Chippendale chair and lied. 'You're looking better, I think.'

'No, not better. But I won't keep you a minute. Richard, I had a talk with the doctor this morning. He's not a bad boy; not at all a bad boy. He was frank with me. I asked him to tell me the worst. I'd have liked to quote to him, "Let me know the number of my days that I may be certified how long I have to live," but I don't think it'd have been a success with him. I fear the dear chap doesn't know his Bible as you and I do. Of course he tried to leave me with some hope, as they always do, but he did manage to say – trying to smile, God bless him – that if I had any arrangements to make, it was always as well to have them over and done with. It ended any worry, he said, and worry was the one thing that did no good to a heart like mine. That was the way he put it, but I saw what he really meant. The party-wall between us and death, Richard, is never very solid at any time, and for me just now it's – well, it's about as thin as it can get.' The next words he covered with a smile. 'It's getting extremely diaphonous, I assure you, but I suppose that's a good thing. How utterly futile and fatuous this flimsy wall makes all our ambitions appear – yes, and all our shames too. And yet we go on hugging both of them right up to the end. Well. . . .' A halt; and I detected his diffidence about coming at the real business. He was talking – talking as he had been used to do in pulpit or confessional rather than broach a difficult matter. 'Well . . . my arrangements for this world are in pretty good order – there is all too little to arrange! – so' – here the smile again – 'it's rather a question of arrangements for the next. This is something you'll understand. I've been lying here thinking I'd like old Gregory Griffyn to hear my confession and be my last director. He was wonderful to us at one time – oh, but you knew all about it, didn't you? You did the collecting; I had forgotten that. You realize, don't you, that there's no man with a more unsparing tongue or a more generous heart than old Gregory?'

I said how well I knew this and, to help him, told how often I had gone seeking illumination or good advice from that clear source.

'Exactly!' he exclaimed, as if pleased to hear that I had often gone the way he proposed to go. 'I knew you would understand. I didn't want to send Natalie or Julie with a kind of urgent message because I thought it might frighten them, but I was sure you'd see that I'd want to make my confession while I was still in good order, to do it properly.'

I thought, and I think still, that he was trying to make this desire for confession and absolution seem quite normal and natural to me. If this disclosure of the truth at last to his chosen priest was the second and final step in his reconciliation with God, well and good; but there was no obligation in it to let *me*, or the family, suspect what the truth might be.

I just nodded, to show that my understanding was what he considered it.

'Yes,' he said, 'I've often thought that when the time came I'd choose old Gregory to make my confession to. So would you perhaps go and ask him to come to me. When he's not too busy.'

'Of course I will. I can go now when he's sure to be at home.'

'Explain to him what I want him for – and would you very much mind coming back and telling me when he's likely to come? So that I can lie here and get myself prepared.'

'You mean you'd like him to come soon? Tonight?'

'Yes, tonight perhaps. But not if it's any difficulty. Tomorrow would do.'

But he seemed to hope he'd come quickly, for he repeated with a laugh, 'In case he's coming tonight, I'll be getting myself ready. And *that's* going to take an hour or two! It's such a long time since I made a confession. Dear, dear. I've neglected my duties sadly of late. Do you know, I've even had to think, lying here, how the

Confiteor went. Give me that book, Richard. . . . And a pencil, perhaps.'

His eyes had swung to a small pile of devotional manuals on the bedside table. One was a Book of Common Prayer, another a manual of meditations, *Come Ye Apart*; the largest, bound in soft black leather, lay aslant on the others, as if lately looked at; it was that famous old compilation, *Pastor in Parochia*, which had been his *vade mecum* in the days of his ministry.

'This?' I asked.

'Yes. A real old friend, that one.'

I handed it to him – it was broken-backed from much use – and I left him labouring with his long, weak fingers to open its pages.

I knew the book well, having often picked it up and glanced through it. I knew that on the fly-leaf was written in Natalie's large hand, 'Edwyn J. Alanside. From his loving wife, on his ordination as priest, Advent 1884'; and I remembered that on the first page of all, after turning the fly-leaf, was a prayer to be said by a pastor when he was coming towards a home to visit the sick or the dying; an old prayer from the Sacramentary of Leo the Great. '*Exaudi nos, Domine sancte, Pater Omnipotens . . . ut quorum adimus habitacula, Tu in eorum Tibi cordibus facias mansionem.* . . . Hear us, holy Lord, Father Omnipotent . . . that into whosesoever homes we enter, Thou in their hearts mayest make a mansion for Thyself.'

On the table was a pencil, which I handed to him. He asked for no paper, but the book had several ruled pages at the end for pencilled notes.

'Thanks, Richard,' he said, though his thoughts had gone far from me now, and were with the pencil in his hand. I went softly, and unobserved, from the room.

Natalie and Julie were still sitting silently in the dining-room when I returned to them. Like others who have become poor Mr. and Mrs. Alanside always used this small dining-room as their living-room leaving the drawing-room with all its fine furnishings of yesterday as a state room seldom visited.

'What is it? What is it?' Natalie asked anxiously, and Julie's eyes were not less curious.

I told them exactly. Nothing less was possible. They must be ready to receive the Bishop.

Natalie was frightened. And with her mouth trembling towards tears and her head shaking in a despair, she said, 'He knows he's dying. That shows he knows. But there! He's been saying so for days past and being so brave about it, just smiling. It's only now he's asking for a priest. . . . Oh, *Julie!* . . . When will the Bishop come, Richard?'

'I'll go to him at once. I'm pretty sure he'll come tonight.'

'Thank you, Richard. Aren't we glad we've got your Richard, Julie? He understands all this sort of business so well. Come, Julie, we'll go and sit with Edwyn.'

I told her he wanted to be alone for a little in case the Bishop came tonight. To prepare himself.

'Oh, I see,' she said. 'Yes. Yes, of course. I understand. But what can the poor dear man find to confess? He never does anything really wrong.'

'The better a man is,' I reminded her for her comfort, 'the more he usually finds to confess. That's what we're always taught in our pastoral theology.'

'Yes, I've heard that said before. But I can never see the sense of it.'

And I thought, 'No, dear lady, you are good and loyal, but it'd need a far clearer spiritual sight than yours to see the truth of it.' Aloud I quoted for her, 'The sinner falleth seven times a day, the just man seventy times seven.' And Julie said, 'I think I can understand that. I understand what Richard means.'

'*I* don't,' Natalie persisted irritably. 'It seems nonsense to me.' But probably she was really thinking of other things.

It was no distance from Friary Lane to Bishop Griffyn's house in The Pallant. Emmeline Harvie answered my knock and led me to his study. I found him there in one of the long deep chairs in that long narrow room, smoking perhaps his fortieth cigarette. When Emmeline had shut the door on us, and I had delivered my message he instantly crushed out the cigarette and rose. 'Thank you, Richard. I'd better come at once. I imagine that with a heart in his state anything may happen at any time. Yes, best come now.'

'I don't think you need hurry, sir. He said something about needing a little time to prepare.'

His face remained expressionless. The same thought must have been in both our minds as we spoke together, and each must have known it was there, but neither showed it to the other. He said only 'Yes, well, he'll have had time enough if I follow soon after you. What is certain, Richard, is that when one resolves on a thing like this one generally wants to do it quickly. What is the time now? Nearly nine. Tell him I'll be round soon after nine. And ask him if he'd like me to come and celebrate the Holy Communion for him in the morning. If so, you and Julie will probably like to be there. With Natalie. Can you wait with them tonight till I know if this is what he would wish?'

I said, Yes; we would wait with Natalie.

I returned to Friary Lane and found them both seated where I had left them, Julie with her hands joined on her lap and gazing before her into nothing, Natalie turning the rings on her third finger, large diamond engagement ring and small wedding ring, round and round and round. When I said that the Bishop would arrive soon Natalie said 'I wonder if he'd like some coffee when it's over. Or tea. Anyhow I'll go and put the kettle on.' And Julie said, 'Don't worry, Mummy. I'll go and do it.'

Which she did, and returned. I sat with them. And, more than half believing that my father-in-law must be suffering up there because of a dark truth he must unveil to priest and friend, I found myself praying again and again for him in my chair, while pretending to turn the pages of a torn old magazine. I felt my long love for him pouring up towards him where he lay alone in that bed. 'God, give him strength. Be close to him and support him.' I turned the pages of the magazine, mostly occupied by beautiful girls, and prayed at intervals between page and page, 'Oh God, help him. . . . Strengthen him. . . . Let it not hurt too much. . . . Help him. . . .'

And so on.

The bell. I went and opened the front door. The Book of Common Prayer orders that a priest on coming into a sick person's house shall say, 'Peace be to this house and to all that dwell in it.'

Bishop Griffyn, on my opening to him, obeyed this injunction but, perhaps out of shyness in my presence, spoke the words very softly and in Latin, '*Pax huic domui et omnibus habitantibus in ea*,' making a tiny sign of the cross towards the dim passage with the outer edge of his hand.

I thought it best to lead him silently up to the bedroom. Opening its door, I said, 'Bishop Griffyn.'

'Good,' came the voice from the bed, and, almost in jest, a quoting of words that Bishop Griffyn would certainly recognize, for they were famous words spoken by the great non-juring Bishop of Casterton centuries before, 'Being called to a sick and I think a dying bed – dear Gregory —' but I heard no more, for I shut the door on them both and returned to the women below.

Sitting with them, trifling with old papers, or just staring at my nails, I tried to keep my mind from anything happening in the room above. That was secret, and I strove to respect its secrecy. My thoughts had no place there. And they have no place there now.

None of us spoke much. Only Natalie, lifting her eyes from some sewing she had found, said, 'He's too young to die. Much too young. But there you are: they've killed him between them. They were always determined to bring him down. And now I hope they're proud of their handiwork. I shall never forgive them – never'; words which matched ill with any forgiveness spoken upstairs.

I did not answer. Nor Julie.

And Natalie, sewing, said, 'I hope you turned the gas low, Julie darling. We don't want that kettle to boil away.'

'It's low,' Julie told her. 'The kettle can only be simmering.'

'We don't know how long he'll be,' Natalie explained, to justify this small anxiety.

A door closed above, and steps creaked on the stairs. It was over. We laid aside our papers, and Natalie her sewing, and waited for the Bishop to come in. Natalie said, 'I wonder if he'd like coffee or tea. I'd like him to have something before he goes.

He came in, smiling easily and pleasantly for our comfort. And I, rising to meet him, remembered how, years ago, after he had put before me his interpretation of that refusal of Fennings, and I had said, 'Yes, I suppose that's the truth, really,' his reply had been, 'Perhaps. Only perhaps. One cannot know. Probably no one will ever know.'

But now he knew. He alone in all the world. And he alone in all the world would ever know. For him only, *Veritas temporis filia*.

§

When Bishop Griffyn asked my father-in-law, repeating my question, whether he would like him to celebrate in his room, he had answered, 'Yes; oh, yes;' with joy, I suspect, for if the truth now known to the Bishop was as I imagine it, he was free to take communion at last. Free at last, and perhaps never more free, for there was so little time left him now in which to lose the 'state of grace'. Next morning we three knelt about that great bed while the Bishop made his altar out of Natalie's elegant little dressing-table, the satin-wood table-desk from the Residentiary, with its slim reeded legs. Robed, he looked tall and majestic before that spare little table in the window. Julie knelt by the bed, sometimes burying her face in its coverlet; Natalie, more upright, knelt on the bed's other side; I knelt at the celebrant's right, ready to serve him with the Elements placed on the small night-table from which all lesser medicines had been removed. Obeying the Prayer Book the Bishop administered the sacrament to us all first and 'last of all to the sick person', who made out of his weak and trembling hands a throne to receive it.

It was his first reception after the long empty years. And his last.

One thing I learned many years afterwards. It came from the ardent but loose talk of Emmeline Harvie, talk all the looser because these matters were now so far in the past. She did not believe that all interesting secrecies need be buried in their graves for ever and ever. Her bishop was dead long since, and her beloved archdeacon too. So tell of them freely. Tell this.

When we three had gone from the room Bishop Griffyn knelt in his turn by the bedside of the dying priest and asked him to give him his blessing. He gave him a first opportunity to act again as a priest; a gentle action designed, I think, to assure his penitent that the forgiveness last night was complete. And the ex-archdeacon laid his hand on Bishop Griffyn's head, a man much older and greatly his senior, and spoke in his failing voice one of the blessings from his old *Pastor in Parochia*. 'God be with you always and strengthen you. God keep you under the shadow of his wings. God fill you with the knowledge of his will in all wisdom and understanding.'

His second, and last, priestly act was in the morning when, Natalie having summoned Julie and me, we all stood about his bed and he said hoarsely, 'I think it is near now, my dears. Quite near now'; and, lifting a shaking hand, made a small, a mere sketched, sign of the cross towards us all in blessing.

With Natalie at his side he died late that night, after a long day in which he seemed happy and at peace, sometimes smiling.

Bishop Griffyn's Eucharist at his bedside was thus his Viaticum.